EVERYMAN,

I WILL GO WITH THEE,

AND BE THY GUIDE,

IN THY MOST NEED

TO GO BY THY SIDE

EVERYMAN'S POCKET CLASSICS

AFRICAN STORIES

EDITED BY BEN OKRI

EVERYMAN'S POCKET CLASSICS
Alfred A. Knopf New York London Toronto

THIS IS A BORZOI BOOK
PUBLISHED BY ALFRED A. KNOPF

This selection by Ben Okri first published in
Everyman's Library, 2025

A list of acknowledgments to copyright owners appears at
the back of this volume.

 Published in the United States by Alfred A. Knopf,
a division of Penguin Random House LLC, New York, and in
Canada by Penguin Random House Canada Limited, Toronto.
Distributed by Penguin Random House LLC, New York. Published
in the United Kingdom by Everyman's Library, 50 Albemarle Street,
London W1S 4BD and distributed by Penguin Random House UK,
20 Vauxhall Bridge Road, London SW1V 2SA.

everymanslibrary.com
www.everymanslibrary.co.uk

ISBN 978-1-101-90833-4 (US)
978-1-84159-637-2 (UK)

A CIP catalogue reference for this book is available from the
British Library

Typography by Peter B. Willberg

Typeset in the UK by Input Data Services Ltd, Bridgwater, Somerset

Printed and bound in Germany by GGP Media GmbH, Pössneck

Contents

PREFACE

The short story is one of the most compelling of literary forms. It is perhaps the most rigorous literary form after the sonnet. It has the destiny of creating, within a few pages, a brief eternity. As from a magic lamp, with a few rubbings of prose, a genie emerges to take the imagination on a journey that becomes one's own. A dream that becomes a reality, or a reality that becomes a dream.

African writers have a unique affinity with the short story form. Maybe it is the literary form that best approximates patterns of the African experience. Maybe also it is the form closest to the oral stories, legends, fables, and tales of origin that are part of traditional life.

The short story is very suited to Africa. For there is something a little fantastical about African reality. This has nothing to do with the exotic, which alienates the reality of the Other. The slightly fantastical nature of African life might have to do with the persistence in the modern world of ancient ways of being that are coherent and ritualistically alive. The exotic implies a deviation from an accepted code of reality. African reality is not a deviation from a commonly agreed world. It is a world unto itself. It is richly diverse and yet in each place, each land, entirely true.

This is another way of saying that African reality is already fictional. It is fictional because the lands breathe stories.

The African short story was born of the intersection of many conditions: the ancient African worlds, the colonial experience, encounters with world literature, post-independence disillusionment, the plethora of magazines that accompanied the emergence of an African middle class, a new African aesthetics elaborated by intellectuals in the wake of independence, the necessity for African writers to define themselves and to question the new ruling elite, and the sense of the oral tradition as representing an authentic literary matrix.

This is not true for all the writers. For the white South African writers, for example, being born on the continent, being entangled in its fate, is enough to generate the urgency that characterizes writing from the land – urgency and a sense of the land itself, its complicated history and politics, and issues of identity and language and power.

Many African writers tended to do other jobs for a living. They were lecturers, journalists, scientists, musicologists, professors, doctors, lawyers, government employees. For this reason the short story was the literary form best suited to writers who had only small snatches of time, writers who did not have the luxury of writing for a living. For such busy lives, poetry and the short story were greatly favoured. This is not to say that the novel languished. Far from it. The novel is the master form of the literature. It is just that the short story was handier.

As a result the short story became the ready form for interrogating African realities, for catching the mood of rural or urban lives, for capturing what was left of traditional mores as they were slowly fading under the assault of westernization. The short story became the portable form for bearing witness to the mysteries of being alive. It was also the training ground for the novel.

The English, American or European writer can tell a story for its own sake. They don't have to be political. They are not compelled to be socially responsive. Flaubert can write a story about an old woman in Rouen without it being a direct or indirect interrogation of the political system. Chekhov can write a story about a woman with a lapdog who was seduced and then abandoned without it being a text about the emancipation of the Russian soul from centuries of autocracy. But it is rare for the African writer not to be telling us, through stories, about the state of African being, in a particular country and a particular time.

It is this quality, this political and cultural responsibility, that gives an edge, a constant relevance, and a sense of perennial engagement to the African short story. The troubled history of modern Africa has made its writers conjoin the functional value of their art with the entertainment that is natural to the short story. This is true whether it is Chinua Achebe, in 'The Voter', satirizing the political process in post-independence Nigeria, or Bessie Head, in 'Jacob: The Story of a Faith-Healing Priest', taking an amused eye to the complicated permutations of spirituality in Botswana, or J. M. Coetzee in 'The Glass Abattoir', directing his caustic pen at the horrors of meat-eating through the tale of a mother's ambiguous literary legacy to her son. It is there in the entanglements of ritual and spirits that run through this selection. Camara Laye's 'The Eyes of the Statue' examines numinous terror in the ruins of an ancient city. 'A Child in the Bush of Ghosts' by Olympe Bhêly-Quénum is the tale of a child encountering the dead in the forest. Its title echoes that of a famous novel by Amos Tutuola. Social commentary and satire feature in Francis Bebey's 'Edda's Marriage' and Guillaume Oyônô-Mbia's 'The Little Railway Station'.

Threads of fantasy are woven through Emmanuel Boundzéki Dongala's 'Jazz and Palm Wine' and Dambudzo Marechera's 'Protista'. Ngũgĩ wa Thiong'o is represented here with 'The Martyr', which emerged from the Mau Mau struggle in Kenya. The trace presence of fables and oral tales is visible in Mouhamadoul Nouktar Diop's 'The Pot of Gold' and Clémentine Nzuji Madiya's 'Ditetembwa'. There are tales of theft gone wrong (David Owoyele's 'The Will of Allah'), of a shopkeeper's yearning for a woman who vaguely promises love (Abdulrazak Gurnah's 'Cages'), a fable about power (Jomo Kenyatta's 'The Gentlemen of the Jungle'), and of a woman awaiting a freedom fighter's return during the era of apartheid in South Africa (Nadine Gordimer's 'Amnesty'). There are funny, poignant and heartbreaking stories about individuals managing their daily lives with bewilderment and courage. They are all unique and they are all African. Nadine Gordimer said somewhere that the short story is just right for our times. The short story is just right for Africa.

But it would be dangerous to generalize about the African short story. The stories are too varied for that and the writers are equally diverse in their attitudes to their craft. All that can be said with any certainty is that the stories collected in this book are entertaining and unflinching in their gaze. They probe while being delightful. Whether they deal in spirits, love, imprisonment, the urban experience, politics, or the colonial past, whether written in English, French, Portuguese, or Arabic, they all shine a refracted light on the human condition. Through these stories you could track, in an indirect way, the history of the continent and the progress of the spirit of its peoples.

It may be paradoxically easier to make stories out of lands that do not breathe stories. But where everything yields stories like the fragrance of certain flowers at twilight, it requires an altogether more rigorous art. Where reality easily lends itself to anecdote, to the tall tale, to exaggeration, a particular discipline is called for to turn the teeming worlds into singular fictions. To carve a single figure from abundance requires an art out of which a new world might emerge.

That is the gift of these stories. Each of the writers could have succumbed to the temptation to overwhelm the senses and the imagination; but tempered by the sorcery of the short story writer's art they gave us brief pages that suggest worlds just beyond the margins. As a reader you will proceed from dream to dream, from reality to reality, in something approaching a controlled fever of the creative spirit.

The watchword of this collection is brevity. Almost all the writers could have given examples of the long form of the short story, but nothing displays the art of the short story more powerfully than compression. The aim is to choose stories which are not only exemplars of the form but which maintain the performance of the art's nomenclature. The stories had to be short while giving the impression of being much longer. The traditional tale in most of Africa displays that paradox of space and narration. Brief experiences might be long in recounting, long experiences short in the telling. But this brevity casts long shadows in the mind.

The African imagination is as fecund as its reality, bristling with the collision of the political and the cultural, of suffering and celebration, of outrages and the spiritual, all intermingled into potent, and often pungent, conditions. These will be experienced in abundance in these tales. Writers from Africa have produced such a cornucopia of good short stories that this may well be the first of two volumes. A second collection is needed to do justice to that fertility.

Another guiding principle has been the sheer pleasure of encountering so many fictional worlds. There is nothing that recommends a volume such as this more than the enjoyment that the stories give. This may be in the telling or in what is told. Like finding oneself on a fast-flowing river, one is borne from tale to tale by the richness of the experience and often by the improbable speed with which the imagination is snatched to unexpected realms of life. When all the stories have been experienced, the reader may feel that they have been taken on a journey of the spirit akin to the magical strangeness of a great novel. Better still, it is hoped that the reader emerges from these pages shaken and refreshed, as if from one of those initiations that only an extraordinary experience in real life can induce.

There can be no better excuse for assembling so many stories than to offer glimpses into the soul of one of the most mysterious and least understood continents. One that is older than Atlantis, more varied than any land, and with the largest land mass in the world; yet whose contemporary existence in most people's minds outside the continent is associated with poverty and wars and injustices.

Africa deserves to be rediscovered afresh. We need readers that will turn the pages of the continent anew and surrender to the imagination and humanity of the worlds revealed. Then Africa's real destiny, veiled for too long, can begin a new chapter in the grand story of the world. But it begins in stories that hint at creativity and resilience and hope, renewed each day, like the wind over the savannahs at dawn.

Ben Okri

CHINUA ACHEBE

THE VOTER

RUFUS OKEKE – Roof for short – was a very popular man in his village. Although the villagers did not explain it in so many words Roof's popularity was a measure of their gratitude to an energetic young man who, unlike most of his fellows nowadays had not abandoned the village in order to seek work, any work, in the towns. And Roof was not a village lout either. Everyone knew how he had spent two years as a bicycle repairer's apprentice in Port Harcourt, and had given up of his own free will a bright future to return to his people and guide them in these difficult times. Not that Umuofia needed a lot of guidance. The village already belonged *en masse* to the People's Alliance Party, and its most illustrious son, Chief the Honourable Marcus Ibe, was Minister of Culture in the out-going government (which was pretty certain to be the in-coming one as well). Nobody doubted that the Honourable Minister would be elected in his constituency. Opposition to him was like the proverbial fly trying to move a dunghill. It would have been ridiculous enough without coming, as it did now, from a complete nonentity.

As was to be expected Roof was in the service of the Honourable Minister for the coming elections. He had become a real expert in election campaigning at all levels – village, local government or national. He could tell the mood and temper of the electorate at any given time. For instance he had warned the Minister months ago about the radical change that had come into the thinking of Umuofia since the last national election.

The villagers had had five years in which to see how quickly and plentifully politics brought wealth, chieftaincy titles, doctorate degrees and other honours some of which, like the last, had still to be explained satisfactorily to them; for in their naïvety they still expected a doctor to be able to heal the sick. Anyhow, these honours and benefits had come so readily to the man to whom they had given their votes free of charge five years ago that they were now ready to try it a different way.

Their point was that only the other day Marcus Ibe was a not too successful mission school teacher. Then politics had come to their village and he had wisely joined up, some said just in time to avoid imminent dismissal arising from a female teacher's pregnancy. Today he was Chief the Honourable; he had two long cars and had just built himself the biggest house anyone had seen in these parts. But let it be said that none of these successes had gone to Marcus's head as well they might. He remained devoted to his people. Whenever he could he left the good things of the capital and returned to his village which had neither running water nor electricity, although he had lately installed a private plant to supply electricity to his new house. He knew the source of his good fortune, unlike the little bird who ate and drank and went out to challenge his personal spirit. Marcus had christened his new house 'Umuofia Mansions' in honour of his village, and he had slaughtered five bulls and countless goats to entertain the people on the day it was opened by the Archbishop.

Everyone was full of praise for him. One old man said: 'Our son is a good man; he is not like the mortar which as soon as food comes its way turns its back on the ground.' But when the feasting was over, the villagers told themselves that they had underrated the power of the ballot paper before and should not do so again. Chief the Honourable Marcus Ibe was not unprepared. He had drawn five months' salary in advance, changed a few hundred pounds into shining shillings and armed his campaign boys with eloquent little jute bags. In the day he made his speeches; at night his stalwarts conducted their whispering campaign. Roof was the most trusted of these campaigners.

'We have a Minister from our village, one of our own sons,' he said to a group of elders in the house of Ogbuefi Ezenwa, a man of high traditional title. 'What greater honour can a village have? Do you ever stop to ask yourselves why we should be singled out for this honour? I will tell you: it is because we are favoured by the leaders of PAP. Whether or not we cast our paper for Marcus, PAP will continue to rule. Think of the pipe-borne water they have promised us . . .'

Besides Roof and his assistant there were five elders in the room. An old hurricane lamp with a cracked, sooty, glass chimney gave out yellowish light in the midst. The elders sat on very low stools. On the floor, directly in front of each of them, lay two shilling pieces. Outside beyond the fastened door, the moon kept a straight face.

'We believe every word you say to be true,' said Ezenwa. 'We shall, every one of us, drop his paper for Marcus. Who would leave an *ọzọ* feast and go to a poor ritual meal? Tell Marcus he has our papers, and our wives' papers too. But what we do say is that two shillings is shameful.' He brought the lamp close and tilted it at the money before him as if to make sure he had not mistaken its value. 'Yes, two shillings is too shameful. If Marcus were a poor man – which our ancestors forbid – I should be the first to give him my paper free, as I did before. But today Marcus is a great man and does his things like a great man. We did not ask him for money yesterday; we shall not ask him tomorrow. But today is our day; we have climbed the iroko tree today and would be foolish not to take down all the firewood we need.'

Roof had to agree. He had lately been taking down a lot of firewood himself. Only yesterday he had asked Marcus for one of his many rich robes – and had got it. Last Sunday Marcus's wife (the teacher that nearly got him in trouble) had objected (like the woman she was) when Roof pulled out his fifth bottle of beer from the refrigerator; she was roundly and publicly rebuked by her husband. To cap it all Roof had won a land case recently because, among other things, he had been chauffeur-driven to the disputed site. So he understood the elders about the firewood.

'All right,' he said in English and then reverted to Ibo. 'Let us not quarrel about small things.' He stood up, adjusted his robes and plunged his hand once more into the bag. Then he bent down like a priest distributing the host and gave one shilling more to every man; only he did not put it into their palms but on the floor in front of them. The men, who had so far not deigned to touch the things, looked at the floor and shook their heads. Roof got up again and gave each man another shilling.

'I am through,' he said with a defiance that was no less effective for being transparently faked. The elders too knew how far to go without losing decorum. So when Roof added: 'Go cast your paper for the enemy if you like!' they quickly calmed him down with a suitable speech from each of them. By the time the last man had spoken it was possible, without great loss of dignity, to pick up the things from the floor . . .

The enemy Roof had referred to was the Progressive Organization Party (POP) which had been formed by the tribes down the coast to save themselves, as the founders of the party proclaimed, from 'total political, cultural, social and religious annihilation'. Although it was clear the party had no chance here it had plunged, with typical foolishness, into a straight fight with PAP, providing cars and loud-speakers to a few local rascals and thugs to go around and make a lot of noise. No one knew for certain how much money POP had let loose in Umuofia but it was said to be very considerable. Their local campaigners would end up very rich, no doubt.

Up to last night everything had been 'moving according to plan', as Roof would have put it. Then he had received a strange visit from the leader of the POP campaign team. Although he and Roof were well known to each other, and might even be called friends, his visit was cold and business-like. No words were wasted. He placed five pounds on the floor before Roof and said, 'We want your vote.' Roof got up from his chair, went to the outside door, closed it carefully and returned to his chair. The brief exercise gave him enough time to weigh the proposition. As he spoke his eyes never left the red notes on the floor. He seemed to be mesmerized by the picture of the cocoa farmer harvesting his crops.

'You know I work for Marcus,' he said feebly. 'It will be very bad . . .'

'Marcus will not be there when you put in your paper. We have plenty of work to do tonight; are you taking this or not?'

'It will not be heard outside this room?' asked Roof.

'We are after votes not gossip.'

'All right,' said Roof in English.

The man nudged his companion and he brought forward an object covered with a red cloth and proceeded to remove the cover. It was a fearsome little affair contained in a clay pot with feathers stuck into it.

'The *iyi* comes from Mbanta. You know what that means. Swear that you will vote for Maduka. If you fail to do so, this *iyi* take note.'

Roof's heart nearly flew out when he saw the *iyi*; indeed he knew the fame of Mbanta in these things. But he was a man of quick decision. What could a single vote cast in secret for Maduka take away from Marcus's certain victory? Nothing.

'I will cast my paper for Maduka; if not this *iyi* take note.'

'Das all,' said the man as he rose with his companion who had covered up the object again and was taking it back to their car.

'You know he has no chance against Marcus,' said Roof at the door.

'It is enough that he gets a few votes now; next time he will get more. People will hear that he gives out pounds, not shillings, and they will listen.'

Election morning. The great day every five years when the people exercise power. Weather-beaten posters on walls of houses, tree trunks and telegraph poles. The few that were still whole called out their message to those who could read. Vote for the People's Alliance Party! Vote for the Progressive Organization Party! Vote for PAP! Vote for POP! The posters that were torn called out as much of the message as they could.

As usual Chief the Honourable Marcus Ibe was doing things in grand style. He had hired a highlife band from Umuru and stationed it at such a distance from the voting booths as just managed to be lawful. Many villagers danced to the music, their ballot papers held aloft, before proceeding to the booths. Chief the Honourable Marcus Ibe sat in the 'owner's corner' of his enormous green car and smiled and nodded. One enlightened villager came up to the car, shook hands with the great man and said in advance, 'Congrats!' This immediately set the pattern. Hundreds of admirers shook Marcus's hand and said 'Corngrass!'

Roof and the other organizers were prancing up and down, giving last-minute advice to the voters and pouring with sweat.

'Do not forget,' he said again to a group of illiterate women who seemed ready to burst with enthusiasm and good humour, 'our sign is the motor-car . . .'

'Like the one Marcus is sitting inside.'

'Thank you, mother,' said Roof. 'It is the same car. The box with the car shown on its body is the box for you. Don't look at the other with the man's head: it is for those whose heads are not correct.'

This was greeted with loud laughter. Roof cast a quick and busy-like glance towards the Minister and received a smile of appreciation.

'Vote for the car,' he shouted, all the veins in his neck standing out. 'Vote for the car and you will ride in it!'

'Or if we don't, our children will,' piped the same sharp, old girl.

The band struck up a new number: 'Why walk when you can ride . . .'

In spite of his apparent calm and confidence Chief the Honourable Marcus was a relentless stickler for detail. He knew he would win what the newspapers called 'a landslide victory' but he did not wish, even so, to throw away a single vote. So as soon as the first rush of voters was over he promptly asked his campaign boys to go one at a time and put in their ballot papers.

'Roof, you had better go first,' he said.

Roof's spirits fell; but he let no one see it. All morning

he had masked his deep worry with a surface exertion which was unusual even for him. Now he dashed off in his springy fashion towards the booths. A policeman at the entrance searched him for illegal ballot papers and passed him. Then the electoral officer explained to him about the two boxes. By this time the spring had gone clean out of his walk. He sidled in and was confronted by the car and the head. He brought out his ballot paper from his pocket and looked at it. How could he betray Marcus even in secret? He resolved to go back to the other man and return his five pounds . . . Five pounds! He knew at once it was impossible. He had sworn on that *iyi*. The notes were red; the cocoa farmer busy at work.

At this point he heard the muffled voice of the policeman asking the electoral officer what the man was doing inside. 'Abi na pickin im de born?'

Quick as lightning a thought leapt into Roof's mind. He folded the paper, tore it in two along the crease and put one half in each box. He took the precaution of putting the first half into Maduka's box and confirming the action verbally: 'I vote for Maduka.'

They marked his thumb with indelible purple ink to prevent his return, and he went out of the booth as jauntily as he had gone in.

OLYMPE BHÊLY-QUÉNUM

A CHILD IN THE BUSH OF GHOSTS

[*To André Breton to whom I first told this story; to the Collège Littré in Avranches and my former schoolmates in that establishment where I wrote this story; but also to the city of Avranches where I learnt a great deal.*]

WHEN I WAS eleven years old, one of my uncles one day took me along with him to his farm. His name was Akpoto. He was a handsome man with large black eyes, sturdy and distinguished-looking.

We had set out early, and yet the African morning sun had beaten us to it. We had covered more than thirteen kilometres on the district council road; then we had taken the pathway that led to Houêto. A small river, fordable at any time of day, cut across the path of fine golden sand which meandered through a high and dense forest.

We had crossed the river and continued walking on sand. I loved the softness of that sandy earth; its velvety surface pleasantly caressed the soles of my bare feet. But the joy I felt in walking on that path gradually gave way to fear as we penetrated ever more deeply into the forest.

When we left the path for a sodden trail, I suddenly had a feeling that the humidity pervaded my whole body, and the sense of fear became intolerable.

I therefore started pestering my uncle with little questions which were as irritating as they were foolish. I kept knocking against him, clung to his hand, or moved clumsily in front of him and thus almost succeeded several times in making him fall . . .

We were crossing a kind of clearing where the sky above remained invisible as in most of our forests. We had already walked too much. For how long? I can't say. I was not yet going to school and, naturally, did not know any French, to the utter indignation of my father, the respectable primary school teacher, who always saw me as sickly and unable to stand the hustle and bustle of a school in session. As far as my uncle was concerned, he was able to determine the time of day from the position of the sun through a special kind of sensory perception, or rather intuition. Therefore after having raised his eyes in vain towards the arches of the towering trees hiding the sky from our eyes, he said to me in his gentle voice which I can still hear: 'Wait for me here, I'll be back in a short while.'

He left me, plunging with big steps into the bush that stretched out as far as the eye could see. He had put a big orange and four guavas into my hands.

Suddenly I felt dead tired. I was gripped by the urge to cry but controlled myself. I've never had much use for cry-babies. There is nothing I detest so much as giving unbridled expression to our sorrows. And I waited. Oh, I certainly waited more than I shall ever be able to wait again, but my uncle did not return. There was plenty of time for me to eat two guavas, then my orange, and then I waited again a very long time before munching my two remaining guavas.

Worn out by the anxiety brought about by seeing nothing but the bush with its frightening calm around me, I sat down on the black forest earth and buried my face in my hands as if I never wanted to see any more of the place where I was. But as the humidity caught hold of me I had to rise again and

I started walking without really having any idea of where I was going.

I ought to have searched for the path we had followed until then but all my senses were gripped by panic and I marched like an automaton. I wished I could have given out a single scream, whistled, sung, or talked loudly, or even just muttered something – anything to assuage the effect of the fear in me, anything to make me feel aware of my person or simply to give me the illusion that I still was myself, a human being, alive, finding myself there by chance, but I could not say anything . . . True to God, it is the only time I remember ever having felt fear.

I walked on relentlessly, unable to rediscover the path covered with sand; neither did I see the river again, its waters rolling with a sweet music, but I suddenly noticed in front of me a big woman wrapped in a white lappa that concealed her face and covered her feet. She advanced towards me; my heart started pounding fast; I felt as if I were receiving heavy blows from a ram inside me that did not quite succeed in splitting my chest open. I started shouting, no, I would have liked to shout; I felt I was shouting but did not hear myself shouting. I wished I could see the earth opening under my feet, but the humus refused to do my bidding. Only then did I concede defeat and stretched out my arms to the woman like a baby to its mother.

To my surprise the woman passed me by in mute indifference. I looked back. She too had turned her head and before I had time to avert my eyes, she had already uncovered her face. I then saw something frightful: an emaciated face, the face of a fleshless skull, which made a horrid and repugnant grimace at me.

I started running head over heels but glanced backwards

from time to time. It was to no avail, for I constantly saw the person at a distance of twenty paces behind me, although she was not running. But my mad gallop did not last very long, for a few moments after that encounter I found myself right in front of the railway tracks. My heart was thumping so violently that it seemed to be about to burst my chest. I looked back again and saw my uncle.

'Where have you been? Why did you abandon me in the forest?' I asked, staring at him in bleak reproach.

He looked at me with pity because he read the anguish in my eyes; he told me, however, that he had not wasted any time at Houêto:

'I ordered my farm labourers at once to catch the chickens you see here and went myself to dig out cassava tubers for your grandmother and great-aunt. As soon as the job was finished, I returned to the clearing and was greatly surprised not to find you. I then continued my return journey, looking everywhere. All of a sudden I heard a rustle in the bush to my left; at first I thought it was a deer but I changed my mind afterwards when I saw a human shape running helter-skelter; it was you. I could have called you but I preferred to follow you with my eyes, for we were moving along parallel lines. A single step, but a big one, separated me from you, my boy. And then, of course, I had nothing to fear for you, for the bush is not dangerous.'

I felt sad at having brought him to the point where he thought he owed me an explanation. But on the other hand, my heart was still throbbing with anger and subdued sobs when I asked him in a trembling voice whether he had seen the river again.

'Yes, of course. It was there even before our ancestors were born, and will certainly remain after we're dead and gone.'

'You may be right, but I did not recross it.'

'What's that you're telling me? You must have forded it without noticing.'

'But it's true, uncle! I didn't see the slightest trace of the river; just look at my legs and feet, they aren't soaked like yours.'

'You surprise me, Codjo!'

'Let's return to the clearing by the path that has brought me here, if you don't believe me,' I said with an assurance that today I find astounding on the part of the child I was.

My uncle tucked his baskets with the cassava and chickens in them under some undergrowth, put me astride his shoulders and we took the path on which I had come, or rather the trail which perhaps would never have come into existence if I had not been the first human being who in my terrorized gallop had savagely flattened the grass along that line.

We had arrived at the clearing, then at the farm much more quickly than we could have managed by walking on the sand-covered pathway.

Akpoto was dumbfounded not to be obliged to pass the river he had been crossing for more than thirty-five years, the source of which he imagined to be somewhere in the forest.

He put me down. My mouth felt dry. I quenched my thirst by drinking from a gourd, and this made me feel the freshness of the water and the pleasure of drinking it more keenly. Then we set out on the return journey, taking once more the kind of game track I had discovered and which had become the fastest way to go to Houêto and back.

'*A walking skeleton, that sort of thing doesn't exist. No dead man comes back to stay among the living; my grandmother and great-grandfather followed one another into death at a month's interval; nobody's ever told me that he has met them during the three years since they stopped coddling me.*' So went my train of thought, and I was convinced that my encounter with the skeleton was merely the result of a hallucination.

Still, I wanted to make sure it was only an illusion and, taking advantage of a moment when my parents' watchfulness had flagged, I sneaked away from our compound where I was getting bored. I liked the open air, the solitude at the seaside or in the bush, and likewise the company of human beings who made no impositions on me but allowed me to make myself useful without feeling duty-bound to do so.

In my parents' house everything was offered to me on a golden platter; I was pampered and idle and felt my uselessness to the full.

I reached the clearing again through the game track and started searching for the source of the river. My mind was totally absorbed in the operation, perhaps because I was what my parents called 'a self-willed child', or perhaps also because I had an ulterior motive: to surprise my uncle by discovering the truth I wanted to find out.

I therefore headed into the bush, slipping over pebbles, sinking into the spongy suction of the soft ground; skipping over creepers, crawling among thorns. In front of me appeared a big chameleon. We looked at each other for a good second and its skin visibly, and gradually, took on the colour of the indigo cloth tied around my neck, which I was wearing over my khaki shorts. At that moment I thought of my revered great-grandfather who in telling tales did not hide his predilection for the chameleon: '*It rarely misses its destination because it knows how to adjust itself to its surroundings and never looks back.*'

What did that mean? I hadn't the slightest idea. I was a spoilt, demanding child whom a too-indulgent great-grandfather had perhaps wanted to convert to patience and gentleness by lectures on moral philosophy. But he had reasoned through the use of symbols which remained a mystery to the child. Still, it was that venerable old man that I thought of that day, and seeing the chameleon take on the colour of my cloth, I not only decided not to look back but also to adapt myself to the bush, to understand its language, to bow to its laws, without, however, forgetting that I was a human being, the only creature who would not be forgiven voluntary subservience. I was born to grow big and to live even beyond death . . .

A small noise startled me; I did not pay any heed and continued making my way through the thorns that tore my cloth. A long snake carelessly passed between my legs, a boa rolled itself around a tree towards which I was heading. I was unafraid, beyond caring. My only concern was to discover the source of the river. I had met the chameleon that perhaps still retained the colour of my garment in memory of our chance encounter or had swapped it for that of some of the distinctly green or red leaves I remembered seeing.

From among creepers and thorns I emerged into another clearing. In its immobility, the canopy of leaves above my head sealed off the place in tragic solitude. I felt the void within me as if I were nothing thenceforth but a wretched carcase draped with black skin. At that moment, the skeleton appeared a few steps away from me, wrapped in its big white lappa which covered its head. I felt no emotion, or more precisely, I was not afraid since I considered it as something I was used to. Still, I rubbed my eyes as if to rid myself of an optical illusion, to make sure of what I was seeing. It drew closer; I did not rush towards it as in our first encounter, for I had to preserve my dignity. In my view, it represented nothing. It was nothingness in motion, and I was a man. This certainty, due to the realization of the difference between us, fortified me not with courage – that I didn't care about – but with cockiness, and I saw my body rising to its level. This was not the time for any more concessions. I felt that the bush was not supposed to be the abode of the dead but of the living. Wasn't I one of them? We converged as on a one-way track where no provision has been made for people to pass one another. I did nothing to let it pass when we were face to face. Then it stretched out its hand to me. At that moment I would have liked to cross my arms, to sport a scornful countenance since last time it too had snubbed me; but I decided to let bygones be bygones and gathered its bony hand in mine.

Instead of forcing me to retrace my steps it did the opposite, still holding my hand. I thus followed it, eager to discover where it was taking me. We wended our way side by side without my feeling the slightest apprehension. After all, what was there to be afraid of? Holding in my hand the hand of a human skeleton? Human. That was just the word I needed. Was I not with something human? Was I not sure now that my first encounter was not simply the effect of a delusion?

No, really, I was no longer afraid. I was eight years old when my grandmother and great-grandfather stopped living. I remember having cried a great deal by their bodies, seated beside the mortal remains of these old people in their barely gnarled height during my vigil, despite my parents' vain efforts to spare me what they called too violent shocks. Yes, I still remember: I hurled myself on my grandmother when they wanted to put her in the coffin; I took her hand and squeezed it very hard so as to communicate all my warmth to her. O the piercing coldness she left in my hands and which is still there, evermore! It was her that I felt again all along, while the skeleton kept my hand in its own. It did not hold it in a tight grip, did not apply any pressure, and we just wandered along like two friends.

Still, I did not forget that I was a man, a human being, a child barely twelve years old, while it was a skeleton. Had it been a man or a woman ? I never found out. Besides, this was of no importance. With wide open eyes I stared at the bush in front of me. Not a single time did it occur to me to have to look at my fellow-traveller. And why should I have looked at its skeletal visage since I was feeling its hand in mine? Had it suddenly vanished I would most assuredly not have worried about its disappearance but would have continued on my way amidst the trees, the thorns and the beasts.

But I have to admit today that I had realized that from the moment we walked together the thorns no longer tore my cloth; everything slipped smoothly off me as it did off the skeleton. A wild boar and his mate emerging from their lair took to flight on seeing us. My uncle had told me that the bush was not dangerous; all the same, we saw more than one pair of lions and panthers, but they had passed us by with something approaching indifference. To be precise, they had invariably passed on my side; they had all sniffed at me and then walked away in haughty grandeur. Why? I wouldn't know. I may have appeared vile-smelling and undesirable to them, unless they just happened not to be hungry just then.

We had been walking like that for a time that seemed reasonably long to me but I was not tired. I did not feel the slightest fatigue. I paid attention to everything. Then, to my great surprise, I stopped seeing the bush around me and realized that we were in an underground tunnel hung with tree-roots. The walls were oozing moisture but the ground was dry. The ear perceived the gentle, distant murmur of a stream. I thought of the river while striding along with my strange companion.

At certain places the walls of the long gallery through which we were proceeding had been discreetly adorned with symbolic graffiti: snakes biting their own tails; arms cut off and placed on top of each other in the form of an X; sexual organs; copulation scenes; shin-bones; human skulls; horses without heads but galloping at full speed, tails and manes flying in the wind; fire shaped like an open lily blossom flaring from a pit; coffins; people performing a ritual dance; a clumsily drawn rectangle representing a mirror.

We turned to the left and I had the impression that we were changing our direction from north to sunrise. A light entering the place from heaven knows where gently lit up the underground passage sloping downwards in front of me. We walked unceasingly, descending the slope, and arrived at a kind of crypt where human skeletons without the tiniest bone missing were stretched out side by side.

My guide stopped in front of one of them, uncovering his cavity-riddled face. I looked straight at him. He bowed slightly to one of the skeletons which sat up, crossed its legs, then its arms; he continued his homage and each one of his fellow-skeletons took the same posture as the preceding one. And I saw seventy-seven skeletons thus sitting up and leaning their backs against the wall of the crypt.

Did they want to impress me? I had experienced fear before, but fear held no more meaning for me. I had heard people talk a lot about death, but since the death of my grandparents I no longer feared it. Death had become for me such a familiar companion that I gave it no more thought. But looking at the skeletons attentively, I had a feeling that each one of them represented a human being I had known, and to which I had perhaps been close. It was good to see them again but I had not come here for them.

'Where is the source of the river?' I suddenly cried in a

tragic voice which struck the walls in a zigzag line, provoking a long and sonorous echo.

And again I heard murmurings of the water, then a groan followed by the sound of a torrent rushing away.

The skulls all seemed to have been raised again to look me straight in the face.

'You see that I have come to visit you without misgivings. I'm not afraid of you because you used to be men; for me you still are, and I don't believe in death!'

I heard my voice re-echo. It ricocheted away from me along the underground passage.

'Why don't you answer? Should you really be so useless?' All I received for an answer was my own voice and its echo which garbled any utterance.

'You hear me?'

'You hear me?'

'– 'ear me?'

'– me?'

'– 'e?'

'Why did you bring me here?'

'– bring me here?'

'– me here?'

'– 'ere?'

I looked around me and noticed that my guide had disappeared; maybe he had quietly slipped back to his little niche among his peers. So I thought of setting out on my return journey but as the passage stretched out farther before me, I preferred not to retrace my steps; so I moved forward. Thus I continued marching at a normal walking pace, looking all the while at the walls covered with graffiti fraught with symbolism. Despite my casual and almost leisurely gait I was feeling tired. I later realized that the way was sloping upwards. Moreover, the certainty that I was advancing towards the sun became more and more acute.

As if in a fog I saw a shadow passing before my eyes; then the shadow became a reality: a majestic skeleton without any clothes on, his right hand clutched to his heart and his left holding a shin-bone with a skull on top.

I stopped short in front of him. He made to let me pass and the moment I was going to continue on my way he slightly stroked my head with the skull resting on the shin-bone. I did not react, did not look back. The light entering the cavern was becoming more and more intense, I breathed in the air charged with a thousand smells from the fields . . . Abruptly I felt myself carried off into a long sleep and saw myself in a place, the name of which someone seemed to murmur into my ear.

'Wassai.'

O Wassai! Wassai! Disturbing, exciting paradise of entwined bodies. Here was a pathway divided into five branches, each leading to clearly defined places. On one side of the main path stood a hedge of hibiscus, bougainvillea and Campeachy separating the path from a vast area planted with kola-nut trees dwarfed by iroko and silk-cotton trees. In the hollows of those giant trees nested night birds; their lugubrious shrieks did not frighten me. Wisps of white smoke rose from the foot of the trees. Little did I care about their origin and meaning! Let the sorcerers abandon themselves to their orgies, let them devour the souls of their victims. I was in Wassai.

On the other side of the road was Wassai, little house of joy without a keeper. I entered. Ravishing young beauties with sturdy breasts, black skin, athletic bodies. And their nimble legs with prettily proportioned muscles, readily intertwining, pushed me gently into voluptuous depths. At Wassai I experienced unforgettable little tremors brought about by girls I did not know, their names have remained unspoken, I've forgotten their seductive faces; the form of their lithe and supple bodies remains in my arms, the freshness of their jet-black skin still vibrates through my nerves. In their midst I underwent my sexual initiation till all the flowers of the world blossomed within me, till the hard egg whose unwonted presence I had felt deep within was hatched. No outburst of rebellious sex will ever surprise me. I have explored all its domains in Wassai, fearsome black flower slowly unfolding in the deep nights of a dwelling without a master.

When I came to myself, I went my way without slowing down my pace and thus I came out into the open air.

Let it be said in passing that I did not for a single moment feel like a prisoner in that underground gallery. But instead of finding myself on even ground, at the edge of the forest as I expected, perhaps because I had scented the wind and the sun, I realized that I was perched high up on a mountainside studded with shrubbery.

A little further down, beneath my feet, a spring gushing out from this imposing height I had not known before flowed into the plain before me with a murmur. And the glittering reflections of lights, a vast imaginary ocean, seemed to undulate on the surface of the stream.

I climbed on all fours up to the summit, stood erect and saw the top of the forest covering the villages all around.

Far away thin columns of smoke rose above the trees. Coming from another world I discovered the immensity of space above the earth; then I went down from the mountain as if gently impelled and held back at the same time by a protecting hand.

I had not succeeded in seeing what I was searching for: the source of the river. Disappointed, I had to rest content with following the stream which flowed into a natural canal, the banks of which were hemmed in by aquatic plants; and I saw the river again which here to my great surprise almost flowed alongside the railway line.

My cloth was in shreds. I followed the railway line and then the usual path to town. I arrived there at nightfall. In front of the door of my parents' house I was stunned to see on either side an earthenware pot containing a decoction such as our customs prescribe for funeral ceremonies; I also heard a dirge gently syncopated by calabash rattles.

I entered and saw a gathering of sad people. The women, including my mother, had untied their hair as a token of mourning. The people gathered there noticed my presence and started up. Some took to their heels, others, paralysed by fear, just looked at me. I stepped forward to my mother who had been quickly joined by my father.

'What has happened? Who has died?'

Dead silence.

'You have to forgive me for leaving without telling you about it.'

'Where have you come from? Are you dead or are you a living person in our midst?' my father asked.

'I'm alive.'

'What, alive?' my mother said, weeping.

'Nobody's dead. Death doesn't exist and if it does, no dead man will ever return,' I replied firmly, but with my most casual expression.

The people had come back, more numerous now than when I had first set foot in the house.

'Where have you come from?'

'Where've you been?'

'We thought you were dead.'

'For the past three days we've been sure about it.'

'The diviners have confirmed it.'

I was somewhat depressed by these comments and asked if the funeral ceremonies had anything to do with me. They said yes.

'The diviners have all been telling you lies. I went for a walk, and I've come back with flesh and blood, body and soul, cured from the fear of death. I apologize for having given you so much worry.'

'My son, tell me honestly where you have come from,' my father said.

'Just from a walk. I didn't realize that it lasted three days.'

'What did you eat?' asked my mother.

'Nothing.'

'Who did you stay with?'

'Nobody.'

'I don't understand you.'

'I've nothing to explain.'

'Why?'

'Such things can't be explained. I am alive and life goes on.'

'Oh, this child!' my mother murmured.

'I'm hungry, mother. You can see I'm alive and kicking since I'm hungry and thirsty.'

'May you never again disappear like that!'

'I promise, but don't ever ask me for an explanation,' I said. And everything was all right again.

How long did this dream last? I shall never know.

NGŨGĨ WA THIONG'O

THE MARTYR

WHEN MR AND MRS GARSTONE were murdered in their home by unknown gangsters, there was a lot of talk about it. It was all on the front pages of the daily papers and figured importantly in the Radio Newsreel. Perhaps this was so because they were the first European settlers to be killed in the increased wave of violence that had spread all over the country. The violence was said to have political motives. And wherever you went, in the market-places, in the Indian bazaars, in a remote African duka, you were bound to hear something about the murder. There were a variety of accounts and interpretations.

Nowhere was the matter more thoroughly discussed than in a remote, lonely house built on a hill, which belonged, quite appropriately, to Mrs Hill. Her husband, an old veteran settler of the pioneering period, had died the previous year after an attack of malaria while on a visit to Uganda. Her only son and daughter were now getting their education at 'Home' – home being another name for England. Being one of the earliest settlers and owning a lot of land with big tea plantations sprawling right across the country, she was much respected by the others if not liked by all.

For some did not like what they considered her too 'liberal' attitude to the 'natives'. When Mrs Smiles and Mrs Hardy came into her house two days later to discuss the murder, they wore a look of sad triumph – sad because Europeans (not just Mr and Mrs Garstone) had been killed, and of triumph, because the essential depravity and ingratitude of the natives had been demonstrated beyond all doubt. No longer could Mrs Hill maintain that natives could be civilized if only they were handled in the right manner.

Mrs Smiles was a lean, middle-aged woman whose tough, determined nose and tight lips reminded one so vividly of a missionary. In a sense she was. Convinced that she and her kind formed an oasis of civilization in a wild country of savage people, she considered it almost her calling to keep on reminding the natives and anyone else of the fact, by her gait, talk and general bearing.

Mrs Hardy was of Boer descent and had early migrated into the country from South Africa. Having no opinions of her own about anything, she mostly found herself agreeing with any views that most approximated those of her husband and her race. For instance, on this day she found herself in agreement with whatever Mrs Smiles said. Mrs Hill stuck to her guns and maintained, as indeed she had always done, that the natives were obedient at heart and *all* you needed was to treat them kindly.

'That's all they need. *Treat them kindly*. They will take kindly to you. Look at my "boys". They all love me. They would do anything I ask them to!' That was her philosophy and it was shared by quite a number of the liberal, progressive type. Mrs Hill had done some liberal things for her 'boys'. Not only had she built some brick quarters (*brick*, mind you) but had also put up a school for the children. It did not matter if the school had not enough teachers or if the children learnt only half a day and worked in the plantations for the other half; it was more than most other settlers had the courage to do!

'It is horrible. Oh, a horrible act,' declared Mrs Smiles

rather vehemently. Mrs Hardy agreed. Mrs Hill remained neutral.

'How could they do it? We've brought 'em civilization. We've stopped slavery and tribal wars. Were they not all leading savage miserable lives?' Mrs Smiles spoke with all her powers of oratory. Then she concluded with a sad shake of the head: 'But I've always said they'll never be civilized, simply can't take it.'

'We should show tolerance,' suggested Mrs Hill. Her tone spoke more of the missionary than Mrs Smiles's looks.

'Tolerant! Tolerant! How long shall we continue being tolerant? Who could have been more tolerant than the Garstones? Who more kind? And to think of all the squatters they maintained!'

'Well, it isn't the squatters who . . .'

'Who did? Who did?'

'They should all be hanged!' suggested Mrs Hardy. There was conviction in her voice.

'And to think they were actually called from bed by their houseboy!'

'Indeed?'

'Yes. It was their houseboy who knocked at their door and urgently asked them to open. Said some people were after him—'

'Perhaps there—'

'No! It was all planned. All a trick. As soon as the door was opened, the gang rushed in. It's all in the paper.'

Mrs Hill looked away rather guiltily. She had not read her paper.

It was time for tea. She excused herself and went near the door and called out in a kind, shrill voice.

'Njoroge! Njoroge!'

Njoroge was her 'houseboy'. He was a tall, broad-shouldered man nearing middle age. He had been in the Hills' service for more than ten years. He wore green trousers, with a red cloth-band round the waist and a red fez on his head. He now appeared at the door and raised his eyebrows in inquiry – an action which with him accompanied the words, 'Yes, Memsahib?' or 'Ndio, Bwana.'

'Leta Chai.'

'Ndio, Memsahib!' and he vanished back after casting a quick glance round all the Memsahibs there assembled. The conversation which had been interrupted by Njoroge's appearance was now resumed.

'They look so innocent,' said Mrs Hardy.

'Yes. Quite the innocent flower but the serpent under it.' Mrs Smiles was acquainted with Shakespeare.

'Been with me for ten years or so. Very faithful. Likes me very much.' Mrs Hill was defending her 'boy'.

'All the same I don't like him. I don't like his face.'

'The same with me.'

Tea was brought. They drank, still chatting about the death, the government's policy, and the political demagogues who were undesirable elements in this otherwise beautiful country. But Mrs Hill maintained that these semi-illiterate demagogues who went to Britain and thought they had education did not know the true aspirations of their people. You could still win your 'boys' by being kind to them.

Nevertheless, when Mrs Smiles and Mrs Hardy had gone, she brooded over that murder and the conversation. She felt uneasy and for the first time noticed that she lived a bit too far from any help in case of an attack. The knowledge that she had a pistol was a comfort.

Supper was over. That ended Njoroge's day. He stepped out of the light into the countless shadows and then vanished into the darkness. He was following the footpath from Mrs Hill's house to the workers' quarters down the hill. He tried to whistle to dispel the silence and loneliness that hung around him. He could not. Instead he heard a bird cry, sharp, shrill. Strange thing for a bird to cry at night.

He stopped, stood stock-still. Below, he could perceive nothing. But behind him the immense silhouette of Memsahib's house – large, imposing – could be seen. He looked back intently, angrily. In his anger, he suddenly thought he was growing old.

'You. You. I've lived with you so long. And you've reduced me to this!' Njoroge wanted to shout to the house all this and many other things that had long accumulated in his heart. The house would not respond. He felt foolish and moved on.

Again the bird cried. Twice!

'A warning to her,' Njoroge thought. And again his whole soul rose in anger – anger against those with a white skin, those foreign elements that had displaced the true sons of the land from their God-given place. Had God not promised Gekoyo all this land, he and his children, forever and ever? Now the land had been taken away.

He remembered his father, as he always did when these moments of anger and bitterness possessed him. He had died in the struggle – the struggle to rebuild the destroyed shrines. That was at the famous 1923 Nairobi Massacre when police fired on a people peacefully demonstrating for their rights. His father was among the people who died. Since then Njoroge had had to struggle for a living – seeking employment here and there on European farms. He had met many types – some harsh, some kind, but all dominating, giving him just what salary they thought fit for him. Then he had come to be employed by the Hills. It was a strange coincidence that he had come here. A big portion of the land now occupied by Mrs Hill was the land his father had shown him as belonging to the family. They had found the land occupied when his father and some of the others had temporarily retired to Muranga owing to famine. They had come back and *Ng'o*! the land was gone.

'Do you see that fig tree? Remember that land is yours. Be patient. Watch these Europeans. They will go and then you can claim the land.'

He was small then. After his father's death, Njoroge had forgotten this injunction. But when he coincidentally came here and saw the tree, he remembered. He knew it all – all by heart. He knew where every boundary went through.

Njoroge had never liked Mrs Hill. He had always resented her complacency in thinking she had done so much for the workers. He had worked with cruel types like Mrs Smiles and Mrs Hardy. But he always knew where he stood with such. But Mrs Hill! Her liberalism was almost smothering. Njoroge hated settlers. He hated above all what he thought was their hypocrisy and complacency. He knew that Mrs Hill was no exception. She was like all the others, only she loved paternalism. It convinced her she was better than the others. But she was worse. You did not know exactly where you stood with her.

All of a sudden, Njoroge shouted, 'I hate them! I hate them!' Then a grim satisfaction came over him. Tonight, anyway, Mrs Hill would die – pay for her own smug liberalism, her paternalism and pay for all the sins of her settler race. It would be one settler less.

He came to his own room. There was no smoke coming from all the other rooms belonging to the other workers. The lights had even gone out in many of them. Perhaps, some were already asleep or gone to the Native Reserve to drink beer. He lit the lantern and sat on the bed. It was a very small room. Sitting on the bed one could almost touch all the corners of the room if one stretched one's arms wide. Yet it was here, *here*, that he with two wives and a number of children had to live, had in fact lived for more than five years. So crammed! Yet Mrs Hill thought that she had done enough by just having the houses built with brick.

'Mzuri, sana, eh?' (very good, eh?) she was very fond of asking. And whenever she had visitors she brought them to the edge of the hill and pointed at the houses.

Again Njoroge smiled grimly to think how Mrs Hill would pay for all this self-congratulatory piety. He also knew that he had an axe to grind. He had to avenge the death of his father and strike a blow for the occupied family land. It was foresight on his part to have taken his wives and children back to the Reserve. They might else have been in the way and in any case he did not want to bring trouble to them should he be forced to run away after the act.

The other Ihii (Freedom Boys) would come at any time now. He would lead them to the house. Treacherous – yes! But how necessary.

The cry of the night bird, this time louder than ever, reached his ears. That was a bad omen. It always portended death – death for Mrs Hill. He thought of her. He remembered her. He had lived with Memsahib and Bwana for more than ten years. He knew that she had loved her husband. Of that he was sure. She almost died of grief when she had learnt of his death. In that moment her settlerism had been shorn off. In that naked moment, Njoroge had been able to pity her. Then the children! He had known them. He had seen them grow up like any other children. Almost like his own. They loved their parents, and Mrs Hill had always been so tender with them, so loving. He thought of them in England, wherever that was, fatherless and motherless.

And then he realized, too suddenly, that he could not do it. He could not tell how, but Mrs Hill had suddenly crystallized into a woman, a wife, somebody like Njeri or Wambui, and above all, a mother. He could not kill a woman. He could not kill a mother. He hated himself for this change. He felt agitated. He tried hard to put himself in the other condition, his former self and see her as just a settler. As a settler, it was easy. For Njoroge hated settlers and all Europeans. If only he could see her like this (as one among many white men or settlers) then he could do it. Without scruples. But he could not bring back the other self. Not now, anyway. He had never thought of her in these terms. Until today. And yet he knew she was the same, and would be the same tomorrow – a patronizing, complacent woman. It was then he knew that he was a divided man and perhaps would ever remain like that. For now it even seemed an impossible thing to snap just like that ten years of relationship, though to him they had been years of pain and shame. He prayed and wished there had never been injustices. Then there would never have been this rift – the rift between white and black. Then he would never have been put in this painful situation.

What was he to do now? Would he betray the 'Boys'? He sat there, irresolute, unable to decide on a course of action. If only he had not thought of her in human terms! That he hated settlers was quite clear in his mind. But to kill a mother of two seemed too painful a task for him to do in a free frame of mind.

He went out.

Darkness still covered him and he could see nothing clearly. The stars above seemed to be anxiously awaiting Njoroge's decision. Then, as if their cold stare was compelling him, he began to walk, walk back to Mrs Hill's house. He had decided to save her. Then probably he would go to the forest. There, he would forever fight with a freer conscience. That seemed excellent. It would also serve as a propitiation for his betrayal of the other 'Boys'.

There was no time to lose. It was already late and the 'Boys' might come any time. So he ran with one purpose – to save the woman. At the road he heard footsteps. He stepped into the bush and lay still. He was certain that those were the 'Boys'. He waited breathlessly for the footsteps to die. Again he hated himself for this betrayal. But how could he fail to hearken to this other voice? He ran on when the footsteps had died. It was necessary to run, for if the 'Boys' discovered his betrayal he would surely meet death. But then he did not mind this. He only wanted to finish this other task first.

At last, sweating and panting, he reached Mrs Hill's house and knocked at the door, crying, 'Memsahib! Memsahib!'

Mrs Hill had not yet gone to bed. She had sat up, a multitude of thoughts crossing her mind. Ever since that afternoon's conversation with the other women, she had felt more and more uneasy. When Njoroge went and she was left alone she had gone to her safe and taken out her pistol, with which she was now toying. It was better to be prepared. It was unfortunate that her husband had died. He might have kept her company.

She sighed over and over again as she remembered her pioneering days. She and her husband and others had tamed the wilderness of this country and had developed a whole mass of unoccupied land. People like Njoroge now lived contented without a single worry about tribal wars. They had a lot to thank the Europeans for.

Yes she did not like those politicians who came to corrupt the otherwise obedient and hard-working men, especially when treated kindly. She did not like this murder of the

Garstones. No! She did not like it. And when she remembered the fact that she was really alone, she thought it might be better for her to move down to Nairobi or Kinangop and stay with friends a while. But what would she do with her boys? Leave them there? She wondered. She thought of Njoroge. A queer boy. Had he many wives? Had he a large family? It was surprising even to her to find that she had lived with him so long, yet had never thought of these things. This reflection shocked her a little. It was the first time she had ever thought of him as a man with a family. She had always seen him as a servant. Even now it seemed ridiculous to think of her houseboy as a father with a family. She sighed. This was an omission, something to be righted in future.

And then she heard a knock on the front door and a voice calling out 'Memsahib! Memsahib!'

It was Njoroge's voice. Her houseboy. Sweat broke out on her face. She could not even hear what the boy was saying for the circumstances of the Garstones' death came to her. This was her end. The end of the road. So Njoroge had led them here! She trembled and felt weak.

But suddenly, strength came back to her. She knew she was alone. She knew they would break in. No! She would die bravely. Holding her pistol more firmly in her hand, she opened the door and quickly fired. Then a nausea came over her. She had killed a man for the first time. She felt weak and fell down crying, 'Come and kill me!' She did not know that she had in fact killed her saviour.

On the following day, it was all in the papers. That a single woman could fight a gang fifty strong was bravery unknown. And to think she had killed one too!

Mrs Smiles and Mrs Hardy were especially profuse in their congratulations.

'We told you they're all bad.'

'They are all bad,' agreed Mrs Hardy. Mrs Hill kept quiet. The circumstances of Njoroge's death worried her. The more she thought about it, the more of a puzzle it was to her. She gazed still into space. Then she let out a slow enigmatic sigh.

'I don't know,' she said.

'Don't know?' Mrs Hardy asked.

'Yes. That's it. Inscrutable.' Mrs Smiles was triumphant. 'All of them should be whipped.'

'All of them should be whipped,' agreed Mrs Hardy.

BESSIE HEAD

JACOB: THE STORY OF A FAITH-HEALING PRIEST

THE QUIET, SLEEPY village of Makaleng was about thirty miles from a big railway station in Northern Botswana. Makaleng village was quiet and sleepy because the people were fat and well-fed. Envious visitors to the village often exclaimed that there must be something wrong with the sky overhead, because whilst the rest of the country was smitten by drought year after year, Makaleng village never failed to receive its yearly quota of twenty-two inches of rain. Whenever people stood in groups and shook their heads sadly about another of those summers of no rain and no crops, someone would always interrupt to say:

'But I've just come from Makaleng village. The people there are eating water-melon and fresh green mealies. And from their lands they are about to harvest bags and bags of corn.'

Thus, Makaleng was one of those far-away wonders of the world which people sometimes visited but never thought of inhabiting. It never occurred to people perishing of drought and hunger to rush there in droves, settle there, and produce their crops and raise their cattle in ease and comfort. As it was, good fortune was added to good fortune in Makaleng. The village had a small population of about five hundred people and a big, broad sandy river cut its way through the central part of the village. In the summer this river flowed in torrents of muddy water, and in winter gigantic pools of water shimmered like mercury in the pot-holes of its sandy bed.

The summer grass of Makaleng was a miracle too. It shot seven feet high into the sky like a thick, dense jungle which terrified the small boys who herded the cattle. The small boys had a secret joke among themselves about the summer grass of Makaleng. They never set foot in it. Early each morning they would stand at its perimeter and drive the cattle into this dark jungle of stalks and leaves to graze. Once the last swishing tail had disappeared, they would retreat as far as possible, hugging their arms around their bony chests so afraid were they of the terror that lived all summer long in the dense grass. For some hours a deep silence would reign over the grazing area; then all of a sudden, the agonized bellows of the cattle and their mad, stampeding feet would send the birds into the air with startled shrieks and make the cattleboys jump for their sticks. A ferocious vampire-fly bred in the long grass and pierced its deep, sharp mouth-parts into the skin of either man or beast to suck up the blood. The pain caused by its sting was excruciating. Yet the cattle never seemed to learn. For once they had stampeded out of the grass and had had the flies beaten off them by the cattle-boys, they allowed themselves to be driven back again into this terrible grazing area. And that's how the cattle were grazed all summer. Maybe cattle-grazing in this manner was a hard job, but if so only the small boys who herded the cattle knew it to be so and maybe by sunset, when they herded the cattle home, they had temporarily forgotten the vampire-fly. They laughed and joked among themselves, and as soon as they entered their yards, they started fights with their sisters.

It's not certain what the authorities thought about the village of Makaleng and its good twenty-two inches of rain, or whether the area was suited to agricultural development or not. Someone had muttered something about the soil; it became too easily waterlogged. Nor did the ordinary people of the country visit Makaleng because the people there were eating fresh green mealies in a drought year. Oh no, Makaleng village was famous in the hearts of ordinary people because it had two prophets.

The one prophet, Jacob, lived on the sunrise side of the village. The other prophet, Lebojang, lived on the sunset side. Prophet Jacob was very poor and lived in a mud hut. He walked around with no shoes. Prophet Lebojang was very rich. He lived in a great mansion and drove around in a very posh car.

It was not the habit of Prophet Lebojang to notice the existence of Prophet Jacob, except that on one occasion Prophet Jacob had entered his yard on the death of a relative. But as Prophet Jacob attended all funerals from the sympathy and kindness of his heart, he was unperturbed by the cold reception given him by Lebojang and his followers, and the fact that he was overlooked when plates of food were handed round. Much more terrible things had Lebojang done to him on his arrival in Makaleng. There was a time when lightning used to stike the hut of Prophet Jacob, though there was not a cloud in the sky. There was a time when an enormous hissing snake would suddenly manifest itself in the hut of Prophet Jacob, but neither lightning nor snakes, nor poisoned food and water could take the life of Prophet Jacob. At first, Prophet Jacob had wanted to flee the hatred of Prophet Lebojang, but one night when the persecution and torture had reached its peak, he heard, so he told two close friends, the Voice of his God in the silence of his hut. It said:

'Haven't I always prepared a table for you in the presence of your enemies? Then why don't you trust me to take care of you?'

And that was enough for Prophet Jacob. He no longer

feared to stay in Makaleng. It was never quite clear to those who loved Prophet Jacob just who his God was. At times he would refer to him as Jesus. At times his God, in moments of inspiration, appeared to be the width and depth of his own experience and suffering. This he in turn called the Voice which had come to him at all the turning points of his life, forcing him into strange and incomprehensible acts.

There was a time when Prophet Jacob had been as rich a man as Prophet Lebojang. He had been the owner of a store in the big railway village thirty miles from Makaleng. He had had a car, a beautiful wife who loved beautiful clothes, and two pretty daughters. To enable him to give his wife all that she desired, Jacob had even established a big beer-brewing business from which he earned huge profits. After twelve years of this rich and sumptuous living, during which time Jacob drank heavily and lived in the roar of prosperity, a bolt from the blue turned him into a man of rags and tatters overnight. It happened like this: one week his wife had a sudden desire to visit relatives living in another part of the country. She took the two small girls with her and Jacob was left alone. The night of the day of his wife's departure he retired early. At about midnight there was a thunderous, crashing sound at the door. Jacob sprang awake and found his bedroom filled with thieves. Some of the thieves held him down while his hands were tied behind his back and his mouth gagged. As he lay helpless on the floor, the thieves quietly and calmly removed every piece of furniture and clothing from the house. They had already completely emptied the store. All he had left was a few hundred rands in the bank, and he lay there weeping in the darkness. In this darkness and silence he heard the Voice of his God.

'Jacob,' it said quietly, 'why have you forgotten me? It

is I who have brought this trouble on you so that you may do my work. From now on you shall only have your daily bread.'

Even though he strained his eyes in the darkness, hoping to get some glimpse of a form which uttered these words, he could see no one. But the words burned into his mind like fire. Not for one moment did he doubt that it was the Voice of his God. And that was enough for Jacob. Amazed neighbours found him the next morning still trussed up and gagged, lying on the floor of his bedroom in the ransacked house behind the ransacked store.

'You must call the police at once,' they said. 'The sooner you report a burglary, the sooner the police will catch up with the thieves.'

But Jacob only stared back at them absent-mindedly. His mind had withdrawn itself from preoccupations with business. Besides, how could he explain the truth to them? How could he tell them he had heard a Voice in the night and that the Voice had claimed responsibility for the thefts? Hadn't the Voice said so? It wasn't a matter that could be mentioned to the police either. It was better to remain silent than to tell the truth. The neighbours watching him remain silent and unmoving on the floor, clucked, clucked sympathetically and shook their heads. Among themselves they said:

'This sudden trouble has unhinged the mind of our friend, Jacob. Look, he can't utter a word.'

Some of the women began to weep loudly. They could not forget the days of starvation in their own homes and the way in which Jacob had never turned a hungry child away from his door. Jacob was widely commended as a good man because of his generosity, and their weeping was meant to be an unspoken rebuke to God. Why did he strike down the good man, always? They wept this way when any of their children died and unconsciously created legends about their saintliness.

Two weeks later, Jacob's wife returned to this changed situation. As she breezed into the house with her high-heeled shoes and big, wide, red-painted mouth, it seemed to Jacob that he was seeing the type of woman he had married for the first time. He said to himself: 'I shall tell her the truth. If she is really my wife, she will give up these ways and join me in the work I have to do.'

'Darling,' she gushed, flinging off a brilliant red turban and kicking off her shoes. 'I've already heard the news. All up and down the line people are talking of nothing else. They even say it has unsettled your mind. I said: "Bosh! we'll make it up in no time." And so here I am, all ready to give it a go.'

She paused and looked at him with a brilliant smile. He looked back at her, almost choked with fear. Had they really not communicated with each other throughout these twelve years of married life? Her mood was so foreign, as though their lives had never flowed together. But what really choked him was his own nature which had constantly sought security; he had never loved any other woman because of this desire for emotional security. Now he was to lose this too. Still, he said the fatal words, so gravely and so finally:

'We are not going back to the old ways of trading in liquor,' he said. 'I have to do the work of the Lord.'

She laughed, ha! ha! ha! in a gay and brittle way. Life had never had any depth for her. She was always in such a rush. She was also a woman of practical common sense with no whims or fancies.

'You aren't serious darling?' she said, with raised eyebrows.

'I am,' he said.

'But who is this Lord?' she said. 'No one has ever seen

him. There's nothing we Africans have but the Lord. We sit down and pray to the Lord all the time but he doesn't bring us one ounce of sugar. It would be a different thing if he came down to earth and we could see him. But no one takes the Lord seriously, darling. He doesn't come down.'

'You may say so,' Jacob replied, 'but I have heard the Voice of the Lord and I cannot disobey it.'

He had in his hand the last R10.000 he had withdrawn from the bank. He handed it to his wife, stood up, and walked out of the empty house not looking back once, not even at his two wide-eyed little girls. The Voice of the Lord had told him to go to Makaleng.

It was not the first time Jacob had tasted wealth and had wealth removed from him, overnight. He was born into wealth. His father was a German who had come to Botswana with an eye to the cattle speculating business. Many a man had reached near millionaire-hood on cattle speculating because it was quick, easy money. The German had married a Motswana woman and established a cattle ranch, mostly used as a transit farm for fattening all the lean cattle he bought as a speculation from the local people. The ranch was not many miles from the village of Makaleng and it did not take him many months to organize his cattle business and have thousands of rands in the bank. His wife also bore him twins, two boys – one of whom she named Jacob, and the other Isaac, these names having been obtained from her studies of the Bible. If questioned about this part of his life, Jacob cannot remember it too well. He vaguely remembers wearing shoes and being well clothed and sleeping in a bed with sheets. But of his father and mother he has little recollection. One day, not long after Jacob and Isaac had turned six years old, his father and mother took a trip by car into the village of Makaleng. As they were crossing the narrow bridge which spanned the broad river in a heavy downpour, the car skidded and went over the edge into the muddy torrent below. Both were killed.

As from nowhere, along came an uncle, the brother of Jacob's mother, weeping bitter tears over the death of his sister. He approached a certain chief of Makaleng and offered to act as guardian of the two boys until they were old enough to inherit their father's wealth. What happened subsequently has often made people say that the then chief of Makaleng village had a share in the robbery of the children's inheritance. It was his duty to see that the guardianship of the children was conducted in an honourable way yet, to the many aghast comments from the people of Makaleng, he only turned a deaf ear. The uncle, the brother of Jacob's mother, became overnight the richest man in Makaleng. His brood of twelve children walked about in shoes and socks. He acquired a brick house and a car and was seen to wave about thick wads of money in the hotel bar of the big railway village. On the other hand, his sister's children, Jacob and Isaac, who now lived with him, were seen to walk about the village without shoes, dressed in the discarded rags and tatters of their uncle's children. What little was left after the wholesale slaughter and sale of the fifty thousand cattle was given to the two small boys, Jacob and Isaac, to herd in the traditional way in the vampire-fly, grazing-ground of Makaleng. Not once after that did the uncle's children have to soil their hands with work. They had acquired two slaves.

Those who are born to suffer, experience suffering to its abysmal depths. The damage to the two children did not stop at the expropriation of their inheritance. It was now claimed by the uncle and all the relatives that since the children were not pure Botswana by birth, they were therefore of an inferior species. They were fed according to their status. They were given plain porridge with salt and water at every meal, day in and day out, year in and year out. Their sleeping quarters were a ramshackle hut at the bottom of their uncle's yard. They slept on pieces of sacking and lived out their whole lives in that dog house.

Jacob is old now. He relates these experiences of his childhood without bitterness. He will also tell you that his uncle, as though prompted by a subconscious guilt, sent him and his brother to the night school of Makaleng village together with all the small cattle-herding boys who could not attend school during the day. He even remembers the way they were taught to sing the alphabet and clap their hands.

There is a point in his story when you begin to doubt Jacob's sanity and that of his God. Somehow you don't doubt his adult experiences and his conversations with God, but you doubt cruelty and stress placed on a young and helpless child. It's when he tells you about what happened when he was twelve years old that a bad light is thrown on Jacob's God. At this time Jacob's twin brother Isaac died, worn out by the poor diet and hard labour. A deep and terrifying loneliness possessed the heart of the small boy who was left behind that night. He had lost the only living being who had shared some love with him in a world peopled by monsters. There is much said about the love and sharing to be found within tribal societies and much of this is true – but true too is Jacob's uncle. Any child trapped in this cycle of cruelty can find no way out except to cry lonely, hot tears in the dark night.

At this point, says Jacob, while he lay alone in his broken-down hut, weeping, he first heard the Voice of his God.

'Jacob,' it said, 'one day I shall call you to do my work. All the suffering you endure now is but a preparation for the work you have to do.'

Jacob sat up startled, dashing the tears from his eyes. At that time also his eyes searched for a presence or form in the room but there was nothing, only the strong impression of having heard a Voice. You lean forward eagerly towards the now old man; his God seems very dubious, so you ask: Did he bring a little piece of meat on the morrow to eat with that dreadful porridge? Did he change the world and give a jersey to a little boy shivering in tattered clothes? To all your questions Jacob responds with a look of baffled surprise. It has not occurred to him to ask his God for anything all these long long years. He has been too busy fulfilling the orders and strange commands of that Voice. It didn't seem as though Jacob's God wanted him to have anything for himself, even when he was little. No meat came. No jersey. It makes you feel something is wrong because even in old age Jacob hasn't got shoes. It makes you feel like breaking down and weeping because even in old age Jacob hasn't got shoes. So you say, almost violently: Does he love you this God? Why do you let him disrupt your life like that?

Jacob keeps silent a moment sorting this out. Then he tells you that every time he heard that Voice a great peace would fill his heart; that peace gave him the courage to do whatever the Voice requested of him. To an outsider there never seemed to be much coherence in what was going on between Jacob and his God. But the way in which he expressed this relationship in deeds arrested the attention. Everything about him was very beautiful and simple and deeply sincere. He had too, one of the oddest churches in the whole wide world.

* * *

On his arrival in the village of Makaleng after parting company from his wife, Jacob set about constructing a mud hut which was to be used both as accommodation for himself and his church. His uncle and the chief of Makaleng who had stolen the inheritance of himself and his brother, were long since dead. At the time of his uncle's death the relatives had squabbled and torn each other to pieces over what remained of the wealth which was not theirs. These relatives lived on the sunset side of the village and were the followers of Prophet Lebojang. The relatives, like Prophet Lebojang, affected in public not to be aware of the sudden and unexpected return of Jacob. He had been away from the village for almost fourteen years, having walked out of his uncle's home as soon as he realized that he could stand on his own two feet and earn his living. But secretly, like all thieves, they were at first intensely interested in the activities of Jacob on the sunrise side of the village, fearing that he might still start a commotion about his stolen inheritance. They also knew about all the black magic spells Prophet Lebojang was casting on Prophet Jacob. No one quite knew why Prophet Lebojang did not have Prophet Jacob killed outright once the black magic powers had failed to destroy him. Some think that the Voice of Prophet Jacob's God might have spoken to Prophet Lebojang and told him under no circumstances to harm Prophet Jacob. This was a rumour in the village, said to have issued from the mouth of Prophet Lebojang.

But the activities of Prophet Jacob on the sunrise side of the village soon had the relatives and Prophet Lebojang rolling on the ground with laughter. After he had completed his hut, Prophet Jacob purchased for himself some cheap material which he shaped into a priestly cloak and in one corner pinned a small cross. He next made a wooden table and carved three wooden candlesticks. Those candlesticks he placed on the table and always, when he wanted to pray, he placed a jug of fresh, clean water near the candlesticks. Curious people would often question him about the water jug and he would reply simply that his God had ordered him to put the water there. After each session of prayer, he was to put the water in bottles and then give it freely to anyone who suffered from ailments or sorrow. His God had assured him that the blessed water would remove all people's troubles.

It took great simplicity of heart to approach a church such as the one conducted by Prophet Jacob. Prophet Jacob had no shoes, so he conducted his services in his bare feet. Many, many strange churches, variants on the Christian religion, exist in Botswana but they all have a bit of glitter and dash. They have funds behind them. Sometimes, like Prophet Lebojang, they put both God and the Devil on the same altar for many years and nothing happens except a great increase in wealth. In contrast to all of them, Prophet Jacob only had the Voice of his God whom he obeyed. From this Voice he received the strictest orders about how to conduct himself. He was never, never under any circumstances to canvass for membership. People would be sent to him. Also, the bare minimum for his daily bread would be given him and this he must break in half and share with whomsoever should step in the door. From these commands Prophet Jacob never deviated one inch.

The next surprise Jacob received was the type of congregation sent to him by his God. One afternoon, towards sunset, as Jacob sat in the silence of his hut, the door was slowly pushed open and six small black heads peered cautiously in.

'We have come to the church, Maruti*' the children said.

* Maruti: a priest.

Jacob leapt to his feet in great joy and hastened to put on his cloak. The words of the children corresponded to a dream he had had. In the dream he had sung a song. It went like this:

Look, I shall be coming again on clouds of glory,
When you see me children,
You must say: Dumelang! Allelujah!

The song had a very gay rhythm. The little girls got carried away by it, their skirts swishing up and down as they kept time to the beat by clapping their hands vigorously. From that day onwards there was a never-ending bustle of activity in the yard of Jacob, and these activities spread themselves thoughout the whole of the sunrise side of the village. The children constantly brought him information of someone ailing there, someone ailing here, and soon it became a not uncommon sight to see Jacob trailing behind a group of children, all singing and making their way to a hut to help someone in sorrow. In all cases the sorrow or ailments would be removed and people would quietly rise up and go about their daily business.

After the first reaction of surprised amusement, no one paid much attention to the church of Jacob because of his poverty and because his congregation was composed entirely of children. No adults joined the church, though through the efforts of the children many of them received a blessing from Jacob's God. A few would approach Jacob wistfully and ask to become members of the church, but he would always reply:

'Please first go to your Maruti and ask his permission.'

This permission was never granted. Yet Jacob's reputation spread quietly and persistently; people pointed out his goodness to like-minded people. Thus, when the lorry brought visitors to Makaleng, half the people made their way to the hut of Jacob and half to the mansion of Lebojang. It was almost as though there were no meeting place between the people who went to Jacob and the people who went to Lebojang. Lebojang's relationship with people was that of a businessman. You paid your money and that was that.

If you dressed well and looked rich, a servant would immediately approach you and lead you into Lebojang's plush lounge. There you would be constantly plied with all the good things from Lebojang's pantry until he was free to interview you. If you were in rags and tatters, you sat out all day in the yard and, the interview being over, you would then wander about the village in search of provisions. Lebojang enriched himself from rich and poor alike but he only gave the good things in his pantry to those who had the least need of them. But whether rich or poor, all came to Lebojang for the same purpose – to make use of his stunning powers.

A woman would travel many miles to report to Lebojang that for a long time she had concealed a purse of money under her mattress. One day she had found the purse of money removed and it had been impossible to trace the thief. Lebojang would keep silent awhile, then fix his penetrating eyes on the woman.

'Do you have a friend named Bontle?' he would ask. And the amazed woman would merely nod her head.

'Well,' Lebojang would say. 'It is she who stole your purse on the 25th of February.'

Or again, a woman would say that she had no end of trouble from her husband, who had suddenly taken to drinking heavily. And Lebojang would say:

'Does he have a friend named Toto . . .? Well, this Toto

has one aim in mind and that is to take you as his sweetheart. Therefore he leads your husband to drink.'

Such was the power of Lebojang; he would come out with names and dates and prophecies. His charges for these services were very high. It did not matter to him that people were secretly poisoned or driven mad by his prophecies; he simply took his money and that was that. But at least these prophecies of names and dates could bear the light of day. Once his other deeds became known people were to ponder deeply on the nature of evil.

The other half of the lorry-load of visitors to Makaleng had no tales of lost purses or drunken husbands but a terrible anguish of heart. They said to Jacob:

'I have so many troubles. I don't know how to sort them out.'

The practical issues were never discussed. A man in that gathering would have no work for a year and his family would be destitute. After seeing Jacob and participating in the worship of his church, the man would strike a job in two or three days; not anything spectacular, but his poverty would be eased. There was something else too that developed in a quite natural way – an exchange of gifts system. No one ever left Jacob's hut without a parcel. Many grateful seekers of help brought gifts to Jacob; a bag of corn, a bag of sugar, a box of eggs, and so on. These gifts in turn filled many destitute people with good things so that they did not leave Jacob's home hungry. Then too, the church really belonged to the children. They would come in towards the close of day, and the adults would sit to one side as respectful spectators while Jacob and the children conversed with the Lord. No one seemed to question the uniqueness of this, how it was possible for children at the age when their teeth fall out, to turn up promptly at sunset for sermons. Not that they comprehended anything, not even Jacob's simple sermons.

So, in this way, following their two strange occupations, a routine and ritual established itself around the lives of the prophets of Makaleng. Prophet Lebojang increased in wealth, until it was said at the time he met his doom that he was a near-millionaire. Prophet Jacob increased only in his love for the Lord. Seemingly, in gratitude for this, the Lord arranged one more turning point in the life of Prophet Jacob. After many years of living alone, the Lord sent him a wife named Johannah.

Johannah was a tall, striking handsome woman with a beautifully carved mouth around which a faint smile always lingered. She also had a thick cluster of eyelashes around her pitch-black eyes. These two striking features had brought her lots of trouble. She was the sort of woman men would look at twice. Less attractive women were more in tune with the feeling of the times; there was no such thing as marriage left. Johannah had always received proposals of marriage and produced four children always with a view to marrying their fathers, but at the critical moment, the man simply disappeared.

For some years Johannah lived in the yard of her elder brother, who was married. Because of her position as an unmarried woman with children, she assumed the major responsibilities of running the home; washing, cooking for the family and mending the clothes of her brother's children as well as her own. Her brother's wife never soiled her hands with work; either she lay in bed until eleven o'clock in the morning or stood up, dressed herself in smart clothes and spent the day visiting relatives and friends. At least, Johannah reasoned, there was no need for her brother to employ a servant for his fancy wife. Johannah was careful to see that there was no waste in food and other household expenses. In spite of all the services she offered, her brother's manner abruptly changed towards her. He was often angry and impatient with his sister because he was nagged by his wife who had said to him:

'Two of Johannah's children have now reached school-going age. Are you going to foot the bill?'

Thus it was that Johannah found herself confronted by a family conference. Relatives gathered in the yard and to them Johannah's brother put his complaint; he could not afford to support all Johannah's children as well as his own. They spent some time discussing her misdeeds with rising wrath, flinging around such terms as harlot and loose woman who took her sins lightly. Johannah listened to it all with an amused smile, especially her sister-in-law's loud, irate tone. Once Johannah was no longer in the yard would she do all the housework? At last Johannah was allowed to speak. She raised her head proudly and quoted an old proverb:

'I agree with all that has been said about me,' she said. 'But I am a real woman and as the saying goes the children of a real woman do not get lean or die.'

Johannah spent many days wandering hither and thither in search of employment but without success. It was during her wanderings from home to home for possible employment as a house servant that she was told about the Prophet Jacob of Makaleng village who had bought work and comfort to the hearts of many people. One morning before dawn she set out on foot to the village of Makaleng, arriving there about mid-morning.

Like all the visitors to Prophet Jacob, she did not notice his poverty nor the simplicity of his church but right away began confiding the troubles and disappointments of her life. Now and then she would cry a little as she recalled one promise of marriage after another and then the stress of being left alone with fatherless children. She cried in such a peculiar way that even Jacob, who was concentrating his mind on her tale of sorrow, diverted his attention to her tears. They kept welling up in abrupt little bundles which were then caught in the thick cluster of her eyelashes and deposited neatly into her lap. Not one splash soiled the smooth curved surface of her cheekbones. They were very much an expression of the concentrated emotional intensity of the woman, as though, like her tears, she only saw one thing at a time, in the immediate present, and could not be troubled much about the past. He noted that it was only on actually recalling a disillusionment in words that an abrupt bundle of tears would appear; everything about her was open and straightforward.

'I have come to see that the faults are all mine,' she said. 'Each time it was I who believed that the father of my child would marry me. I have paid heavily for this error of judgement. But the saying is still there: the children of a real woman cannot fall into the fire.'

Then she lapsed into an abrupt waiting silence keeping her pretty eyes in a steadfast gaze on her lap. Jacob also hesitated. She was the only visitor of the day and she had arrived early. He never said prayers for visitors without the children as they were now an inextricable part of his life. Perhaps the woman would like to prepare some food for herself. She looked extremely hungry.

'Yes indeed,' he said, slowly. 'There are many good sayings in the world. There is the saying that the foot cannot always find its way home. It may be that I should pass your village one day and be afflicted by hunger. You would soon rush to the cooking pot to prepare something for me. Therefore I am paying you for this kindness before it is done. In the corner you will find a bag of corn and next to that a dish of meat. Prepare some food and eat.'

A brief expression of pleased surprise flitted across the woman's face. She arose in one neat self-contained movement and set about to do as he had ordered with a grave, absorbed manner.

'So it's true,' she thought, as she dipped into the bag of corn. 'The man's goodness is expressed in deeds as well as words. How lucky for me that I took this journey. My sorrows are taken away from me this very minute.'

She had far to go on the return journey and without much waste of time Jacob sent a message to the children so that as soon as she had eaten she might receive the prayers and blessed water. In the twinkling of an eye the yard was filled from all directions with rushing feet. Johannah paused in the act of stirring the porridge to stare at the children in amazement. So this was true too; the Prophet kept a church of children. The woman who had told her this had merely shrugged and smiled. Most curious people had, out of a profound respect for Prophet Jacob, refrained from questioning him about this matter.

'I shall certainly bring my children to this church,' Johannah thought to herself. 'There is only goodness here.'

An hour later Johannah was on her way home with a swift, light step. It seemed as though a soft wind blew her home. On her head she carried a quantity of corn for herself and her children and some eggs, sugar, and tea. In her heart she carried a vivid memory of the children's singing.

'How lucky I am,' she thought. 'How wonderful this day has been.'

Alone that night in his hut Jacob found that a wandering

mood possessed him. It was always the hour when his soul had soared in peace and freedom, detached from the cares of the day. But on this night it remained firmly on the earth, amusing and entertaining itself with trifles. At first it said:

'Oh, so people cry in all kinds of different ways. Some cry as though they are spitting tears out onto the dry ground.'

Then he would catch himself at this trifling amusement and mutter aloud:

'But I am in old age now. I must be fifty-five,' and he would sigh heavily thinking of his creeping old age. Then the game would start again:

'Porridge is always porridge but some people are better at cooking it than others . . .'

This went on for some time and Jacob was unaware that he was actually smiling to himself. This state of affairs was suddenly interrupted by the Voice of his God sounding loudly and clearly in his ears. It said:

'You are a very foolish man Jacob. How could you let your future wife depart so quickly?'

Being somewhat caught off-balance, for the first time Jacob replied to his God. He said:

'But I am already in old age. She looks about twenty-nine.'

And he turned with a startled expression and stared over his shoulder. But there was no further sound except . . . except an impression of soft laughter. Feeling shaken and confused, Jacob stood up and prepared his blankets on the floor.

A month went by and then one Sunday morning Johannah arrived once again with the early-morning lorry-load of visitors to Makaleng, this time bringing her four children with her. She looked very smart in a new cotton frock and brand-new low-heeled shoes. Just a day after she had paid her first visit to Prophet Jacob, she had found a job as a cook and housekeeper for a wealthy person for R10.00 a month. Somehow Prophet Jacob had already known in his heart of her coming, but since the other visitors who also crowded into his yard did not know this secret of his heart there was no one to point out that Prophet Jacob pointedly omitted to gaze in the direction of Johannah. But there was an intense joy in his heart and a glow like a candle flame in his eyes. The joy in the heart of Prophet Jacob soon affected everyone. A surprise feast was arranged on the spur of the moment. Someone suddenly walked out and bought a goat; another rice, and another some vegetables for salad while the women ran about making preparations for the feast. The children also appeared with their freshly scrubbed faces and clean Sunday clothes and sat among the guests clapping their hands and singing the songs taught to them by Jacob. The villagers of Makaleng were amazed. Never had they heard such a commotion issue from the yard of Prophet Jacob.

'Perhaps Prophet Jacob is holding a marriage feast,' they said. 'Perhaps one of his visitors is getting married.'

And they hastened to wash and make their way to the yard of Prophet Jacob. But no bride and groom were in evidence. There was only joy. Not even prayers were said that day, nor was anyone given the blessed water. Each one was blessed by the joy in his own heart. By sunset, when the lorry turned up to take the visitors back to their own villages, no one wanted to leave. At last the lorry driver had to get out of his lorry and scold the people.

'Look here, people,' he shouted, 'no one pays me for overtime. I have to get back to my wife and children.'

With many wistful, lingering glances, the visitors slowly climbed into the lorry. They kept on repeating to themselves that they would surely visit Prophet Jacob the following

Sunday. Since Prophet Jacob was so foolhardy as to omit gazing in any direction that might contain the presence of Johannah, he failed to see that she was not present among the visitors who climbed onto the lorry. But he stood for a long while gazing after it until the flaming red sun dropped down behind the flat horizon. The darkness and gloom that swept down on his heart was like the sudden descent of the black night on Makaleng. He sighed heavily and slowly shuffled towards his lonely hut. It was a good thing for Prophet Jacob that he had a strong heart, for as he pushed open the door of his hut the flaming sun reversed itself and shone again like a dazzling light in the gloom. There was Johannah seated on the floor with her children. Prophet Jacob could not utter a word. He stood for a long while at the door like one stunned. Johannah cried many bundles of neat tears because she could not account for her actions, only that it seemed like her death to climb into the lorry and go away. But, being fearful of this silence, she said painfully:

'You must forgive me. I am so happy here.'

Imagine the amazement of the villagers of Makaleng! That following Monday morning they had to rub their eyes in disbelief and doubt their sanity, for there was Prophet Jacob in his yard with a woman constructing a mud hut. Prophet Jacob had been celebate for so long that they had ceased to regard him as a normal man. Some of the scandal-mongers of the village, hoping to get the full details of this unexpected development, immediately picked up their hoes and dishes and made their way to the yard of Prophet Jacob to help in the construction of the hut. By midday the walls were complete and Prophet Jacob had already set up the framework for the thatched roof. The scandal-mongers were entertained that afternoon by all the women of the village.

'It's true,' they said. 'Prophet Jacob has acquired a new wife.'

Once the impact of it struck their sense of humour, they began to roll on the ground, laughing till the tears poured out of their eyes. In this manner it became an accepted fact that Johannah was the legal wife of Prophet Jacob.

As for Jacob, a whole new world of learning and living opened up for him. He soon found that his home was run peacefully with clockwork precision, by a woman full of the traditions and customs of the country. Jacob had no full knowledge of these customs as his upbringing had been that of an outcast living apart from the household and it was as though he was transported back into a childhood he might have had had his mother lived. His first wife had been a very different type of woman from Johannah, very modern and daring and very de-tribalized. If there were such things as customs which governed the behaviour of children and adults, she knew nothing about this. Now, from Johannah, he was to learn that there were strict, hard-and-fast laws, governing the conduct of family life. In spite of Johannah having produced so many fatherless children, she had indoctrinated them all with the customs of her own childhood so that they were among the most disciplined children on earth. It was an easy, almost effortless act for the children to accept Jacob as their father because according to custom all adult people were regarded as the mothers and fathers of all children.

Jacob was amazed to note how nothing was ever out of place in his home, in spite of its having been invaded so suddenly by so many children. If a guest arrived and was served tea, it would not be long before one of the children appeared and removed the forgotten tea-tray from the floor. Then the cups and pots would be immediately rinsed out and stacked neatly away. There was always a quiet hustle and bustle to and fro. There were always chores for the little girls and boys. There was always wood and water to fetch, corn to stamp and floors to sweep, and never for a moment did the children sit idle during the daylight. Thinking of the hardship of his own childhood when he had longed to play, Jacob one day questioned his wife:

'Why so much work for the children?' he asked. 'When do they have time to play?'

She kept silent a while, staring steadfastly into her lap. Then she said, smiling faintly:

'We must teach the children the real things, husband. Is life play? No, it is hardship. Therefore it's better for the children to learn this lesson while young so that they will stand up to the hardship.'

There seemed to be much sense in her reasoning, yet it made Jacob ponder about the eagerness with which the children attended his church. It seemed to him then that his church was the only place in which they could relax, sing, and play together. He determined to have no more sermons, only singing and play. Perhaps the Lord had seen all the hardships children endured. But he did not mention this to his wife as half his mind approved of the way she brought up the children. Half of the customs too agreed with the many good things the Lord had pointed out to Jacob. From their mother's training, they broke the crust of bread and shared it equally with each other or any other child who happened to be passing by. Jacob pondered on all these things shown him by his new wife, and also the customs which she followed so strictly to teach her children the correct way of living with others.

One other thing caused a stir of amazement in Makaleng village. Jacob now had a family but his occupation brought him no funds. There were two boys of school-going age who needed clothes and school fees. Therefore Jacob spent each morning doing odd jobs about the village to have a small amount of money in hand for whatever his family might need. The women of the village said Johannah was indeed blessed to have such a good man. If Prophet Jacob had condescended to be a priest like Prophet Lebojang, he could have got people to contribute handsomely to his church. But Prophet Jacob always said: 'Please get permission from your Maruti before you join my church.' And which priest would give this permission when it meant losing one of his pay packets?

Not long after these discussions of the people of Makaleng, the world came crashing down on Prophet Lebojang. It all began simply enough. A certain man of Makaleng village, named Kelepile, was detained on business in the big railway village thirty miles away. He had missed the last transport home and decided to make the journey by foot. As he approached Makaleng he noticed a big car parked on one side of the road and from the bushes nearby he heard voices raised in argument. Being merely curious about what people could be doing in the bushes at night, he turned and crept near. Soon he was able to hear the conversation quite clearly.

An alien voice was saying: 'It's always the case with you, Lebojang. You always want the best parts of the body.'

Lebojang appeared to be very cross. He said, 'I'm telling you, Bogosi, you won't get the money if you don't hand the heart over to me.'

The man, Kelepile, waited to hear no more. In fact, his legs were shaking with terror. He has often said that he cannot recollect how they brought him with such speed into Makaleng village. He knew well enough that the conversation was about a ritual murder, just committed. The first thought in his mind had been to save his own life but to his amazement he found his shaking legs taking him to the police station. And this was how it came about that the police surrounded Lebojang and two other men, one of whom was a witch-doctor by profession and the other a chief. They arrested the three men with the cut-up parts of a dead child in their hands. This was the first time that the doers of these evil deeds had been caught in the act. Often the mutilated bodies were found but the murderers were seldom caught.

The position was desperate. The chief and witch-doctor immediately turned state witness and shifted the blame to Lebojang. The witch-doctor was so obliging as to point out to the authorities the graves of twenty other victims to fix the case against Lebojang. They said they did this sort of murder to make potions for the cattle of rich men, like the chief, to increase. Lebojang could even make rain. Lebojang's potions had long been recommended as the best in the land. He had been making these potions and killing men, women, and children for twenty years. He had also been the priest of a Christian church with a big blue cross down the back of his cloak.

Lebojang was sentenced to death. But the story did not end there. A strange thing happened after Lebojang's death. People say the soul of Lebojang returned from the grave. At night, it kept on knocking on the doors of all the people to whom he had sold potions. Some of these people packed their belongings and fled. Some went insane. Some people also say that Lebojang's soul is like that of Lazarus. Lebojang only wanted to tell the people whom he awoke at night – his fellow ritual murderers – to desist from taking the lives of people because of the agony he was suffering now.

CAMARA LAYE

THE EYES OF THE STATUE

SHE STOPPED WALKING for a moment – ever since she had set out, she had been feeling as though she had earned a moment's rest – and she took stock of her surroundings. From the top of the hill on which she stood, she saw spread out before her a great expanse of country.

Far away in the distance was a town or rather the remains of a town, for there was no trace of movement to be seen near it, none of the signs of activity which would suggest the presence of a town. Perhaps it was merely distance which hid from her sight all the comings and goings, and possibly once within the town she would be borne along on the urgent flood of activity. Perhaps . . .

'From this distance anything is possible,' she was surprised to hear herself say aloud.

She mused on how, from such a vast distance, it seemed still as though anything could happen, and she fervently believed that if any changes were to take place, they would occur in the intervals when the town was hidden by the trees and undergrowth.

There had been many of these intervals and they were nearly always such very long intervals, so long that it was now by no means certain that she was approaching the town by the most direct route, for there was absolutely nothing to guide her and she had to struggle continually against the intertwining branches and tangled thorns and pick her way around a maze of swamps. She had tried very hard to cross the swamps but all she had succeeded in doing was getting her shoes and the hem of her skirt soaking wet and she had been obliged to retrace her steps hurriedly, so treacherous was the surface of the ground.

She couldn't really see the town and she wasn't going straight towards it except for the rare moments when she topped a rise. There the ground was sparsely planted with broom and heath and she was far above the thickly wooded depths of the valleys. But no sooner had she finished scrambling up the hills than she had to plunge once more into the bushes and try to force her way through the impenetrable undergrowth where everything was in her way, cutting off her view and making her walk painful and dangerous again.

'Perhaps I really ought to go back,' she said to herself; and certainly that would have been the most sensible thing to do. But in fact she didn't slacken her pace in the least, as though something away over there was calling to her, as though the distant town were calling. But how could an empty town summon her? A silent deserted town!

For the closer she came to it, the more she felt that it must really be a deserted city, a ruined city in fact. The height of the bushes and the dense tangled undergrowth about her feet convinced her. If the town had still been inhabited, even by a few people, its surroundings would never have fallen into the confusion through which she had been wandering for hours. Surely she would have found, instead of this tangled jungle, the orderly outskirts of which other towns could boast. But here there were neither roads nor paths; everything betokened disorder and decay.

Yet once more she wondered whatever forced her to continue her walk, but she could find no reply. She was following an irresistible urge. She would have been hard put to it to say how this impulse had arisen or indeed to decide just how long she had been obeying it. And perhaps it was the case that if only she followed the impulse for long enough she would no longer be capable of defying it, although there was no denying that it was grossly irrational. At any rate the urge must have been there for a very long time, as she could tell from the tiredness of her limbs and moreover it was still very close. Couldn't she feel it brimming up within her, pressing on her breast with each eager breath she drew? Then all of a sudden she realized that she was face to face with it.

'The urge is me,' she cried.

She proclaimed it defiantly, but without knowing what she was defying, and triumphantly, although unaware of her opponent. Whom had she defied, and what could she be triumphing over? It was not simply that she was identifying herself with the strange compulsion in order to get to know more of it and of herself. She was obliged to admit that the urge was indefinable, as her own being for ever escaped definition.

After one final struggle with the branches and obstacles, and after skirting one more morass, she suddenly emerged in front of the city, or what remained of it. It was really only the traces of a town, no more than the traces, and in fact just what she had feared to find ever since she set out, but so sad, so desolate, she could never have imagined such desolation. Scarcely anything but rough heaps of walls remained. The porticoes were crumbling and most of the roofs had collapsed; only a column here or a fragment of a wall there proclaimed the former splendour of the peristyles. As for the remaining buildings, they seemed to waver uncertainly, as though on the very point of tumbling. Trees had thrust their branches through broken windows, great tufts of weeds pushed the blocks and the marble slabs upwards, the statues had fallen from their niches, all was ruined and burst asunder.

'I wonder why these remains seem so different from the forests and bush I have come through already?' she said to herself. There was no difference except for the desolation and loss, rendered all the more poignant by the contrast with what had once been. 'What am I searching for here?' she asked herself once more. 'I ought never to have come.'

'Many people used to come here once,' said an old man who appeared out of the ruins.

'Many people?' she said. 'I have not seen a single soul.'

'Nobody has been here for a very long time,' said the old man. 'But there was a time when crowds of people visited the ruins. Is that what you have come for?'

'I was coming towards the city.'

'It certainly was a great city once. But you have arrived too late. Surely you must have been delayed on the road.'

'I should not have been so late but for my battles with the trees and undergrowth and all my detours around the swamps. If only they hadn't held me back . . .'

'You should have come by the direct route.'

'The direct route?' she exclaimed. 'You cannot have any idea of the wilderness round this place.'

'All right, all right,' he said. 'I do have some idea of it. As a matter of fact when I saw that people had stopped coming, I guessed how it was. Perhaps there isn't any road left?'

'There isn't even a bush path!'

'What a pity,' he said. 'It was such a fine town, the most beautiful city in all the continent.'

'And now, what is it?' she said.

'What is it?' he replied dismally.

With his stick he began to mow down the nettles which rose thick and menacing about them.

'Look at this,' he said.

She saw, in the midst of the nettles, a fallen statue, green with moss, a humiliated statue. It cast upon her a dead, grey glance. Presently she became aware that the look was not really dead, only blind, as the eyes were without pupils, and it was in fact a living gaze, as alive as a look could be. A cry came from it, an appealing cry. Was the statute bewailing its loneliness and neglect? The lips drooped pitiably.

'Who is it?' she asked.

'He was the ruler who lived in this place. His rooms can still be seen.'

'Why don't you set up the statue over there?' she said. 'It would be better there than among all these nettles.'

'That is what I wanted to do. As soon as the statue fell from its alcove I wanted to put it back, but I simply hadn't the strength. These stone sculptures are terribly heavy.'

'I know,' she replied, 'and after all it is merely a stone sculpture.'

But was it merely carved stone? Could sculptured stone have cast upon her such a piercing glance? Perhaps, then, it wasn't mere stone. And even if it were nothing more than mere stone, the fact remained that for all the nettles and moss and the vagaries of fortune which it had endured, this stone would still outlast man's life. No, it could not be mere stone. And with this sort of distress in its look, this cry of distress . . .

'Would you care to visit his rooms?' asked the old man.

'Yes, take me there,' she answered.

'Pay particular attention to the columns,' he told her. 'No doubt there is only one hall left here now, but when you consider the number of broken and fallen columns it does look as though there used to be at least ten halls.'

With the end of his stick he pointed out the marble

stumps and debris of broken slabs buried in the grass.

'This gateway must have been exceedingly high,' he said, gazing upwards.

'It can't have been higher than the palace, surely,' she said.

'How can we tell? I haven't seen it any more than you have. By the time I arrived here it had already fallen into the grass; but those who were here before my time declared that it was an astonishing entrance. If you could put all this debris together again I dare say you would get a surprise. But who could tackle such a task?'

He shrugged his shoulders and continued: 'You would need to be a giant, to have the hands and the strength of a giant.'

'Do you really believe that a giant . . .?'

'No,' he replied. 'Only the ruler himself, who had it erected, could do it. He could certainly manage it.'

She gazed at the niches where great tufts of grass had been bold enough to replace the statues. There was one space, larger than all the rest, where the weeds grew particularly ostentatiously, like a flaming torch.

'That is the niche, over there, where he used to stand before his fall among the nettles,' he remarked.

'I see,' she said. 'But now there is nothing left but wild grass and the memory of his agony.'

'He used to find this city and his palace trying enough. He personally supervised the building of the entire place. He intended this town to be the biggest and this palace the highest. He wanted them built to his own scale. Now he is dead, his heart utterly broken.'

'But could he have died any other way?'

'No, I suppose he carried his own death within him, like us all. But he had to carry the fate of a felled Goliath.'

By this time they had reached the foot of a staircase and he pointed out a little door at the end of the corridor on the left.

'That is where I live,' he told her. 'It is the old porter's lodge. I suppose I could have found somewhere a little more spacious and less damp, but after all, I am not much more than a caretaker. In fact, a guide is only a caretaker.'

So saying, he began to make his way painfully up the steps. He was a decrepit old man.

'You are looking at me? I know I'm not much better than the palace! All this will crumble down one day. Soon all this will crumble down on my head and it won't be a great loss! But perhaps I shall crumble before the palace.'

'The palace is older,' she said.

'Yes, but it is more robust. They don't build like that nowadays.'

'What have you been saying?' she demanded. 'You are not stone! Why compare your body to a palace?'

'Did I compare myself to a palace? I don't think so. My body is certainly no palace, not even a ruined one. Perhaps it is like the porter's lodge where I live, and perhaps I was wrong to call it damp and dark, perhaps I should have said nothing about it. But I must pause for breath. These stairs. At my age no one likes climbing stairs.'

And he wheezed noisily, pressing his hand over his heart as though to subdue its frantic beating.

'Let us go,' he said at last, 'up the few remaining steps.'

They climbed a little higher and reached a landing with a great door opening off it, a door half wrenched from its hinges.

'Here are the rooms,' he said.

She saw an immense apartment, frightfully dilapidated. The roof had partly collapsed, leaving the rafters open to the sky. Daylight streamed in upon the debris of tiles and rubbish strewn upon the floor. But nothing could take from the chamber its harmonious proportions, with its marble panels, its tapestry and paintings, the bold surge of its columns, and the deep alcoves between them. It was still beautiful, in spite of being three-quarters ruined. The torn and rotten tapestries and the peeling paintings were still beautiful: so were the cracked stained-glass windows. And although the panelling was practically torn away, the grandeur of the original conception remained.

'Why have you let everything deteriorate so far?' she asked.

'Why indeed? But now it is too late to do anything about it.'

'Is it really too late?'

'Now that the master is no longer here . . .' He tapped the panels with his stick.

'I don't know how the walls are still standing,' he said. 'They may last a fair time yet. But the rain floods through the roof and windows and loosens the stones. And then when the winter storms come! It is those violent storms that destroy everything.'

He dislodged a scrap of mortar.

'Just look, it's no more than a bit of grey dust. I can't think why the blocks don't fall apart. The damp has destroyed everything.'

'Was this the only room the master had?' she asked.

'He had hundreds of them and all of them richly furnished. I've pushed the movable stuff into one of the smaller rooms which was less damaged.'

He opened a door concealed in the panelling.

'Here is some of it,' he said.

She beheld a jumble of carved furniture, ornaments, carpets and crockery.

'Gold dishes, please note. The master would eat off nothing but gold. And look at this. Here he is in his robes of state.' He pointed to a canvas where the face of the statue was portrayed.

The eyes were marvellously expressive. They were so even in the statue, although the sculptor had given them no pupils, but here they were infinitely more expressive and the look which they gave was one of anguish. 'Is no one left near me?' they seemed to ask. And the droop of the mouth replied, 'No one.' The man had known they would all forsake him, he had long foreseen it. Nevertheless she, she had come! She had fought through the bush and she had wandered round the swamps, she had felt fatigue and despair overwhelming her, but she had triumphed over all these obstacles and she had come, she had come at last. Had he not guessed she would come? Yet possibly this very foresight had but accentuated the bitter line of his set lips. 'Yes,' said those lips, 'someone will come, when all the world has ceased to call. But someone who will be unable to soothe my distress.'

She swung round. This reproach was becoming unbearable, and not only this reproach, which made all her goodwill seem useless, but the cry of abandonment, the wild lonely appeal in his look.

'We can do nothing, nothing at all for him,' the old man declared. And she replied: 'Is there ever anything we can do?' She sighed. In her innermost being she felt the anguish of this look; one might have thought it was she who cried, that the cry of loneliness welled up from her own lonely heart.

'Perhaps you can do something,' he said. 'You are still young. Although you may not be able to do anything for yourself, you might perhaps help others.'

'You know very well that I cannot even do that,' she said.

She seemed overwhelmed, as though she bore the ruins on her own shoulders.

'Are there still more rooms?' she asked him.

'Lots of them. But it is getting late, the sun is sinking.'

Daylight was fading fast. The light had become a soft, rosy glow, a light which was kinder to details, and in it the great room took on a new aspect. The paintings and panels regained a freshness which was far from theirs by right. This sudden glow was the gentlest of lights. But not even this light could calm a tormented heart.

'Come along,' called the old man.

'Yes,' she answered.

She imagined that once she went out of this hall and its adjoining storeroom her heart would perhaps calm down. She thought that perhaps she might forget the great cry coming from the storeroom. Yes, if only she could get away from this palace, leave these ruins, surely she could forget it. But was not the cry inside herself?

'The cry is within me,' she exclaimed.

'Stop thinking about it,' advised the old man. 'If you hear anything it's because the silence has got on your nerves. Tomorrow you will hear nothing.'

'But it is a terrible cry.'

'The swans have an awful cry too,' he remarked.

'Swans?'

'Yes, the swans. To look at them gliding over the water you might never believe it. Have you ever happened to hear them cry? But, of course not, you are scarcely more than a child, and, with less sense than one, you probably imagine that they sing. Listen, formerly there were lots of swans here, they were at the very gate of the palace. Sometimes, the lake was covered with them like white blossoms. Visitors used to throw scraps to them. Once the tourists stopped coming, the swans died. No doubt they had lost the habit of searching for food themselves and so they died. Very well, never, do you hear me, never, did I hear a single song coming from the pond.'

'Why do you have to tell me all this? Have I ever told you that I believe swans sing? You didn't need to speak to me like that.'

'No, maybe I shouldn't have said it, or I should have said it less suddenly at least. I'm sorry. I even believed that swans sing myself once. You know how it is, I am old and lonely and I have got into the habit of talking to myself. I was talking to myself, then. I once believed that the lord of this palace, before he died, sang a swan-song. But no, he cried out. He cried so loudly that . . .'

'Please tell me no more,' she begged.

'All right, I suppose we shouldn't think about all that. But let's go.'

He carefully closed the storeroom door and they made their way towards the exit.

'Did you mean to leave the door of the big room open?' she asked once they had reached the landing.

'It hasn't been shut for a long time,' he replied. 'Besides, there is nothing to fear. No one comes here now.'

'But I came.'

He glanced at her.

'I keep wondering why you came,' he said. 'Why did you?'

'How can I tell?' she said.

Her visit was futile. She had crossed a desert of trees, and bush and swamps. And why? Had she come at the summoning of that anguished cry from the depth of the statue's and the picture's eyes? What way was there of finding out? And moreover it was an appeal in which she could not respond, an appeal beyond her power to satisfy. No, this impulse which had moved her to hasten towards the town had been mad from the start.

'I don't know why I came,' she repeated.

'You shouldn't take things to heart like that. These painters and carvers are so crafty, you know, they can make you work out the portrait, for instance. Have you noticed the look in the eyes? We begin by wondering where they found such a look and eventually we realize they have taken it from ourselves; and these are the paradoxes they would be the first to laugh at. You should laugh too.'

'But these paradoxes, as you call them, which come from the depth of our being, what if we cannot find them there?'

'What do you find within yourself?' he answered her.

'I have already told you: unbearable loneliness.'

'Yes,' he said, 'there is something of that in each one of us.'

'But in me . . .'

'No, not more than in anyone else,' he insisted. 'Don't imagine that others are any less alone. But who wants to admit that? All the same, it is not an unendurable state of affairs. It is quite bearable in fact. Solitude! Listen, solitude isn't what you imagine. I don't want to run away from my solitude. It is the last desirable thing left me, it is my only wealth, a great treasure, an ultimate good.'

'Is he just saying that to comfort me?' she wondered. 'But it is no consolation, a shared solitude can be no consolation. The sharing only makes the solitude doubly lonely.'

Aloud she said: 'That doesn't console me in the least.'

'I didn't think it would,' he replied. They had by now reached the foot of the staircase and the old man showed her the little corridor leading to his room.

'My lodge is here.'

'Yes, I know,' she said. 'You've told me already.'

'But I haven't told you everything: I didn't say that my room is right beneath the staircase. When visitors used to climb up there in throngs they were walking over my lodge. Do you understand?'

'Yes.'

'No, you don't understand at all, you don't realize that they were marching on my head, wiping their feet on my hair. I had plenty of hair in those days.'

'But they weren't really wiping their feet,' she said. 'They . . .'

'Don't you think it was humiliating enough anyway?'

She did not know how to reply. The old man seemed slightly crazy: some of what he said was very sensible, but a lot of it was sheer nonsense. 'That solitude has gone to his head,' she told herself, and she looked at him afresh. He was certainly very old. There must be times when age and loneliness together . . . Aloud she remarked: 'I don't know.' And then, all of a sudden: 'What made you say that solitude is an ultimate good?'

'How very young you are,' was his only reply. 'You should never have come here.' He made off towards his lodge, saying: 'I'm going to prepare a meal.'

'I shall rest here awhile,' she said as she climbed the steps.

'Yes, do have a rest, you've certainly earned one. I shall call you when the food is ready.'

She sat down and gazed at the evil weeds. The nettles were by far the most numerous and reminded her of the ocean. They were like a great green sea which surged around the palace trying to drown it, and ultimately they would completely engulf it. What could mere stones do against such a powerful wave? A wave with the deceptive smoothness of velvety leaves, a wave which hid its poisons and its sorcery beneath a velvet touch. It seemed to her fevered imagination that the wave was already rising. Or was it simply the darkness? Was it night, which was burying the lowest steps? No, it was really the wave of nettles, imperceptibly advancing in its assault upon the palace. A transient attack, no doubt. Probably this sea of nettles had tides like the ocean. And perhaps it wasn't merely a simple tide. Perhaps . . .

She leapt to her feet. The tide was about her ankles. She climbed several steps and the tide rose as quickly.

'Caretaker!' she screamed.

But she could no longer see the porter's lodge. Perhaps the sea had already entered the room while she was sitting down. She couldn't be certain now whether it had a door which shut. Even suppose it did have, how could a door stop such a wave?

'What is to become of me?' she asked herself. She climbed a few more steps, but the tide continued to pursue her, it really was following her. She paused; perhaps if she stopped the tide in its turn might stop rising. But instead it flowed right up to her, covering her shoes. Feverishly she resumed her upward flight and gained the landing opposite the doorway of the main hall. But to her horror she realized that the wave was there almost as soon. It was inches away. Must she drown in those horrible weeds?

She rushed to open the storeroom door, only to find that the sea had beaten her and had borne everything away, literally washed off the face of the earth. There was no longer any storeroom left! It had been engulfed beneath the flood of nettles, with its furniture and tapestries and dishes, and the portrait as well. Only the cry, the great cry of anguish remained, and it had become vaster and louder, more piercing and heart-rending than ever. It swelled to fill the whole earth! It seemed to her as though nothing could silence it any more and that whatever she did she could never escape. Her heart could never escape again. Yet at the same time she tried to bolt the door upon it as though in spite of all she knew she might evade it yet. But what could she escape to? There was no way of escape left open, it was either the cry or the flood. She was a prey to this cry and in no time she would be the victim of the flood. She was trapped between two floods, the one which swallowed up the storeroom and was lying in wait menacingly on its threshold, and the other one which had pursued her step by step up the stairs and across the great hall. She had no choice but to cast herself into one of these two floods which were soon to merge. Placed as she was, she could neither advance nor retreat.

'Caretaker!' she cried.

But did she actually shriek? No sound came from her lips. Terror was throttling her, it had her by the throat, she only imagined she had shouted.

At the second attempt she could not even pretend to herself that she had shouted. She no longer even had the will to cry out. She realized that her terror was so extreme that she could never shout again. Nevertheless she continued to struggle hopelessly, she fought and struggled silently and in vain.

And meanwhile the flood was steadily rising beyond her ankles and up her legs. Confident of its power it rose more rapidly than ever.

Then, while she was struggling and trying desperately to regain her voice, she suddenly caught sight of the statue. The sea of weeds had lifted it and was tossing it on its waves.

She stopped struggling to watch it and at once she could see that its eyes were looking at her just as they had done when the old man had first thrust aside the nettles. It was the same look, the same cry of distress and bitter loneliness.

She longed to awake from her nightmare and she tried once more to call for help, but in vain. Must she really die alone beneath the flood of weeds, all alone? She hid her face in her arms.

A little later she felt a blow on her forehead and she felt as if her skull were bursting.

Translated by Una Maclean

DORIS LESSING

A SUNRISE ON THE VELD

EVERY NIGHT THAT winter he said aloud into the dark of the pillow: Half past four! Half past four! till he felt his brain had gripped the words and held them fast. Then he fell asleep at once, as if a shutter had fallen; and lay with his face turned to the clock so that he could see it first thing when he woke.

It was half past four to the minute, every morning. Triumphantly pressing down the alarm-knob of the clock, which the dark half of his mind had outwitted, remaining vigilant all night and counting the hours as he lay relaxed in sleep, he huddled down for a last warm moment under the clothes, playing with the idea of lying abed for this once only. But he played with it for the fun of knowing that it was a weakness he could defeat without effort; just as he set the alarm each night for the delight of the moment when he woke and stretched his limbs, feeling the muscles tighten, and thought: Even my brain – even that! I can control every part of myself.

Luxury of warm rested body, with the arms and legs and fingers waiting like soldiers for a word of command! Joy of knowing that the precious hours were given to sleep voluntarily! – for he had once stayed awake three nights running, to prove that he could, and then worked all day, refusing even to admit that he was tired; and now sleep seemed to him a servant to be commanded and refused.

The boy stretched his frame full-length, touching the wall

at his head with his hands, and the bedfoot with his toes; then he sprang out, like a fish leaping from water. And it was cold, cold.

He always dressed rapidly, so as to try and conserve his night-warmth till the sun rose two hours later; but by the time he had on his clothes his hands were numbed and he could scarcely hold his shoes. These he could not put on for fear of waking his parents, who never came to know how early he rose.

As soon as he stepped over the lintel, the flesh of his soles contracted on the chilled earth, and his legs began to ache with cold. It was night: the stars were glittering, the trees standing black and still. He looked for signs of day, for the greying of the edge of a stone, or a lightening in the sky where the sun would rise, but there was nothing yet. Alert as an animal he crept past the dangerous window, standing poised with his hand on the sill for one proudly fastidious moment, looking in at the stuffy blackness of the room where his parents lay.

Feeling for the grass-edge of the path with his toes, he reached inside another window farther along the wall, where his gun had been set in readiness the night before. The steel was icy, and numbed fingers slipped along it, so that he had to hold it in the crook of his arm for safety. Then he tiptoed to the room where the dogs slept, and was fearful that they might have been tempted to go before him; but they were waiting, their haunches crouched in reluctance at the cold, but ears and swinging tails greeting the gun ecstatically. His warning undertone kept them secret and silent till the house was a hundred yards back: then they bolted off into the bush, yelping excitedly. The boy imagined his parents turning in their beds and muttering: Those dogs again! before they were dragged back in sleep; and he smiled scornfully. He always looked back over his shoulder at the house before he passed a wall of trees that shut it from sight. It looked so low and small, crouching there, under a tall and brilliant sky. Then he turned his back on it, and on the frowsting sleepers, and forgot them.

He would have to hurry. Before the light grew strong he must be four miles away; and already a tint of green stood in the hollow of a leaf, and the air smelled of morning and the stars were dimming.

He slung the shoes over his shoulder, veld skoen that were crinkled and hard with the dews of a hundred mornings. They would be necessary when the ground became too hot to bear. Now he felt the chilled dust push up between his toes, and he let the muscles of his feet spread and settle into the shape of the earth, and he thought: I could walk a hundred miles on feet like these! I could walk all day, and never tire!

He was walking swiftly through the dark tunnel of foliage that in daytime was a road. The dogs were invisibly ranging the lower travelways of the bush, and he heard them panting. Sometimes he felt a cold muzzle on his leg before they were off again, scouting for a trail to follow. They were not trained, but free-running companions of the hunt, who often tired of the long stalk before the final shots, and went off on their own pleasure. Soon he could see them, small and wild-looking in a wild strange light, now that the bush stood trembling on the verge of colour, waiting for the sun to paint earth and grass afresh.

The grass stood to his shoulders; and the trees were showering a faint silvery rain. He was soaked; his whole body was clenched in a steady shiver.

Once he bent to the road that was newly scored with animal trails, and regretfully straightened, reminding himself that the pleasure of tracking must wait till another day.

He began to run along the edge of a field, noting jerkily how it was filmed over with fresh spiderweb, so that the long reaches of great black clods seemed netted in glistening grey. He was using the steady lope he had learned by watching the natives, the run that is a dropping of the weight of the body from one foot to the next in a slow balancing movement that never tires, nor shortens the breath; and he felt the blood pulsing down his legs and along his arms, and the exultation and pride of body mounted in him till he was shutting his teeth hard against a violent desire to shout his triumph.

Soon he had left the cultivated part of the farm. Behind him the bush was low and black. In front was a long vlei, acres of long pale grass that sent back a hollowing gleam of light to a satiny sky. Near him thick swathes of grass were bent with the weight of water, and diamond drops sparkled on each frond.

The first bird woke at his feet and at once a flock of them sprang into the air calling shrilly that day had come; and suddenly behind him, the bush woke into song, and he could hear the guinea-fowl calling far ahead of him. That meant they would not be sailing down from their trees into thick grass, and it was for them he had come: he was too late. But he did not mind. He forgot he had come to shoot. He set his legs wide, and balanced from foot to foot, and swung his gun up and down in both hands horizontally, in a kind of improvised exercise, and let his head sink back till it was pillowed in his neck muscles, and watched how above him small rosy clouds floated in a lake of gold.

Suddenly it all rose in him: it was unbearable. He leapt up into the air, shouting and yelling wild, unrecognizable noises. Then he began to run, not carefully, as he had before, but madly, like a wild thing. He was clean crazy, yelling mad with the joy of living and a superfluity of youth. He rushed down the vlei under a tumult of crimson and gold, while all the birds of the world sang about him. He ran in great leaping strides, and shouted as he ran, feeling his body rise into the crisp rushing air and fall back surely on to sure feet; and thought briefly, not believing that such a thing could happen to him, that he could break his ankle any moment, in this thick tangled grass. He cleared bushes like a duiker, leaped over rocks; and finally came to a dead stop at a place where the ground fell abruptly away below him to the river. It had been a two-mile-long dash through waist-high growth, and he was breathing hoarsely and could no longer sing. But he poised on a rock and looked down at stretches of water that gleamed through stooping trees, and thought suddenly, I am fifteen! Fifteen! The words came new to him; so that he kept repeating them wonderingly, with swelling excitement; and he felt the years of his life with his hands, as if he were counting marbles, each one hard and separate and compact, each one a wonderful shining thing. That was what he was: fifteen years of this rich soil, and this slow-moving water, and air that smelt like a challenge whether it was warm and sultry at noon, or as brisk as cold water, like it was now.

There was nothing he couldn't do, nothing! A vision came to him, as he stood there, like when a child hears the word 'eternity' and tries to understand it, and time takes possession of the mind. He felt his life ahead of him as a great and wonderful thing, something that was his; and he said aloud, with the blood rising to his head: All the great men of the world have been as I am now, and there is nothing I can't become, nothing I can't do; there is no country in the world I cannot make part of myself, if I choose. I contain the world. I can make of it what I want. If I choose, I can change everything that is going to happen: it depends on me, and what I decide now.

The urgency, and the truth and the courage of what his voice was saying exulted him so that he began to sing again, at the top of his voice, and the sound went echoing down the river gorge. He stopped for the echo, and sang again: stopped and shouted. That was what he was! – he sang, if he chose; and the world had to answer him.

And for minutes he stood there, shouting and singing and waiting for the lovely eddying sound of the echo; so that his own new strong thoughts came back and washed round his head, as if someone were answering him and encouraging him: till the gorge was full of soft voices clashing back and forth from rock to rock over the river. And then it seemed as if there was a new voice. He listened, puzzled, for it was not his own. Soon he was leaning forward, all his nerves alert, quite still: somewhere close to him there was a noise that was no joyful bird, nor tinkle of falling water, nor ponderous movement of cattle.

There it was again. In the deep morning hush that held his future and his past, was a sound of pain, and repeated over and over: it was a kind of shortened scream, as if someone, something, had no breath to scream. He came to himself, looked about him, and called for the dogs. They did not appear: they had gone off on their own business, and he was alone. Now he was clean sober, all the madness gone. His heart beating fast, because of that frightened screaming, he stepped carefully off the rock and went towards a belt of trees. He was moving cautiously, for not so long ago he had seen a leopard in just this spot.

At the end of the trees he stopped and peered, holding his gun ready; he advanced, looking steadily about him, his eyes narrowed. Then, all at once, in the middle of a step, he faltered, and his face was puzzled. He shook his head impatiently, as if he doubted his own sight.

There, between two trees, against a background of gaunt black rocks, was a figure from a dream, a strange beast that was horned and drunken-legged, but like something he had never even imagined. It seemed to be ragged. It looked like a small buck that had black ragged tufts of fur standing up irregularly all over it, with patches of raw flesh beneath . . . but the patches of rawness were disappearing under moving black and came again elsewhere; and all the time the creature screamed, in small gasping screams, and leaped drunkenly from side to side, as if it were blind.

Then the boy understood: it *was* a buck. He ran closer, and again stood still, stopped by a new fear. Around him the grass was whispering and alive. He looked wildly about, and then down. The ground was black with ants, great energetic ants that took no notice of him, but hurried and scurried towards the fighting shape, like glistening black water flowing through the grass.

And, as he drew in his breath and pity and terror seized him, the beast fell and the screaming stopped. Now he could hear nothing but one bird singing, and the sound of the rustling, whispering ants.

He peered over at the writhing blackness that jerked convulsively with the jerking nerves. It grew quieter. There were small twitches from the mass that still looked vaguely like the shape of a small animal.

It came into his mind that he should shoot it and end its pain; and he raised the gun. Then he lowered it again. The buck could no longer feel; its fighting was a mechanical protest of the nerves. But it was not that which made him put down the gun. It was a swelling feeling of rage and misery and protest that expressed itself in the thought: If I had not come it would have died like this: so why should I interfere? All over the bush things like this happen; they happen all the time; this is how life goes on, by living things dying in anguish. He gripped the gun between his knees and felt in his own limbs the myriad swarming pain of the twitching animal that could no longer feel, and set his teeth, and said over and over again under his breath: I can't stop it. I can't stop it. There is nothing I can do.

He was glad the buck was unconscious and had gone past suffering so that he did not have to make a decision to kill it even when he was feeling with his whole body: this is what happens, this is how things work.

It was right – that was what he was feeling. *It was right and nothing could alter it.*

The knowledge of fatality, of what has to be, had gripped him and for the first time in his life; and he was left unable to make any movement of brain or body, except to say: 'Yes, yes. That is what living is.' It had entered his flesh and his bones and grown into the farthest corners of his brain and would never leave him. And at that moment he could not have performed the smallest action of mercy, knowing as he did, having lived on it all his life, the vast unalterable cruel veld, where at any moment one might stumble over a skull or crush the skeleton of some small creature.

Suffering, sick, and angry, but also grimly satisfied with his new stoicism, he stood there leaning on his rifle, and watched the seething black mound grow smaller. At his feet, now, were ants trickling back with pink fragments in their mouths, and there was a fresh acid smell in his nostrils. He sternly controlled the uselessly convulsing muscles of his empty stomach, and reminded himself: the ants must eat too! At the same time he found that the tears were streaming down his face, and his clothes were soaked with the sweat of that other creature's pain.

The shape had grown small. Now it looked like nothing

recognizable. He did not know how long it was before he saw the blackness thin, and bits of white showed through, shining in the sun – yes, there was the sun, just up, glowing over the rocks. Why, the whole thing could not have taken longer than a few minutes.

He began to swear, as if the shortness of the time was in itself unbearable, using the words he had heard his father say. He strode forward, crushing ants with each step, and brushing them off his clothes, till he stood above the skeleton, which lay sprawled under a small bush. It was clean-picked. It might have been lying there years, save that on the white bones were pink fragments of gristle. About the bones ants were ebbing away, their pincers full of meat.

The boy looked at them, big black ugly insects. A few were standing and gazing up at him with small glittering eyes.

'Go away!' he said to the ants, very coldly. 'I am not for you – not just yet, at any rate. Go away.' And he fancied that the ants turned and went away.

He bent over the bones and touched the sockets in the skull; that was where the eyes were, he thought incredulously, remembering the liquid dark eyes of a buck. And then he bent the slim foreleg bone, swinging it horizontally in his palm.

That morning, perhaps an hour ago, this small creature had been stepping proud and free through the bush, feeling the chill on its hide even as he himself had done, exhilarated by it. Proudly stepping the earth, tossing its horns, frisking a pretty white tail, it had sniffed the cold morning air. Walking like kings and conquerors it had moved through this free-held bush, where each blade of grass grew for it alone, and where the river ran pure sparkling water for its slaking.

And then – what had happened? Such a swift surefooted thing could surely not be trapped by a swarm of ants?

The boy bent curiously to the skeleton. Then he saw that the back leg that lay uppermost and strained out in the tension of death was snapped midway in the thigh, so that broken bones jutted over each other uselessly. So that was it! Limping into the ant-masses it could not escape, once it had sensed the danger. Yes, but how had the leg been broken? Had it fallen, perhaps? Impossible, a buck was too light and graceful. Had some jealous rival horned it?

What could possibly have happened? Perhaps some Africans had thrown stones at it, as they do, trying to kill it for meat, and had broken its leg. Yes, that must be it.

Even as he imagined the crowd of running, shouting natives, and the flying stones, and the leaping buck, another picture came into his mind. He saw himself, on any one of these bright ringing mornings, drunk with excitement, taking a snap shot at some half-seen buck. He saw himself with the gun lowered, wondering whether he had missed or not; and thinking at last that it was late, and he wanted his breakfast, and it was not worthwhile to track miles after an animal that would very likely get away from him in any case.

For a moment he would not face it. He was a small boy again, kicking sulkily at the skeleton, hanging his head, refusing to accept the responsibility.

Then he straightened up, and looked down at the bones with an odd expression of dismay, all the anger gone out of him. His mind went quite empty: all around him he could see trickles of ants disappearing into the grass. The whispering noise was faint and dry, like the rustling of a cast snakeskin.

At last he picked up his gun and walked homewards. He was telling himself half defiantly that he wanted his breakfast. He was telling himself that it was getting very hot, much too hot to be out roaming the bush.

Really, he was tired. He walked heavily, not looking where he put his feet. When he came within sight of his home he stopped, knitting his brows. There was something he had to think out. The death of that small animal was a thing that concerned him, and he was by no means finished with it. It lay at the back of his mind uncomfortably.

Soon, the very next morning, he would get clear of everybody and go to the bush and think about it.

BEN OKRI

INCIDENTS AT THE SHRINE

ANDERSON HAD BEEN waiting for something to fall on him. His anxiety was such that for the first time in several years he went late to work. It was just his luck that the Head of Department had chosen that day for an impromptu inspection. When he got to the museum he saw that his metal chair had been removed from its customary place. The little stool on which he rested his feet after running endless errands was also gone. His official messenger's uniform had been taken off the hook. He went to the main office and was told by one of the clerks that he had been sacked, and that the supervisor was not available. Anderson started to protest, but the clerk got up and pushed him out of the office.

He went aimlessly down the corridors of the Department of Antiquities. He stumbled past the visitors to the museum. He wandered amongst the hibiscus and bougainvillea. He didn't look at the ancestral stoneworks in the museum field. Then he went home, dazed, confused by objects, convinced that he saw many fingers pointing at him. He went down streets he had never seen in his life and he momentarily forgot where his compound was.

When he got home he found that he was trembling. He was hungry. He hadn't eaten that morning and the cupboard was empty of food. He couldn't stop thinking about the loss of his job. Anderson had suspected for some time that the supervisor had been planning to give his job to a distant relation. That was the reason why the supervisor was always berating him on the slightest pretext. Seven years in the city had begun to make Anderson feel powerless because he didn't belong to the important societies, and didn't have influential relatives. He spent the afternoon thinking about his condition in the world. He fell asleep and dreamt about his dead parents.

He woke up feeling bitter. It was late in the afternoon and he was hungry. He got out of bed and went to the market to get some beef and tripe for a pot of stew. Anderson slid through the noise of revving motors and shouting traders. He came to the goatsellers. The goats stood untethered in a small corral. As Anderson went past he had a queer feeling that the goats were staring at him. When he stopped and looked at them the animals panicked. They kicked and fought backwards. Anderson hurried on till he found himself at the meat stalls.

The air was full of flies and the stench was overpowering. He felt ill. There were intestines and bones in heaps on the floor. He was haggling the price of tripe when he heard confused howls from the section where they sold generators and videos. The meat-seller had just slapped the tripe down on the table and was telling him to go somewhere else for the price he offered, when the fire burst out with an explosion. Flames poured over the stalls. Waves of screaming people rushed in Anderson's direction. He saw the fire flowing behind them, he saw black smoke. He started to run before the people reached him.

He heard voices all around him. Dry palm fronds crackled in the air. Anderson ducked under the bare eaves of a stall, tripped over a fishmonger's basin of writhing eels, and fell into a mound of snailshells. He struggled back up. He ran past the fortune-tellers and the amulet traders. He was shouldering his way through the bamboo poles of the lace-sellers when it struck him with amazing clarity that the fire was intent upon him because he had no power to protect himself. And soon the fire was everywhere. Suddenly, from the midst of voices in the smoke, Anderson heard someone calling his names. Not just the one name, the ordinary one which made things easier in the city – Anderson; he heard all the others as well, even the ones he had forgotten: Jeremiah, Ofuegbu, Nutcracker, Azzi. He was so astonished that when he cut himself, by brushing his thigh against two rusted nails, he did not know how profusely he bled till he cleared out into the safety of the main road. When he got home he was still bleeding. When the bleeding ceased, he felt that an alien influence had insinuated itself into his body, and an illness took over.

He became so ill that most of the money he had saved in all the years of humiliation and sweat went into the hands of the quack chemists of the area. They bandaged his wound. They gave him tetanus injections with curved syringes. They gave him pills in squat, silvery bottles. Anderson was reduced to creeping about the compound, from room to toilet and back again, as though he were terrified of daylight. And then, three days into the illness, with the taste of alum stale in his mouth, he caught a glimpse of himself in the mirror. He saw the gaunt face of a complete stranger. Two days later, when he felt he had recovered sufficiently, Anderson packed his box and fled home to his village.

The Image-maker

Anderson hadn't been home for a long time. When the lorry driver dropped him at the village junction, the first things he noticed were the ferocity of the heat and the humid smell of rotting vegetation. He went down the dirt track that led to the village. A pack of dogs followed him for a short while and then disappeared. Cowhorns and the beating of drums sounded from the forest. He saw masks, eaten by insects, along the grass verge.

He was sweating when he got to the obeche tree where, during the war, soldiers had shot a woman thought to be a spy. Passing the well which used to mark the village boundary, he became aware of three rough forms running after him. They had flaming red eyes and they shouted his names.

'Anderson! Ofuegbu!'

He broke into a run. They bounded after him.

'Ofuegbu! Anderson!'

In his fear he ran so hard that his box flew open. Scattered behind him were his clothes, his medicines, and the modest gifts he had brought to show his people that he wasn't entirely a small man in the world. He discarded the box and sped on without looking back. Swirls of dust came towards him. And when he emerged from the dust, he saw the village.

It was sunset. Anderson didn't stop running till he was safely in the village. He went on till he came to the pool office with the signboard that read: MR ABAS AND CO. LICENSED COLLECTOR. Outside the office, a man sat in a depressed cane chair. His eyes stared divergently at the road and he snored gently. Anderson stood panting. He wanted to ask directions to his uncle's place, but he didn't want to wake the owner of the pool office.

Anderson wasn't sure when the man woke up, for suddenly he said: 'Why do you have to run into our village like a madman?'

Anderson struggled for words. He was sweating.

'You disturb my eyes when you come running into our village like that.'

Anderson wiped his face. He was confused. He started to apologize, but the man looked him over once, and fell back into sleep, with his eyes still open. Anderson wasn't sure what to do. He was thirsty. With sweat dribbling down his face, Anderson tramped on through the village.

Things had changed since he'd been away. The buildings had lost their individual colours to that of the dust. Houses had moved several yards from where they used to be. Roads ran diagonally to how he remembered them. He felt he had arrived in a place he had almost never known.

Exhausted, Anderson sat on a bench outside the market. The roadside was full of ants. The heat mists made him sleepy. The market behind him was empty, but deep within it he heard celebrations and arguments. He listened to alien voices and languages from the farthest reaches of the world. Anderson fell asleep on the bench and dreamt that he was being carried through the village by the ants. He woke to find himself inside the pool office. His legs itched.

The man whom he had last seen sitting in the cane chair, was now behind the counter. He was mixing a potion of local gin and herbs. There was someone else in the office: a stocky man with a large forehead and a hardened face.

He stared at Anderson and then said: 'Have you slept enough?'

Anderson nodded. The man behind the counter came round with a tumbler full of herbal mixtures.

Almost forcing the drink down Anderson's throat, he said: 'Drink it down. Fast!'

Anderson drank most of the mixture in one gulp. It was very bitter and bile rushed up in his mouth.

'Swallow it down!'

Anderson swallowed. His head cleared a little and his legs stopped itching.

The man who had given him the drink said: 'Good.' Then he pointed to the other man and said: 'That's your uncle. Our Image-maker. Don't you remember him?'

Anderson stared at the Image-maker's face. The lights shifted. The face was elusively familiar. Anderson had to subtract seven years from the awesome starkness of the Image-maker's features before he could recognize his own uncle.

Anderson said: 'My uncle, you have changed!'

'Yes, my son, and so have you,' his uncle said.

'I'm so happy to see you,' said Anderson.

Smiling, his uncle moved into the light at the doorway. Anderson saw that his left arm was shrivelled.

'We've been expecting you,' his uncle said.

Anderson didn't know what to say. He looked from one to the other. Then suddenly he recognized Mr Abas, who used to take him fishing down the village stream.

'Mr Abas! It's you!'

'Of course it's me. Who did you think I was?'

Anderson stood up.

'Greetings, my elders. Forgive me. So much has changed.'

His uncle touched him benevolently on the shoulder and said: 'That's all right. Now, let's go.'

Anderson persisted with his greeting. Then he began to apologize for his bad memory. He told them that he had been pursued at the village boundary.

'They were strange people. They pursued me like a common criminal.'

The Image-maker said: 'Come on. Move. We don't speak of strange things in our village. We have no strange things here. Now, let's go.'

Mr Abas went outside and sat in his sunken cane chair. The Image-maker led Anderson out of the office.

They walked through the dry heat. The chanting of worshippers came from the forest. Drums and jangling bells sounded faintly in the somnolent air.

'The village is different,' Anderson said.

The Image-maker was silent.

'What has happened here?'

'Don't ask questions. In our village we will provide you with answers before it is necessary to ask questions,' the Image-maker said with some irritation.

Anderson kept quiet. As they went down the village Anderson kept looking at the Image-maker: the more he looked, the more raw and godlike the Image-maker seemed. It was as though he had achieved an independence from human agencies. He looked as if he had been cast in rock, and left to the wilds.

'The more you look the less you see,' the Image-maker said.

It sounded, to Anderson, like a cue. They had broken into a path. Ahead of them were irregular rows of soapstone monoliths. Embossed with abstract representations of the human figure, the monoliths ranged from the babies of their breed to the abnormally large ones. There were lit candles and varied offerings in front of them. There were frangipani and iroko trees in their midst. There were also red-painted poles which had burst into flower.

His uncle said: 'The images were originally decorated with pearls, lapis lazuli, amethysts and magic glass which twinkled wonderful philosophies. But the pale ones from across the seas came and stole them. This was whispered to me in a dream.'

Anderson gazed at the oddly elegant monoliths and said: 'You resemble the gods you worship.'

His uncle gripped him suddenly.

'We don't speak of resemblances in our village, you hear?'

Anderson nodded. His uncle relaxed his grip. They moved on.

After a while his uncle said: 'The world is the shrine and the shrine is the world. Everything must have a centre. When you talk rubbish, bad things fly into your mouth.'

They passed a cluster of huts. Suddenly the Image-maker bustled forward. They had arrived at the main entrance to a circular clay shrinehouse. The Image-maker went to the niche and brought out a piece of native chalk, a tumbler and a bottle of herbs. He made a mash which he smeared across Anderson's forehead. On a nail above the door, there was a bell which the Image-maker rang three times.

A voice called from within the hut.

The Image-maker sprayed himself forth in a list of his incredible names and titles. Then he requested permission to bring to the shrine an afflicted 'son of the soil'.

The voices asked if the 'son of the soil' was ready to come in.

The Image-maker was silent.

A confusion of drums, bells, cowhorns, came suddenly from within. Anderson fainted.

Then the Image-maker said to the voices: 'He is ready to enter!'

They came out and found that Anderson was light. They bundled him into the shrinehouse and laid him on a bed of congealed palm oil.

The Image

When Anderson came to he could smell burning candles, sweat and incense. Before him was the master Image, a hallucinatory warrior monolith decorated in its original splendour of precious stones and twinkling glass. At its base were roots, kola nuts and feathers. When Anderson gazed at the master Image he heard voices that were not spoken and he felt drowsiness come over him.

Candles burned in the mist of blue incense. A small crowd of worshippers danced and wove Anderson's names in songs. Down the corridors he could hear other supplicants crying out in prayer for their heart's desires, for their afflictions and problems. They prayed like people who are ill and who are never sure of recovering. It occurred to Anderson that it must be a cruel world to demand such intensity of prayer.

Anderson tried to get up from the bed, but couldn't. The master Image seemed to look upon him with a grotesque face. The ministrants closed in around him. They praised the master Image in songs. The Image-maker gave a sudden instruction and the ministrants rushed to Anderson. They spread out their multiplicity of arms and embraced Anderson in their hard compassions. But when they touched Anderson he screamed and shouted in hysteria. The ministrants embraced him with their remorseless arms and carried him through the corridors and out into the night. They rushed him past the monoliths outside. They took him past creeks and waterholes. When they came to a blooming frangipani tree, they dumped him on the ground. Then they retreated with flutters of their smocks, and disappeared as though the darkness were made of their own substance.

Anderson heard whispers in the forest. He heard things falling among the branches. Then he heard footsteps that seemed for ever approaching. He soon saw that it was Mr Abas. He carried a bucket in one hand and a lamp in the other. He dropped the bucket near Anderson.

'Bathe of it,' Mr Abas said, and returned the way he had come.

Anderson washed himself with the treated water. When he finished the attendants came and brought him fresh clothes. Then they led him back to the shrinehouse.

The Image-maker was waiting for him. Bustling with urgency, his bad arm moving restlessly like the special instrument of his functions, the Image-maker grabbed Anderson and led him to an alcove.

He made Anderson sit in front of a door. There was a hole greased with palm oil at the bottom of the door. The Image-maker shouted an instruction and the attendants came upon Anderson and held him face down. They pushed him towards the hole; they forced his head and shoulders through it.

In the pain Anderson heard the Image-maker say: 'Tell us what you see!'

Anderson couldn't see anything. All he could feel was the grinding pain. Then he saw a towering tree. There was a door on the tree trunk. Then he saw a thick blue pall. A woman emerged from the pall. She was painted over in native chalk. She had bangles all the way up her arms. Her stomach and waist were covered in beads.

'I see a woman,' he cried.

Several voices asked: 'Do you know her?'

'No.'

'Is she following you?'

'I don't know.'

'Is she dead?'

'I don't know.'

'Is she dead?'

'No!'

There was the merriment of tinkling bells.

'What is she doing?'

She had come to the tree and opened the door. Anderson suffered a fresh agony. She opened a second door and tried the third one, but it didn't open. She tried again and when it gave way with a crash Anderson finally came through – but he lost consciousness.

Afterwards, they fed him substantially. Then he was allowed the freedom to move round the village and visit some of his relations. In the morning the Image-maker sent for him. The attendants made him sit on a cowhide mat and they shaved off his hair. They lit red and green candles and made music around him. Then the Image-maker proceeded with the extraction of impurities from his body. He rubbed herbal juices into Anderson's shoulder. He bit into the flesh and pulled out a rusted little padlock which he spat into an enamel bowl. He inspected the padlock. After he had washed out his mouth, he bit into Anderson's shoulder again and pulled out a crooked needle. He continued like this till he had pulled out a piece of broken glass, a twisted nail, a cowrie, and a small key. There was some agitation as to whether the key would fit the padlock, but it didn't.

When the Image-maker had finished he picked up the bowl, jangled the objects, and said: 'All these things, where do they come from? Who sent them into you?'

Anderson couldn't say anything.

The Image-maker went on to cut light razor strokes on Anderson's arm and he rubbed protective herbs into the bleeding marks. He washed his hands and went out of the alcove. He came back with a pouch, which he gave to Anderson with precise instructions of its usage.

Then he said: 'You are going back to the city tomorrow. Go to your place of work, collect the money they are owing you, and look for another job. You will have no trouble. You understand?'

Anderson nodded.

'Now, listen. One day I went deep into the forest because my arm hurt. I injured it working in a factory. For three days I was in the forest praying to our ancestors. I ate leaves and fishes. On the fourth day I forgot how I came there. I was lost and everything was new to me. On the fifth day I found the Images. They were hidden amongst the trees and tall grasses. Snakes and tortoises were all around. My pain stopped. When I found my way back and told the elders of the village what I had seen they did not believe me. The Images had been talked about in the village for a long time but no one had actually seen them. That is why they made me the Image-maker.'

He paused, then continued.

'Every year, around this time, spirits from all over the world come to our village. They meet at the marketplace and have heated discussions about everything under the sun. Sometimes they gather round our Images outside. On some evenings there are purple mists round the iroko tree. At night we listen to all the languages, all the philosophies, of the world. You must come home now and again. This is where you derive power. You hear?'

Anderson nodded. He hadn't heard most of what was said. He had been staring at the objects in the enamel bowl.

The Image-eaters

Anderson ate little through the ceremonies that followed the purification of his body. After all the dancing and feasting to the music of cowhorns and tinkling bells, they made him lie down before the master Image. Then the strangest voice he had ever heard thundered the entire shrinehouse with its full volume.

'ANDERSON! OFUEGBU! YOU ARE A SMALL MAN. YOU CANNOT RUN FROM YOUR FUTURE. GOVERNMENTS CANNOT EXIST WITHOUT YOU. ALL THE DISASTERS OF THE WORLD REST ON YOU AND HAVE YOUR NAME. THIS IS YOUR POWER.'

The ministrants gave thanks and wept for joy.

Anderson spent the night in the presence of the master Image. He dreamt that he was dying of hunger and that there was nothing left in the world to eat. When Anderson ate of the master Image he was surprised at its sweetness. He was surprised also that the Image replenished itself.

In the morning Anderson's stomach was bloated with an imponderable weight. Shortly before his departure the Image-maker came to him and suggested that he contribute to the shrine fund. When Anderson made his donation, the Image-maker gave his blessing. The ministrants prayed for him and sang of his destiny.

Anderson had just enough money to get him back to the city. When he was ready to leave, Anderson felt a new heaviness come upon him. He thanked his uncle for everything and made his way through the village.

He stopped at the pool office. Mr Abas was in his sunken cane chair, his eyes pursuing their separate lines of vision. Anderson wasn't sure if Mr Abas was asleep.

He said: 'I'm leaving now.'

'Leaving us to our hunger, are you?'

'There is hunger where I am going,' Anderson said.

Mr Abas smiled and said: 'Keep your heart pure. Have courage. Suffering cannot kill us. And travel well.'

'Thank you.'

Mr Abas nodded and soon began to snore. Anderson went on towards the junction.

As he walked through the heated gravity of the village Anderson felt like an old man. He felt that his face had stiffened. He had crossed the rubber plantation, had crossed the boundary, and was approaching the junction, when the rough forms with blazing eyes fell upon him. He fought them off. He lashed out with his stiffened hands and legs. They could easily have torn him to pieces, because their ferocity was greater than his. There was a moment in which he saw himself dead. But they suddenly stopped and stared at him. Then they pawed him, as though he had become allied with them in some way. When they melted back into the heat mists, Anderson experienced the new simplicity of his life, and continued with his journey.

GRACE OGOT

THE GREEN LEAVES

IT WAS A DREAM. Then the sounds grew louder. Nyagar threw the blanket off his ears and listened. Yes, he was right. Heavy footsteps and voices were approaching. He turned round to wake up his wife. She was not there. He got up and rushed to the door. It was unlocked. Where was Nyamundhe? 'How could she slip back to her hut so quietly?' he wondered. 'I've told her time and again never to leave my hut without waking me up to bolt the door. She will see me tomorrow!'

'*Ero, ero*, there, there!' The noise was quite close now – about thirty yards away. Nyagar put a sheet round his well-developed body, fumbled for his spear and club, and then left the hut.

'*Piti, piti. Piti, piti.*' A group was running towards his gate. He opened the gate and hid by the fence. Nyagar did not want to meet the group directly, as he was certain some dangerous person was being pursued.

Three or four men ran past the gate, and then a larger group followed. He emerged from his hiding-place and followed them.

'These bastards took all my six bulls,' he heard one voice cursing.

'Don't worry – they will pay for it,' another voice replied.

Nyagar had caught up with the pursuing crowd. He now realized that the three or four men he had seen run past his gate were cattle thieves. They rounded a bend. About thirty yards away were three figures who could only be the thieves.

'They must not escape,' a man shouted.

'They will not,' the crowd answered in chorus.

The gap was narrowing. The young moon had disappeared, and it was quite dark.

'Don't throw a spear,' an elder warned. 'If it misses, they can use it against us.'

The thieves took the wrong turning. They missed the bridge across the River Opok, which separated the people of Masala from those of Mirogi. Instead they turned right. While attempting to cross the river, they suddenly found themselves in a whirlpool. Hastily they scrambled out of the water.

'*Ero*, *ero*,' a cry went out from the pursuers.

Before the thieves could find a safe place at which to cross the river, the crowd was upon them. With their clubs they smote the thieves to the ground. The air was filled with the howls of the captured men. But the crowd showed no mercy.

During the scuffle, one of the thieves escaped and disappeared into the thick bush by the river.

'Follow him! Follow him!' someone shouted.

Three men ran in the direction in which he had disappeared, breathing heavily. The bush was thick and thorny. They stood still and listened. There was no sound. They beat the bush around with their clubs – still no sound. He had escaped.

Another thief took out his knife and drove it into the shoulder-blade of one of the pursuers, who fell back with the knife still sticking in him. In the ensuing confusion, the thief got up and made straight for the whirlpool. To everybody's amazement, he was seen swimming effortlessly across it to the other side of the river.

Nyagar plucked the knife out from Omoro's shoulder and

put his hand over the wound to stop the bleeding. Omoro, still shaken, staggered to his feet and leaned on Nyagar. Streaks of blood were still running along his back, making his buttocks wet.

One thief was lying on the grass, groaning. As the other two had escaped, the crowd were determined to make an example of this one. They hit him several times on the head and chest. He groaned and stretched out his arms and legs as if giving up the ghost.

'Aa, aa,' Omoro raised his voice. 'Let not the enemy die in your hands. His spirit would rest upon our village. Let him give up the ghost when we have returned to our huts.'

The crowd heeded Omoro's warning. They tore green leaves from nearby trees and covered the victim completely with them. They would call the entire clan in the morning to come and bury him by the riverside.

The men walked back home in silence. Omoro's shoulder had stopped bleeding. He walked, supported by two friends who volunteered to take him home. It was still not light, but their eyes were by now accustomed to the darkness. They reached Nyagar's home – the gate was still ajar.

'Remember to be early tomorrow,' a voice told him. 'We must be on the scene to stop the women before they start going to the river.'

Nyagar entered his home, while the others walked on without looking back. The village was hushed. The women must have been awake, but they dared not talk to their husbands. Whatever had happened, they thought, they would hear about it in the morning. Having satisfied themselves that their husbands were safely back, they turned over and slept.

Nyagar entered his hut, searched for his medicine bag and found it in a corner. He opened it, and pulled out a bamboo container. He uncorked the container, and then scooped out some ash from it. He placed a little on his tongue, mixed it well with saliva and then swallowed. He put some on his palm and blew it in the direction of the gate. As he replaced the bamboo container in the bag, his heart felt at peace.

He sat on the edge of his bed. He started to remove his clothes. Then he changed his mind. Instead he just sat there, staring vacantly into space. Finally he made up his mind to go back to the dead man alone.

He opened the door slowly, and then closed it quietly after him. No one must hear him.

He did not hesitate at the gate, but walked blindly on.

'Did I close the gate?' he wondered. He looked back. Yes, he had closed it – or it looked closed.

Apart from a sinister sound which occasionally rolled through the night, everything was silent. Dawn must have been approaching. The faint and golden gleams of light which usually herald the birth of a new day could be seen in the east shooting skywards from the bowels of the earth. 'He must have a lot of money in his pocket,' Nyagar said aloud. He knew that stock thieves sold stolen cattle at the earliest opportunity.

'The others were foolish not to have searched him.' He stopped and listened. Was somebody coming? No. He was merely hearing the echo of his own footsteps.

'Perhaps the other two thieves who had escaped are now back at the scene,' he thought nervously. 'No, they can't be there – they wouldn't be such idiots as to hang around there.'

The heap of green leaves came in sight. A numb paralysing pain ran through his spine. He thought his heart had stopped beating. He stopped to check. It was still beating, all right. He was just nervous. He moved on faster, and the echo of his footsteps bothered him.

When Nyagar reached the scene of murder, he noticed that everything was exactly as they had left it earlier. He stood there for a while, undecided. He looked in all directions to ensure that no one was coming. There was nobody. He was all alone with the dead body. He now felt nervous. 'Why should you disturb a dead body?' his inner voice asked him. 'What do you want to do with money? You have three wives and twelve children. You have many cattle and enough food. What more do you want?' the voice persisted. He felt even more nervous, and was about to retreat when an urge stronger than his will egged him on.

'You have come all this far for one cause only, and the man is lying before you. You only need to put your hand in his pockets, and all the money will be yours. Don't deceive yourself that you have enough wealth. Nobody in the world has enough wealth.'

Nyagar bent over the dead man, and hurriedly removed the leaves from him. His hand came in contact with the man's arm which lay folded on his chest. It was still warm. A chill ran through him again, and he stood up. It was unusual for a dead person to be warm, he thought. However, he dismissed the thought. Perhaps he was just nervous and was imagining things. He bent over the man again, and rolled him on his back. He looked dead all right.

He fumbled quickly to find the pockets. He dipped his hand into the first pocket. It was empty. He searched the second pocket – that, too, was empty. A pang of disappointment ran through his heart. Then he remembered that cattle traders often carried their money in a small bag stringed with a cord round their neck.

He knelt beside the dead man and found his neck. Sure enough there was a string tied around his neck, from which hung a little bag. A triumphant smile played at the corners of his mouth. Since he had no knife with which to cut the string, he decided to remove it over the man's head. As Nyagar lifted the man's head, there was a crashing blow on his right eye. He staggered for a few yards and fell unconscious to the ground.

The thief had just regained consciousness and was still very weak. But there was no time to lose. He managed to get up on his feet after a second attempt. His body was soaked in blood, but his mind was now clear. He gathered all the green leaves and heaped them on Nyagar. He then made for the bridge which he had failed to locate during the battle.

He walked away quickly – the spirit should not leave the body while he was still on the scene. It was nearly dawn. He would reach the river Migua in time to rinse the blood off his clothes.

Before sunrise, the clan leader Olielo sounded the funeral drum to alert the people. Within an hour more than a hundred clansmen had assembled at the foot of the *Opok* tree where the elders normally met to hear criminal and civil cases. Olielo then addressed the gathering.

'Listen, my people. Some of you must have heard of the trouble we had in our clan last night. Thieves broke into Omogo's kraal and stole six of his ploughing oxen.'

'Oh!' the crowd exclaimed.

Olielo continued, 'As a result, blood was shed, and we now have a body lying here.'

'Is this so?' one elder asked.

'Yes, it is so,' Olielo replied. 'Now listen to me. Although our laws prohibit any wanton killing, thieves and adulterers we regard as animals. If anyone kills one of them he is not guilty of murder. He is looked upon as a person who has rid society of an evil spirit, and in return society has a duty to protect him and his children. You all know that such a person must be cleansed before he again associates with other members of society. But the white man's laws are different. According to his laws, if you kill a man because you find him stealing your cattle or sleeping in your wife's hut, you are guilty of murder – and therefore you must also be killed. Because he thinks his laws are superior to ours, we should handle him carefully. We have ancestors – the white man has none. That is why they bury their dead far away from their houses.

'This is what we should do. We shall send thirty men to the white man to tell him that we have killed a thief. This group should tell him that the whole clan killed the thief. Take my word, my children. The white man's tricks work only among a divided people. If we stand united, none of us will be killed.'

'The old man has spoken well,' they shouted. Thirty men were elected, and they immediately left for the white man's camp.

More people, including some women, had arrived to swell the number of the group. They moved towards the river where the dead thief lay covered in leaves, to await the arrival of the white man.

Nyamundhe moved near her co-wife. 'Where is Nyagar? My eye has not caught him.'

His co-wife peered through the crowd, and then answered, 'I think he has gone with the thirty. He left home quite early. I woke up very early this morning, but the gate was open. He had left the village.'

Nyamundhe recollected that as they entered the narrow path which led to the river, their feet felt wet from the morning dew. And bending across the path as if saying prayers to welcome the dawn, were long grasses which were completely overpowered by the thick dew. She wanted to ask her co-wife where their husband could have gone but, noticing her indifference, she had decided to keep quiet.

'I did not like that black cat which dashed in front of us when we were coming here,' Nyamundhe said to her co-wife.

'Yes, it is a bad sign for a black cat to cross one's way first thing in the morning.'

They heard the sound of a lorry. They looked up and saw a cloud of dust and two police lorries approaching.

The two lorries pulled up by the heap of green leaves. A European police officer and four African officers stepped down. They opened the back of one of the lorries and the thirty men who had been sent to the police station by the clan came out.

'Where is the clan elder?' the white officer demanded.

Olielo stepped forward.

'Tell me the truth. What happened? I don't believe a word of what these people are saying. What did you send them to tell me?'

Olielo spoke sombrely and slowly in Dholuo, pronouncing every word distinctly. His words were translated by an African police officer.

'I sent them to inform you that we killed a thief last night.'

'What! You killed a man?' the white man moved towards Olielo. The other policeman followed him.

'You killed a man?' the white officer repeated.

'No, we killed a thief.' Olielo maintained his ground.

'How many times have I told you that you must abandon this savage custom of butchering one another? No one is a thief until he has been tried in a court of law and found guilty. Your people are deaf.' The white man pointed at Olielo with his stick in an ominous manner.

'This time I shall show you how to obey the law. Who killed him?' the white officer asked angrily.

'All of us,' answered Olielo, pointing at the crowd.

'Don't be silly. Who hit him first?'

The crowd was getting restless. The people surged forward menacingly towards the five police officers.

'We all hit the thief,' they shouted.

'If you want to arrest us, you are free to do so. You'd better send for more lorries.'

'Where is the dead man?' the white man asked Olielo.

'There,' Olielo replied, pointing at the heap of leaves.

The police moved towards the heap. The crowd also pushed forward. They wanted to get a glimpse of him before the white man took him away.

The last time a man had been killed in the area the police took the corpse to Kisumu where it was cut up into pieces and then stitched up again. Then they returned it to the people saying, 'Here is your man – bury him.' Some people claimed that bile is extracted from such bodies and given to police tracker dogs; and that is why the dogs can track a thief to his house. Many people believed such stories. They were sure that this body would be taken away again by the police.

The European officer told the other police officer to uncover the body. They hesitated for a while, and then obeyed.

Olielo looked at the body before them unbelievingly. Then he looked at his people, and at the police. Was he normal? Where was the thief? He looked at the body a second time. He was not insane. It was the body of Nyagar, his cousin, who lay dead, with a sizeable wooden stick driven through his right eye.

Nyamundhe broke loose from the crowd and ran towards the dead body. She fell on her husband's body and wept bitterly. Then turning to the crowd, she shouted, 'Where is the thief you killed? Where is he?'

As the tension mounted, the crowd broke up into little groups of twos and threes. The women started to wail; and the men who had killed the thief that night looked at one another in complete disbelief. They had left Nyagar entering his village while they walked on. They could swear to it. Then Olielo, without any attempt to conceal his tear-drenched face, appealed to his people with these words, 'My countrymen, the evil hand has descended upon us. Let it not break up our society. Although Nyagar is dead, his spirit is still among us.'

But Nyamundhe did not heed the comforts of Jaduong' Olielo nor did she trust the men who swore that they had seen Nyagar enter his village after the incident with the thieves. She struggled wildly with the police who carried the corpse of her husband and placed it on the back of the lorry to be taken to Kisumu for a post-mortem. A police officer comforted her with the promise that a village-wide enquiry would start at once into the death of her husband.

But Nyamundhe shook her head. 'If you say you will give him back to me alive, then I will listen.'

Nyamundhe tore her clothes and stripped to the waist. She walked slowly behind the mourners, weeping and chanting, her hands raised above her head.

My lover the son of Ochieng'
The son of Omolo
The rains are coming down
Yes, the rains are coming down
The nights will be dark
The nights will be cold and long.
Oh! the son-in-law of my mother
I have no heart to forgive,
I have no heart to pardon

All these mourners cheat me now
Yes, they cheat me
But when the sun goes to his home and
Darkness falls, they desert me.
In the cold hours of the night
Each woman clings to her man
There is no one among them
There is none
There is no woman who will lend me a
Husband for the night
Ah, my lover, the son of Ochieng'
The son-in-law of my mother.

SEMBÈNE OUSMANE

TRIBAL MARKS

WE HAVE MADE it a habit to meet every night at Mane's. While sipping Moorish tea we tackle any topic that comes our way, and the fact that we might know precious little about it does not worry us unduly . . . But these past few weeks the great problems of the Mali Federation, the Algerian war, the forthcoming session of the UNO, all had been relegated to the background of our preoccupations. Even women, who would normally take up one quarter of our discussions, were eclipsed. Saër, a serious and phlegmatic person, had put us a poser: 'Why do we have tribal marks?'

It must be mentioned here that Saër is half Senegalese and half Upper Voltan and that he does not bear any tribal marks himself. It is also true that none of us was adorned in this way. Nevertheless, during the whole year that we have been meeting at Mane's, I have never heard such a heated discussion, nor have I been so inundated with torrents of words. Just listening to us one would have thought that the future of the whole African continent was at stake. For weeks on end while these nightly get-togethers lasted, the most stupendous and unexpected arguments were advanced. Some of us went to the surrounding villages or pushed even further inland to consult the oldest men, the griots, those very people who are referred to as the 'libraries' of our country, to provide us with the key to a mystery buried in the past.

Saër refuted all arguments with chapter and verse.

Some said with fiery conviction that 'it was a sign of

nobility'. Others held that 'it was a sign of bondage'. Somebody explained, 'It was purely decorative. In a certain tribe people would strictly refuse to accept any man or woman without these signs . . . either as facial marks or body-adornments.' Some jokers, giving themselves a serious air, told the following story: 'There was once a rich African king who sent his son to study in Europe. The king's son left as a child but came back as a grown man. Obviously he was an educated person or, let's say it right away, an intellectual. He looked down on the ways and customs of his ancestors. The king was annoyed and wondered how he could save his wayward son for the sacred institution of kingship. He consulted the senior adviser of the kingdom . . . And one morning on the public square the son's face was marked . . .'

Nobody believed that story. Its author willy-nilly had to drop it.

Another speaker started after the jokers had given up: 'I went to the French Institute for Black Africa and swotted up the subject, but didn't find anything. I only discovered the significant fact that in the upper classes of our society the wives of certain GENTLEMEN have their facial marks removed. They travel to Europe to see their beautician, for the new tenets of African beauty no longer square with the former aesthetic norms in our country. Our women are getting Americanized. The influence of those black dames on Fifth Avenue and 137th Avenue makes itself felt. As this trend gains ground, so our tribal marks lose their citizenship rights among us and are bound to disappear.'

Another topic of discussion was the variety of tribal marks, which was even apparent in one and the same tribe. There are facial as well as body marks. This fact led to the crucial question: 'If these marks were symbols of belonging to a noble or high caste on the one hand or a low caste on the other, why didn't they survive in the Americas?'

'At last!' Saër broke in, 'now we're getting somewhere.'

'Let's hear it, we're tired of just scouting around,' several voices could be heard in unison.

'All right,' Saër said, and paused. The servant as usual passed round glasses of hot tea. The fragrance of mint filled the room.

'All right,' Saër said again. 'We have touched upon the Americas. Among the men and women who have distinguished themselves through research on Negro slavery, not one has mentioned those marks, so far as I'm aware. In South America, where the practice of voodoo or witchcraft among the slave community has survived to this day, we find no trace of them. In the Caribbean, the black people don't have any facial marks either. Whether you take Haiti, Cuba, San Domingo or any of those places . . . nothing doing. Now if we turn back to Africa before the era of the slave-trade, say to the period of the empires of Ghana, Mali, Gao, the Hausa States, Bornu, Benin, the Mossi kingdoms and so forth, none of the travellers who visited any of them actually mentions this practice. So where do you think these marks come from?'

The audience had stopped sipping their hot tea and listened with rapt attention.

'But if we study the period of the slave-trader impartially, we will find that for the slave-traders the physical condition of the slave was of paramount importance. They had to be strong and without any visible deficiency. We know for example that during the entire trade cycle, both at the internal market in Africa and at the external market on the far side of the Atlantic, the slave would be examined, weighed and fingered like an animal. The prospective buyer would not condone the slightest imperfection of the merchandise, except for the mark left by the branding-iron of the slave-trading company or nation delivering the goods. No other blemishes on the body of the beast were tolerated. The salesmanship these fellows developed was truly remarkable. The slave would be scrubbed down and given a special skin treatment – they called it whitewashing in those days – which raised the price. How then did we come by these graphic symbols on our bodies? . . .'

We were unable to supply an answer. Saër's hypotheses on tribal marks were buttressed by solid arguments. The most talkative among us as well as those who tended to be more thoughtful, all kept silent.

'Carry on, Saër,' we shouted for fear of remaining without an answer.

This is the story he told us.

The captain of the slave ship *The African* had been riding at anchor in the bay for days, waiting to complete his cargo so that he could set sail for New England. He had more than fifty full-grown slaves and thirty young girls aboard. The captain's licensed purchasing agents were roving the hinterland for further supplies. The captain, the ship's doctor and a few men had remained on board. On that particular day they all happened to be in the doctor's cabin. Their chatter could be heard from the fo'c's'le.

Amoo bent down further and stole a look at the men following behind him. He was solidly built, his body all muscle, and fit for any hardship. He firmly gripped the handle of his axe and with the other hand he touched his big cutlass, then took a few stealthy steps forward. On the port side his armed men who had dropped lithely from the bulwark netting could now be seen emerging one by one; on the starboard side Momutu, the commander of the boarding party with his wide-brimmed hat, his blue uniform with red trimmings, and holding a big gun in his hand, signalled to his squad to surround the cabin. The ship's cooper had appeared out of nowhere. In an attempt to get away he threw himself into the sea. The black men down in the canoes grabbed him and pierced him with a lance.

On deck the fight had started when a shipping agent seeking to engage the attackers in hand-to-hand combat had his guts spilled out in the process. The men of the boarding party were armed with rifles and Spanish cutlasses. The captain and the rest of his men had locked themselves up in the doctor's cabin. Momutu laid siege to them and let them have a volley from time to time. A hellish noise reigned on the ship. Plundering was in full swing. When the shooting started, the number of black combatants increased. Coming from the shore, canoes glided towards *The African* and left again heavily loaded with goods.

Momutu called together his lieutenants, four hefty fellows armed to the teeth: 'We have to start freeing the captives and bringing them out of the hold.'

'What about that one?' the lieutenant next to him asked.

'That one?' Momutu repeated, pointing to Amoo who was standing near the hatch. 'We'll see about him later. He is looking for his daughter. Hey, you there, open the hold . . . and don't give any arms to the people of the coast! Pile up everything!'

The air was full of the smell of gunpowder and sweat. With furious determination, Amoo tried to force the hatch open. Axes and crowbars did the rest, and it was finally smashed.

At the bottom of the hold lay the men, shackled, and their ankles linked together by a long chain. As soon as they had heard the shots being fired, they had shouted with joy and fear. A rotten stench filled the hold. Between-decks where the young girls were accommodated, screams of terror could be heard. Amid this deafening noise, Amoo could distinguish his daughter's voice. Bathed in sweat he struck at the hatches with all his strength.

'Hey, brother, this way,' a man called out to him. 'Are you in such a big hurry to see your daughter?'

'Yes, I am,' he replied, and his eyes glittered restlessly.

After long hours of intense activity the hold was finally thrown wide open. Momutu's men began to bring up the captives and assemble them on deck, where the slave-traders' wares were piled up: barrels of brandy, crates of knives, and boxes full of glass beads, silk, parasols and gaudy dresses of doubtful quality. Momutu's men formed a circle around everything and lined up the prisoners. Amoo had found his daughter Iomé. The two of them stood back from the crowd. Amoo was well aware of the fact that Momutu had only freed the men and the girls in order to sell them again. It was he who had lured the captain of *The African* into his bay under false pretences.

'Now we're going to land. I warn you that you are my prisoners. The moment one of you tries to escape or commit suicide, I'll get hold of his neighbour and cut his skin to shreds,' Momutu said.

The sun, reflected by an enormous silvery sheet of water, was sinking towards the horizon. On the land-side loomed a dark line of trees. The loot was being carried into the boats. Momutu, the uncontested leader, gave orders. Some fellows were keeping guard around the cabin. Every couple of minutes a volley of shots directed at the cabin made it clear to those crouching inside that the besiegers were still on board. When all was finished, Momutu lit a long wick which connected two barrels of gunpowder. The captain, not hearing any more noise, tried to leave the cabin and promptly received a shot in the middle of his chest. The last canoes made for the shore. When they were half-way, the explosions rang out: *The African* was blown sky-high.

It was pitch-dark when the entire freight of the ship had been unloaded. The prisoners were herded together and guarded by pickets. They still had their feet and hands shackled. All through the night one heard their whispering and weeping punctuated by the vicious swish of the lash. At some distance away Momutu and his accomplices were doing their accounts. The prize had been worth the effort. They evaluated their capital income while downing an enormous number of pints of brandy by starlight.

Momutu bade Amoo come to him.

'You'll have a few drinks with us,' Momutu told him when he arrived, carrying his sleeping daughter on his back. They loomed in front of Momutu like nameless shadows.

'I have to set out on my return journey. I live far from here and the coast is not a safe place. It's two months now that I have been working for you,' Amoo said, refusing the drink.

'Is it true that you killed your wife to prevent her being captured?' a fellow stinking with alcohol said.

A groan was the answer.

'And you've risked your life more than once just to save your daughter!'

'She's all I have. I have seen my whole family sold one by one and carried away Heaven knows where. I grew up in fear, fleeing from one place to another with my clan to escape slavery. In my clan there are no slaves . . . we are all equal.'

'It's because you don't live on the coast,' somebody interrupted him, prompting Momutu to break into hilarious laughter. 'Have a swig. A true warrior, that's what you are.

I saw you split that shipping agent into two. Your axe really hits home unfailingly.'

'Stay with me. You're tough and you know what you want,' Momutu started again, offering him the cask of brandy. He politely declined. 'You know what our job is like. We roam the savanna taking prisoners whom we sell to the whites. Some captains, unfortunately, know me. Others are lured to this place and my men see to it that they're tricked into leaving the ship. The ship is plundered and the captives taken over . . . the whites, well, they're killed. It's an easy job. The outcome of every operation is a foregone conclusion. I've returned your daughter to you. She's a nice piece. She's worth several iron bars.' (Up to the eighteenth century payments were made, in addition to trumpery stuff, in bags of cowrie shells, the cowrie shells being later superseded by iron bars. According to some sources the barter currency in other markets had always been iron bars.)

'I admit that I have killed, but never to sell or to make prisoners. That's your job. Not mine. I want to return to my village.'

'What a strange fellow! All he can think of is his village, his wife and his daughter.'

Amoo could only see their eyeballs gleaming. He knew that these people were ready to seize him and his daughter to resell them to the first slave-trader that happened to come along. He was not quite up to their tricks.

'I wanted to leave tonight . . .'

'Not on your life,' Momutu said harshly. The alcohol was beginning to have its effect. But when he realized the angry state he was in, he softened his voice. 'There remains just one more fight,' he said. 'Some of my men have set out with the rest of the whites to take slaves. We have to intercept them. After that you'll be free.'

'I am going to put her to rest. She's gone through a lot,' Amoo said and withdrew.

'Has she eaten? . . .'

'We have both eaten our fill . . . We'll wake up early.'

They vanished into the night but from a distance a shadow kept them under surveillance.

'A strapping fellow like him ought to fetch us four casks.'

'More than that,' another one chimed in, 'a number of iron bars, not counting the goods.'

'Let's take it easy. Tomorrow after the battle we'll get hold of him and his daughter. His daughter is quite valuable. Under no circumstance must they get away. Such pieces can't be had on this coast for love or money.'

A freshness conducive to sleep wafted in from the open sea, the night hovered dark around them, the stars were shining. From time to time a piercing shriek of pain could be heard, followed by a crack of the whip. Amoo lay down with Iomé outside the two camps. His eyes were alert although he looked sleepy. In dozens of fights he had taken part in to redeem his daughter, Momutu had had occasion to appreciate his worth. He had astounding strength and suppleness. Three times three moons ago the slave-hunters had come and raided his village and carried away all able-bodied people. He had managed to escape because he happened to be away in the bush that day. When he returned, his mother-in-law, whose life had been spared because of her elephantiasis, told him everything.

The moment he had won back his daughter on the slave-ship, he lost all self-control and let his tears flow freely. His left hand firmly clasped his daughter's wrist while in the other hand he had held the battle-axe covered with gore from the cutting edge right up to his fingers. His heart beat fast. Iomé must have been nine or ten years old. She too had shed copious tears. He had soothed her:

'We're going home to the village. You must not cry. You will do what I tell you, you understand?'

'Yes, father.'

'Don't cry any more. It's all over. I'm here.'

And now in the dead of night Iomé slept peacefully, her head on her father's thigh. Amoo unsheathed his axe and put it within easy reach. He sat propped up against a tree trunk, his wakefulness pitched around him like a force-field of magnetic rays. At the faintest noise his fingers clasped the handle of his weapon. He only slept intermittently.

Before a whitish light lit up the eastern sky, Momutu had roused his men. One detachment was detailed to escort the captives and the trade goods and take them to a safe place. Amoo and Iomé stood at a distance. The girl was tall for her age and had deep-set eyes; her short hair was done lengthwise into a pair of plaits which divided her head into two sections. She nestled between her father's legs. She had seen her former companions. Maybe she did not know the fate that awaited them but the sound of the lash did not leave any doubt in her mind about the condition they were in.

'They are going to wait for us farther away. We have to be careful so that the scouts of the whites won't take us by surprise,' Momutu said, sidling up to Amoo. 'Why are you holding on to your child? You could have entrusted her to one of my men.'

'I prefer to keep her with me. She gets easily frightened,' Amoo replied, looking at the caravan moving off.

'She is beautiful.'

'She is indeed.'

'As beautiful as her mother?'

'Not quite.'

Momutu turned around and inspected the remainder of his troop, who numbered about thirty. Then the column marched off. The men advanced in parallel lines. Momutu was well-known in the ebony trade. No merchant and no captain trusted him. Before engaging in the trade on his own account, he had been a recruitment agent. Then he became a 'master of language' – an interpreter who sailed between the fortresses and the stockades where the prisoners were crowded together.

They marched the whole morning. Amoo and his daughter followed behind. When Iomé was tired, her father would put her on his back or on his shoulders. Amoo knew he was being watched. The men who marched in front of him were uncouth, shabby and grotesque with their long rifles. They had crossed the savanna and the land of the big trees where whole colonies of vultures were perched. Soon the men had stopped talking altogether. All that could be heard in the bush was the jabbering of the birds and sometimes a howl echoing in the distance. They reached the big forest, steeped in humidity and hostile silence. Momutu gave orders to pitch camp and his men fanned out over a wide area.

'Are you tired, brother? And the little girl?'

Iomé raised her heavy eyelashes to their guard, then looked at her father.

'Just a little,' Amoo replied while his eyes were roving around for a resting-place. He saw a branch lying at the foot of a tree and took Iomé over to it, the guard dogging their steps.

Momutu had meagre food rations of tubers shared out. After the meal he came to see Amoo. The child was asleep.

'How's your daughter?'

'She's resting,' Amoo said. He was carving a doll with his knife.

'She's well-built,' Momutu said sitting down beside him. He took off his wide-brimmed hat, his black boots were dirty all over. 'We'll recuperate here and then we'll get them. They can't help passing this way.'

Amoo was more and more on his guard. He nodded agreement. His eyes did not leave Iomé a single moment while his knife was giving life to the piece of wood.

'You'll be a free man when it's all over. Are you sure you want to return to your village?'

'Yes, I am.'

'You haven't got anybody left there,' Momutu said and went right on before Amoo could answer. 'I too once had a village . . . just at the edge of a forest. In that village were my mother and my father, relatives . . . and the whole clan! We used to eat meat and fish. The farms were well cultivated. But as the years passed by, the village went to ruin. Nothing but moaning and groaning. The only things I have ever heard since I was born were cries, all I ever saw was agitated flight into the bush. You enter the forest and die of illness, or stay in the savanna and get caught . . . What was I to do? I have made my choice. I'd rather be with the hunters than with the hunted any day.'

Amoo did not understand. He, too, knew that life was like that. One was never safe, never sure whether one would live to see another day. And something else also bothered him: to what use did they really put the men and women who were carried away? It was said that the whites made boots from their skin.

They talked for a long time, or rather Momutu rambled on without stopping. He bragged about his exploits and his nights of drunkenness. Amoo only listened. He found it increasingly difficult to understand Momutu's character. Momutu was like a petty king. For him power only manifested itself through the use of force and coercion. After a long time – too long for Amoo's taste – a messenger came and informed the boss that the whites were approaching. Momutu gave his orders: everyone except the captives was to be killed. In a split second the whole bush fell silent. Only the impotent voice of the wind kept up its wailing.

Now the raiding-party with its victims also entered the forest. Four Europeans, each armed with two pistols and carrying a musket in his hands, marched in front, followed by the long file of male and female prisoners, tied together by a wooden fork and a neck-iron, the tail-end of which rested on the shoulder of the prisoner in front. Three more Europeans brought up the rear while a fourth, who seemed to be ill, was stretched out in a hammock carried by four blacks.

As the first volley of shots rang out from the tops of the trees, the whole forest resounded with echoes. Shouts arose down below, then there was a short scuffle. Amoo, who was holding his daughter by his hand, took advantage of the general confusion to slay his bodyguard and disappear with Iomé . . .

They had kept running, avoiding any baneful encounters, penetrating ever more deeply into the forest, crossing rivers and streams. Amoo was going in a south-easterly direction. His knife and his axe had never been so useful to him as they were these days. They would travel for the major part of the night, at dawn and at dusk. Never in broad daylight.

Three weeks later they arrived at their village, consisting of some thirty huts huddled close together between the bush and the source of the river. Few men and women were around at that time of day. The village, which had so often been drained of its life-force, was depopulated. When

Amoo and Iomé appeared on the threshold of his mother-in-law's house, the old woman, dragging her crippled leg, gave off screams that alerted the other villagers. They came to see what was the matter, a rickety lot, and scared to death. All stood frozen to the spot on seeing Amoo and Iomé and shouted with surprise. Tearful cries and questions flew hither and thither in the house. Iomé was treated like the most precious object and dragged aside by her grandmother. Her answers came in fits and starts, between bursts of tears.

Amoo had been invited to a palaver session by the village elders. During his talk with them he recounted the ups and downs of his adventurous journey.

'Since my birth, and well before that of my father and my grandfather, the whole country has only been living in expectation of being captured and sold to the whites. The whites are barbarians,' an apparently ageless elder said.

'Will it ever stop?' another asked. 'I've seen all my children being carried off. I don't remember how many times we have changed the site of the village. It's impossible to penetrate the forest any more deeply . . . The wild beasts . . . Sickness . . .'

'I prefer the wild beasts to the slave-hunters. Five or six rainy seasons ago we were safe here. Now that's finished. At three and a half days' march from this village there's a slave factory now,' a third man added.

They fell silent, their wizened faces tortured and rutted with sorrow, bearing the indelible mark of the times. They were satisfied that there was an urgent necessity to move but while one group was for immediate action, others evoked the hazards of living in the heart of the forest without water, in the absence of able-bodied men, and the fact that they would have to abandon the tombs of their dead ancestors.

The chief with his gnarled baton, his flat-topped degenerate-looking skull with a protuberance near the neck, proposed that they should spend the rainy season in the old village while scouts would be sent out to find a new site. To leave just like that without choosing the place would be the height of folly. There were also sacrifices to be made. Finally the men agreed. During the short period they had to remain they consented to step up the cultivation of the land, pool their livestock and put it in a common enclosure. The old man recommended the use of the old women to keep watch over the village.

Amoo's and Iomé's return had given the community a new lease of life. Communal labour, the pulling up of weeds, repairing the enclosures, all these activities started again. People set out for work and returned together. The women were not idle; while some went about their normal chores, others were detailed to be on the look-out for the sudden arrival of the raiders. These were indigenous employees who could be identified by their uniforms in the national colours of the country they were working for. People simply called them 'slave-hunters'. The villagers looked in the direction of the coast only with the deepest apprehension.

The first rains fell. The fertile, generous earth gave life to the seeds sown. But although nothing in the behaviour of the villagers betrayed any shadow of anxiety or fear, their minds remained on the alert. Every night they were kept awake by the certainty of an imminent invasion.

Amoo was sharing his hut with Iomé. He too only went to bed armed. Any harmless rattle caused by the wind put the child into a state of extreme agitation. Amoo put heart and soul into his work. As for Iomé, everybody insisted on letting her rest, and the little girl gradually regained her strength. Her black cheeks acquired a new lustre, tiny folds of fatty tissue began to develop around her neck, and her hitherto bony joints took on flesh and became rounded.

Days and weeks went by peacefully. The narrow strips of land wrested from nature through strenuous effort offered a new promise. Cassava plants were shooting up. Foodstuffs, palm-oil, shea-butter, baskets full of beans, pots of honey, all the things that would be needed in the new village were being gathered. The men who had been sent out to search for a suitable site returned. They had discovered a choice piece of ground beneath the mountain but above the savanna, with a pleasant stream flowing nearby. The land was arable, there was ample pasture, and the children would be safe from the raiders.

The men and women were happy. The chief had fixed the departure date. The prospect of finding a safe haven dulled their sense of danger. Fire, which had previously been forbidden at night so as not to give away the village, burned with a red glare. Laughter rang out. The children dared to go out without being under the constant watch of their parents, for all the parents could think of was the forthcoming departure. It was only a matter of days now. In the palaver hut the question was raised under what favourable sign the removal was to take place. Every man and woman was concerned about the spirits of their homestead, their totems and ancestral graves . . .

That day was not, however, a day of sacred ceremonies. It was a day like any other with brilliant sunshine, trees draped in tender foliage swaying in the wind, clouds sailing on high, humming-birds frolicking around, and monkeys gambolling at their best. The village breathed that air of life and feeling that haunts the traveller for years to come like a stranded ship.

And yet it was the day. The raiders had appeared out of

nowhere frightening away the animals which instinctively ran towards the forest in a mad stampede. Men, women and children gave off animal noises in response to the rifle fire. Scattered and lost as they were, flight was all they could think of, and only the great forest offered them refuge.

Amoo unsheathed his axe, pushing Iomé and her grandmother before him. The old woman, being an invalid, made little headway. They had fled behind the huts, between the enclosures, and reached the edge of the forest. Amoo hurried the women noiselessly forward. On the outskirts of the village they ran into Momutu's men . . . his number one lieutenant. Amoo, moving faster, struck him down . . . but the whole pack kept pursuing them.

Amoo penetrated more deeply into the forest but the branches handicapped the women in their flight. Had he been on his own he would have been able to make a dash for freedom but he could not abandon his child. He thought of his wife. He had killed her that she might be free. His mother-in-law reminded him of his wife. Ridding himself of the old woman was like leaving his wife. Many times the old woman stopped to regain her breath. Her wooden leg got heavier and heavier. Amoo steadied her and gave her a breathing spell. Iomé kept silent and did not leave her father; she clung to him.

What idea crossed Amoo's mind? He took Iomé gently by the chin and looked deeply into the child's eyes. Their fixed gaze seemed to last an eternity. Tears streamed from Amoo's eyes.

'Mother, we can't go any further. In front of us we face certain death if the three of us stay together . . . Behind us, it's slavery for Iomé and me . . .'

'I can't move any more,' the old woman said, taking her granddaughter. She raised a troubled face to Amoo.

'Mother, Iomé could still escape. She and yourself . . . Your own skin isn't worth much, so the whites won't be able to cut it into leather for their boots.'

'Letting Iomé run off alone would mean certain death for her . . . and what of yourself?'

'Don't worry! The rest is my own business.'

'You aren't going to kill us, are you?' the woman cried.

'No, mother. But I know what to do . . . to ensure that Iomé remains free. We have to hurry. These people are coming nearer, I can hear them talking.'

It was as if all the lightnings of heaven had exploded in his brain. Amoo felt the ground slipping away from under his feet. He gripped the handle of his knife, took a few steps towards a shrub called bantamare by the Wolofs and known for the antiseptic quality of its leaves, pulled off a handful of them and then returned to the two who were staring at him. His eyes were clouded with tears.

'Don't be afraid, Iomé . . .'

'Are you going to kill her as you did her mother?' the mother-in-law cried again.

'No . . . Iomé, you are going to suffer, but you'll never be a slave. You understand?'

By way of an answer the child stared fixedly at the blade of the knife. She remembered the ship . . . the blood-stained axe.

Without further hesitation, keeping the little girl tightly wedged between his muscular legs, Amoo went ahead and scarified her body. The child's screams could be heard from the heart of the forest. She screamed till she lost her voice. Amoo had barely had time to finish when the slavers seized him. He had wrapped up the child in leaves. Amoo was dragged to the coast along with other captives. Iomé and her grandmother returned to the village. Thanks to the old woman's knowledge of herbs, Iomé's body soon healed, but the marks remained.

When the slavers returned several months later, Iomé was taken prisoner and then released again. She was entirely worthless to them because her skin no longer had the requisite purity.

Many miles away the news spread. People came from the most distant villages to consult the grandmother. And as the years and centuries passed by, many different patterns of tribal marks appeared on the bodies of our ancestors.

This is how our ancestors got their tribal marks. They refused to be slaves.

Saër had finished his account.

Over to you now, gentle reader.

MOUHAMADOUL NOUKTAR DIOP

THE POT OF GOLD

THAT DAY, DJIBI was hard at work cultivating his field in the middle of the bush, behind the village of Samtentak.

As usual, Djibi had got up early, and, leaving the village, made his way to his plot of land which had to be cleared, for soon the first rains would fall on the land.

It was the end of the dry season.

The winter would bring moisture and the earth had to be ready for the coming sowing.

Like so many other peasants, Djibi, with his axe, his chopper and his hand-plough, struggled to root out the young grass, to hack down the dead tree-trunks and to grub up the thick bushes which had grown everywhere and refused to be killed by the long drought.

He then used these uprooted plants to enclose his field. After two weeks of back-breaking work he had made a low hedge all around his land with an opening, which served as a gate, for the path to go through.

In the middle of Djibi's plot stood a huge baobab tree, and he loved to rest in the shade of its thick foliage. The people of Diambentak said that this very baobab tree, several centuries old, was once the palaver tree of another village whose ruins had long since been lost in the sand. From time to time Djibi would find among other unidentifiable objects, fragments of crockery, pieces of pestles, the remains of calabashes and mortars. The ancient walls of red earth had crumbled in the rain and all that was left was this plot on which Djibi grew groundnuts.

All the men of Samtentak had advised him not to cultivate this land, telling him that he ought to respect the memory of his forefathers and abandon to the bush this place where at the time of the Damals of Cayor and the Bracs of Walo there had existed a large and populous village, which had now crumbled into dust. But Djibi did not listen to them, or rather he turned a deaf ear. The earth, enriched by years of deposits, produced fine harvests. Each year, his barns were full of marvellous crops. Khoudia, his wife, seeing that the ancestral spirits were not angry and let them grow rich, no longer dared ask her husband to choose another plot of land.

The midday sun blazed down pitilessly on Djibi's body. He stopped pushing his plough through the burning soil and wiped the sweat from his forehead. From early morning he had been struggling against the dry grass which at all costs he wanted to tear up before the first rains fell. He had nearly finished clearing his *lougan*, and he was well satisfied as he looked at the extent of his field, enclosed in its hedge of thorns.

In the distance, in the flames of the beating sun, the village of Samtentak rose up, with its thatched huts. The figure of a woman came rapidly along the path leading from these houses bathed in the midday heat. She walked quickly, carrying on her head a calabash which shone in the sunshine.

This was Khoudia, Djibi's wife.

Alert and lively, she walked upright and majestically, her breasts swelling provocatively. Khoudia, too proud of herself, was envied by her neighbours. Despite her lack of height, she had an unquestionable authority over her husband, and everybody was afraid of her sharp tongue, ever ready to enumerate the faults of any person who had dared to make her angry.

When Djibi saw her coming, he left his plough and went to sit under the baobab tree where Khoudia soon joined him. She put the calabash down, knelt as a sign of respect, got up and said:

'Here is your meal, Djibi.'

'I told you that I am not going to eat today. Why have you come?'

'I hope you are not sorry that I have come. Working from morning to noon always makes you very hungry. Sit down and eat, Djibi.'

'You know, you are right, my clever wife. Do not get angry, I'll eat your *lakh*.'

Djibi sat down on a scrap of matting and started to eat his meal of *lakh* (boiled millet and sour milk), reaching into the calabash with his hand which he had washed with water from the kettle.

Leaning against the trunk of the enormous baobab, Khoudia watched her husband calming his hunger under the ancient branches of the tree.

'The rains are late this year,' she said.

'Yes, and I am very worried, Khoudia. I am very much afraid that the winter winds will not be right for good crops. Look at the sky, not a single cloud. O Lord, when will you bring rain? We are waiting impatiently for it; have pity on us poor peasants!'

Khoudia burst out laughing.

'You are not going to cry, are you? Calm yourself, Djibi. God has heard our prayers. He will certainly fulfil them, for the priests have recited the Koran in the village mosque. They have called for rain and soon it will rush in from the horizon with a loud growling and will soak the earth.'

'I only hope that you are right. If only I had enough money to open a shop, I would have built up a trading stock and we could have gone and established ourselves in a city, probably Thiès, where my brother would have welcomed us.'

Khoudia started when she heard these words.

'You mean that you want to leave the land?'

'Yes, I know she does not deserve it, but despite the good crops every year, it is a hard life and I have too many worries.'

At that moment Khoudia cried out suddenly:

'Look, Djibi, look at that hare!'

'What?' answered her husband between two mouthfuls.

He turned and looked in the direction his wife was pointing just in time to see the short tail of a hare disappearing into a bush.

'You must kill it, Djibi,' she ordered.

'You know very well that it is impossible; a diombor in hiding is very difficult to find.'

'It went into that hole, I saw it. Perhaps it is not very deep.'

The man, after licking his fingers, got up despite himself, took up his plough and went to the bush, followed by his wife. He parted the branches and saw the mouth of a hole.

'My little hare, I've got you,' he said, and set about widening the hole, causing clumps of soil to fall into the subterranean passage. Soon, after having dug quite deep, he confessed that he could not reach the bottom of the hole.

'Carry on anyway,' said Khoudia.

'I tell you I cannot go any further!' he cried.

'Well, you are free to do what you like, but I warn you, if you don't carry on, you will regret it.'

'I understand, damn you! Look, I'm carrying on, but where is the hare?'

Suddenly the iron of the plough struck something hard

and at the same time the long wooden handle vibrated in Djibi's hands.

'What's this? What is happening? What is it?' he said, stooping down. He got up almost at once and said to his wife:

'Look, we've dug up a pot!'

'Oh, there's a stroke of luck for me!' said Khoudia. 'Isn't it broken?'

'No.'

'Well, bring it up then. If it is whole, I can put it to good use.'

'Isn't it wonderful? To think that you wanted me to abandon a place like this, which gives us such good crops and which today gives me a pot!'

'Hurry up!' said Khoudia impatiently.

Djibi raised the pot with great difficulty, and took it out of the hole. How heavy it was! His arm muscles stood out beneath the skin, so great was his effort. When he put it down, Khoudia leant over eagerly. Like all pots of its kind, this one had no lid. She started to clear away the sand that blocked its mouth. Soon a faint gleam shone in the pot. What was inside?

Husband and wife crouched over it. The pot was full of yellow pebbles. They realized what this meant; they knew very well what they had just unearthed.

'Gold!' shouted Djibi.

'It's gold!' repeated Khoudia.

'We've found a jar full of gold! See how big the nuggets are!' they both shouted.

Round-eyed, they danced round the pot, looking at the unhoped-for treasure which Providence had given them, and which would make them the richest in the village of Samtentak.

In former days, people used to bury their wealth in the ground in places known only to themselves. This treasure had obviously been buried there by some fortunate man, afraid of being robbed, for it is well known that the greatest secrecy was always observed about the places where fabulous riches were hidden.

'God bless this man who has given us this wonderful treasure!' cried Djibi.

'What are we going to do with it?' asked Khoudia.

'What are we going to do with it? What are you saying? We'll pretend we never found anything at all! It would be useless, even harmful, to tell our neighbours that we've become rich. Outwardly let us continue to appear poor. Then you'll see how we'll live for the rest of our days in luxury, without anybody suspecting it. Wife, the white people have said: "To live happily, let us live in hiding." I tell you this, so as not to tempt thieves, the envious and the evil. You can call that selfishness, if you like. But I beg you to hold your tongue. Will you obey me?'

'Of course I won't breathe a word of it to anyone. Do you think I'm mad enough to do that?' she asked.

'Don't get cross . . . I'll wait till nightfall to bring the pot to our hut. It would be dangerous to risk it now, since I should certainly be stopped and asked why I, a man, am carrying a pot. If it weren't so heavy you could have carried it. But we'll wait for nightfall. Now go back to the village. Once again, hold your tongue.'

'Do you think I'm as silly as that?' she retorted.

Back in the shade of the baobab tree, Khoudia eagerly picked up the calabash from which her husband had eaten. Joyfully, she started down the road to the village, strutting proudly, full to bursting of the important news of the discovery of the pot of gold.

Impatience gnawed at Djibi as he watched the sun go slowly down towards the horizon. His nervousness increased as night approached. Already several peasants, returning from their fields, were arriving back at Samtentak. One of them, after skirting the enclosure, entered Djibi's plot. Djibi, put out, watched him coming. In different circumstances, he would have welcomed him with a smile, for the man coming towards him was his friend. When he was quite close, he exclaimed:

'What's the matter, Djibi? Why aren't you coming back to the village?'

Djibi, without answering, gave an embarrassed smile. The other stood before him, carrying a rake balanced on his shoulder.

'Come on, let's go back together, Djibi.'

'No,' he replied, opening his mouth for the first time. 'You go ahead, Mor-Diop. I'll come later.'

'But why are you still here? Night is falling.'

Mor-Diop, the same size as Djibi, was as strongly built and wore the same clothes: rags! Suddenly, while he was wondering about his friend's strange behaviour, his glance fell on the pot, the mouth of which had been blocked up with a bunch of flowers to hide its contents.

'Wow!' he exclaimed. 'Who ever saw such a pot? What's in it?'

He bent down eagerly.

'Stop!' roared Djibi. 'Leave it alone!'

'Why should I?' said the other in astonishment, his hand quickly removing the flowers. A soft gleam shone from the inside. He leant further over and recognized the precious metal.

'Gold!' he yelled.

But he cried out in surprise, for Djibi, seized with sudden

wrath, struck him an unexpected blow on the shoulder.

'Get up, I tell you, you inquisitive wretch!'

'What did you hit me for?' Mor-Diop asked.

'I ought even to kill you, you old bastard!' said Djibi.

'Huh! Insults too! Just because I discovered that you have found gold in your field?' replied his friend.

'Enough of that. On your way!' retorted Djibi and threatened him with a meaningful gesture.

'So that's how you welcome a friend?' said Mor-Diop. 'Shout as much as you like. I'm not moving from here.'

'Be off, I tell, you son of a jackal!'

'That's enough from you, you snake!'

'Mor-Diop, don't try me too far . . .' threatened Djibi.

'If it's a fight you want, I'm quite ready. I'm not afraid.'

The two men, face to face, stood watching each other sourly. The blood mounted to their faces. In the middle of the field, the silhouettes of the two fighters stood out against the evening air. All at once, as though moved by an implacable fit of violence, they threw themselves at one another, their limbs entwined. The two wild beings gripped one another savagely. They rolled together on the ground.

'Take that, you dirty spy!'

'And that's for you, you old devil!'

'What? So . . . Aren't you ashamed of biting me?'

'And you, scratching me?'

Eventually they were back on their feet again. A blow from Djibi sent his opponent reeling; the latter got up and charged blindly, like a maddened rhinoceros. Djibi, who was stronger, took him calmly, grasped his wrists in a vice-like grip, and forced him to stand up in front of him.

'Stop, Mor-Diop, we're behaving like children.'

'You started it first. You are to blame!'

'If we carry on, one of us will die!'

'Well then, let's stop, if you want to.'

They eyed one another more watchfully, then without any warning each let out a short laugh, a little forced, admittedly. Mor-Diop's face darkened again very quickly. Without a word, he picked up his rake, glanced insistently at the pot, and took his leave. Meanwhile, Djibi gathered himself together and shouted: 'You won't say a thing to anyone, will you?'

The night ate up the countryside and the fields. Soon, the round circle of the full moon rose in the sky and bathed the earth in a brightness which made the leaves stand out black. The birds were silent in their nests. Everything seemed calm and at rest under the soft caress of the bright evening.

With an uneasy conscience, Djibi carried the pot home, groaning a little under the weight of his burden.

When he reached the village he carefully skirted several houses, and then he went down a dark alley. In the huts oil lamps burned, and calm voices were heard in the night. Full of fear, Djibi tiptoed along, afraid of meeting someone. Suddenly a thick shape appeared in front of him, and he hurriedly hid in the shadow at the corner of a palisade. The man passed by without seeing him: it was Bailo, the village blacksmith.

At last Djibi reached home. He entered the hut he shared with his wife. Khoudia was waiting for him, and seemed annoyed, her face full of ill-concealed anger. In the lamplight, Djibi, at first surprised by her attitude, quickly saw the reason: there, in his house was Mor-Diop, sitting on a mat, awkwardly smoking a white man's cigarette.

'What are you doing here?' said Djibi, angrily putting down the pot.

'I was waiting for you,' said Mor-Diop in a calm voice.

'Why wait for me?' asked Djibi.

'You are my friend, you've become rich. Whether you're generous towards me or not, I know how to keep quiet; it's my bounden duly. I've just explained this to Khoudia who hasn't understood me. Never mind, I hope you do. Chance has wished that I, your friend, should know your secret. Don't worry, I'm as much concerned about your interests as if they were my own. We are almost like two brothers, the same blood flows in our veins.'

'What do you want?' asked Djibi.

'Nothing, except a complete reconciliation: forgive me, I ask nothing more. Let's be friends as before.'

At once all Djibi's suspicions fell from him. So Mor-Diop, instead of threatening to reveal his secret, was assuring him that he would keep quiet, and that he asked nothing for his silence. He was a real friend. Djibi was touched, his expression changed.

'I'm sorry too, Mor-Diop. But did you think I could be so ungrateful as to let my friend live in misery now that, Heaven be praised, I'm rich? Come! I swear you shall have your share.'

'Forgive me, Mor-Diop, for my bad behaviour just now,' moaned Khoudia.

'My brother,' Djibi said, 'the calabash of couscous is waiting. Come and eat.'

'Gladly,' replied Mor-Diop.

On their knees around the food, Khoudia and the two men began to eat together. Yet the peace which had always existed between them seemed to have vanished with the discovery of the pot of gold. From time to time Khoudia gave a mirthless laugh which increased the tension in the air. Djibi looked sideways at his guest who showed a calmness and good spirits which, despite everything, did not come from the heart.

Outside in the bright moonlight the village slept.

The crickets sang, and the single note of their chirruping was interrupted by the sound of a human voice, the call of a household animal or the sad screech of a night bird.

The land was cold.

Slowly, sleep descended on the village of Samtentak.

'Cock-a-doodle-doo!'

The raucous voice of an old cock announced the dawn.

Khoudia got up and left the hut in the soft light. The rhythmic sound of pestle on mortar echoed around. Doves cooed in the dew-bathed foliage. A few birds twittered cautiously.

Soon the sun rose slowly from the east. Its soft beams reached out to the fields, the village and the bush. Far, far away on the plain, a Fulani man with a stick followed his herd of red and white cows into the distance.

Samtentak, under the soft touch of the morning resounded with the noise of the women gathered around the mortars.

Khoudia took a large pan and, leaving the house, joined the crowd of jabbering housewives going to the well. Khoudia, upright and lively, walked with them, going from one to another to exchange a word. From time to time they all burst out laughing. An old woman, carrying her earthenware pitcher with great difficulty, was reciting the latest gossip from the night before.

Suddenly Khoudia noticed Farma, the conceited woman who claimed to be the richest in the village. She wore silver bracelets on her arms, which she loved to swing so that her jewels rang out. Gold ornaments hung from her ears. Khoudia had never been able to get on with her. Farma deserved a good lesson, and who better to give her one than Khoudia, now that her husband had a pot of gold?

Khoudia, out to annoy, went up to Farma who was

walking slowly along, carrying her empty calabash under her arm.

'How's your conscience, Farma? Do you have to dress up like a bride to go to the well?' she asked.

'What?' exclaimed Farma, startled. 'What are you saying, Khoudia? I'm warning you; treat me carefully. If I put on jewels every day, even to go to the well, it's because I've got plenty, while you . . .'

'That's enough. Do you still believe that I, Khoudia, don't have any ornaments? If I wanted to, I could own a thousand times more jewels than you.'

'Ha! Listen to this crazy woman, this liar!'

Farma clapped her hands. The others, fascinated, made a circle round the two quarrelling women. Khoudia saw that everyone was beginning to make fun of her. How could she own a thousand times as many jewels as Farma, the most elegant woman in the village? She smarted under their scorn which clearly favoured her rival.

For a few seconds she hesitated, struggling to control herself, then, infuriated by the mocking expressions of those insolent faces, Khoudia began to shout more and more, revealing all the things she should have kept secret for the safety of her own home.

'If you don't believe me,' she continued, 'far from exaggerating, I haven't even told the whole truth. Since yesterday my husband has become the richest man in the village. Yes, digging for a hare, he found a pot full of gold! With this fortune am I not able to wear a thousand times as many jewels as Farma, this stuck-up hussy whose mouth has to be stopped with a pepper?'

An incredulous silence greeted these words. Khoudia carried on:

'You don't believe me, do you?'

'Have you gone mad?' shouted Farma.

'I'm not asking anything of you,' replied Khoudia. 'If you can't take my word for it, come to my house, all of you. My husband, who need never work again, has gone to clear the scrub on his land so as to avoid suspicion. I shouldn't have told you our secret. Now it's too late. Come and see anyway.'

The women were reluctant to turn back on the way to the well; Khoudia must really have gone mad. Was she telling the truth? Curiosity won in the end and they retraced their steps and followed Djibi's wife who led them to her hut. She drew out an old pot from under the bed. When they saw the contents they all shouted greedily. It really was gold!

Khoudia was indeed right. She had not lied. When she saw this, Farma, furious with spite, fled from the house. Soon the whole village knew what had happened to Djibi. In their homes the women waited impatiently for their menfolk to return from the fields so that they could tell them the news.

So it was, on the following morning, when Djibi was getting ready to return to his work, that a crowd of peasants invaded his home. They stood in the yard, talking and gesticulating wildly. Each of them carried a spade, or a hoe, and they wanted Djibi to listen to them.

'What's the matter, men?' asked Djibi, coming out of his hut.

In reply, several excited voices were heard above the crowd.

'You've found a pot of gold in your field. We aren't asking you to share it with us. But we're going to the same place, and we're going to dig there. There must be more treasure on the site of the old village . . .'

'What? You want to dig in my field?'

Several voices gave their insistent replies.

'Of course! . . .'

'Why not?'

'We must try our luck!'

Djibi considered it. After all, what did it matter if they went to dig in his field? Had not he, Djibi, become rich? For the sake of appearances, he made a show of being angry. In the frenzy of their impatience, the men rushed out of the house without further delay and made their way towards the field.

Djibi was left alone with Khoudia. She, a little ashamed of herself, lowered her head in front of her husband. But he, without attempting to scold her, said:

'I've just come to a decision. We'll wait till nightfall then leave the village for good. When you have a fortune as big as ours, it's dangerous to have neighbours greedy for gold. Goodbye, brothers of Samtentak! Dig to your hearts' content. Just let me tell you this: in one year, it's impossible to dig up two crocks of gold. I swear it, on the name of my father!'

Scarcely had the peasants started digging, each in a different place, when the sky became covered with black clouds. The sun, veiled by this moving canopy, disappeared above the bush.

Was it going to rain?

Without a second's rest, everybody carried on using his spade or hoe. Soil flew in all directions from the holes which soon grew into ditches. Driven on by the hope of a find, the men of Samtentak toiled ceaselessly, shouting whenever they struck something hard, thinking it must be a pot. Soon Djibi's plot became a vast depression surrounded by heaps of sand, which the tornado soon scattered in all directions. Interrupting their furious labour, the peasants looked up to see the thick clouds in the darkened sky. The wind became stronger, carrying away the soil and tearing the leaves off the bushes, twisting and turning in the dust.

There were a few claps of thunder, which shook the earth, and a branch of the baobab tree broke with a dry snapping sound.

'Quick, back to the village!'

They hurried out of the huge trench and staggered back through the gusts of wind. Even before they had reached Samtentak, the rain began to fall heavily, and the noise of the thunder was deafening. The water smashed down on to the parched earth, which swallowed it up immediately. In spite of not having found any gold, the peasants rejoiced at the coming of the rain, and though they were soaked from head to foot, they laughed at the thunder like big children.

Back in their huts, they all waited impatiently for the dawn when, with all their families, they would go to their own fields and begin the sowing.

Only Djibi and Khoudia did not go to their plot, for they had long since fled, taking their treasure with them.

Their field became a huge pond. The rainwater collected in the depression made by the spades and hoes of the gold-seekers, and in that place there was a beautiful pool, so clear that on that morning not a single passing shepherd could resist the temptation to water his flock there.

ABDULRAZAK GURNAH

CAGES

THERE WERE TIMES when it felt to Hamid as if he had been in the shop always, and that his life would end there. He no longer felt discomfort, nor did he hear the secret mutterings at the dead hours of night which had once emptied his heart in dread. He knew now that they came from the seasonal swamp which divided the city from the townships, and which teemed with life. The shop was in a good position, at a major crossroads from the city's suburbs. He opened it at first light when the earliest workers were shuffling by, and did not shut it again until all but the last stragglers had trailed home. He liked to say that at his station he saw all of life pass him by. At peak hours he would be on his feet all the time, talking and bantering with the customers, courting them and taking pleasure in the skill with which he handled himself and his merchandise. Later he would sink exhausted on the boxed seat which served as his till.

The girl appeared at the shop late one evening, just as he was thinking it was time to close. He had caught himself nodding twice, a dangerous trick in such desperate times. The second time he had woken up with a start, thinking a large hand was clutching his throat and lifting him off the ground. She was standing in front of him, waiting with a look of disgust in her face.

'Ghee,' she said after waiting for a long, insolent minute. 'One shilling.' As she spoke she half-turned away, as if the sight of him was irritating. A piece of cloth was wrapped round her body and tucked in under the armpits. The soft cotton clung to her, marking the outline of her graceful shape. Her shoulders were bare and glistened in the gloom. He took the bowl from her and bent down to the tin of ghee. He was filled with longing and a sudden ache. When he gave the bowl back to her, she looked vaguely at him, her eyes distant and glazed with tiredness. He saw that she was young, with a small round face and slim neck. Without a word, she turned and went back into the darkness taking a huge stride to leap over the concrete ditch which divided the kerb from the road. Hamid watched her retreating form and wanted to cry out a warning for her to take care. How did she know that there wasn't something there in the dark? Only a feeble croak came out as he choked the impulse to call to her. He waited, half-expecting to hear her cry out but only heard the retreating slap of her sandals as she moved further into the night.

She was an attractive girl, and for some reason as he stood thinking about her and watched the hole in the night into which she had disappeared, he began to feel disgust for himself. She had been right to look at him with disdain. His body and his mouth felt stale. There was little cause to wash more than once every other day. The journey from bed to shop took a minute or so, and he never went anywhere else. What was there to wash for? His legs were misshapen from lack of proper exercise. He had spent the day in bondage, months and years had passed like that, a fool stuck in a pen all his life. He shut up the shop wearily, knowing that during the night he would indulge the squalor of his nature.

The following evening, the girl came to the shop again. Hamid was talking to one of his regular customers, a man much older than him called Mansur who lived nearby and on some evenings came to the shop to talk. He was half-blind with cataracts, and people teased him about his affliction, playing cruel tricks on him. Some of them said of Mansur that he was going blind because his eyes were full of shit. He could not keep away from boys. Hamid sometimes wondered if Mansur hung around the shop after something, after him. But perhaps it was just malice and gossip. Mansur stopped talking when the girl approached, then squinted hard as he tried to make her out in the poor light.

'Do you have shoe polish? Black?' she asked.

'Yes,' Hamid said. His voice sounded congealed, so he cleared his throat and repeated Yes. The girl smiled.

'Welcome, my love. How are you today?' Mansur asked. His accent was so pronounced, thick with a rolling flourish, that Hamid wondered if it was intended as a joke. 'What a beautiful smell you have, such perfume! A voice like *zuwarde* and a body like a gazelle. Tell me, *msichana*, what time are you free tonight? I need someone to massage my back.'

The girl ignored him. With his back to them, Hamid heard Mansur continue to chat to the girl, singing wild praises to her while he tried to fix a time. In his confusion Hamid could not find a tin of polish. When he turned round with it at last, he thought she had been watching him all the time, and was amused that he had been so flustered. He smiled, but she frowned and then paid him. Mansur was talking beside her, cajoling and flattering, rattling the coins in his jacket pocket, but she turned and left without a word.

'Look at her, as if the sun itself wouldn't dare shine on her. So proud! But the truth is she's easy meat,' Mansur said, his body gently rocking with suppressed laughter. 'I'll be having that one before long. How much do you think she'll take? They always do that, these women, all these airs and disgusted looks . . . but once you've got them into bed, and you've got inside them, then they know who's the master.'

Hamid found himself laughing, keeping the peace among men. But he did not think she was a girl to be purchased. She was so certain and comfortable in every action that he could not believe her abject enough for Mansur's designs. Again and again his mind returned to the girl, and when he was alone he imagined himself intimate with her. At night after he had shut up the shop, he went to sit for a few minutes with the old man, Fajir, who owned the shop and lived in the back. He could no longer see to himself and very rarely asked to leave his bed. A woman who lived nearby came to see to him during the day, and took free groceries from the shop in return, but at night the ailing old man liked to have Hamid sit with him for a little while. The smell of the dying man perfumed the room while they talked. There was not usually much to say, a ritual of complaints about poor business and plaintive prayers for the return of health. Sometimes when his spirits were low, Fajir talked tearfully of death and the life which awaited him there. Then Hamid would take the old man to the toilet, make sure his chamber-pot was clean and empty, and leave him. Late into the night, Fajir would talk to himself, sometimes his voice rising softly to call out Hamid's name.

Hamid slept outside in the inner yard. During the rains he cleared a space in the tiny store and slept there. He spent his nights alone and never went out. It was well over a year since he had even left the shop, and before then he had only gone out with Fajir, before the old man was bedridden. Fajir had taken him to the mosque every Friday, and Hamid remembered the throngs of people and the cracked pavements steaming in the rain. On the way home they went to the market, and the old man named the luscious fruit and the brightly coloured vegetables for him, picking up some of them to make him smell or touch. Since his teens, when he first came to live in this town, Hamid had worked for the old man. Fajir gave him his board and he worked in the shop. At the end of every day, he spent his nights alone, and often thought of his father and his mother, and the town of his birth. Even though he was no longer a boy, the memories made him weep and he was degraded by the feelings that would not leave him be.

When the girl came to the shop again, to buy beans and sugar, Hamid was generous with the measures. She noticed and smiled at him. He beamed with pleasure, even though he knew that her smile was laced with derision. The next time she actually said something to him, only a greeting, but spoken pleasantly. Later she told him that her name was Rukiya and that she had recently moved into the area to live with relatives.

'Where's your home?' he asked.

'Mwembemaringo,' she said, flinging an arm out to indicate that it was a long way away. 'But you have to go on back-roads and over hills.'

He could see from the blue cotton dress she wore during the day that she worked as a domestic. When he asked her where she worked, she snorted softly first, as if to say that the question was unimportant. Then she told him that until she could find something better, she was a maid at one of the new hotels in the city.

'The best one, the Equator,' she said. 'There's a swimming pool and carpets everywhere. Almost everyone staying there is a *mzungu*, a European. We have a few Indians too, but none of these people from the bush who make the sheets smell.'

He took to standing at the doorway of his backyard bed-chamber after he had shut the shop at night. The streets were empty and silent at that hour, not the teeming, dangerous places of the day. He thought of Rukiya often, and sometimes spoke her name, but thinking of her only made him more conscious of his isolation and squalor. He remembered how she had looked to him the first time, moving away in the late evening shadow. He wanted to touch her . . . Years in darkened places had done this to him, he thought, so that now he looked out on the streets of the foreign town and imagined that the touch of an unknown girl would be his salvation.

One night he stepped out into the street and latched the door behind him. He walked slowly towards the nearest street-lamp, then to the one after that. To his surprise he did not feel frightened. He heard something move but he did not look. If he did not know where he was going, there was no need to fear since anything could happen. There was comfort in that.

He turned a corner into a street lined with shops, one or two of which were lit, then turned another corner to escape the lights. He had not seen anyone, neither a policeman nor a night watchman. On the edge of a square he sat for a few minutes on a wooden bench, wondering that everything should seem so familiar. In one corner was a clock tower, clicking softly in the silent night. Metal posts lined the sides of the square, impassive and correct. Buses were parked in rows at one end, and in the distance he could hear the sound of the sea.

He made for the sound, and discovered that he was not far from the waterfront. The smell of the water suddenly made him think of his father's home. That town too had been by the sea, and once he had played on the beaches and in the shallows like all the other children. He no longer thought of it as somewhere he belonged to, somewhere that was his home. The water lapped gently at the foot of the sea-wall, and he stopped to peer at it breaking into white froth against the concrete. Lights were still shining brightly on one of the jetties and there was a hum of mechanical activity. It did not seem possible that anyone could be working at that hour of the night.

There were lights on across the bay, single isolated dots that were strung across a backdrop of darkness. Who lived there? he wondered. A shiver of fear ran through him. He tried to picture people living in that dark corner of the city. His mind gave him images of strong men with cruel faces, who peered at him and laughed. He saw dimly lit clearings where shadows lurked in wait for the stranger, and where later, men and women crowded over the body. He heard the sound of their feet pounding in an old ritual, and heard their cries of triumph as the blood of their enemies flowed into the pressed earth. But it was not only for the physical threat they posed that he feared the people who lived in the dark across the bay. It was because they knew where they were, and he was in the middle of nowhere.

He turned back towards the shop, unable to resist, despite everything, a feeling that he had dared something. It became a habit that after he had shut up the shop at night and had seen to Fajir, he went for a stroll to the waterfront. Fajir did not like it and complained about being left alone, but Hamid ignored his grumbles. Now and then he saw people, but they hurried past without a glance. During the day, he kept an eye out for the girl who now so filled his hours. At night he imagined himself with her. As he strolled the silent streets, he tried to think she was there with him, talking and smiling, and sometimes putting the palm of her hand on his neck. When she came to the shop, he always put in something extra, and waited for her to smile. Often they spoke, a few words of greeting and friendship. When there were shortages he served her from the secret reserves he kept for special customers. Whenever he dared he complimented her on her appearance, and squirmed with longing and confusion when she rewarded him with radiant smiles. Hamid laughed to himself as he remembered Mansur's boast about the girl. She was no girl to be bought with a few shillings, but one to be sung to, to be won with display and courage. And neither Mansur, half-blind with shit as he was, nor Hamid, had the words or the voice for such a feat.

Late one evening, Rukiya came to the shop to buy sugar. She was still in her blue work-dress, which was stained under the arms with sweat. There were no other customers, and she did not seem in a hurry. She began to tease him gently, saying something about how hard he worked.

'You must be very rich after all the hours you spend in the shop. Have you got a hole in the yard where you hide your money? Everyone knows shopkeepers have secret hoards . . . Are you saving to return to your town?'

'I don't have anything,' he protested. 'Nothing here belongs to me.'

She chuckled disbelievingly. 'But you work too hard, anyway,' she said. 'You don't have enough fun.' Then she smiled as he put in an additional scoopful of sugar.

'Thank you,' she said, leaning forward to take the package from him. She stayed that way for a moment longer than necessary, then she moved back slowly. 'You're always giving me things. I know you'll want something in return. When you do, you'll have to give me more than these little gifts.'

Hamid did not reply, overwhelmed with shame. The girl laughed lightly and moved away. She glanced round once, grinning at him before she plunged into the darkness.

AMA ATA AIDOO

TWO SISTERS

AS SHE SHAKES out the typewriter cover and covers the machine with it, the thought of the bus she has to hurry to catch goes through her like a pain. It is her luck, she thinks. Everything is just her luck. Why, if she had one of those graduates for a boyfriend, wouldn't he come and take her home every evening? And she knows that a girl does not herself have to be a graduate to get one of those boys. Certainly, Joe is dying to do exactly that – with his taxi. And he is as handsome as anything, and a good man, but you know . . . Besides, there are cars and there are cars. As for the possibility of the other actually coming to fetch her – oh well. She has to admit it will take some time before she can bring herself to make demands of that sort on *him*. She has also to admit that the temptation is extremely strong. Would it really be so dangerously indiscreet? Doesn't one government car look like another? The hugeness of it? Its shaded glass? The uniformed chauffeur? She can already see herself stepping out to greet the dead-with-envy glances of the other girls. To begin with, she will insist on a little discretion. The driver can drop her under the *neem* trees in the morning and pick her up from there in the evening . . . anyway, she will have to wait a little while for that and it is all her luck.

There are other ways, surely. One of these, for some reason, she has sworn to have nothing of. Her boss has a car and does not look bad. In fact, the man is all right. But she keeps telling herself that she does not fancy having some old and dried-out housewife walking into the office one afternoon to tear her hair out and make a row . . . Mm, so for the meantime it is going to continue to be the municipal bus with its grimy seats, its common passengers and impudent conductors . . . Jesus! She doesn't wish herself dead or anything as stupidly final as that. Oh no. She just wishes she could sleep deep and only wake up on the morning of her glory.

The new pair of black shoes are more realistic than their owner, though. As she walks down the corridor, they sing:

Count, count, count your blessings.
Count, Mercy, count your blessings
Count, Mercy, count your blessings
Count, count, count your blessings.

The sing along the corridor, into the avenue, across the road, and into the bus. And they resume their song along the gravel path as she opens the front gate and crosses the cemented courtyard to the door.

'Sissie!' she called.

'*Hei* Mercy.' And the door opened to show the face of Connie, big sister, six years or more older and now heavy with her second child. Mercy collapsed into the nearest chair.

'Welcome home. How was the office today?'

'Sister, don't ask. Look at my hands. My fingers are dead with typing. Oh God, I don't know what to do.'

'Why, what is wrong?'

'You tell me what is right. Why should I be a typist?'

'What else would you be?'

'What a strange question. Is typing the only thing one can do in this world? You are a teacher, are you not?'

'But . . . but . . .'

'But what? Or you want me to know that if I had done better in the exams, I could have trained to be a teacher too, eh, sister? Or even a proper secretary?'

'Mercy, what is the matter? What have I done? What have I done? Why have you come home so angry?'

Mercy broke into tears.

'Oh I am sorry. I am sorry, Sissie. It's just that I am sick of everything. The office, living with you and your husband. I want a husband of my own, children. I want . . . I want . . .'

'But you are so beautiful.'

'Thank you. But so are you.'

'You are young and beautiful. As for marriage, it's you who are postponing it. Look at all these people who are running after you.'

'Sissie, I don't like what you are doing. So stop it.'

'Okay, okay, okay.'

And there was a silence.

'Which of them could I marry? Joe is – mm, fine – but, but I just don't like him.'

'You mean . . .'

'Oh, Sissie!'

'Little sister, you and I can be truthful with one another.'

'Oh yes.'

'What I would like to say is that I am not that old or wise. But still I could advise you a little. Joe drives someone's car now. Well, you never know. Lots of taxi drivers come to own their taxis, sometimes fleets of cars.'

'Of course. But it's a pity you are married already. Or I could be a go-between for you and Joe!'

And the two of them burst out laughing. It was when she rose to go to the bedroom that Connie noticed the new shoes.

'*Ei*, those are beautiful shoes. Are they new?'

From the other room, Mercy's voice came interrupted by the motions of her body as she undressed and then dressed again. However, the uncertainty in it was due to something entirely different.

'Oh, I forgot to tell you about them. In fact, I was going to show them to you. I think it was on Tuesday I bought them. Or was it Wednesday? When I came home from the office, you and James had taken Akosua out. And later I forgot all about them.'

'I see. But they are very pretty. Were they expensive?'

'No, not really.' This reply was too hurriedly said.

And she said only last week that she didn't have a penny on her. And I believed her because I know what they pay her is just not enough to last anyone through any month, even minus rent . . . I have been thinking she manages very well. But these shoes. And she is not the type who would borrow money just to buy a pair of shoes, when she could have gone on wearing her old pairs until things get better. Oh, I wish I knew what to do. I mean, I am not her mother. And I wonder how James will see these problems.

'Sissie, you look worried.'

'Hmm, when don't I? With the baby due in a couple of months and the government's new ruling on salaries and all. On top of everything, I have reliable information that James is running after a new girl.'

Mercy laughed. 'Oh, Sissie. You always get reliable information on these things.'

'But yes. And I don't know why.'

'Sissie, men are like that.'

'They are selfish.'

'No, it's just that women allow them to behave the way they do instead of seizing some freedom themselves.'

'But I am sure that even if we were free to carry on in the same way, I wouldn't make use of it.'

'But why not?'

'Because I love James. I love James and I am not interested in any other man.' Her voice was full of tears.

But Mercy was amused. 'Oh God. Now listen to that. It's women like you who keep all of us down.'

'Well, I am sorry but it's how the good God created me.'

'Mm. I am sure that I can love several men at the same time.'

'Mercy!'

They burst out laughing again. And yet they are sad. But laughter is always best.

Mercy complained of hunger and so they went to the kitchen to heat up some food and eat. The two sisters alone. It is no use waiting for James. And this evening a friend of Connie's has come to take out the baby girl, Akosua, and had threatened to keep her until her bedtime.

'Sissie, I am going to see a film.' This from Mercy.

'Where?'

'The Globe.'

'Are you going with Joe?'

'No.'

'Are you going alone?'

'No.'

Careful Connie.

'Whom are you going with?'

Careful Connie, please. Little sister's nostrils are widening dangerously. Look at the sudden creasing up of her mouth and between her brows. Connie, a sister is a good thing. Even a younger sister. Especially when you have no mother or father.

'Mercy, whom are you going out with?'

'Well, I had food in my mouth! And I had to swallow it down before I could answer you, no?'

'I am sorry.' How softly said.

'And anyway, do I have to tell you everything?'

'Oh no. It's just that I didn't think it was a question I should not have asked.'

There was more silence. Then Mercy sucked her teeth with irritation and Connie cleared her throat with fear.

'I am going out with Mensar-Arthur.'

As Connie asked the next question, she wondered if the words were leaving her lips. 'Mensar-Arthur?'

'Yes.'

'Which one?'

'*How many do you know?*'

Her fingers were too numb to pick up the food. She put the plate down. Something jumped in her chest and she wondered what it was. Perhaps it was the baby.

'Do you mean that Member of Parliament?'

'Yes.'

'But, Mercy . . .'

Little sister only sits and chews her food.

'But, Mercy . . .'

Chew, chew, chew.

'But, Mercy . . .'

'What?'

She startled Connie.

'He is so old.'

Chew, chew, chew.

'Perhaps, I mean, perhaps that really doesn't matter, does it? Not very much anyway. But they say he has so many wives and girlfriends.'

Please little sister. I am not trying to interfere in your private life. You said yourself a little while ago that you wanted a man of your own. That man belongs to so many women already . . .

That silence again. Then there was only Mercy's footsteps as she went to put her plate in the kitchen sink, running water as she washed her plate and her hands. She drank some water and coughed. Then, as tears streamed down her sister's averted face, there was the sound of her footsteps as she left the kitchen. At the end of it all, she banged a door. Connie only said something like, 'O Lord, O Lord,' and continued sitting in the kitchen. She had hardly eaten anything at all. Very soon Mercy went to have a bath. Then Connie heard her getting ready to leave the house. The shoes. Then she was gone. She needn't have carried on like that, eh? Because Connie had not meant to probe or bring on a quarrel. What use is there in this old world for a sister, if you can't have a chat with her? What's more, things like this never happen to people like Mercy. Their parents were good Presbyterians. They feared God. Mama had not managed to give them all the rules of life before she died. But Connie knows that running around with an old and depraved public man would have been considered an abomination by the parents.

A big car with a super-smooth engine purred into the drive. It actually purrs, this huge machine from the white man's land. Indeed, its well-mannered protest as the tires slid onto the gravel seemed like a lullaby compared to the loud thumping of the girl's stiletto shoes. When Mensar-Arthur saw Mercy, he stretched his arm and opened the door to the passenger seat. She sat down and the door closed with a civilized thud. The engine hummed into motion and the car sailed away.

After a distance of a mile or so from the house, the man started a conversation.

'And how is my darling today?'

'I am well,' and only the words did not imply tragedy.

'You look solemn today, why?'

She remained silent and still.

'My dear, what is the matter?'

'Nothing.'

'Oh . . .' He cleared his throat again. 'Eh, and how were the shoes?'

'Very nice. In fact, I am wearing them now. They pinch a little but then all new shoes are like that.'

'And the handbag?'

'I like it very much, too . . . My sister noticed them. I mean the shoes.' The tragedy was announced.

'Did she ask you where you got them from?'

'No.'

He cleared his throat again. 'Where did we agree to go tonight?'

'The Globe, but I don't want to see a film.'

'Is that so? Mm, I am glad because people always notice things.'

'But they won't be too surprised.'

'What are you saying, my dear?'

'Nothing.'

'Okay, so what shall we do?'

'I don't know.'

'Shall I drive to the Seaway?'

'Oh yes.'

He drove to the Seaway. To a section of the beach they knew very well. She loves it here. This wide expanse of sand and the old sea. She has often wished she could do what she fancied: one thing she fancies. Which is to drive very near to the end of the sands until the tires of the car touched the water. Of course it is a very foolish idea, as he pointed out sharply to her the first time she thought aloud about it.

It was in his occasional I-am-more-than-old-enough-to-be-your-father tone. There are always disadvantages. Things could be different. Like if one had a younger lover. Handsome, maybe not rich like this man here, but well off, sufficiently well off to be able to afford a sports car. A little something very much like those in the films driven by the white racing drivers. With tires that can do everything . . . and they would drive to exactly where the sea and the sand meet.

'We are here.'

'Don't let's get out. Let's just sit inside and talk.'

'Talk?'

'Yes.'

'Okay. But what is it, my darling?'

'I have told my sister about you.'

'Good God. Why?'

'But I had to. I couldn't keep it to myself any longer.'

'Childish. It was not necessary at all. She is not your mother.'

'No. But she is all I have. And she has been very good to me.'

'Well, it was her duty.'

'Then it is my duty to tell her about something like this. I may get into trouble.'

'Don't be silly,' he said. 'I normally take good care of my girlfriends.'

'I see,' she said, and for the first time in the one month since she agreed to be this man's lover, the tears which suddenly rose into her eyes were not forced.

'And you promised you wouldn't tell her.' It was Father's voice now.

'Don't be angry. After all, people talk so much, as you said a little while ago. She was bound to hear it one day.'

'My darling, you are too wise. What did she say?'

'She was pained.'

'Don't worry. Find out something she wants very much but cannot get in this country because of the import restrictions.'

'I know for sure she wants an electric motor for her sewing machine.'

'Is that all?'

'That's what I know of.'

'Mm. I am going to London next week on some delegation, so if you bring me the details on the make of the machine, I shall get her the motor.'

'Thank you.'

'What else is worrying my Black Beauty?'

'Nothing.'

'And by the way, let me know as soon as you want to leave your sister's place. I have got you one of the government estate houses.'

'Oh . . . oh,' she said, pleased, contented for the first time since this typically ghastly day had begun, at half past six in the morning.

Dear little child came back from the playground with her toe bruised. Shall we just blow cold air from our mouth on it or put on a salve? Nothing matters really. Just see that she does not feel unattended. And the old sea roars on. This is a calm sea, generally. Too calm in fact, this Gulf of Guinea. The natives sacrifice to him on Tuesdays and once a year celebrate him. They might save their chickens, their eggs, and their yams. And as for the feast once a year, he doesn't pay much attention to it either. They are always celebrating one thing or another and they surely don't need him for an excuse to celebrate one day more. He has seen things happen along these beaches. Different things. Contradictory things.

Or just repetitions of old patterns. He never interferes in their affairs. Why should he? Except in places like Keta, where he eats houses away because they leave him no choice. Otherwise, he never allows them to see his passions. People are worms, and even the God who created them is immensely bored with their antics. Here is a fifty-year-old 'big man' who thinks he is somebody. And a twenty-three-year-old child who chooses a silly way to conquer unconquerable problems. Well, what did one expect of human beings? And so, as those two settled on the back seat of the car to play with each other's bodies, he, the Gulf of Guinea, shut his eyes with boredom. It is right. He could sleep, no? He spread himself and moved farther ashore. But the car was parked at a very safe distance and the rising tides could not wet its tires.

James has come home late. But then he has been coming back late for the past few weeks. Connie is crying and he knows it as soon as he enters the bedroom. He hates tears, for, like so many men, he knows it is one of the most potent weapons in women's bitchy and inexhaustible arsenal. She speaks first.

'James.'

'Oh, are you still awake?' He always tries to deal with these nightly funeral parlor doings by pretending not to know what they are about.

'I couldn't sleep.'

'What is wrong?'

'Nothing.'

So he moves quickly and sits beside her. 'Connie, what is the matter? You have been crying again.'

'You are very late again.'

'Is that why you are crying? Or is there something else?'

'Yes.'

'Yes to what?'

'James, where were you?'

'Connie, I have warned you about what I shall do if you don't stop examining me, as though I were your prisoner, every time I am a little late.'

She sat up. 'A little late! It is nearly two o'clock.'

'Anyway, you won't believe me if I told you the truth, so why do you want me to waste my breath?'

'Oh well.' She lies down again and turns her face to the wall. He stands up but does not walk away. He looks down at her. So she remembers every night: they have agreed, after many arguments, that she should sleep like this. During her first pregnancy, he kept saying after the third month or so that the sight of her tummy the last thing before he slept always gave him nightmares. Now he regrets all this. The bed creaks as he throws himself down by her.

'James.'

'Yes.'

'There is something much more serious.'

'You have heard about my newest affair?'

'Yes, but that is not what I am referring to.'

'Jesus, is it possible that there is anything more important than that?'

And as they laugh they know that something has happened. One of those things which, with luck, will keep them together for some time to come.

'He teases me on top of everything.'

'What else can one do to you but tease when you are in this state?'

'James! How profane!'

'It is your dirty mind which gave my statement its shocking meaning.'

'Okay! But what shall I do?'

'About what?'

'Mercy. Listen, she is having an affair with Mensar-Arthur.'

'Wonderful.'

She sits up and he sits up.

'James, we must do something about it. It is very serious.'

'Is that why you were crying?'

'Of course.'

'Why shouldn't she?'

'But it is wrong. And she is ruining herself.'

'Since every other girl she knows has ruined herself prosperously, why shouldn't she? Just forget for once that you are a teacher. Or at least remember she is not your pupil.'

'I don't like your answers.'

'What would you like me to say? Every morning her friends who don't earn any more than she does wear new dresses, shoes, wigs, and what-have-you to work. What would you have her do?'

'The fact that other girls do it does not mean that Mercy should do it, too.'

'You are being very silly. If I were Mercy, I am sure that's exactly what I would do. And you know I mean it, too.'

James is cruel. He is terrible and mean. Connie breaks into fresh tears and James comforts her. There is one point he must drive home, though.

'In fact, encourage her. He may be able to intercede with the Ministry for you so that after the baby is born they will not transfer you from here for some time.'

'James, you want me to use my sister!'

'She is using herself, remember.'

'James, you are wicked.'

'And maybe he would even agree to get us a new car from abroad. I shall pay for everything. That would be better than paying a fortune for that old thing I was thinking of buying. Think of that.'

'You will ride in it alone.'

'Well . . .'

That was a few months before the coup. Mensar-Arthur did go to London for a conference and bought something for all his wives and girlfriends, including Mercy. He even remembered the motor for Connie's machine. When Mercy took it to her she was quite confused. She had wanted this thing for a long time, and it would make everything so much easier, like the clothes for the new baby. And yet one side of her said that accepting it was a betrayal. Of what, she wasn't even sure. She and Mercy could never bring the whole business into the open and discuss it. And there was always James supporting Mercy, to Connie's bewilderment. She took the motor with thanks and sold even her right to dissent. In a short while, Mercy left the house to go and live in the estate house Mensar-Arthur had procured for her. Then, a couple of weeks later, the coup. Mercy left her new place before anyone could evict her. James never got his car. Connie's new baby was born. Of the three, the one who greeted the new order with undisguised relief was Connie. She is not really a demonstrative person but it was obvious from her eyes that she was happy. As far as she was concerned, the old order as symbolized by Mensar-Arthur was a threat to her sister and therefore to her own peace of mind. With it gone, things could return to normal. Mercy would move back to the house, perhaps start to date someone more – ordinary, let's say. Eventually, she would get married and then the nightmare of those past weeks would be forgotten. God being so good, he brought the coup early before the news of the affair could spread and brand her sister . . .

The arrival of the new baby has magically waved away the difficulties between James and Connie. He is that kind of man, and she that kind of woman. Mercy has not been seen for many days. Connie is beginning to get worried . . .

James heard the baby yelling – a familiar noise, by now – the moment he opened the front gate. He ran in, clutching to his chest the few things he had bought on his way home.

'We are in here.'

'I certainly could hear you. If there is anything people of this country have, it is a big mouth.'

'Don't I agree? But on the whole, we are well. He is eating normally and everything. You?'

'Nothing new. Same routine. More stories about the overthrown politicians.'

'What do you mean, nothing new? Look at the excellent job the soldiers have done, cleaning up the country of all that dirt. I feel free already and I am dying to get out and enjoy it.'

James laughed mirthlessly. 'All I know is that Mensar-Arthur is in jail. No use. And I am not getting my car. Rough deal.'

'I never took you seriously on that car business.'

'Honestly, if this were in the ancient days, I could brand you a witch. You don't want me, your husband, to prosper?'

'Not out of my sister's ruin.'

'Ruin, ruin, ruin! Christ! See, Connie, the funny thing is that I am sure you are the only person who thought it was a disaster to have a sister who was the girlfriend of a big man.'

'Okay; now all is over, and don't let's quarrel.'

'I bet the coup could have succeeded on your prayers alone.'

And Connie wondered why he said that with so much bitterness. She wondered if . . .

'Has Mercy been here?'

'Not yet, later, maybe. Mm. I had hoped she would move back here and start all over again.'

'I am not surprised she hasn't. In fact, if I were her, I wouldn't come back here either. Not to your nagging, no thank you, big sister.'

And as the argument progressed, as always, each was forced into a more aggressive defensive stand.

'Well, just say what pleases you, I am very glad about the soldiers. Mercy is my only sister, brother; everything. I can't sit and see her life going wrong without feeling it. I am grateful to whatever forces there are which put a stop to that. What pains me now is that she should be so vague about where she is living at the moment. She makes mention of a girlfriend but I am not sure that I know her.'

'If I were you, I would stop worrying because it seems Mercy can look after herself quite well.'

'Hmm' was all she tried to say.

Who heard something like the sound of a car pulling into the drive? Ah, but the footsteps were unmistakably Mercy's. Are those shoes the old pair which were new a couple of months ago? Or are they the newest pair? And here she is herself, the pretty one. A gay Mercy.

'Hello, hello, my clan!' And she makes a lot of her nephew. 'Dow-dah-dee-day! And how is my dear young man today? My lord, grow up fast and come to take care of Auntie Mercy.'

Both Connie and James cannot take their eyes off her. Connie says, 'He says to Auntie Mercy he is fine.'

Still they watch her, horrified, fascinated, and wondering what it's all about. Because they both know it is about something.

'Listen, people, I brought a friend to meet you. A man.'

'Where is he?' from James.

'Bring him in,' from Connie.

'You know, Sissie, you are a new mother. I thought I'd come and ask you if it's all right.'

'Of course,' say James and Connie, and for some reason they are both very nervous.

'He is Captain Ashley.'

'Which one?'

'*How many do you know?*'

James still thinks it is impossible. 'Eh . . . do you mean the officer who has been appointed the . . . the . . .'

'Yes.'

'Wasn't there a picture in *The Crystal* over the weekend of his daughter's wedding? And another one of him with his wife and children and grandchildren?'

'Yes.'

'And he is heading a commission to investigate something or other?'

'Yes.'

Connie just sits there with her mouth open that wide . . .

MIA COUTO

THE BIRDS OF GOD

BEGGING YOUR PARDON, I don't know anything more like a pilgrim than the river. The waves pass by on a journey which has no end. For how long has it been water's job to do that? Alone in his old dugout, Ernesto Timba measured his life. At the age of twelve he had entered the school of pulling fish from the water. Ever in the waft of the current, his shadow had reflected the laws of the river dweller for the last thirty years. And what was it all for? Drought had exhausted the earth, the seeds were not fulfilling their promise. When he returned from fishing, he had nothing to defend himself from his wife and children, who impaled him with their eyes. Eyes like those of a dog, he was loath to admit, but the truth is that hunger makes men like animals.

While he contemplated his suffering, Timba made his craft glide slowly along. Under the *mafurreira* tree, there on the bank where the river narrows, he brought the boat to rest so that he might drive away his sad thoughts. He allowed his paddle to nibble the water and the dugout clung to the stillness. But he could not stop his thoughts:

'*What life have I lived? Water, water, just nothing else.*'

As it rocked to and fro, the dugout caused his anguish to multiply.

'*One day they'll fish me out of the water, swallowed up by the river.*'

He foresaw his wife and children watching him being

pulled from the mud, and it was as if the roots of the water were being torn up.

Overhead, the *mafurreira* retained the sun's fierce dispatch. But Timba wasn't listening to the tree, his eyes were peeping into his soul. And it was as if they were blind, for pain is a dust which drains light away. Still higher above, morning called and he caught the smell of the intense blue.

'*If only I belonged to the sky*,' he sighed

And he felt the burden of thirty years of tiredness upon his life. He remembered the words of his father, uttered to teach him courage:

'*See the hunter there, what he does? He prepares his spear the moment he sees the gazelle. But the fisherman can't see the fish inside the river. The fisherman believes in something he can't see.*'

That was the lesson of the bound-to-be of life and he now recalled those wise words. It was getting late and hunger told him it was time to go home. He began to move his arm while casting a last glance upwards, beyond the clouds. It was then that a huge bird passed over the sky. It was like a king, pleased with its own majesty. The creature, high on the wing, held his eyes and an uncanny anxiety took root within him. He thought:

'*If that bird were to fall on my canoe now!*'

He uttered these words aloud. Hardly had he finished speaking than the bird shook its huge wings and quickly flew in a downward spiral towards the boat. It fell as if expelled from life. Timba picked up the damaged bird and holding it in his hands, saw that the blood had not yet unbuttoned its body. In the boat, the animal gradually recovered, until it stood up and climbed onto the prow to take stock of its survival. Timba grabbed it, and weighed its flesh in order to work out how many meals it would provide. He put the idea out of his mind, and with a shove, helped the bird to take off.

'*Be off with you, bird, go back from where you came!*'

But the bird turned round and headed back to the boat. The fisherman once again drove it away. Yet again it returned. Ernesto Timba began to despair.

'*Get back to your life, you bloody bird.*'

Nothing. The bird didn't move. It was then that the fisherman began to wonder: that thing wasn't a bird, it was a sign from God. The warning from heaven would destroy his peace of mind for ever.

Accompanied by the animal, he returned to the village. His wife celebrated his homecoming:

'*Let's have the bird for lunch!*'

Delighted, she called the children:

'*Little ones, come and see the dicky-bird.*'

Without answering, Timba placed the bird on the mat and went to the back of the house to fetch some wooden boards, wire and reeds. Then he set to work to build a cage so large that even a man could fit inside standing up straight. He put the animal inside and fed it the fish he had caught.

His wife was flabbergasted; the man was mad. Time passed and Timba only cared about the bird.

His wife would ask, pointing at the bird:

'*Seeing as how hunger is pinching us, don't you want to kill it?*'

Timba would raise his arm, emphatically. '*Never! Whoever touched the bird would be punished by God, would be marked down for life.*'

And so the days passed by, while the fisherman awaited fresh signs of divine intentions. Countless times he lingered in the moist afternoon heat while the river sat there in front of him. When the sun went down, he would go and check the cage where the animal was growing ever fatter. Little by little, he began to notice a shadow of sadness fall over the sacred bird. He realized the creature was suffering because it was lonely. One night he asked God to send the solitary fowl a companion. The following day, the cage had a new inmate, a female. Timba silently thanked the heavens for this new gift. At the same time, anxiety took root in him: why had God entrusted him to keep these animals? What might be the message they brought?

He thought and thought. That sign, that lightning flash of white plumage, could only mean that heaven's humour was about to change. If men would agree to dispense their kindness to those messengers from heaven, then the drought would end and the season of rains would begin. It had befallen him, a poor fisherman of the river, to play host to God's envoys. It was his task to show that men could still be good. Yes, that true goodness cannot be measured in times of abundance but when hunger dances in the bodies of men.

His wife, who had returned from the *machamba*, interrupted his thoughts:

'*So there are two of them now, are there?*'

She came over, sat down on the same mat and looking long and hard into her companion's eyes, said:

'*Husband, the pot's on the fire. I'm asking you for the neck of one of them, just one.*'

It was a waste of time. Timba promised severe punishment to whoever mistreated the divine birds.

In time, the couple had chicks. There were three of them, clumsy and ugly, their gullets ever open: enough appetite to empty the river. Timba toiled on behalf of their parents. The household provisions, already so scarce, were diverted to feed the coop.

In the village, the rumour went around: Ernesto Timba was stark raving mad. His own wife, after many a threat, left home taking with her all the children. Timba didn't even seem to notice his family's absence. He was more concerned with ensuring his poultry's protection. He detected a spirit of envy around him, vengeance hatching itself. Was it his fault that he had been chosen? They said he had gone crazy. But he who is chosen by God always wanders off his path.

Then, one afternoon when he had finished his work on the river, a feeling of uncertainty set his mind aflame: the birds! He set off home at a rush. When he got near, he saw a pall of smoke rising through the trees around his house. He paddled his dugout towards the river bank, jumped out without even tying it up, and began to run towards the scene of the tragedy. When he arrived, all he saw was wreckage and ashes. The wood and wire had been chewed up by the flames. From between the boards a wing, untouched by the fire, sought to save itself. The bird must have hurled itself against the wall of flames and the wing had got away, an arrow ominously pointing towards disaster. It was not swaying to and fro, as is the obsession of dead things. It was rigid, full of certainty.

Timba stepped back, appalled. He shouted for his wife, for his children, and then, on discovering that there was nobody else to shout for, he wept such copious tears of rage that his eyes hurt.

Why? Why had they harmed those birds, pretty as they were? And there and then, amidst all the ash and the smoke, he addressed himself to God:

'*You're going to be angry, I know. You're going to punish your children. But look: I'm asking you to forgive them. Let me be the one to die, me. Leave the others to suffer what they are already suffering. You can forget the rain even, you can leave the dust lying on the ground, but please don't punish the men of this land.*'

The following day, they found Ernesto hugging the current of the river, chilled by the early morning mist. When they tried to raise him, they found him heavy and impossible to separate from the water. The strongest men were brought to the task, but their efforts were in vain. The body was stuck to the surface of the river. A strange feeling of dread spread among those present. To hide their fear, someone said:

'*Go and tell his wife. Tell the others that the village madman has died.*'

And they withdrew. As they were climbing the bank, the clouds clashed, the sky seemed to cough sullenly as if it were sick. In different circumstances, they would have celebrated the coming of the rain. Not now. For the first time, their faiths joined together pleading that it might not rain.

Impassive, the river flowed on into the distance, laughing at the ignorance of men. Ernesto Timba, gently lulled by the current, was carried downstream, and shown the by-ways he had only glimpsed in dreams.

Translated by David Brookshaw

JOMO KENYATTA

THE GENTLEMEN OF THE JUNGLE

ONCE UPON A time an elephant made a friendship with a man. One day a heavy thunderstorm broke out, the elephant went to his friend, who had a little hut at the edge of the forest, and said to him: 'My dear good man, will you please let me put my trunk inside your hut to keep it out of this torrential rain?' The man, seeing what situation his friend was in, replied: 'My dear good elephant, my hut is very small, but there is room for your trunk and myself. Please put your trunk in gently.' The elephant thanked his friend, saying: 'You have done me a good deed and one day I shall return your kindness.' But what followed? As soon as the elephant put his trunk inside the hut, slowly he pushed his head inside, and finally flung the man out in the rain, and then lay down comfortably inside his friend's hut, saying: 'My dear good friend, your skin is harder than mine, and as there is not enough room for both of us, you can afford to remain in the rain while I am protecting my delicate skin from the hailstorm.'

The man, seeing what his friend had done to him, started to grumble; the animals in the nearby forest heard the noise and came to see what was the matter. All stood around listening to the heated argument between the man and his friend the elephant. In this turmoil the lion came along roaring, and said in a loud voice: 'Don't you all know that I am the King of the Jungle! How dare any one disturb the peace of my kingdom?' On hearing this the elephant, who was one of the high ministers in the jungle kingdom, replied in a soothing voice, and said: 'My lord, there is no disturbance of the peace in your kingdom. I have only been having a little discussion with my friend here as to the possession of this little hut which your lordship sees me occupying.' The lion, who wanted to have 'peace and tranquillity' in his kingdom, replied in a noble voice, saying: 'I command my ministers to appoint a Commission of Enquiry to go thoroughly into this matter and report accordingly.' He then turned to the man and said: 'You have done well by establishing friendship with my people, especially with the elephant, who is one of my honourable ministers of state. Do not grumble any more, your hut is not lost to you. Wait until the sitting of my Imperial Commission, and there you will be given plenty of opportunity to state your case. I am sure that you will be pleased with the findings of the Commission.' The man was very pleased by these sweet words from the King of the Jungle, and innocently waited for his opportunity, in the belief that naturally the hut would be returned to him.

The elephant, obeying the command of his master, got busy with other ministers to appoint the Commission of Enquiry. The following elders of the jungle were appointed to sit in the Commission: (1) Mr Rhinoceros; (2) Mr Buffalo; (3) Mr Alligator; (4) The Rt Hon. Mr Fox to act as chairman; and (5) Mr Leopard to act as Secretary to the Commission. On seeing the personnel, the man protested and asked if it was not necessary to include in this Commission a member from his side. But he was told that it was impossible, since no one from his side was well enough educated to understand the intricacy of jungle law. Further, that there was nothing to fear, for the members of the Commission were all men of repute for their impartiality in justice, and as they were gentlemen chosen by God to look after the interests of races less adequately endowed with teeth and claws, he might rest assured that they would investigate the matter with the greatest care and report impartially.

The Commission sat to take the evidence. The Rt Hon. Mr Elephant was first called. He came along with a superior air, brushing his tusks with a sapling which Mrs Elephant had provided, and in an authoritative voice said: 'Gentlemen of the Jungle, there is no need for me to waste your valuable time in relating a story which I am sure you all know. I have always regarded it as my duty to protect the interests of my friends, and this appears to have caused the misunderstanding between myself and my friend here. He invited me to save his hut from being blown away by a hurricane. As the hurricane had gained access owing to the unoccupied space in the hut, I considered it necessary, in my friend's own interests, to turn the undeveloped space to a more economic use by sitting in it myself; a duty which any of you would undoubtedly have performed with equal readiness in similar circumstances.'

After hearing the Rt Hon. Mr Elephant's conclusive evidence, the Commission called Mr Hyena and other elders of the jungle, who all supported what Mr Elephant had said. They then called the man, who began to give his own account of the dispute. But the Commission cut him short, saying: 'My good man, please confine yourself to relevant issues. We have already heard the circumstances from various unbiased sources; all we wish you to tell us is whether the undeveloped space in your hut was occupied by any one else before Mr Elephant assumed his position?' The man began to say: 'No, but—' But at this point the Commission declared that they had heard sufficient evidence from both sides and retired to consider their decision. After enjoying a delicious meal at the expense of the Rt Hon. Mr Elephant, they reached their verdict, called the man, and declared as follows: 'In our opinion this dispute has arisen through a regrettable misunderstanding due to the backwardness of your ideas. We consider that Mr Elephant has fulfilled his sacred duty of protecting your interests. As it is clearly for your good that the space should be put to its most economic use, and as you yourself have not reached the stage of expansion which would enable you to fill it, we consider it necessary to arrange a compromise to suit both parties. Mr Elephant shall continue his occupation of your hut, but we give you permission to look for a site where you can build another hut more suited to your needs, and we will see that you are well protected.'

The man, having no alternative, and fearing that his refusal might expose him to the teeth and claws of members of the Commission, did as they suggested. But no sooner had he built another hut than Mr Rhinoceros charged in with his horn lowered and ordered the man to quit. A Royal Commission was again appointed to look into the matter, and the same finding was given. This procedure was repeated until Mr Buffalo, Mr Leopard, Mr Hyena and the rest were all accommodated with new huts. Then the man decided that he must adopt an effective method of protection, since Commissions of Enquiry did not seem to be of any use to him. He sat down and said, '*Ng'enda thi ndagaga motegi*,' which literally means 'there is nothing that treads on the earth that cannot be trapped,' or in other words, you can fool people for a time, but not for ever.

Early one morning, when the huts already occupied by the jungle lords were all beginning to decay and fall to pieces, he went out and built a bigger and better hut a little distance away. No sooner had Mr Rhinoceros seen it than he came rushing in, only to find that Mr Elephant was already inside, sound asleep. Mr Leopard next came to the window, Mr Lion, Mr Fox and Mr Buffalo entered the doors, while Mr Hyena howled for a place in the shade and Mr Alligator basked on the roof. Presently they all began disputing about their rights of penetration, and from disputing they came to fighting, and while they were all embroiled together the man set the hut on fire and burnt it to the ground, jungle lords and all. Then he went home, saying: 'Peace is costly, but it's worth the expense,' and lived happily ever after.

TAYEB SALIH

A HANDFUL OF DATES

I MUST HAVE been very young at the time. While I don't remember exactly how old I was, I do remember that when people saw me with my grandfather they would pat me on the head and give my cheek a pinch – things they didn't do to my grandfather. The strange thing was that I never used to go out with my father, rather it was my grandfather who would take me with him wherever he went, except for the mornings when I would go to the mosque to learn the Koran. The mosque, the river and the fields – these were the landmarks in our life. While most of the children of my age grumbled at having to go to the mosque to learn the Koran, I used to love it. The reason was, no doubt, that I was quick at learning by heart and the Sheikh always asked me to stand up and recite the *Chapter of the Merciful* whenever we had visitors, who would pat me on my head and cheek just as people did when they saw me with my grandfather.

Yes, I used to love the mosque, and I loved the river too. Directly we finished our Koran reading in the morning I would throw down my wooden slate and dart off, quick as a genie, to my mother, hurriedly swallow down my breakfast, and run off for a plunge in the river. When tired of swimming about I would sit on the bank and gaze at the strip of water that wound away eastwards and hid behind a thick wood of acacia trees. I loved to give rein to my imagination and picture to myself a tribe of giants living behind that wood, a people tall and thin with white beards and sharp noses, like my grandfather. Before my grandfather ever replied to my many questions he would rub the tip of his nose with his forefinger; as for his beard, it was soft and luxuriant and as white as cotton-wool – never in my life have I seen anything of a purer whiteness or greater beauty. My grandfather must also have been extremely tall, for I never saw anyone in the whole area address him without having to look up at him, nor did I see him enter a house without having to bend so low that I was put in mind of the way the river wound round behind the wood of acacia trees. I loved him and would imagine myself, when I grew to be a man, tall and slender like him, walking along with great strides.

I believe I was his favourite grandchild: no wonder, for my cousins were a stupid bunch and I – so they say – was an intelligent child. I used to know when my grandfather wanted me to laugh, when to be silent; also I would remember the times for his prayers and would bring him his prayer-rug and fill the ewer for his ablutions without his having to ask me. When he had nothing else to do he enjoyed listening to me reciting to him from the Koran in a lilting voice, and I could tell from his face that he was moved.

One day I asked him about our neighbour Masood. I said to my grandfather: 'I fancy you don't like our neighbour Masood?'

To which he answered, having rubbed the tip of his nose: 'He's an indolent man and I don't like such people.'

I said to him: 'What's an indolent man?'

My grandfather lowered his head for a moment, then looking across at the wide expanse of field, he said: 'Do you see it stretching out from the edge of the desert up to the Nile bank? A hundred feddans. Do you see all those date palms? And those trees – sant, acacia, and sayal? All this fell into Masood's lap, was inherited by him from his father.'

Taking advantage of the silence that had descended upon my grandfather, I turned my gaze from him to the vast area defined by his words. 'I don't care,' I told myself, 'who owns those date palms, those trees or this black, cracked earth – all I know is that it's the arena for my dreams and my playground.'

My grandfather then continued: 'Yes, my boy, forty years ago all this belonged to Masood – two-thirds of it is now mine.'

This was news to me for I had imagined that the land had belonged to my grandfather ever since God's Creation.

'I didn't own a single feddan when I first set foot in this village. Masood was then the owner of all these riches. The position has changed now, though, and I think that before Allah calls to Him I shall have bought the remaining third as well.'

I do not know why it was I felt fear at my grandfather's words – and pity for our neighbour Masood. How I wished my grandfather wouldn't do what he'd said! I remembered Masood's singing, his beautiful voice and powerful laugh that resembled the gurgling of water. My grandfather never used to laugh.

I asked my grandfather why Masood had sold his land.

'Women,' and from the way my grandfather pronounced the word I felt that 'women' was something terrible. 'Masood, my boy, was a much-married man. Each time he married he sold me a feddan or two.' I made the quick calculation that Masood must have married some ninety women. Then I remembered his three wives, his shabby appearance, his lame donkey and its dilapidated saddle, his djellaba with the torn sleeves. I had all but rid my mind of the thoughts that jostled in it when I saw the man approaching us, and my grandfather and I exchanged glances.

'We'll be harvesting the dates today,' said Masood. 'Don't you want to be there?'

I felt, though, that he did not really want my grandfather to attend. My grandfather, however, jumped to his feet and I saw that his eyes sparkled momentarily with an intense brightness. He pulled me by the hand and we went off to the harvesting of Masood's dates.

Someone brought my grandfather a stool covered with an ox-hide, while I remained standing. There was a vast number of people there, but though I knew them all, I found myself for some reason, watching Masood: aloof from the great gathering of people he stood as though it were no concern of his, despite the fact that the date palms to be harvested were his own. Sometimes his attention would be caught by the sound of a huge clump of dates crashing down from on high. Once he shouted up at the boy perched on the very summit of the palm who had begun hacking at a clump with his long, sharp sickle: 'Be careful you don't cut the heart of the palm.'

No one paid any attention to what he said and the boy seated at the very summit of the date palm continued, quickly and energetically, to work away at the branch with his sickle till the clump of dates began to drop like something descending from the heavens.

I, however, had begun to think about Masood's phrase 'the heart of the palm'. I pictured the palm tree as something with feeling, something possessed of a heart that throbbed. I remembered Masood's remark to me when he had once seen me playing about with the branch of a young palm tree: 'Palm trees, my boy, like humans, experience joy and suffering.' And I had felt an inward and unreasoned embarrassment.

When I again looked at the expanse of ground stretching before me I saw my young companions swarming like ants around the trunks of the palm trees, gathering up dates and eating most of them. The dates were collected into high mounds. I saw people coming along and weighing them into measuring bins and pouring them into sacks, of which I counted thirty. The crowd of people broke up, except for Hussein the merchant, Mousa the owner of the field next to ours on the east, and two men I'd never seen before.

I heard a low whistling sound and saw that my grandfather had fallen asleep. Then I noticed that Masood had not changed his stance, except that he had placed a stalk in his mouth and was munching at it like someone surfeited with food who doesn't know what to do with the mouthful he still has.

Suddenly my grandfather woke up, jumped to his feet and walked towards the sacks of dates. He was followed by Hussein the merchant, Mousa the owner of the field next to ours, and the two strangers. I glanced at Masood and saw that he was making his way towards us with extreme slowness, like a man who wants to retreat but whose feet insist on going forward. They formed a circle round the sacks of dates and began examining them, some taking a date or two to eat. My grandfather gave me a fistful, which I began munching. I saw Masood filling the palms of both hands with dates and bringing them up close to his nose, then returning them.

Then I saw them dividing up the sacks between them. Hussein the merchant took ten; each of the strangers took five. Mousa the owner of the field next to ours on the eastern side took five, and my grandfather took five. Understanding nothing, I looked at Masood and saw that his eyes were darting about to left and right like two mice that have lost their way home.

'You're still fifty pounds in debt to me,' said my grandfather to Masood. 'We'll talk about it later.'

Hussein called his assistants and they brought along donkeys, the two strangers produced camels, and the sacks of dates were loaded on to them. One of the donkeys let out a braying which set the camels frothing at the mouth and complaining noisily. I felt myself drawing close to Masood, felt my hand stretch out towards him as though I wanted to touch the hem of his garment. I heard him make a noise in his throat like the rasping of a lamb being slaughtered. For some unknown reason, I experienced a sharp sensation of pain in my chest.

I ran off into the distance. Hearing my grandfather call after me, I hesitated a little, then continued on my way. I felt at that moment that I hated him. Quickening my pace, it was as though I carried within me a secret I wanted to rid myself of. I reached the river bank near the bend it made behind the wood of acacia trees. Then, without knowing why, I put my finger into my throat and spewed up the dates I'd eaten.

Translated by Denys Johnson-Davies

EZEKIEL (ES'KIA) MPHAHLELE

THE COFFEE-CART GIRL

THE CROWD MOVED like one mighty being, and swayed and swung like the sea. In front, there was the Metropolitan Steel Windows Ltd. All eyes were fixed on it. Its workers did not hear one another: perhaps they didn't need to, each one interested as he was in what he was saying – and that with his blood. All he knew was that he was on strike: for what? If you asked him he would just spit and say: 'Do you think we've come to play?'

Grimy, oily, greasy, sweating black bodies squeezed and chafed and grated. Pickets were at work; the law was brandishing batons; cars were hooting a crazy medley.

'Stand back, you monkeys!' cried a black man pinned against a pillar. 'Hey, you black son of a black hen!'

The coffee-cart girl was absorbed in the very idea of the Metropolitan Steel Windows strike, just as she was in the flood of people who came to buy her coffee and pancakes: she wasn't aware of the swelling crowd and its stray atoms which were being flung out of it towards her cart until she heard an ear-splitting crash behind her. One of the row of coffee-carts had tipped over and a knot of men fallen on it. She climbed down from her cart, looking like a bird frightened out of its nest.

A woman screamed. Another crash. The man who had been pinned against the pillar had freed himself and he found himself standing beside the girl. He sensed her predicament. Almost rudely he pushed her into the street, took the cart by the stump of a shaft and wheeled it across the street, shouting generally, 'Give way, you black monkeys.' Just then a cart behind him went down and caved in like matchwood.

'Oh, thank you so much, mister!'

'Ought to be more careful, my sister.'

'How can I thank you! Here, take coffee and a pancake.'

'Thank you, my sister.'

'Look, they're moving forward, maybe to break into the factory!' When next she looked back he was gone. And she hadn't even asked him his name: how unfriendly of her, she thought . . .

Later that winter morning the street was cleared of more people. The workers had gone away. There had been no satisfactory agreement. Strikes were unlawful for black people anyhow.

'Come back to work, or you are signed off, or go to gaol,' had come the stock executive order. More than half had been signed off.

It was comparatively quiet now in this squalid West End sector of the city. Men and women continued their daily round. A dreary smoky mist lingered in suspension, or clung to the walls; black sooty chimneys shot up malignantly; there was a strong smell of bacon; the fruit and vegetable shops resumed trade with a tremulous expectancy; old men stood Buddha-like at the entrances with folded arms and a vague grimace on their faces, seeming to sneer at the world in general and their contemptible mercantile circle in particular; and the good earth is generous enough to contain all the human sputum these good suffering folk shoot out of their mouths at the slightest provocation. A car might tear down the cross-street and set up a squall and weep dry horse manure so that it circled in the air in a momentary spree, increasing the spitting gusto . . .

'Hullo.'
'Hullo, want coffee?'
'Yes, and two hot buns.'

She hardly looked at him as she served him. For a brief spell her eyes fell on the customer. Slowly she gathered up the scattered bits of memory and unconsciously the picture was framed. She looked at him and found him scanning her.

'Oh!' She gave a gasp and her hand went to her mouth. 'You're the good uncle who saved my cart!'

'Don't uncle me, please. My name is Ruben Lemeko. The boys at the factory call me China. Yours?'

'Zodwa.'

His eyes travelled from her small tender fingers as she washed a few things, to her man's jersey which was a faded green and too big for her, her thin frock, and then to her peach-coloured face, not well fed, but well framed and compelling under a soiled black beret. As he ate hungrily she shot a side-glance at him occasionally. There was something sly in those soft, moist, slit eyes, but the modest stoop at the shoulders gave him a benign appearance; otherwise he would have looked twisted and rather fiendish. There was something she felt in his presence: a repelling admiration. She felt he was the kind of man who could be quite attractive so long as he remained more than a touch away from the contemplator; just like those wax figures she once saw in the chamber of horrors.

'Signed off at the Metropolitan?'

'Hm.' His head drooped and she could read dejection in the oily top of his cap. 'Just from the insurance fund office.' She pitied him inwardly; a sort of pity she had never before experienced for a strange man.

'What to do now?'

'Like most of us,' looking up straight into her eyes, 'beat the road early mornings just when the boss's breakfast is settling nicely in the stomach. No work, no government papers, no papers, no work, then out of town.'

'It's hard for everybody, I guess.'

'Ja.'

'I know. When you feel hungry and don't have money, come past here and I'll give you coffee and pancake.'

'Thanks, er – let me call you Pinkie, shall I?'

'Hm,' she nodded automatically.

He shook her hand. 'Grow as big as an elephant for your goodness, as we say in our idiom.' He shuffled off. For a long time, until he disappeared, she didn't take her eyes off the stooping figure, which she felt might set any place on fire. Strange man Pinkie thought idly as she washed up.

China often paused at Pinkie's coffee-cart. But he wouldn't let her give him coffee and pancakes for nothing.

'I'm no poorer than you,' he said. 'When I'm really in the drain pipes you may come to my help.'

As she got used to him and the idea of a tender playfellow who is capable of scratching blood out of you, she felt heartily sorry for him; and he detected it, and resented it and felt sorry for her in turn.

'Right, Pinkie, I'll take it today.'

'You'll starve to death in this cruel city.'

'And then? Lots of them starve; think of this mighty city, Pinkie. What are we, you and me? If we starved and got sick and died, who'd miss you and me?'

Days when China didn't come, she missed him. And then she was afraid of something; something mysterious that crawls into human relations, and before we know it it's there, and because it is frightening it does not know how to announce itself without causing panic and possibly breaking down bonds of companionship. In his presence she tried to take refuge in an artless sisterly pity for him. And although he resented it, he carried on a dumb show. Within, heaven and earth thundered and rocked, striving to meet; sunshine and rain mingled; milk and gall pretended friendship; fire and water went hand in hand; tears and laughter hugged each other in a fit of hysterics; the screeching of the hang-bird started off with the descant of a dove's cooing; devils waved torches before a chorus of angels. Pinkie and China panicked at the thought of a love affair and remained dumb.

'Pinkie, I've got a job at last!'

'I'm happy for you, China!'

'You'll get a present, first money I get. Ach, but I shouldn't have told you. I wanted to surprise you.' He was genuinely sorry.

'Don't worry, China, I'll just pretend I'm surprised really, you'll see.' They laughed.

Friday came.

'Come, Pinkie, let's go.'

'Where to?'

'I'll show you.' He led her to the cheapjack down the street.

'Mister, I want her to choose anything she wants.'

The cheapjack immediately sprang up and in voluble cataracts began to sing praises upon his articles.

'All right, mister, let me choose.' Pinkie picked up one article after another, inspected it, and at last she selected a beautiful long bodkin, a brooch, and a pair of bangles. Naidoo, the cheapjack, went off into rhapsodies again on Pinkie's looks when China put the things on her himself, pinning the bodkin on her beret. He bought himself a knife, dangling from a fashionable chain. They went back to the coffee-cart.

From this day onwards, Naidoo became a frequent customer at Pinkie's coffee-cart. He often praised her cakes and coffee. Twice at lunch-time China found him relating some anecdotes which sent Pinkie off into peals of laughter.

'Where you work, my prend?' asked Naidoo one day. He was one of the many Indians who will say 'pore-pipty' for 'four fifty', 'pier foms' for 'five forms', 'werry wital' for 'very vital'.

'Shoe factory, Main Street.'

'Good pay?'

'Where do you find such a thing in this city?'

'Quite right, my prend. Look at me: I was wanted to be a grocer, and now I'm a cheapjack.'

'I'm hungry today, Pinkie,' China said one day. He was clearly elated over something.

'It's so beautiful to see you happy, China, what's the news?'

'Nothing. Hasn't a man the right to be jolly sometimes?'

'Of course. Just wondered if anything special happened.'

He looked at her almost transparent pink fingers as she washed the coffee things.

'Hey, you've a lovely ring on your finger, where's the mine?'

Pinkie laughed as she looked at the glass-studded ring, fingered it and wiped it.

'From Naidoo.'

'What?'

'It's nothing, China. Naidoo didn't have any money for food, so he offered me this for three days' coffee and cakes.' She spoke as if she didn't believe her own self. She sensed a gathering storm.

'You lie!'

'Honestly China, now what would I be lying for?'

So! he thought, she couldn't even lie to keep their friendship: how distant she sounded. His fury mounted.

'Yes, you lie! Now listen Pinkie, you're in love with that cheapjack. Every time I found him here he's been damn happy with you, grinning and making eyes at you. Yes, I've watched him every moment.'

He approached the step leading into the cart.

'Do you see me? I've loved you since I first saw you, the day of the strike.' He was going to say more, but something rose inside him and choked him. He couldn't utter a word more. He walked slowly; a knife drawn out, with a menacing blade, pointed towards her throat. Pinkie retreated deeper into her cart, too frightened to plead her case.

At that very moment she realized fully the ghastliness of a man's jealousy, which gleamed and glanced on the blade and seemed to have raised a film which steadied the slit eyes. Against the back wall she managed to speak.

'All right, China, maybe you've done this many times before. Go ahead and kill me; I won't cry for help, do what you like with me.'

She panted like a timid little mouse cornered by a cat. He couldn't finish the job he had set out to do. Why? He had sent two men packing with a knife before. They had tried to fight, but this creature wasn't resisting at all. Why, why, why? He felt the heat pounding in his temples; the knife dropped, and he sank on to a stool and rested his head on the wall, his hands trembling.

After a moment he stood up, looking away from Pinkie. 'I'm sorry, Pinkie, I pray you never in your life to think about this day.'

She looked at him, mystified.

'Say you forgive me.' She nodded twice.

Then she packed up for the day, much earlier than usual.

The following day China did not visit Pinkie; nor the next. He could not decide to go there. Things were all in a barbed wire tangle in his mind. But see her he must, he thought. He would just go and hug her; say nothing but just press her to himself because he felt too mean even to tell her not to be afraid of him any more.

The third day the law came. It stepped up the street in goose-march fashion. The steel on its heels clanged on the pavement with an ominous echo. It gave commands and everything came to an end at once. Black man's coffee-cart was not to operate any more in the city. '. . . Makes the city look ugly,' the city fathers said.

For several days China, unaware of what had happened, called on Pinkie, but always found the coffee-carts empty and deserted. At last he learned everything from Naidoo, the cheapjack.

He stepped into her coffee-cart and sat on the stool.

He looked into the cheerless pall of smoke. Outside life went on as if there had never been a Pinkie who sold coffee and pancakes.

Dare he hope that she would come back, just to meet him? Or was it going to turn out to have been a dream? He wondered.

We'll meet in town, some day, China thought. I'll tell her all about myself, all about my wicked past; she'll get used to me, not be afraid of me any more . . .

And still he sat in the coffee-cart which was once Pinkie's all through the lunch-hour . . .

DAVID OWOYELE

THE WILL OF ALLAH

THERE HAD BEEN a clear moon. Now the night was dark. Dogo glanced up at the night sky. He saw that scudding black clouds had obscured the moon. He cleared his throat. 'Rain tonight,' he observed to his companion. Sule, his companion, did not reply immediately. He was a tall powerfully-built man. His face, as well as his companion's, was a stupid mask of ignorance. He lived by thieving as did Dogo, and just now he walked with an unaccustomed limp. 'It is wrong to say that,' Sule said after a while, fingering the long, curved sheath-knife he always wore on his upper left arm when, in his own words, he was 'on duty'. A similar cruel-looking object adorned the arm of his comrade. 'How can you be sure?' 'Sure?' said Dogo, annoyance and impatience in his voice. Dogo is the local word for tall. This man was thickset, short and squat, anything but tall. He pointed one hand up at the scurrying clouds. 'You only want to look up there. A lot of rain has fallen in my life: those up there are rain clouds.'

They walked on in silence for a while. The dull red lights of the big town glowed in crooked lines behind them. Few people were abroad, for it was already past midnight. About half a mile ahead of them the native town, their destination, sprawled in the night. Not a single electric light bulb glowed on its crooked streets. This regrettable fact suited the books of the two men perfectly. 'You are not Allah,' said Sule at last. 'You may not assert.'

Sule was a hardened criminal. Crime was his livelihood, he had told the judge this during his last trial that had earned him a short stretch in jail. 'Society must be protected from characters like you,' he could still hear the stern judge intoning in the hushed courtroom. Sule had stood in the dock, erect, unashamed, unimpressed; he'd heard it all before. 'You and your type constitute a threat to life and property and this court will always see to it that you get your just deserts, according to the Law.' The judge had then fixed him with a stern gaze, which Sule coolly returned: he had stared into too many so-called judges' eyes to be easily intimidated. Besides, he feared nothing and no one except Allah. The judge thrust his legal chin forward. 'Do you never pause to consider that the road of crime leads only to frustration, punishment and suffering? You look fit enough for anything. Why don't you try your hand at earning an honest living for a change?' Sule had shrugged his broad shoulders. 'I earn my living the only way I know,' he said. 'The only way I've chosen.' The judge had sat back, dismayed. Then he leaned forward to try again. 'Is it beyond you to see anything wrong in thieving, burglary, crime?' Again Sule had shrugged. 'The way I earn my living I find quite satisfactory.' 'Satisfactory!' exclaimed the judge, and a wave of whispering swept over the court. The judge stopped this with a rap of his gavel. 'Do you find it satisfactory to break the law?' 'I've no choice,' said Sule. 'The law is a nuisance. It keeps getting in one's way.' 'Constant arrest and imprisonment – do you find it satisfactory to be a jailbird?' queried the judge, frowning most severely. 'Every calling has its hazards,' replied Sule philosophically. The judge mopped his face. 'Well, my man, you cannot break the law. You can only attempt to break it. And you will only end up by getting broken.' Sule nodded. 'We have a saying like that,' he remarked conversationally. 'He who attempts to shake a stump only shakes himself.' He glanced up at the frowning judge. 'Something like a thick stump – the law, eh?' The judge had given him three months. Sule had shrugged. 'The will of Allah be done . . .'

A darting tongue of lightning lit up the overcast sky for a second. Sule glanced up. 'Sure it looks like rain. But you do not say: It will rain. You are only a mortal. You only say: If it is the will of Allah, it will rain.' Sule was a deeply religious man, according to his lights. His religion forbade being dogmatic or prophetic about the future, about anything. His fear of Allah was quite genuine. It was his firm conviction that Allah left the question of a means of livelihood for each man to decide for himself. Allah, he was sure, gives some people more than they need so that others with too little could help themselves to some of it. It could certainly not be the intention of Allah that some stomachs remain empty while others are overstuffed.

Dogo snorted. He had served prison sentences in all the major towns in the country. Prison had become for him a home from home. Like his companion in crime, he feared no man, but unlike him, he had no religion other than self-preservation. 'You and your religion,' he said in derision. 'A lot of good it has done you.' Sule did not reply. Dogo knew from experience that Sule was touchy about his religion, and the first intimation he would get that Sule had lost his temper would be a blow on the head. The two men never pretended that their partnership had anything to do with love or friendship or any other luxurious idea: they operated together when their prison sentences allowed because they found it convenient. In a partnership that each believed was for his own special benefit, there could be no fancy code of conduct. 'Did you see the woman tonight?' Dogo asked, changing the subject, not because he was afraid of Sule's displeasure but because his grasshopper mind had switched to something else. 'Uh-huh,' granted Sule. 'Well?' said Dogo when he did not go on. 'Bastard!' said Sule, without any passion. 'Who? Me?' said Dogo thinly. 'We were talking about the woman,' replied Sule.

They got to a small stream. Sule stopped, washed his arms and legs, his clean-shaven head. Dogo squatted on the bank, sharpening his sheath-knife on a stone. 'Where do you think you are going?' 'To yonder village,' said Sule, rinsing out his mouth. 'Didn't know you had a sweetheart there,' said Dogo. 'I'm not going to any woman,' said Sule. 'I am going to collect stray odds and ends – if it is the will of Allah.'

'To steal, you mean?' suggested Dogo.

'Yes,' conceded Sule. He straightened himself, pointed a brawny arm at Dogo: 'You are a burglar, too . . . and a bastard besides.'

Dogo, calmly testing the edge of the knife on his arm, nodded. 'Is that part of your religion, washing in midnight streams?' Sule didn't reply until he had climbed on to the farther bank, 'Wash when you find a stream; for when you cross another is entirely in the hands of Allah.' He limped off, Dogo following him. 'Why did you call her a bastard?' Dogo asked. 'Because she is one.' 'Why?' 'She told me she sold the coat and the black bag for only fifteen shillings.' He glanced down and sideways at his companion. 'I suppose you got on to her before I did and told her what to say?' 'I've not laid eyes on her for a week,' protested Dogo. 'The coat is fairly old. Fifteen shillings sounds all right to me. I think she has done very well indeed.' 'No doubt,' said Sule. He didn't believe Dogo. 'I'd think the same way if I'd already shared part of the proceeds with her . . .'

Dogo said nothing. Sule was always suspicious of him, and he returned the compliment willingly. Sometimes their suspicion of each other was groundless, other times not. Dogo shrugged. 'I don't know what you are talking about.' 'No. I don't suppose you would,' said Sule drily. 'All I'm interested in is my share,' went on Dogo. 'Your second share, you mean,' said Sule. 'You'll both get your share – you cheating son without a father, as well as that howling devil of a woman.' He paused before he added, 'She stabbed me in the thigh – the bitch.' Dogo chuckled softly to himself. 'I've been wondering about that limp of yours. Put a knife in your thigh, did she? Odd, isn't it?' Sule glanced at him sharply. 'What's odd about it?' 'You getting stabbed just for asking her to hand over the money.' 'Ask her? I didn't ask her. No earthly use asking anything of characters like that.' 'Oh?' said Dogo. 'I'd always thought all you had to do was ask. True, the coat wasn't yours. But you asked her to sell it. She's an old "fence" and ought to know that you are entitled to the money.' 'Only a fool would be content with fifteen shillings for a coat and a bag,' said Sule. 'And you are not a fool, eh?' chuckled Dogo. 'What did you do about it?' 'Beat the living daylight out of her,' rasped Sule. 'And quite right, too,' commented Dogo. 'Only snag is you seem to have got more than you gave her.' He chuckled again. 'A throbbing wound is no joke,' said Sule testily. 'And who's joking? I've been stabbed in my time, too. You can't go around at night wearing a knife and not expect to get stabbed once in a while. We should regard such things as an occupational hazard.' 'Sure,' grunted Sule. 'But that can't cure a wound.' 'No, but the hospital can,' said Dogo. 'I know. But in the hospital they ask questions before they cure you.'

They were entering the village. In front of them the broad path diverged into a series of tracks that twined away between the houses. Sule paused, briefly, took one of the paths. They walked along on silent feet, just having a look around. Not a light showed in any of the crowded mud houses. Every little hole of a window was shut or plugged, presumably against the threatening storm. A peal of languid thunder rumbled over from the east. Except for a group of goats and sheep, which rose startled at their approach, the two had the village paths to themselves. Every once in a while Sule would stop by a likely house; the two would take a careful look around; he'd look inquiringly down at his companion, who would shake his head, and they would move on.

They had been walking around for about a quarter of an hour when a brilliant flash of lightning almost burned out their eyeballs. That decided them. 'We'd better hurry,' whispered Dogo. 'The storm's almost here.' Sule said nothing. A dilapidated-looking house stood a few yards away. They walked up to it. They were not put off by its appearance. Experience had taught them that what a house looked like was no indication of what it contained. Some stinking hovels had yielded rich hauls. Dogo nodded at Sule. 'You stay outside and try to keep awake,' said Sule. He nodded at a closed window. 'You might stand near that.'

Dogo moved off to his post. Sule got busy on the crude wooden door. Even Dogo's practised ear did not detect any untoward sound, and from where he stood he couldn't tell when Sule gained entry into the house. He remained at his post for what seemed ages – it was actually a matter of minutes. Presently he saw the window at his side open slowly. He froze against the wall. But it was Sule's muscular hands that came through the window, holding out to him a biggish gourd. Dogo took the gourd and was surprised at its weight. His pulse quickened. People around here trusted gourds like this more than banks. 'The stream,' whispered Sule through the open window. Dogo understood. Hoisting the gourd on to his head, he made off at a fast trot for the stream. Sule would find his way out of the house and follow him.

He set the gourd down carefully by the stream, took off its carved lid. If this contained anything of value, he thought, he and Sule did not have to share it equally. Besides, how did he know Sule had not helped himself to a little of its contents before passing it out through the window? He thrust his right hand into the gourd and next instant he felt a vicious stab on his wrist. A sharp exclamation escaped from him as he jerked his arm out. He peered at his wrist closely then slowly and steadily he began to curse. He damned to hell and glory everything under the sun in the two languages he knew. He sat on the ground, holding his wrist, cursing softly. He heard Sule approaching and stopped. He put the lid back on the gourd and waited. 'Any trouble?' he asked, when the other got to him. 'No trouble,' said Sule. Together they stooped over the gourd. Dogo had to hold his right wrist in his left hand but he did it so Sule wouldn't notice. 'Have you opened it?' Sule asked. 'Who? Me? Oh, no!' said Dogo. Sule did not believe him and he knew it. 'What can be so heavy?' Dogo asked curiously. 'We'll see,' said Sule.

He took off the lid, thrust his hand into the gaping mouth of the gourd and felt a sharp stab on his wrist. He whipped his hand out of the gourd. He stood up. Dogo, too, stood up and for the first time Sule noticed Dogo's wrist held in the other hand. They were silent for a long time, glaring at each other. 'As you always insisted, we should go fifty-fifty in everything,' said Dogo casually. Quietly, almost inaudibly, Sule started speaking. He called Dogo every name known to obscenity. Dogo for his part was holding up his end quite well. They stopped when they had run out of names. 'I am going home,' Dogo announced. 'Wait!' said Sule. With his uninjured hand he rummaged in his pocket, brought out a box of matches. With difficulty he struck one, held the flame over the gourd, peered in. He threw the match away. 'It is not necessary,' he said. 'Why not?' Dogo demanded. 'That in there is an angry cobra,' said Sule. The leaden feeling was creeping up his arm fast. The pain was tremendous. He sat down. 'I still don't see why I can't go home,' said Dogo. 'Have you never heard of the saying that what the cobra bites dies at the foot of the cobra? The poison is that good: just perfect for sons of swine like you. You'll never make it home. Better sit down and die here.' Dogo didn't agree but the throbbing pain forced him to sit down.

They went silent for several minutes while the lightning played around them. Finally Dogo said, 'Funny that your last haul should be a snake-charmer's gourd.' 'I think it's funnier still that it should contain a cobra, don't you?' said Sule. He groaned. 'I reckon funnier things will happen before the night is done,' said Dogo. 'Uh!' he winced with pain. 'A couple of harmless deaths, for instance,' suggested Sule. 'Might as well kill the bloody snake,' said Dogo. He attempted to rise and pick up a stone from the stream; he couldn't. 'Ah, well,' he said, lying on his back. 'It doesn't matter anyway.'

The rain came pattering down. 'But why die in the rain?' he demanded angrily. 'Might help to die soaking wet if you are going straight to hell from here,' said Sule. Teeth clenched, he dragged himself to the gourd, his knife in his good hand. Closing his eyes, he thrust knife and hand into the gourd, drove vicious thrusts into the reptile's writhing body, breathing heavily all the while. When he crawled back to lie down a few minutes later the breath came whistling out of his nostrils; his arm was riddled with fang-marks; but the reptile was dead. 'That's one snake that has been charmed for the last time,' said Sule. Dogo said nothing.

Several minutes passed in silence. The poison had them securely in its fatal grip, especially Sule, who couldn't suppress a few groans. It was only a matter of seconds now. 'Pity you have to end up this way,' mumbled Dogo, his senses dulling. 'By and large, it hasn't been too bad – you thieving scoundrel!' 'I'm soaked in tears on account of you,' drawled Sule, unutterably weary. 'This seems the end of the good old road. But you ought to have known it had to end some time, you rotten bastard!' He heaved a deep sigh. 'I shan't have to go up to the hospital in the morning after all,' he mumbled, touching the wound in his thigh with a trembling hand. 'Ah,' he breathed in resignation, 'the will of Allah be done.' The rain came pattering down.

NADINE GORDIMER

AMNESTY

WHEN WE HEARD he was released I ran all over the farm and through the fence to our people on the next farm to tell everybody. I only saw afterwards I'd torn my dress on the barbed wire, and there was a scratch, with blood, on my shoulder.

He went away from this place eight years ago, signed up to work in town with what they call a construction company – building glass walls up to the sky. For the first two years he came home for the weekend once a month and two weeks at Christmas; that was when he asked my father for me. And he began to pay. He and I thought that in three years he would have paid enough for us to get married. But then he started wearing that T-shirt, he told us he'd joined the union, he told us about the strike, how he was one of the men who went to talk to the bosses because some others had been laid off after the strike. He's always been good at talking, even in English – he was the best at the farm school, he used to read the newspapers the Indian wraps soap and sugar in when you buy at the store.

There was trouble at the hostel where he had a bed, and riots over paying rent in the townships and he told me – just me, not the old ones – that wherever people were fighting against the way we are treated they were doing it for all of us, on the farms as well as the towns, and the unions were with them, he was with them, making speeches, marching. The third year, we heard he was in prison. Instead of getting married. We didn't know where to find him, until he went on trial. The case was heard in a town far away. I couldn't go often to the court because by that time I had passed my Standard 8 and I was working in the farm school. Also my parents were short of money. Two of my brothers who had gone away to work in town didn't send home; I suppose they lived with girlfriends and had to buy things for them. My father and other brother work here for the Boer and the pay is very small, we have two goats, a few cows we're allowed to graze, and a patch of land where my mother can grow vegetables. No cash from that.

When I saw him in the court he looked beautiful in a blue suit with a striped shirt and brown tie. All the accused – his comrades, he said – were well dressed. The union bought the clothes so that the judge and the prosecutor would know they weren't dealing with stupid ycs-baas black men who didn't know their rights. These things and everything else about the court and trial he explained to me when I was allowed to visit him in jail. Our little girl was born while the trial went on and when I brought the baby to court the first time to show him, his comrades bugged him and then hugged me across the barrier of the prisoners' dock and they had clubbed together to give me some money as a present for the baby. He chose the name for her, Inkululeko.

Then the trial was over and he got six years. He was sent to the Island. We all knew about the Island. Our leaders had been there so long. But I have never seen the sea except to colour it in blue at school, and I couldn't imagine a piece of earth surrounded by it. I could only think of a cake of dung, dropped by the cattle, floating in a pool of rainwater they'd crossed, the water showing the sky like a looking-glass, blue. I was ashamed only to think that. He had told me how the glass walls showed the pavement trees and the other buildings in the street and the colours of the cars and the clouds as the crane lifted him on a platform higher and higher through the sky to work at the top of a building.

He was allowed one letter a month. It was my letter because his parents didn't know how to write. I used to go to them where they worked on another farm to ask what message they wanted to send. The mother always cried and put her hands on her head and said nothing, and the old man, who preached to us in the veld every Sunday, said tell my son we are praying, God will make everything all right for him. Once he wrote back, That's the trouble – our people on the farms, they're told God will decide what's good for them so that they won't find the force to do anything to change their lives.

After two years had passed, we – his parents and I – had saved up enough money to go to Cape Town to visit him. We went by train and slept on the floor at the station and asked the way, next day, to the ferry. People were kind; they all knew that if you wanted the ferry it was because you had somebody of yours on the Island.

And there it was – there was the sea. It was green *and* blue, climbing and falling, bursting white, all the way to the sky. A terrible wind was slapping it this way and that; it hid the Island, but people like us, also waiting for the ferry, pointed where the Island must be, far out in the sea that I never thought would be like it really was.

There were other boats, and ships as big as buildings that go to other places, all over the world, but the ferry is only for the Island, it doesn't go anywhere else in the world, only to the Island. So everybody waiting there was waiting for the Island, there could be no mistake we were not in the right place. We had sweets and biscuits, trousers and a warm coat for him (a woman standing with us said we wouldn't be allowed to give him the clothes) and I wasn't wearing, any more, the old beret pulled down over my head that farm girls wear, I had bought relaxer cream from the man who comes round the farms selling things out of a box on his bicycle, and my hair was combed up thick under a flowered scarf that didn't cover the gold-coloured rings in my ears. His mother had her blanket tied round her waist over her dress, a farm woman, but I looked just as good as any of the other girls there. When the ferry was ready to take us, we stood all pressed together and quiet like the cattle waiting to be let through a gate. One man kept looking round with his chin moving up and down, he was counting, he must have been afraid there were too many to get on and he didn't want to be left behind. We all moved up to the policeman in charge and everyone ahead of us went on to the boat. But when our turn came and he put out his hand for something, I didn't know what.

We didn't have a permit. We didn't know that before you come to Cape Town, before you come to the ferry for the Island, you have to have a police permit to visit a prisoner on the Island. I tried to ask him nicely. The wind blew the voice out of my mouth.

We were turned away. We saw the ferry rock, bumping the landing where we stood, moving, lifted and dropped by all that water, getting smaller and smaller until we didn't know if we were really seeing it or one of the birds that looked black, dipping up and down, out there.

The only good thing was one of the other people took the sweets and biscuits for him. He wrote and said he got them. But it wasn't a good letter. Of course not. He was cross with me; I should have found out, I should have known about the permit. He was right – I bought the train tickets, I asked where to go for the ferry, I should have known about the permit. I have passed Standard 8. There was an advice office to go to in town, the churches ran it, he wrote. But the farm is so far from town, we on the farms don't know about these things. It was as he said; our ignorance is the way we are kept down, this ignorance must go.

We took the train back and we never went to the Island – never saw him in the three more years he was there. Not once. We couldn't find the money for the train. His father died and I had to help his mother from my pay. For our people the worry is always money, I wrote. When will we ever have money? Then he sent such a good letter. That's what I'm on the Island for, far away from you, I'm here so that one day our people will have the things they need, land, food, the end of ignorance. There was something else – I could just read the word 'power' the prison had blacked out. All his letters were not just for me; the prison officer read them before I could.

He was coming home after only five years!

That's what it seemed to me, when I heard – the five years was suddenly disappeared – nothing! – there was no whole year still to wait. I showed my – our – little girl his photo again. That's your daddy, he's coming, you're going to see him. She told the other children at school, I've got a daddy, just as she showed off about the kid goat she had at home.

We wanted him to come at once, and at the same time we wanted time to prepare. His mother lived with one of his uncles; now that his father was dead there was no house of his father for him to take me to as soon as we married. If there had been time, my father would have cut poles, my mother and I would have baked bricks, cut thatch and built a house for him and me and the child.

We were not sure what day he would arrive. We only

heard on my radio his name and the names of some others who were released. Then at the Indian's store I noticed the newspaper, *The Nation*, written by black people, and on the front a picture of a lot of people dancing and waving – I saw at once it was at that ferry. Some men were being carried on other men's shoulders. I couldn't see which one was him. We were waiting. The ferry had brought him from the Island but we remembered Cape Town is a long way from us. Then he did come. On a Saturday, no school, so I was working with my mother, hoeing and weeding round the pumpkins and mealies, my hair, that I meant to keep nice, tied in an old *doek*. A combi came over the veld and his comrades had brought him. I wanted to run away and wash but he stood there stretching his legs, calling, hey! hey! with his comrades making a noise around him, and my mother started shrieking in the old style aie! aie! and my father was clapping and stamping towards him. He held his arms open to us, this big man in town clothes, polished shoes, and all the time while he hugged me I was holding my dirty hands, full of mud, away from him behind his back. His teeth hit me hard through his lips, he grabbed at my mother and she struggled to hold the child up to him. I thought we would all fall down! Then everyone was quiet. The child hid behind my mother. He picked her up but she turned her head away to her shoulder. He spoke to her gently but she wouldn't speak to him. She's nearly six years old! I told her not to be a baby. She said, That's not him.

The comrades all laughed, we laughed, she ran off and he said, She has to have time to get used to me.

He has put on weight, yes; a lot. You couldn't believe it. He used to be so thin his feet looked too big for him. I used to feel his bones but now – that night – when he lay on me he was so heavy, I didn't remember it was like that. Such a long time. It's strange to get stronger in prison; I thought he wouldn't have enough to eat and would come out weak. Everyone said, Look at him! – he's a man, now. He laughed and banged his fist on his chest, told them how the comrades exercised in their cells, he would run three miles a day, stepping up and down on one place on the floor of that small cell where he was kept. After we were together at night we used to whisper a long time but now I can feel he's thinking of some things I don't know and I can't worry him with talk. Also I don't know what to say. To ask him what it was like, five years shut away there; or to tell him something about school or about the child. What else has happened, here? Nothing. Just waiting. Sometimes in the daytime I do try to tell him what it was like for me, here at home on the farm, five years. He listens, he's interested, just like he's interested when people from the other farms come to visit and talk to him about little things that happened to them while he was away all that time on the Island. He smiles and nods, asks a couple of questions and then stands up and stretches. I see it's to show them it's enough, his mind is going back to something he was busy with before they came. And we farm people are very slow; we tell things slowly, he used to, too.

He hasn't signed on for another job. But he can't stay at home, with us; we thought, after five years over there in the middle of that green and blue sea, so far, he would rest with us a little while. The combi or some car comes to fetch him and he says don't worry, I don't know what day I'll be back. At first I asked, what week, next week? He tried to explain to me: in the Movement it's not like it was in the union, where you do your work every day and after that you are busy with meetings; in the Movement you never know where you will have to go and what is going to come up next. And the same with money. In the Movement, it's not like a job, with regular pay – I know that, he doesn't have to tell me – it's like it was going to the Island, you do it for all our people who suffer because we haven't got money, we haven't got land – look, he said, speaking of my parents', my home, the home that has been waiting for him, with his child: look at this place where the white man owns the ground and lets you squat in mud and tin huts here only as long as you work for him – *Baba* and your brother planting his crops and looking after his cattle, Mama cleaning his house and you in the school without even having the chance to train properly as a teacher. The farmer owns us, he says. I've been thinking we haven't got a home because there wasn't time to build a house before he came from the Island; but we haven't got a home at all. Now I've understood that.

I'm not stupid. When the comrades come to this place in the combi to talk to him here I don't go away with my mother after we've brought them tea or (if she's made it for the weekend) beer. They like her beer, they talk about our culture and there's one of them who makes a point of putting his arm around my mother, calling her the mama of all of them, the mama of Africa. Sometimes they please her very much by telling her how they used to sing on the Island and getting her to sing an old song we all know from our grandmothers. Then they join in with their strong voices. My father doesn't like this noise travelling across the veld; he's afraid that if the Boer finds out my man is a political, from the Island, and he's holding meetings on the Boer's land, he'll tell my father to go, and take his family with him. But my brother says if the Boer asks anything just tell him it's a prayer meeting. Then the singing is over; my mother knows she must go away into the house.

I stay, and listen. He forgets I'm there when he's talking and arguing about something I can see is important, more important than anything we could ever have to say to each other when we're alone. But now and then, when one of the other comrades is speaking I see him look at me for a moment the way I will look up at one of my favourite children in school to encourage the child to understand. The men don't speak to me and I don't speak. One of the things they talk about is organizing the people on the farms – the workers, like my father and brother, and like his parents used to be. I learn what all these things are: minimum wage, limitation of working hours, the right to strike, annual leave, accident compensation, pensions, sick and even maternity leave. I am pregnant, at last I have another child inside me, but that's women's business. When they talk about the Big Man, the Old Men, I know who these are: our leaders are also back from prison. I told him about the child coming; he said, And this one belongs to a new country, he'll build the freedom we've fought for! I know he wants to get married but there's no time for that at present. There was hardly time for him to make the child. He comes to me just like he comes here to eat a meal or put on clean clothes. He picks up the little girl and swings her round and there! – it's done, he's getting into the combi, he's already turning to his comrade that face of his that knows only what's inside his head, those eyes that move quickly as if he's chasing something you can't see. The little girl hasn't had time to get used to this man. But I know she'll be proud of him, one day!

How can you tell that to a child six years old? But I tell her about the Big Man and the Old Men, our leaders, so she'll know that her father was with them on the Island, this man is a great man, too.

On Saturday, no school and I plant and weed with my mother, she sings but I don't; I think. On Sunday there's no work, only prayer meetings out of the farmer's way under the trees, and beer drinks at the mud and tin huts where the farmers allow us to squat on their land. I go off on my own as I used to do when I was a child, making up games and talking to myself where no one would hear me or look for me. I sit on a warm stone in the late afternoon, high up, and the whole valley is a path between the hills, leading away from my feet. It's the Boer's farm but that's not true, it belongs to nobody. The cattle don't know that anyone says he owns it, the sheep – they are grey stones, and then they become a thick grey snake moving – don't know. Our huts and the old mulberry tree and the little brown mat of earth that my mother dug over yesterday, way down there, and way over there the clump of trees round the chimneys and the shiny thing that is the TV mast of the farmhouse – they are nothing, on the back of this earth. It could twitch them away like a dog does a fly.

I am up with the clouds. The sun behind me is changing the colours of the sky and the clouds are changing themselves, slowly, slowly. Some are white, blowing themselves up like bubbles. Underneath is a bar of grey, not enough to make rain. It gets longer and darker while the other clouds are all pink, it grows a thin snout and long body and then the end of it is a tail. There's a huge grey rat moving across the sky, eating the sky.

The child remembered the photo; she said, That's not him. I'm sitting here where I came often when he was on the Island. I came to get away from the others, to wait by myself.

I'm watching the rat, it's losing itself, its shape, eating the sky, and I'm waiting. Waiting for him to come back.

Waiting. I'm waiting to come back home.

HENRI LOPÈS

THE PLOT

HOW TO GET it across to my colleagues that one shouldn't in any circumstances . . .?

Still, I was sure this time. For two years I had been filing reports on him. The director never paid any heed to them. Whenever he made a data analysis, all that concerned Dr Mobata was eliminated. To his mind there was never sufficient evidence.

Why did he act like that? After all, Mobata and himself were not of the same tribe.

But this time I had the piece of information that clinched it. I was able to go ahead and arrest this agent of Moscow. I had the proof that our local Communists in league with a foreign power were at the bottom of the affair. A few months before the presidential elections this was bound to earn me promotion.

I trembled with pleasurable anticipation. I sought out the copies of all my reports on the doctor to wave them at the boss. I had never given up reminding him that Mobata was a Communist, that he was organizing a network and that quite often, under cover of medical treatment, meetings were actually held in his consulting room.

Incidentally, the director himself did not deny that Mobata was a Red, an avowed Communist. Had he not studied in the Soviet Union? That's what his record said anyway. But despite all that, the director excused him by saying that he was highly qualified, that we lacked manpower of his calibre and that you couldn't censure a man for his ideas. He would add that thinking on Communist lines as such didn't constitute an offence as long as the person concerned didn't try to organize a clandestine movement to overthrow the government of the day. According to him, the doctor was an idealist who with time and experience would adopt more reasonable political ideas. He concluded that at any rate the best means of favouring such a development would be not to persecute him.

And then came this affair. A plot to plunge the whole country into fire and bloodshed and overthrow the government. The ringleader, Nabangou, had managed to escape but the majority of the commandos detailed to swing into action had fallen into our hands.

I had first smelt a rat when one of our men informed me that the doctor's name had been found in the pocket diary of one of the conspirators. Obviously this clue, taken by itself, didn't prove a thing. But then Mobata's houseboy came forward with evidence. He claimed that Nabangou, the leader of the plot, had been received for consultation every single day of the week preceding the attempted coup and that each time the doctor had kept him for nearly an hour, a thing he wouldn't normally do with his other patients.

This time there could not be a shadow of doubt. I felt very fidgety and wanted to make sure the bird wouldn't fly away. I decided to take charge of the detachment sent to arrest him myself. Incidentally, if it had been up to me only, it would have been done there and then. But once more the director delayed the operation with one of those arguments which are typical of intellectuals and which are stuffed into their heads when they go over to Europe for higher studies or staff training.

'It's illegal to arrest somebody in his own home during the night . . .'

Well, we had to wait till morning. It definitely was a long night for me.

He didn't protest – as if he knew that our nerves were on edge and that we were ready to clobber him at the slightest provocation. And he took his time, no doubt to drive home the point that he wasn't scared. He kissed his wife who hung on to him a while. He said something to her I couldn't make out. I'm pretty sure it was in their language which I don't understand. He finally squatted down to strain his kid to his breast, looking at him for a moment. 'Come on, let's go! We've no time to lose,' I shouted.

I just couldn't stand all this pecking and carrying-on. But that's the way those intellectuals are. They have certain habits that make a man less than a man. Or maybe they're just trying to move us to pity, to prove that with those fancy feelings they have towards their family and others, their cause is bound to be human and just. So on the staircase I jostled him a bit. He nearly went down.

'I'm not an animal, am I?'

'Shut up and keep moving!'

If he thought he could start sermonizing, he had got it all wrong. At any rate the moment was badly chosen. I was in no mood to take it. He had just woken up and would have stayed in bed for another hour on this Sunday morning if we hadn't been tactless enough to rouse him. As for me, I hadn't slept for two nights running.

When we got to my office, I put my gun on the table and gave him a vicious stare. He remained unruffled, while electric discharges coursed through my nervous system.

'Sit down here, doctor . . . Don't be afraid . . . We don't

want to do you any harm. That is, if you're ready to cooperate. I suppose you know why we've hauled you in?'

'I haven't the slightest idea. But I think you'll be kind enough to tell me.'

'Listen, doctor. We're human here in this outfit. We understand those we arrest. But we don't like wasting time. If you talk, we'll leave you alone and take it into consideration.'

'If you could kindly express yourself more clearly, I'd be able to follow.'

'Don't play the tough guy, doc.' I think that was the moment I banged my fist on the table. 'Don't play the tough guy. We'll see pretty soon which one's the stronger.'

At this point Inspector Nzengo barged in.

'Come on, spill the beans, man! What was your role in the plot? What are the names of the other leaders? If you answer right, we'll leave you alone.'

'What plot?'

'Ah, you pretend not to know what all this is about!' My foot pressed a button under my desk and at the same moment a projector poured its blinding white light into the doctor's face.

'How many plots d'you think there are?'

'. . .'

'You think I'm a fool? You pretend not to know that we all nearly got bumped off the other night by that Nabangou gang?'

'I heard it on the radio.'

'Yessir! Just fancy that! So you heard it on the radio, did you really?'

'Not much of it, if I may say so. I have a lot of work, you know, and I don't devote as much time to politics as I would like to.'

'How then do you explain that your name and address

were found in the diary of one of the fellows we caught? And a month ago Nabangou came to your consulting-room every day for a whole week.'

This time the doctor was visibly shaken.

'Ah, now you see that it is better to talk. We know a lot about you, my friend. You'd better make a clean breast of it while the going is good.'

'But anybody can put down a doctor's address in his diary. What I deny is having received Mr Nabangou in my consulting-room. It's at least a year ago that he last came for treatment . . .'

'Who are the patients you received last Wednesday?'

'. . .'

'You want us to refresh your memory?'

'Inspector, what's the third word of the fifth line of our national anthem?'

'What d'you mean?'

'Do you know it?'

'. . .'

'And yet you've heard the anthem. We're in the same position, if you ask me point-blank the names of my patients. But I'll consult my agenda . . .'

A slap sealed his mouth.

'Who d'you think you're kidding? You'll also deny no doubt that you're a Communist? Now, if you're a Communist, you're against the President. You declared one night at a dinner party that he was *selling out* – those were your own words – *selling out* the country to what you called the American capitalists.'

'I confess that . . .'

'Put that down! He confesses. Put down that he admits to being a Communist and an organizer of the plot.'

'No, I admit the possibility of having declared in the

course of a conversation that foreign capital seemed to me . . .'

'Don't try playing the wise guy again.'

He was really beginning to annoy me. I hadn't had a wink for two nights, and only the hot coffee my wife had sent me from home in a thermos flask together with a number of cigarettes far above my normal quota kept me going. The slightest irritation jarred on my nerves. I needed somebody on whom to work off the electric charge racing through my system.

I stepped over to him, grabbed him by the collar and gave him a series of slaps that sent his spectacles flying. I had unsettled him. I thought he was going to give in. But I noticed that he tried to control his feelings. I knew this type of person. They may look as if you could knock them over with a straw but they have an iron will and are as stubborn as hell.

They'd rather croak than admit defeat.

'You said, Inspector . . . you said I was a Communist . . .'

'It wasn't me that said it. It's the plain truth.'

'. . . That's just it. I'm not denying it . . .'

'Take a note of it, will you?'

'. . . How then could I collaborate with Nabangou who's a tribalist?'

'For Heaven's sake, doc, who d'you think you're fooling?' I shouted at the top of my voice. 'It's up to us to ask questions, not you . . .'

The telephone rang. The director was calling me.

'OK, fellows, I'll be back soon. You look after him meanwhile. That will refresh his memory for sure.'

I left him in the hands of Zakunda and Mibolo. Two champions when it comes to interrogation. One used to work with the French in Algeria, who taught him quite a few tricks. As for the other, I have to admit that he's a fiend. Each month he dreams up a more refined type of torture.

When I entered, the director pushed back the book he had in front of him. He never reads law books or detective stories but only serious works that must give you the pip. I managed to see the title, *Comrade General Sun*, by J. Stephen-Alexis. He offered me a seat.

'My dear Inspector, I see you have arrested Dr Mobata.' He lit a cigarette and took a long drag. 'Is he also mixed up in this plot?'

'They found his address on one of the prisoners. You'll admit that's suspicious.'

He didn't look convinced at all, the director. But I felt him to be ill at ease. He didn't dare look me straight in the eye. Although he had broached the subject quite openly, he was now hedging. He told me of his aversion to torture, that this process caused the attitude of the accused to be hardened against those who practised it, so that even opponents who were still relatively harmless when arriving here turned absolutely ferocious after passing through our hands. To his mind torture degraded man. Certainly, it was his duty to watch over the security of the State but not to set men below dumb beasts.

'But he's not a man, he's a Communist.'

He didn't reply but gave me an injured look.

'Chief, you definitely don't make our job any easier. And then, you know, it's hard to get this across to our boys. Of course, if it was up to them, they'd simply liquidate all the prisoners.'

'It's our duty to prevent them from doing so. We are in a position of authority, Inspector, and not a delirious mob.'

And he launched once more into a long sermon, half of which I've forgotten. I kept telling myself, 'To hell with all these intellectual arguments! That's what you get if they put Doctors of Law in charge of the CID. They've read too many books and lack stamina. They hold the curious notion that one can get tough-minded people to talk without hurting them . . .'

'And do you think that if they had got away with their plot, they would've spared us? Our heads would certainly have been the first to fall. These stories about offering the left cheek after you've been struck on the right are a load of Sunday School drivel.'

The director was not short of arguments to parry mine. He spoke of the educational role of the police, of sadistic habits to be eradicated, of new, wholesome ones to be created and a whole lot of stuff which sounded like rubbish to me. I wondered if he wasn't a bit of a Red himself. To cut a long story short, he kept me in his office for two hours.

When he let me go, Zakunda and Mibolo had given the doctor the works. I found him stretched out on the floor, unconscious. His eyes were swollen. A trickle of blood was running from his mouth. The boys told me that he still hadn't talked.

It took three buckets of water to bring him round. He opened his eyes. He resembled someone who emerges from a nightmare. He looked at me like an animal in agony and blood spilt out of his mouth.

'Are you going to talk now?' Mibolo roared.

I had to intervene. Even if the boss was wrong, I was obliged to obey him. This was to my mind a concession I could afford to make. If with such a shrewd fellow I found it difficult to prove his connection with the plotters, he on the other hand would be hard put to prove his innocence.

'Take him to a cell and let him rot till tomorrow. Maybe it'll do him good to sleep on it . . .'

And I went off to bed. I slept all night. I needed it to recover. The next morning I even arrived late at the office. I immediately asked for the records of the night's interrogations. The man on whom the address had been found persisted in denying that he knew Dr Mobata. What was more, the ringleader of the plot had finally been arrested.

A patrol had intercepted him in a car one hundred kilometres from here. Though disguised as a woman, he had nevertheless been recognized when he had only a short distance left to get to the border. As soon as he was arrested, he admitted everything. But each time he was questioned about Dr Mobata's involvement, he exonerated him.

All the same this doctor looked like a real plotter!

There was a knock at the door. An officer of the peace stood to attention, his chest stuck out, his head thrust backward, and saluted me.

'Stand easy!'

'The director wishes to see you, Sir.'

I found him in a relaxed mood. He spoke to me slowly and calmly about the conclusions of the enquiry. For each statement he showed me documentary evidence. It was obvious that Dr Mobata had nothing to do with this affair. The houseboy who had volunteered the information had started spluttering when confronted with Nabangou, and had finally admitted that he had hoped to make some money that way, but that he had in the first place wanted to get his own back on his master for giving him the sack.

'My dear Inspector, I leave to you the pleasure of announcing to the doctor his discharge.'

The boss had won once more. I was fuming with rage. The policeman I ordered to fetch Mobata knew it. My nervous irritation grew worse because it took him a long time to return. I decided to go down to the cell in the basement myself. When I arrived I sensed at once that something had happened. The two policemen were squatting in front of the cell's heavy iron door which they had opened. When they saw me, they stood up.

'What's going on here?'

They didn't answer. They pointed at the body lying prostrate on the floor. Dr Mobata had killed himself. The classical trick of those who can't stand torture. He had slashed a vein.

I am fairly sure that this was the first time a dead man really gave me a shock. I had the impression that I was suffocating. My head was bursting. I felt like shouting like a madman, like knocking myself against the walls and crying.

'Why are you hanging around like this, you clods? Don't you see he's dead? Take him away quickly, quickly!'

I must have pushed the policemen who didn't know what was wrong.

Of course the director gave me a proper dressing-down. Still, the government covered me. An official version was devised to make this death legitimate. Nobody knows the truth. But I think that since that day I have changed. I couldn't eat for two days. My wife told me that she found me strange. At first I shrugged my shoulders but then I noticed that my kids were also starting to look at me strangely.

When I kiss them, I am under the impression that their innocent eyes search mine to see what's going on inside my head. Maybe they too find me strange. I have asked for a transfer to a bush station. Since that event, I no longer dare to interrogate any of the accused. It reminds me too much of the doctor, and that makes me sad. But what gives me the greatest pain is the fact that I don't know how to persuade my colleagues not to use torture. If I try, they'll simply laugh at me . . .

CLÉMENTINE NZUJI MADIYA

DITETEMBWA

IN THE OLDEN days in the village of Mikalaayi, not far from the small waterfalls at Mapoolo, there lived a gari-seller. She used to wake up very early in the morning before sunrise to pound her cassava and make it into gari. At the crack of dawn she could already be seen sieving it, and as soon as the sun made its appearance she would set out on her way to the market where she sold it in small measures.

One day she awoke as usual before dawn. She washed herself and got dressed, stood before her mortar and started pounding the cassava. Suddenly she felt something like a burn on her arm holding the pestle. She stopped pounding and looked at her hurting arm. Just when she had located the spot that hurt, she felt another burn slightly above the first one and saw at the same moment Ditetembwa, the black wasp, leaving her arm. In her fright she gave off a yell and let the pestle slip from her hand.

Now it so happened that next to the mortar stood a winnowing-basket with a calabash of water right in the middle of it. The pestle fell on the winnowing-basket. The winnowing-basket twirled around, and with it the calabash. The water poured out of the calabash. It flowed into a snake-hole. The snake darted out of its hole and fled into the forest.

Well now, at that hour before dawn the lords of the forest usually visit their realm, hence the snake in its flight encountered the elephant. But not having seen it, the elephant stepped on the reptile, which repaid him with a deep bite.

Thereupon it was the elephant's turn to take to flight, and he bumped with all his weight against the tree.

The tree came crashing down into the underbrush and fell into the stream where a family of frogs was living. Father Frog, exasperated by the disturbance, emitted a croak. It was taken up immediately by his entire household, so that a real croaking concert was the result.

Meanwhile, far away in the village, the cock, who was used to being awakened by old Mr Frog, thought it was time to get up and inform the people of the village that the day was beginning. He therefore crowed. His crowing, like an alarm-clock the whole village trusted, rang out as a morning salutation. Right away everyone launched lustily into his early morning duties. The farmers set out for their fields. The girls daintily descended the path to the water, pots and calabashes poised on their heads.

On the side where the sun rises, God sensed an unusual commotion intruding on his dreams. He awoke, listened and heard noises that sounded like the rhythmical footfalls of girls going to the stream. He rubbed his eyes and pinched his cheek to feel whether he was really awake. He listened again and this time heard distinctly the noise of axes and hoes clanging together in the farmers' baskets. Then God realized that the village people had begun their daily activities. He approached the pathway where he saw a group of hunters with arrows in their game-bags, about to set traps. He asked them: 'Good people, what's happening? Where are you going thus in the dead of night?'

They answered: 'Didn't you hear the cock crow? Day is breaking, and we shall set our traps.'

God said: 'That's not possible. It is still night, the sun which wakes me always does so before the first cock-crow but this time it has not yet appeared.'

The hunters replied: 'If that's the way it is, go and ask the cock why he has roused us earlier today.'

God bade the cock come, and asked him: 'Why did you crow so early today? Look at the way everybody is up and about already.'

The cock replied: 'It's not my fault, Boss. I heard the frogs croaking and thought that it was time for me to wake the humans.'

Then God said to him: 'Go, it's not your fault. But tell old Mr Frog to come here.'

The cock went and told old Mr Frog to come and report urgently to God.

God asked him: 'Why did you croak before the normal time today? Look here, the cock has followed your example and has woken up the people.'

Old Mr Frog replied: 'This thing, Boss, was really beyond my control. A big tree fell into the stream and right on top of my house. My family had a narrow escape.'

Then God told him: 'Go, it is not your fault. Bring the tree here.'

Old Mr Frog quickly went to notify the tree that God was waiting for him. So the tree appeared before God, who asked him: 'Why did you fall on the house of old Mr Frog? You see, he croaked, the cock crowed and the people have woken up.'

The tree replied: 'Oh, Master, I'll gladly turn into firewood if this is my fault. My excuse is that I was sleeping peacefully when the elephant came and bumped against me with all his weight, thus uprooting me. Since I couldn't keep upright, I fell into the stream.'

God told him: 'I understand, it's not your fault. Call the elephant who knocked you over.'

The tree went to tell the elephant that God was asking for

him. The elephant appeared before God, who asked him: 'Why did you knock over the tree? It fell on the house of old Mr Frog, and he croaked with fear. The cock, hearing him, crowed and has awakened the people who were asleep.'

The elephant answered him: 'O Lord, Sun that no one can look in the face! May I be cut up for meat if it's my fault! I was walking peacefully in my realm when suddenly I felt under my paw the painful bite of a snake. Obviously I fled across the forest without knowing where I was going, and that's why I bumped into the tree on my way and knocked it down.'

God told him: 'Yes, I see. Go and tell the snake that I am waiting for him to explain things.'

The snake appeared before God, and God asked him: 'What happened this night? Why did you bite the elephant? You see, he took to flight and knocked down the tree on his way. The tree fell into the stream, right onto the house of old Mr Frog who croaked with displeasure. The cock thought that Mr Frog wanted to wake him up, so he started crowing and the people have woken up.'

The snake defended himself in these terms: 'It wasn't my fault, Boss. I was snoring peacefully in my hole when all of a sudden I felt something wet flowing over me. I woke up and saw that it was water. I thought it was a flood and fled before it was too late. As I was slithering along my way, the elephant stepped on my tail, and then of course I bit him.'

God told the snake: 'All right, go and call the water.'

The water arrived and God said to it: 'You owe me an explanation. What was your business entering the snake's hole and disturbing him like that? You see what happened: he ran away and on his way the elephant stepped on him. He bit the elephant who in turn took to his heels and knocked down the tree. The tree fell on Mr Frog's house and Mr

Frog croaked with anger. The cock, awakened by the croak, crowed and the people have woken up.'

The water answered: 'May I evaporate if it's my fault. When I was waiting in the calabash I found myself suddenly poured out by the calabash without understanding why. This is why I had to flow helplessly into the snake's hole.'

God said: 'I understand. Go home and send the calabash to me.'

The calabash appeared and gave its own explanation: 'My master, I was waiting quietly in the winnowing-basket for my mistress to use the water I was carrying. Without being given a chance to know why, I suddenly felt the pestle bouncing on me, I was knocked over and the water I contained ran out. I was not in a position to control it, and that's how it ran into the snake's hole.'

God said: 'I realize it's not your fault. Go and tell the pestle that I'm waiting for an explanation.'

The pestle arrived and took the following line of defence: 'God, I could not do otherwise, the woman who was holding me let go of me all of a sudden and then I fell on the winnowing-basket and the calabash full of water.'

God said: 'You may go home but call the gari-seller for me.'

The woman appeared before God and apologized profusely: 'O Almighty God, Life-force, Sun which no one can look in the face! Everybody in the village knows me and my habits. I rise day after day before cock-crow, frog-croak and sunrise. Normally the thud of my mortar does not disturb anyone because I always manage to start pounding between the onset of man's third deep sleep and the hour of awakening. Today I started at that hour as usual. Everything was going fine until Ditetembwa, the big black wasp, came to sting my arm. Then I let go of the pestle, and it fell on the winnowing-basket in the middle of which was placed a calabash full of water . . . There's no need to repeat the rest because you know all about it.'

After she had given her explanation thus, the gari-seller raised the wrapper which covered her injured arm. It was a painful sight, the arm was sorely swollen and her sad face showed an agony of suffering.

God bade her return home and call Ditetembwa, the big black wasp, who appeared at once. God asked her:

'Why did you sting the gari-seller? Look at the whole chain of trouble you have brought upon the world.'

'Zzz . . . zzz . . . I mean . . . zzz.'

'I want an answer.'

The black wasp could not produce a valid answer.

Therefore, in order to punish her, God took her belly in his left hand, her chest in his right hand and pulled with all his might until the waist of Ditetembwa, the big black wasp, became as thin as a thread.

DANIEL MANDISHONA

A WASTED LAND

UNCLE NICHOLAS CAME back from England after the war in January 1981. He spent the entire fourteen hours that the journey lasted trussed up in a straitjacket between two burly cabin crew. On arrival at the airport he was met by a four-car police escort and taken straight to the psychiatric unit at Harare Hospital. For his waiting relatives, most of whom had not seen him for twenty-five years, it was a traumatic homecoming.

I had been born in his absence and only knew him from a sepia-edged black and white photograph which he had sent to my father on his arrival. It was of him and a friend standing ankle-deep in fresh fields with pigeons perched on their heads and arms. Throughout most of my childhood my memory of him consisted of that hazy, unsatisfactory likeness that was twenty years out of date. Yet it told me nothing about his behavioural quirks: how he talked, how he walked, how he laughed; whether he drank or smoked. In short, I could not visualize the whole without knowing its parts.

When he killed himself in March 1982 by cutting his wrists, all I was left with were confused memories of weekly visits to the hospital bed of a druggy and pathetic old man, who soiled himself and had to be chained to the bed posts to curtail the intermittent orgies of self-inflicted violence provoked by deep bouts of melancholy. It was an inescapable yet poignant irony that he had gone overseas to better himself, not to come back in disgrace to swell the ranks of burned-out, unhinged 'been-tos' with minds contaminated by too much learning.

For the last eight years of his exile he had stopped writing altogether. My father wrote to him regularly but in the end stopped because all his letters were returned saying there was no such person known at that address. Nobody knew what Uncle Nicholas was doing or where he was doing it. Eventually, it seemed, nobody cared much. We knew he was still alive because he sent the occasional Christmas card, and sometimes we went to the post office to collect boxes of second-hand clothes he bought at street markets. When my paternal grandmother died he did not know about it until my father sent a message with a woman who had won a British Council scholarship to study pharmacy at the same college that was Uncle Nicholas's last known abode.

Up to this day nobody knows why he went mad, or why in the end he thought it necessary to take his own life. His madness gradually got worse and in the end, out of sheer desperation, Father had to take him out of the hospital and put him into the care of a traditional witchdoctor. At night he hardly slept, consumed as he was by terrifying nightmares in which he was pursued by the demons that had taken up residence in his unhinged mind and so corrupted his language that all he was capable of was a dialect of carnal profanities. He slept a lot, ate very little and soon managed to reduce himself to a gaunt mass of bones.

The witchdoctor left one rainy night and never came back.

Later on we were to learn – through unsubstantiated rumour, naturally – that after completing his studies he had moved on to Manchester, taken an English wife, and fathered several children. The story was all the more incredible because in Rhodesia he was still married to my Aunt Emily, with whom he had three grown-up children. Another rumour, from a different source, said he had subsequently spent six years in a British jail for wife-battery and child-abuse. This seemed to explain his long silence in the middle of the 70s. When he came out his wife had the marriage annulled on the grounds of his cruelty. She sought a court order that prevented him from seeing his own children. He foolishly threatened to kill her and got himself deported. Those who had nothing better to do than speculate about the reasons for his madness identified the woman's callousness as the pebble that dislodged the avalanche of derangement that finally overwhelmed him.

Sometimes I would look at that old black and white photograph, which my father had relegated from pride of place in the living room to the back of his bedroom door, and wonder how such a brilliant and gifted man could have been capable of the cruelties that were alleged of him. Yet it is quite often said that the calmest features hide the most scheming minds. In the early years my father made sure that everybody in the street and beyond knew that his 'kid brother' Nicholas Musoni – the precociously gifted former herd-boy who wrote prize-winning essays on the Pioneer Column and the Great Trek and the Battle of Blood River – was studying clinical pharmacology at the University of London; that when he completed his doctorate he would be the first indigenous black Rhodesian to hold such a qualification. On most occasions the boast was met by politely bemused blank stares: Pharmacology? – was it something to do with farming, perhaps . . .? Father's simplified explanation was to tell people that Uncle Nicholas was learning how to make Cafenol and Disprin.

Yes, Uncle Nicholas, even though he might not have

known it himself, was a man on the verge of creating momentous history.

But in the days after Uncle Nicholas's death and before his own suicide my father rarely talked about him. When he did he no longer referred to him as 'my kid brother' but as 'that unfortunate brother of mine'. It was almost as if he felt that by propagating this subtle but unbrotherly denunciation he could distance himself from the accusatory fingers that were looking for somewhere to point. He after all had been the instigator of Uncle Nicholas's decision to study abroad. In truth, there had been nowhere for him to go after he had been expelled from the University of Rhodesia for his political activities. The letters he wrote in his first year abroad were all opened by the Special Branch before they were delivered, usually a good month from the date of the postmark. Once, we even got a Christmas card from him a week before Easter.

Despite the fact that he was thousands of miles away in England, Uncle Nicholas was as much a victim of the war as us who were right here in the middle of the bloody conflict. Wars claim their victims in many different ways. They have tentacles that reach beyond the definable violence of battlefields and muddy trenches. They continue to claim casualties long after the physical wounds of shrapnel and gunfire have healed. There is no doubt in my mind that the enforced exile that alienated Uncle Nicholas played a crucial part in his illness. As the doctors at the hospital told Father the day they discharged him, there was nothing physically wrong with him. Whatever he had was all in his head. He was much too young when he left for London. Too young and too inexperienced to cope with the exhilarating freedoms of his new world; a world that was so different from the one he had left behind.

* * *

I was ten when the war started and twenty-one when it ended. In between I lost most of my youth and some of my best friends. Ishmael, Garikayi, Kingston, Jabulani, Abednigo. These were people I had known since childhood without realizing that they harboured grudges far deeper than mine. When they were all killed on the same night trying to cross the Mozambique/Rhodesia border I felt cheated and angry because they had left me out of their doomed plan. And yet I also knew that had they invited me to join I would have found a reason for not going. I was simply not strong enough, or perhaps I was just a coward.

The first time I realized there was a war on was when some of Father's people came down from the villages and vowed never to return. Before that I had always thought of the war as something that happened to other people – like freak accidents, natural disasters and fatal diseases. These people from operational area villages spoke of landmines and dusk-to-dawn curfews; of the mangled corpses of civilians 'caught in cross-fire' and of road blocks manned by sadistic soldiers; of stealthy midnight air-raids that dropped bombs that peeled off skin and burnt the flesh to the bone. Raids that flattened whole villages and filled orphanages with children who would grow up without ever knowing who their parents were or what they looked like.

The country was a wasteland of pain and heartache. Events were happening much too fast for them to be seen as anything other than an incoherent jumble of random circumstances that rolled headlong into each other, cart-wheeling towards even worse disasters. The conflict became an indecisive tussle of divergent wills; of peripheral battles vying to influence an outcome that was already decided.

The violence was the worst part.

It so bludgeoned our senses that in the end we became immune to it, like a tired horse that can no longer respond to the stinging pain of the jockey's whip. Each passing day I watched my mother grow old with the violence; embittered, disconsolate, unforgiving. For it was a violence that encapsulated in its obscene wholeness the disarray that military confrontation breeds. The nationalist politicians indulged in visualized displays of reciprocal insults that only served as a tool for the unsympathetic press to explore the dark depths of their ignorance. They waved militant placards and when on television droned on and on and on like demented sleep-talkers. They proclaimed a fragile unity yet the only thing they had in common, like travellers on the same road, was the destination – not the means of getting there nor the best course to take.

They were an assortment of vainglorious misfits stultified by a communal dearth of intellect. They were men of many promises but few deeds, each pulling in his own direction, each vying to impose his own will. Their speeches were long on emotion and rhetoric but short on ideas. They talked unrealistically of dismantling by proletarian revolution a political system that had been in place for over a century. A political order that was so deeply rooted in the very fabric of the society it had created that it could only be destroyed at considerable expense to the society itself.

The nationalist politicians and the government were like a parasite and its host animal who need each other because of the mutual benefit of an otherwise harmful co-existence. They talked and talked and got nowhere. We listened to both of them, hoping some day they would remove their blinkers and start to make sense. We could see that their promised land would be a tainted utopia, a paradise of emptiness. Yet somehow we listened to them and followed them like columns of compliant somnambulists to the edge of the chasm. Perhaps we were naive to do so, but the situation dictated a response fashioned not by reason but by impulse: the impulse of survival. After the war the same people were to swiftly change sides and stand on rostrums and claim credit for a victory that everybody knew was not theirs.

It is truly amazing how expediency can make people have different memories of the same thing.

I remember going to the funerals of relatives who broke one curfew too many and ended up riddled with bullets in dusty roadside ditches.

We lived in Bindura at the time. It was an old colonial house; so old that sometimes when it rained the walls shook and the windows rattled and the zinc roof produced the most astounding din. Each night we arranged cups and saucers and buckets on the floor to catch the new leaks. We spent many Christmases huddled by the fire in the front room, roasting peanuts to while away the tedium of long slow nights. By staying up late and waking early we sustained the illusion that the days were long and the nights short. Our mother told us stories of her own childhood, growing up in a country that would perhaps be irrevocably lost to us. When we went to bed we pressed our ears hard against the walls and listened to the thunder-roll of gun-battles raging in valleys full of ghost towns long deserted by all sane people. In the long silences that followed sporadic lulls in hostilities our lives were full of fear and uncertainty. Yet even the silence had its own smells; its own ghostly cadences that hung to every long moment.

We celebrated New Year's Eve wondering how many of us would make it through the horrors of the next twelve months. We watched army helicopters gliding like sinister dragonflies on daily manoeuvres to flush out the unseen enemy, rotors swirling in the haze, flattening the grass. Our race-fixated masters had us by the scruff of the neck and they would not let go. Having shut the outside world out – and us in – they were, like caged animals in a zoo, the undisputed masters of their insular kingdom.

Even before Uncle Nicholas's death, we all knew that Father's businesses weren't doing too well. We knew he couldn't get supplies for the two grocery shops that provided our livelihood. The truck drivers, understandably, had reservations about driving along roads that took them through the treacherous terrain of the war zone. There was a fortnightly army convoy that came our way but the supplies, when they arrived, ran out in three or four days. The few drivers who dared drive through the operational areas at night demanded exorbitant payments of 'danger money'. After all, they said, they were risking life and limb. It did not matter that they were on the same side as the guerillas. Landmines and bazookas were colour-blind.

He was a proud man, my father. Perhaps it was this unfortunate tribal trait that fostered within his stubborn head a self-deluding and dangerous overestimation of his own capabilities. He soon found himself, indefatigable optimist that he was, marooned alone in a sea of chronic pessimism. Beleaguered and yet stoically heroic, he dealt with the considerable strain of his fluctuating fortunes by calmly playing down his many failures and exaggerating the few successes. My mother worried constantly about him, for she had known him far too long to be fooled by the elaborate masquerade of normality with which he sought to hide his quite substantial anxieties.

Yet within his bounteous heart he harboured humanitarian sympathies that went beyond the call of duty. People came down from the villages and he was sufficiently moved by their plight to unselfishly borrow money and help them start new lives away from the incessant boom of guns and mortar shells. But in the end he became a victim of his own exemplary altruism. People simply took advantage of him.

When the war intensified the supplies stopped altogether. A convoy was ambushed near Devil's Hill and fifteen Rhodesian army soldiers killed. So our side was winning the war, but at what cost? The shops had row upon row of empty shelves as business slackened considerably. There was no bread, sugar, eggs, soap, salt, milk, butter. In fact, there was nothing. Disgruntled regulars took their custom elsewhere. The point was soon reached where the monthly lease repayments on the buildings far exceeded the profits the businesses themselves were making. The three girls Father employed, distant cousins brought in as a favour after special pleading from their parents who were worried that continued unemployment might lead them into premature motherhood, were now threatening to take their erstwhile benefactor to court for non-payment of wages. They appreciated their employer's plight but insisted that their own difficulties were now just as pressing.

One afternoon an unmarked van from Zimbabwe Furnitures arrived to cart away our threadbare living room suite. Mother told prying neighbours that it was going back to be reupholstered. She too had started telling little lies to maintain the family's good name. That night she sat alone by the fire and cried herself to sleep. We sold things in the house so Father could pay off his debts. He said his insolvency was a temporary hiccup; a minor occupational blip he would soon overcome. But by then I think even he knew that he was fooling no one. He had to borrow money off one loan shark to pay off another. It became an endless spiral of debt. Sometimes he spent hours in the shops and came back bleary-eyed and pensive. He was a broken man.

I hated the war for what it was doing to him, and what it was making him do to us.

On the day of Uncle Nicholas's funeral Father had to go to court again. One of his unpaid creditors had run out of patience and sympathy and issued a writ. The funeral itself was delayed because of heavy seasonal rain. They put the coffin in the living room with its top open and body garlanded by flowers. There was a heavy, overpowering scent in the air. I went in alone and stared at Uncle Nicholas's dead mad face. It was smooth, like a chiselled slab of pasty grey skin. The facial muscles had been frozen into a rigid, lopsided snarl that gave his normally pious features the appearance of a petrified gargoyle. His hands were clasped across his chest as if in prayer, the cuffs of his favourite shirt judiciously covering the wrists he had slashed with the bread knife.

His eldest daughter, Michelle, had arrived unannounced from Manchester the previous day for the funeral. She exhausted herself being friendly to the point of sycophancy with everybody she spoke to but it was all in vain. Aunt Emily, Uncle Nicholas's widow, had made sure that the girl would feel unwelcome by shamelessly orchestrating a verbal boycott directed at her and her white boyfriend. Most of the people Michelle spoke to spoke back in Shona even though they knew fully well that she was a stranger to both the country and its language. I felt sorry for her, yet at the same time I was also ashamed at allowing myself to be party to such a disgraceful conspiracy. But Aunt Emily had made it known, quite emphatically, that she held the girl's mother solely responsible for my uncle's fatal madness. It was an unfair charge but Aunt Emily had always been inclined towards mindless vindictiveness.

Outside the house women in black veils stood patiently on the deep veranda. Some sang hymns, others chatted about the continuing drought. The men held subdued conversations that centred on the estate of the departed man. By mid-afternoon Father had still not returned. The rain by that time had stopped. A straggly rainbow appeared on the edge of the sky but its colours were not quite right; they were frayed and indistinct. My left eye had an autonomous twitch that portended unfavourable news. The rain stopped an hour later and the hearse arrived to lead the procession to the cemetery.

My father had still not returned.

Bernard . . . Run to the shop, said my mother, and phone the court to see what has happened to your father. We cannot bury his brother without him there . . .

I took the shop keys and dashed off to the smaller of the two grocery shops. There was a telephone in a back office which Father used to ring up the Mount Darwin Indian wholesalers who supplied most of his stock. And that was where I found him, slumped across the counter with his wrists cut and his shirtsleeves drenched in brilliant splashes of clotted blood. He was surrounded by unpaid invoices and court summonses. He had been drinking heavily. Several bottles of Bols brandy were on the floor. The Chinese doctor who came from Bindura Hospital said he had been dead for four or five hours at least. There was a bottle of rat poison by his side, long opened but still emitting a faint pungent odour. He had drunk that too. Your father must have really wanted to die, said the doctor, making his astute observation sound as if it was a compliment.

The time of death coincided with the time he had left the house. I knew then that he had never intended to go to the court. That evening I went back to the shop and removed all the court summonses I could find from the office and burnt them in the backyard. I did not think it either fair or necessary for my mother's heartbreak to be compounded by the revelation that our comfortable lifestyle had been fraudulently financed.

The judge declared him a bankrupt in his absence and ordered sequestration of all movable assets. All the court cases against him were dropped because there was nobody to prosecute. Bailiffs arrived over the next few days to apportion the remaining things in the shops and the house to pay off his creditors. They literally left us in the clothes we were standing in. Mother had to borrow money from relatives to pay for the funeral. Michelle came to tell us that she had booked into a cheaper motel and would be staying for the second funeral. Mother was so touched by this gesture that she dropped her pretended hostility and even invited Michelle and her boyfriend to a meal. But they never came. When I went to their motel I was told they had left urgently. I wrote her a letter, speculatively using one of Uncle Nicholas's old addresses, but it came back saying there was no such person known at that address.

We moved house after that but we could not erase the memory of Father's death. One cannot rid a room of its bad associations by rearranging the furniture. Father died in April 1981, exactly a year after Independence. Those debts accumulated during the war proved too much even for a man of his resilience. Like Uncle Nicholas and so many others, he survived the war only to die of its effects when the peace arrived.

AHMED ESSOP

HAJJI MUSA AND THE HINDU FIRE-WALKER

'ALLAH HAS SENT me to you, Bibi Fatima.'

'Allah, Hajji Musa?'

'I assure you, Allah, my good lady. Listen to me carefully. There is something wrong with you. Either you have a sickness or there is an evil spell cast over your home. Can you claim that there is nothing wrong in your home, that your family is perfectly healthy and happy?'

'Well, Hajji Musa, you know my little Amir has a nasty cough that even Dr Kamal cannot cure and Soraya seems to have lost her appetite.'

'My good woman, you believe me now when I say Allah has sent me to you?'

Bibi Fatima's husband, Jogee, entered the room. Hajji Musa took no notice of him and began to recite (in Arabic) an extract from the Koran. When he had done he shook hands with Jogee.

'Listen to me, Bibi Fatima and brother Jogee. Sickness is not part of our nature, neither is it the work of our good Allah. It is the work of that great evil-doer Iblis, some people call him Satan. Well, I, by the grace of Allah' (he recited another extract from the Koran), 'have been given the power to heal the sick and destroy evil. That is my work in life, even if I get no reward.'

'But Hajji Musa, you must live.'

'Bibi Fatima, Allah looks after me and my family. Now bring me two glasses of water and a candle.'

She hurried to the kitchen and brought the articles.

'Now bring me the children.'

'Jogee, please go and find Amir in the yard while I look for Soraya.'

Husband and wife went out. Meanwhile Hajji Musa drew the curtains in the room, lit the candle and placed the two glasses of water on either side of the candle. He took incense out of his pocket, put it in an ash-tray and lit it.

When husband and wife returned with the children they were awed. There was an atmosphere of strangeness, of mystery, in the room. Hajji Musa looked solemn. He took the candle, held it about face level and said:

'Look, there is a halo around the flame.'

They looked and saw a faint halo.

He placed the candle on the table, took the glasses of water, held them above the flame and recited a verse from the Koran. When he had done he gave one glass to the boy and one to the girl.

'Drink, my children,' he said. They hesitated for a moment, but Bibi Fatima commanded them to drink the water.

'They will be well,' he said authoritatively. 'They can now go and play.'

He extinguished the candle, drew the curtains, and sat down on the settee. And he laughed, a full-throated, uproarious, felicitous laugh.

'Don't worry about the children. Allah has performed miracles and what are coughs and loss of appetites.' And he laughed again.

Bibi Fatima went to the kitchen to make tea and Jogee and I kept him company. She returned shortly with tea and cake.

'Jogee,' she said, 'I think Hajji Musa is greater than Dr

Kamal. You remember last year Dr Kamal gave me medicines and ointments for my aching back and nothing came of it?'

'Hajji Musa is not an ordinary doctor.'

'What are doctors of today,' Hajji Musa said, biting into a large slice of cake, 'but chancers and frauds? What knowledge have they of religion and the spiritual mysteries?'

'Since when have you this power to heal, Hajji Musa?'

'Who can tell the ways of Allah, Bibi Fatima. Sometimes his gifts are given when we are born and sometimes when we are much older.'

'More tea?'

She filled the cup. He took another slice of cake.

'Last month I went to Durban and there was this woman, Jasuben, whom the doctors had declared insane. Even her own yogis and swamis had given her up. I took this woman in hand and today she is as sane as anyone else.'

'Hajji Musa, you know my back still gives me trouble. Dr Kamal's medicine gave me no relief. I have even stopped making roti and Jogee is very fond of roti.'

'You should let me examine your back some day,' the healer said, finishing his tea.

'Why not now?'

'Not today,' he answered protestingly. 'I have some business to attend to.'

'But Hajji Musa, it will only take a minute or two.'

'Well that's true, that's true.'

'Will you need the candle and water?'

'Yes.'

She hurriedly went to refill the glass with water.

'Please, Jogee and Ahmed, go into the kitchen for a while,' she said, returning.

We left the room, Jogee rather reluctantly. She shut the door. I sat down on a chair and looked at a magazine lying on the table. Jogee told me he was going to buy cigarettes and left. He was feeling nervous.

I was sitting close to the door and could hear Hajji Musa's voice and the rustle of clothing as he went on with the examination.

'I think it best if you lie down on the settee so that I can make a thorough examination. . . . Yes, that is better. . . . Is the pain here . . .? Bibi Fatima, you know the pain often has its origin lower down, in the lumbar region. Could you ease your ijar a little . . .? The seat of the pain is often here. . . . Don't be afraid.'

'I can feel it getting better already, Hajji Musa.'

'That is good. You are responding very well.'

There was silence for some time. When Jogee returned Hajji Musa was reciting a prayer in Arabic. Jogee puffed at his cigarette.

When Bibi Fatima opened the door she was smiling and looked flushed.

'Your wife will be well in a few days,' Hajji Musa assured the anxious man. 'And you will have your daily roti again. Now I must go.'

'Hajji Musa, but we must give you something for your trouble.'

'No nothing, Bibi Fatima. I forbid you.'

She was insistent. She told Jogee in pantomime (she showed him five fingers) how much money he should give. Jogee produced the money from his pocket, though inwardly protesting at his wife's willingness to pay a man who asked no fees. Bibi Fatima put the money into Hajji Musa's pocket.

In appearance Hajji Musa was a fat, pot-bellied, short, dark man, with glossy black wavy hair combed backwards with fastidious care. His face was always clean shaven. For some reason he never shaved in the bathroom, and every morning one saw him in the yard, in vest and pyjama trousers, arranging (rather precariously) his mirror and shaving equipment on the window-sill outside the kitchen and going through the ritual of cleaning his face with the precision of a surgeon. His great passion was talking and while shaving he would be conducting conversations with various people in the yard: with the hawker packing his fruit and vegetables in the cart; with the two wives of the motor mechanic Soni; with the servants coming to work.

Hajji Musa was a well-known man. At various times he had been a commercial traveller, insurance salesman, taxi driver, companion to dignitaries from India and Pakistan, Islamic missionary, teacher at a seminary, shopkeeper, matchmaker and hawker of ladies' underwear.

His career as a go-between in marriage transactions was a brief inglorious one that almost ended his life. One night there was fierce knocking at his door. As soon as he opened it an angry voice exploded: 'You liar! You come and tell me of dat good-for-nutting Dendar boy, dat he good, dat he ejucated, dat he good prospect. My foot and boot he ejucated. He sleep most time wit bitches, he drink and beat my daughter. When you go Haj? You nutting but liar. You baster! You baster!' And suddenly two shots from a gun rang out in quick succession. The whole incident took place so quickly that no one had any time to look at the man as he ran through the yard and escaped. When people reached Hajji Musa's door they found him prostrate, breathing hard and wondering why he was still alive (the bullets had passed between his legs). His wife and eight children were in a state of shock. They were revived with sugared water.

Hajji Musa's life never followed an even course: on some days one saw him riding importantly in the chauffeur-driven

Mercedes of some wealthy merchant in need of his services; on others, one saw him in the yard, pacing meditatively from one end to the other, reciting verses from the Koran. Sometimes he would visit a friend, tell an amusing anecdote, laugh, and suddenly ask: 'Can you give me a few rands till tomorrow?' The friend would give him the money without expecting anything of tomorrow, for it was well known that Hajji Musa, liberal with his own money, never bothered to return anyone else's.

Hajji Musa considered himself a specialist in the exorcism of evil jinn. He deprecated modern terms such as neurosis, schizophrenia, psychosis. 'What do doctors know about the power of satanic jinn? Only God can save people who are no longer themselves. I have proved this time and again. You don't believe me? Then come on Sunday night to my house and you will see.'

On Sunday night we were clustered around Hajji Musa in the yard. As his patient had not yet arrived, he regaled us with her history.

'She is sixteen. She is the daughter of Mia Mohammed the Market Street merchant. She married her cousin a few years ago. But things went wrong. Her mother-in-law disliked her. For months she has been carted from doctor to doctor, and from one psychiatrist to another, those fools. Tonight you will see me bring about a permanent cure.'

After a while a car drove into the yard, followed by two others. Several men – two of them tall, bearded brothers – emerged from the car, approached Hajji Musa and shook hands with him. They pointed to the second car.

'She is in that car, Hajji Musa.'

'Good, bring her into the house.' And he went inside.

There were several women in the second car. All alighted but one, who refused to come out. She shook her face and hands and cried, 'No! No! Don't take me in there, please! By Allah, I am a good girl.'

The two brothers and several women stood beside the opened doors of the car and coaxed the young lady to come out.

'Sister, come, we are only visiting.'

'No, no, they are going to hit me.'

'No one is going to hit you,' one of the women said, getting into the car and sitting beside her. 'They only want to see you.'

'They can see me in the car. I am so pretty.'

Everyone living in the yard was present to witness the spectacle, and several children had clambered onto the bonnet of the car and were shouting: 'There she is! There she is! She is mad! She is mad!'

'Come now, Jamilla, come. The people are laughing at you,' one of the brothers said sternly.

Hajji Musa now appeared wearing a black cloak emblazoned with sequin-studded crescent moons and stars, and inscribed with Cufic writing in white silk. His sandals were red and his trousers white. His turban was of green satin and it had a large round ruby (artificial) pinned to it above his forehead.

He proceeded towards the car, looked at Jamilla, and then said to the bearded brothers, 'I will take care of her.' He put his head into the interior of the car. Jamilla recoiled in terror. The lady next to her held her and said, 'Don't be frightened. Hajji Musa intends no harm.'

'Listen, sister, come into the house, I have been expecting you.'

'No! No! I want to go home.' Jamilla began to cry.

'I won't let anyone hurt you.'

Hajji Musa tried to grab her hand, but she pushed herself

backwards against the woman next to her and screamed so loudly that for a moment the healer seemed to lose his nerve. He turned to the brothers.

'The evil jinn is in her. Whatever I do now, please forgive me.'

He put his foot into the interior of the car, gripped one arm of the terrified Jamilla and smacked her twice with vehemence.

'Come out jinn! Come out jinn!' he shouted and dragged her towards the door of the car. The woman beside Jamilla pushed her and punched her on her back.

'Please help,' Hajji Musa said, and the two brothers pulled the screaming Jamilla out of the car.

'Drive the jinn into the house!' And they punched and pushed Jamilla towards the house. She pleaded with several spectators for help and then in desperation clung to them. But they shook her off and one or two even took the liberty of punching her and pulling her hair.

Jamilla was pushed into the house and the door closed on her and several of the privileged who were permitted to witness the exorcism ceremony. As soon as she passed through a narrow passage and entered a room she quietened.

The room was brilliantly lit and a fire was burning in the grate. A red carpet stretched from wall to wall and on the window-sill incense was burning in brass bowls. In front of the gate were two brass plates containing sun-dried red chillies.

We removed our shoes and sat down on the carpet. Jamilla was made to sit in front of the grate. She was awed and looked about at the room and the people. Several women seated themselves near her. Hajji Musa then began to recite the chapter 'The Jinn' from the Koran. We sat with bowed heads. When he had done he moved towards the grate. His wife came into the room with a steel tray and a pair of tongs. Hajji Musa took some burning pieces of coal and heaped them on the tray. Then he scattered the red chillies over the coals. Smoke rose from the tray and filled the room with an acrid, suffocating smell. He seated himself beside Jamilla and asked the two brothers to sit near her as well. He pressed Jamilla's head over the tray and at the same time recited a verse from the Koran in a loud voice. Jamilla choked, seemed to scream mutely and tried to lift her head, but Hajji Musa held her.

As the smell of burning chillies was unbearable, some of us went outside for a breath of fresh air. Aziz Khan said to us:

'That primitive ape is prostituting our religion with his hocus-pocus. He should be arrested for assault.'

We heard Jamilla screaming and we returned quickly to the room. We saw Hajji Musa and the two brothers beating her with their sandals and holding her face over the coals.

'Out Iblis! Out Jinn!' Hajji Musa shouted and belaboured her.

At last Jamilla fell into a swoon.

'Hold her, Ismail and Hafiz.' Hajji Musa sprinkled her face with water and read a prayer. Then he asked the two brothers to pick her up and take her into an adjoining room. They laid her on a bed.

'When she wakes up the jinn will be gone,' Hajji Musa predicted confidently.

We went outside for a while. Aziz Khan asked a few of us to go with him in his car to the police station. But on the way he surprised us by changing his mind.

'It's not our business,' he said, and drove back to the yard.

When we returned Jamilla had opened her eyes and was sobbing quietly.

'Anyone can ask Jamilla if she remembers what happened to her.'

Someone asked her and she shook her head.

'See,' said the victorious man, 'it was the evil jinn that was thrashed out of her body. He is gone!'

There had been the singing of hymns, chanting and the jingling of bells since the late afternoon, and as evening approached there was great excitement in the yard. Everyone knew of the great event that was to take place that evening: the Hindu fire-walker was going to give a demonstration.

'There is nothing wonderful about walking on fire,' Hajji Musa declared in a scornful tone. 'The Hindus think they are performing miracles. Bah! Miracles!' And he exploded in laughter. 'What miracles can their many gods perform, I ask you? Let them extract a jinn or heal the sick and then talk of miracles.'

'But can you walk on fire or only cook on fire?' Dolly asked sardonically. There was laughter and merriment.

'Both, my dear man, both. Anyone who cooks on fire can walk on fire.'

'If anyone can, let him try,' said the law student Soma. 'In law, words are not enough; evidence has to be produced.'

'Funny you lawyers never get done with words. After gossiping for days you ask for a postponement.'

Everyone laughed boisterously.

'Hajji Musa,' Dolly tried again, 'can you walk on fire?'

'Are you joking, Dolly? When I can remove a jinn, what is walking on fire? Have you seen a jinn?'

'No.'

'See one and then talk. Evil jinn live in hell. What is walking on fire to holding one of hell's masters in your hands?'

'I say let him walk on fire and then talk of jinn,' said

Rama the dwarfish Hindu watchmaker, but he walked away fearing to confront Hajji Musa.

'That stupid Hindu thinks I waste my time in performing tricks. I am not a magician.'

A fire was now lit in the yard. Wood had been scattered over an area of about twenty feet by six feet. An attendant was shovelling coal and another using the rake to spread it evenly.

Meanwhile, in a room in the yard, the voices of the chanters were rising and the bells were beginning to jingle madly. Every now and then a deeper, more resonant chime would ring out, and a voice would lead the chanters to a higher pitch. In the midst of the chanters, facing a small altar on which were placed a tiny earthenware bowl containing a burning wick, a picture of the god Shiva surrounded by votive offerings of marigold flowers, rice and coconut, sat the fire-walker in a cross-legged posture.

The yard was crowded. Chairs were provided but these were soon occupied. The balconies were packed and several agile children climbed onto rooftops and seated themselves on the creaking zinc. A few dignitaries were also present.

The chanters emerged from the doorway. In their midst was the fire-walker, his eyes focused on the ground. He was like a man eroded of his own will, captured by the band of chanters. They walked towards the fire which was now glowing, flames leaping here and there.

The chanters grouped themselves near the fire and went on with their singing and bell-ringing, shouting refrains energetically. Then, as though life had suddenly flowed into him, the fire-walker detached himself from the group and went towards the fire. It was a tense moment. The chanters were gripped by frenzy. The coal-bed glowed. He placed his right foot on the fire gently, tentatively, as though measuring its intensity, and then walked swiftly over from end to end. He was applauded. Two boys now offered him coconuts in trays. He selected two, and then walked over the inferno again, rather slowly this time, and as he walked he banged the coconuts against his head several times until they cracked and one saw the snowy insides. His movement now became more like a dance than a walk, as though his feet gloried in their triumph over the fire. The boys offered him more coconuts and he went on breaking them against his head.

While the fire-walker was demonstrating his salamander-like powers, an argument developed between Aziz Khan and Hajji Musa.

'He is not walking over the fire,' Hajji Musa said. 'Our eyes are being deceived.'

'Maybe your eyes are being deceived, but not mine,' Aziz answered.

'If you know anything about yogis then you will know how they can pass off the unreal for the real.'

'What do you mean by saying if I know anything about yogis?'

'He thinks he knows about everything under the sun,' Hajji Musa said jeeringly to a friend. He turned to Aziz. 'Have you been to India to see the fakirs and yogis?'

'No, and I don't intend to.'

'Well, I have been to India and know more than you do.'

'I have not been to India, but what I do know is that you are a fraud.'

'Fraud! Huh!'

'Charlatan! Humbug!'

'I say, Aziz!' With a swift movement Hajji Musa clutched Aziz Khan's wrist.

'You are just a big-talker and one day I shall shut your mouth for you.'

'Fraud! Crook! You are a disgrace to Islam. You with your chillies and jinn!'

'Sister . . .!' This remark Hajji Musa uttered in Gujarati.

'Why don't you walk over the fire? It's an unreal fire.' And Aziz laughed sardonically.

'Yes, let him walk,' said the watchmaker. 'Hajji Musa big-talker.'

'The fire is not as hot as any of your jinn, Hajji Musa,' Dolly said slyly, with an ironic chuckle.

'Dolly, anyone can walk on fire if he knows the trick.'

'I suppose you know,' Aziz said tauntingly.

'Of course I do.'

'Then why don't you walk over the fire?'

'Jinn are hotter!' Dolly exclaimed.

'Fraud! Hypocrite! Degraded infidel, you will never walk. I dare you!'

'I will show you, you fool. I will show you what I can do.'

'What can you show but your lying tongue, and beat up little girls!'

'You sister . . .! I will walk.'

While the argument had been raging, many people had gathered around them and ceased to look at the Hindu fire-walker. Now, when Hajji Musa accepted the challenge, he was applauded.

Hajji Musa removed his shoes and socks and rolled up his trousers. All eyes in the yard were now focused on him. Some shouted words of encouragement and others clapped their hands. Mr Darsot, though, tried to dissuade him.

'Hajji Musa, I don't think you should attempt walking on fire.'

But Dolly shouted in his raucous voice:

'Hajji Musa, show them what you are made of!'

Hajji Musa, determined and intrepid, went towards the

fire. The Hindu fire-walker was now resting for a while, his body and clothes wet with sweat and juice from broken coconuts, and the chanters' voices were low. When Hajji Musa reached the fire he faltered. His body tensed with fear. Cautiously he lifted his right foot over the glowing mass. But any thought he might have had of retreat, of giving up Aziz Khan's challenge and declaring himself defeated, was dispelled by the applause he received.

Crying out in a voice that was an invocation to God to save him, he stepped on the inferno:

'Allah is great!'

What happened to Hajji Musa was spoken of long afterwards. Badly burnt, he was dragged out of the fire, drenched with water and smothered with rags, and taken to hospital.

We went to visit him. We expected to find a man humiliated, broken. We found him sitting up in bed, swathed in bandages, but as ebullient and resilient as always, with a bevy of young nurses eagerly attending to him.

'Boys, I must say fire-walking is not for me. Showmanship . . . that's for magicians and crowd-pleasers . . . those seeking cheap publicity.'

And he laughed in his usual way until the hospital corridors resounded.

J. M. COETZEE

THE GLASS ABATTOIR

ONE

HE IS WOKEN in the early hours of the morning by the telephone. It is his mother. He is used by now to these late-night calls: she keeps eccentric hours and thinks the rest of the world keeps eccentric hours too.

'How much do you think it would cost, John, to build an abattoir? Not a big one, just a model, as a demonstration.'

'A demonstration of what?'

'A demonstration of what goes on in an abattoir. Slaughter. It occurred to me that people tolerate the slaughter of animals only because they get to see none of it. Get to see, get to hear, get to smell. It occurred to me that if there were an abattoir operating in the middle of the city, where everyone could see and smell and hear what goes on inside it, people might change their ways. A glass abattoir. An abattoir with glass walls. What do you think?'

'You are speaking of a real abattoir, with real animals being slaughtered, experiencing real death?'

'Real, all of it. As a demonstration.'

'I don't think there is the faintest chance that you would get permission to build such a thing. Not the faintest. Aside from the fact that people don't want to be reminded of how the food comes to be on their plate, there is the question of blood. When you cut an animal's throat, blood gushes out. Blood is sticky and messy. It attracts flies. No local authority will tolerate rivers of blood in their city.'

'There won't be rivers of blood. It will just be a

demonstration abattoir. A handful of killings per day. An ox, a pig, half a dozen chickens. They could make a deal with a restaurant nearby. Fresh-killed meat.'

'Drop the idea, Mother. You won't get anywhere with it.'

Three days later a package arrives in the mail. It contains a mass of papers: pages torn out of newspapers; photocopies; a journal in his mother's handwriting labelled 'Journal 1990–1995'; some stapled-together documents. There is a brief covering note: 'When you have time, glance over this stuff and tell me if you think something can be made of it.'

One of the documents is called 'The Glass Abattoir'. It starts with words attributed to someone named Keith Thomas. As early as the Middle Ages, says Thomas, municipal authorities in Europe began to regard the slaughter of animals in public as an offensive nuisance and took steps to remove the shambles to outside the town walls.

The words *offensive nuisance* are underlined in ink.

He skims through the document. It contains a more fully elaborated proposal for the abattoir his mother had described on the telephone, with a plan of its layout. Pinned to the plan are photographs of hangar-like buildings, presumably an existing abattoir. In the middle distance is a truck of the kind used for transporting livestock, empty and without a driver.

He calls his mother. It is four in the afternoon here, nine in the evening there, a civilized time for both of them. 'The papers you sent have arrived,' he says. 'Can you tell me what I am supposed to do with them?'

'I was in a panic when I sent them,' his mother says. 'It struck me that if I were to die tomorrow, the cleaning-woman from the village might sweep everything off my desk and burn it. So I packed the papers up and sent them to you.

You can ignore them. The panic is over. It is perfectly normal to have accesses of dread as one grows older.'

'So there is nothing wrong, Mother, nothing I ought to know about? Nothing but a passing access of dread?'

'Nothing.'

TWO

THE SAME EVENING he picks up the journal and leafs through it. It starts with several pages of prose headed 'Djibouti 1990'. He settles down to read.

'I am in Djibouti in north-east Africa,' he reads. 'On a visit to the market I watch a young man, very tall, like most people in this part of the world, naked above the waist, bearing in his arms a handsome young goat. The goat, which is pure white, sits peacefully there, gazing around, enjoying the ride.

'Behind the market stalls is an area where the earth and stones are stained dark red, almost black, with blood. Nothing grows there, not a weed, not a blade of grass. It is the slaughter-place, where goats and sheep and poultry are killed. It is to this slaughter-place that the man is bringing his goat.

'I do not follow them. I know what happens there: I have seen it already and have no wish to see it again. The young man will gesture to one of the slaughter-men, who will take the goat from him and hold the body to the ground, gripping the four legs tightly. The young man will take the knife from the scabbard that slaps against his thigh and without preamble slit the goat's throat, then watch while the body convulses and the life-blood pumps out.

'When the goat is finally still he will chop off his head,

slit open his abdomen, pull out his inner organs into the tin basin that the slaughter-man will hold, run a wire through his hocks, hang him from the convenient pole, and peel off his skin. Then he will cut him in half, lengthwise, and bring the two halves, plus the head with its open but glazed eyes, to the market itself, where on a good day these physical remains will fetch nine hundred Djiboutian francs or five US dollars.

'Conveyed to the home of its buyer, the body will be cut into small pieces and roasted over coals, while the head will be boiled in a cauldron. What is not found to be edible, principally the bones, will be thrown to the dogs. And that will be the end. Of the goat as he was in the pride of his days no trace will remain. It will be as if he had never existed. No one will remember him save myself – a stranger who happened to see him, and happened to be seen by him, on his way to his death.

'That stranger, who has not forgotten him, now turns to his shade and asks two questions. First: *What were you thinking as you rode to market that morning in your master's arms? Did you really not know where he was taking you? Could you not smell the blood? Why did you not struggle to escape?*

'And the second question is: *What do you think was going on in that young man's mind as he carried you to market – you whom he had known since the day you were born, who were one of the flock he led out to forage every morning and brought home every evening? Did he breathe any word of apology for what he was about to do to you?*

'Why do I ask these questions? Because I want to understand what you and your brothers and sisters think of the deal that your forefathers struck with humankind many generations ago. In terms of that deal, humankind undertook to protect you against your natural enemies, the lion and the jackal. In return your forefathers undertook that, when the time came, they would yield up their bodies to their protectors to be devoured; furthermore, that their progeny unto the hundredth and the thousandth generation would do the same.

'It strikes me as a bad deal, weighted too heavily against your tribe. If I were a goat I would prefer to take my chance with the lions and the jackals. But I am not a goat and do not know how a goat's mind works. Perhaps it is the way of the goat to think, *The fate that befell my parents and grandparents may not befall me*. Perhaps the way of the goat is to live in hope.

'Or perhaps a goat's mind does not work at all. We must take that possibility seriously, as certain philosophers do – human philosophers. The goat does not think, properly speaking, philosophers say. Whatever mentation occurs within the goat, if we had access to it, would be unrecognizable to us, alien, incomprehensible. Hope, expectation, foreboding – these are forms of mentation unknown to the goat. If the goat kicks and struggles at the very end, when the knife comes out, it is not because he has suddenly understood that his life is about to end. It is a simple reactive aversion to the overwhelming smell of blood, to the stranger who grips his feet and holds him down.

'Of course it is hard, if you are not a philosopher, to believe that a goat, a creature who seems so like us in so many ways, can go through life from beginning to end without thinking. One consequence is that, when it comes to the matter of abattoirs, we in the enlightened West do our best to preserve the ignorance of the goat or the sheep or the pig or the ox as long as is possible, trying to keep it from being alarmed until finally, as it sets foot on the killing floor and sees the blood-splashed stranger with the knife, alarm becomes unavoidable. Ideally we would want the beast to be stunned – its mind incapacitated – so that it will never ever grasp what is going on. So that it will not realize that the time has arrived for it to pay up, to fulfil its part of the immemorial deal. So that its last moments on earth shall not be filled with doubt and confusion and terror. So that it will die, as we put it, "without suffering".

'The males in the herds of animals we own are routinely castrated. Being castrated without anaesthetic is a great deal more painful than having your throat cut, and the pain endures far longer, yet no one creates a song and dance about castration. What is it, then, that we find unacceptable about the pain of death? More specifically, if we are prepared to inflict death on the other, why do we wish to save the other from pain? What is it that is unacceptable to us about inflicting the pain of dying, on top of death itself?

'In English there exists the word *squeamish*, which my Spanish dictionary translates as *aprensivo*. In English, *squeamish* forms a contrastive pair with *soft-hearted*. A person who does not like to see a beetle being squashed can be called either soft-hearted or squeamish depending on whether you admire that person's sympathy for the beetle or find it silly. When workers in abattoirs discuss animal-welfare people, people who are concerned that the animal's last moments on earth should be without pain or terror, they call them squeamish, not soft-hearted. They are generally contemptuous of such people. *Death is death*, say the abattoir workers.

'*Would you like your own last moments on earth to be filled with pain and terror?* the animal-rights people demand of the abattoir workers. *We are not animals*, reply the abattoir workers. *We are human beings. It is not the same for us as for them.*'

THREE

HE PUTS THE journal aside and looks through the rest of the documents, most of which seem to be book reviews or essays on various writers. The shortest is entitled 'Heidegger'. He has never read Heidegger but has heard he is impenetrably difficult. What does his mother have to say about Heidegger?

'Concerning animals, Heidegger observes that their access to the world is limited or deprived: the German word he uses is *arm*, poor. Their access is not just poor in comparison with ours, it is absolutely poor. Though he makes this claim about animals in general, there is reason to believe that when he made this observation he had such creatures as ticks or fleas specifically in mind.

'By *poor* he seems to mean that the animal's world-experience has to be limited, by comparison with ours, because the animal cannot act autonomously, can only respond to stimuli. The tick's senses may be alive, but they are alive only to certain stimuli, for instance the odour in the air or the tremor in the ground that betrays the approach of a warm-blooded creature. To the rest of the world the tick may as well be deaf and blind. That is why, in Heidegger's language, the tick is *weltarm*, poor in world.

'What of me? I can think my way into a dog's being, or so I believe; but can I think my way into the being of a tick? Can I share the intensity of the tick's awareness, as its senses strain to smell or hear the approach of its desire? Do I want to follow Heidegger and measure the thrilling, single-minded intensity of the tick's awareness against my own dispersed human consciousness that flits continually from one object to another? Which is the better? Which would I prefer? Which would Heidegger himself prefer?

'Heidegger had a famous or notorious affair with Hannah Arendt while she was a student of his. In his letters to her, those that have survived, he says not a word about their intimacies. Nevertheless I ask: what was Heidegger seeking through Hannah, or through any other of his mistresses, if it was not that moment when consciousness concentrates itself in thrilling, single-minded intensity before being extinguished?

'I am trying to be fair to Heidegger. I am trying to learn from him. I am trying to get a grasp on his difficult German words, his difficult German thoughts.

'Heidegger says that to the animal (for instance the tick) the world consists, on the one hand, of certain stimuli (smells, sounds), and on the other hand of all that which is not a stimulus and therefore may as well not exist. For this reason we can think of the animal (the tick) as enslaved – enslaved not to smells and sounds themselves but to an appetite for the blood whose proximity the smells and sounds signal.

'Total enslavement to appetite is patently not true of higher animals, which exhibit a curiosity about the world around them that extends well beyond the objects of their appetite. But I want to avoid talk of higher and lower. I want to understand this man Heidegger, towards whom I float the web of my own curiosity, like a spider.

'Because it is enslaved to its appetites, says Heidegger, the animal cannot act in and on the world, properly speaking: it can only *behave*, and furthermore can behave only within the world that is defined by the extent, the reach, of its senses. The animal cannot apprehend the other as and in itself; the other can never reveal itself to the animal as what it is.

'Why is it that, every time that I (like a spider) send out my mind trying to grasp Heidegger, I see him in bed with his hot-blooded student, the two of them naked under one of those capacious German eiderdowns on a rainy Thursday afternoon in Württemberg? Coitus is completed; they lie side by side, she listening while he talks, on and on, about the animal to whom the world is either a stimulus, a tremor in the earth or a whiff of sweat, or else nothing, blankness, inexistence. He talks, she listens, trying to understand him, full of goodwill towards her teacher-lover.

'Only to us, he says, does the world reveal itself as it is.

'She turns towards him and touches him, and suddenly he is full of blood again; he cannot have enough of her, his appetite for her is unquenchable.'

That is all. That is the abrupt end of his mother's three-page Heidegger piece. He hunts through the papers, but there is no fourth page.

On an impulse he telephones her. 'I have been reading your piece on Heidegger. I found it interesting, but what is it? Is it fiction? A piece of abandoned work? What am I supposed to make of it?'

'I suppose you can call it abandoned work,' his mother replies. 'It started seriously, then it changed. That is the trouble with most of the stuff I write nowadays. It starts as one thing and ends as another.'

'Mother,' he says, 'I am not a writer, as you know very well, nor am I an expert on Heidegger. If you sent me your story about Heidegger in the hope that I would tell you what to do with it, I am sorry to say I can't help.'

'But don't you think there is the germ of something there? The man who thinks the tick's experience of the world is impoverished, worse than impoverished, who thinks the tick has no awareness of the world beyond incessantly sniffing the air as it waits for a source of blood to arrive, yet who hungers, himself, for those moments of ecstasy when his awareness of the world shrinks to nothing and he loses himself in mindless sensual transports . . .? Do you not see the irony?'

'I do, Mother. I do see the irony. But is the point you are making not a trite one? Let me spell it out for you. Unlike insects, we human beings have a divided nature. We have animal appetites but we also have reason. We would like to live a life of reason – Heidegger would like to live a life of reason, Hannah Arendt would like to live a life of reason – but sometimes we cannot, because sometimes we are overtaken by our appetites. We are overtaken and we give in, we surrender. Then, when our appetites are satisfied, we return to the life of reason. What more is there to say than that?'

'It depends, my boy, it depends. Can we speak like grown-ups, you and I? Can we speak as if we both know what is meant by the life of the senses?'

'Go ahead.'

'Think about the moment in question, the moment when you are alone with the truly beloved, the truly desired. Think of the moment of consummation. Where is what you call reason at that moment? Is it utterly obliterated, and are we indistinguishable at that moment from the tick engorged with blood? Or, behind it all, does the spark of reason still glimmer, unextinguished, biding its time, waiting to flare up again, waiting for the moment when you separate yourself from the body of the beloved and resume your own life? If the latter, what has it done with itself, this spark of reason, while the body has been away, disporting itself? Has it been waiting impatiently to reassert itself; or has it on the contrary been filled with melancholy, wanting to expire, to die, but not knowing how? Because – speaking as one adult to another – is it not that which inhibits our consummations – that persistent little flickering of reason, of rationality? We want to dissolve into our animal nature but we cannot.'

'Therefore?'

'Therefore I think about this man Martin Heidegger who wants to be proud of being a man, *ein Mensch*, who tells us how he creates a world about him, *weltbildend*, how we can be like him, *weltbildend* too, but who actually is not sure, through and through, that he wants to be *ein Mensch*, who has moments when he wonders whether, in the larger perspective, it might not be better to be a dog or a flea and surrender yourself to the torrent of being.'

'The torrent of being. You have left me behind. What is that? Explain.'

'The torrent. The flood. Heidegger has intimations of what that experience would be like, the experience of the torrent of being, but he resists them. Instead he calls it an impoverished experience of being. He calls it impoverished because it is unvaried. What a joke! He sits at his desk and writes and writes. *Das Tier benimmt sich in einer Umgebung, aber nie in einer Welt*: the animal acts (or behaves) within an environment but never within a world. He lifts his pen. There is a knock at the door. It is the knock he has been listening for all the while he has been writing, his senses alert to it. Hannah! The beloved! He tosses the pen aside. She has come! His desire is here!'

'And?'

'That is all. I haven't been able to take it any further. All the stuff I sent you is like that. I can't take it to the next step. Something is lacking in me. I used to be able to take things to the next step, but I no longer seem to have it in me, that ability. The cogs are seizing up, the lights are going out. The mechanism that I used to rely on to take me to the next step no longer seems to work. Don't be alarmed. It is nature – nature's way of telling me it is time to come home.

'That's another experience Martin Heidegger wasn't

prepared to reflect on: the experience of being dead, of not being present in the world. It's an experience all of its own. I could tell him about it if he were here – at least about its early manifestations.'

FOUR

A DAY LATER he leafs through his mother's journal again, settles on the last entry, dated July 1, 1995.

'Yesterday I went to a lecture by a man named Gary Steiner. He spoke about Descartes and the continuing influence of Descartes on our way of thinking about animals, even the more enlightened among us. (Descartes, one recalls, said that human beings have rational souls while animals do not. From which it followed that while animals are capable of feeling pain they are incapable of suffering. According to Descartes, pain is an unpleasant physical sensation which triggers an automatic response, a cry or a howl; whereas suffering is a different matter, on a higher plane, the plane of the human.)

'I found the lecture interesting. But then Professor Steiner started to go into detail about Descartes' anatomical experiments, and suddenly I could bear it no longer. He described an experiment that Descartes carried out on a live rabbit, which I presume was strapped down to a board or nailed to it so that it could not move. Descartes opened the rabbit's chest with a scalpel, snipping off the ribs one by one and removing them to expose the beating heart. Then he made a little incision in the heart itself, and for a second or two, before the heart stopped beating, was able to observe the system of valves by means of which the blood is pumped.

'I listened to Professor Steiner and then I stopped

listening. My mind went elsewhere. I wanted urgently to fall to my knees; but we were in a lecture theatre with the seats very close to each other so that there was no space to kneel. "Excuse me, excuse me," I said to my neighbours, and worked my way out of the auditorium. In the foyer, which was empty, I was at last able to kneel and ask for pardon, on my own behalf, on Mr Steiner's behalf, on René Descartes' behalf, on behalf of all our murderous gang. There was a song hammering in my ears, an old prophecy:

> A dog starved at his master's gate
> Predicts the ruin of the state.
> A horse misused upon the road
> Calls to heaven for human blood.
> Each outcry from the hunted hare
> A fibre from the brain does tear . . .
> He who shall hurt the little wren
> Shall never be beloved by men . . .
> Kill not the moth nor butterfly
> For the Last Judgment draweth nigh.

'The Last Judgment! What mercy will Descartes' rabbit, martyred in the cause of science three hundred and seventy-eight years ago this year, and in God's hands since that day with his torn-open breast, show toward us? What mercy do we deserve?'

He, John, the son of the woman who fell on her knees in July of 1995 and asked for forgiveness, and then afterwards wrote the words he has just read, takes out his pen. At the foot of the page he writes: 'A fact about rabbits, attested by science. When the fox's jaws close on the rabbit's neck, it goes into a state of shock. Nature has so arranged it, or God, if you prefer to speak of God, has so arranged it, that the fox can tear open the rabbit's belly and feed on his innards and the rabbit will feel nothing, nothing at all. No pain, no suffering.' He underlines the words *A fact about rabbits*.

His mother has given no indication that she wants her journal back. But destiny is inscrutable. Maybe he will be the earlier of the two to die, struck down as he crosses the street. Then *she*, for a change, will have to read *his* thoughts.

FIVE

HE HAS COME to the end of his reading. It is one in the morning here, six in the morning there. His mother is very likely still asleep. Nevertheless, he picks up the telephone.

He has a prepared speech. 'Thank you for sending the packet of documents, Mother. I have read through most of them, and I believe I see what you would like me to do. You would like me to hammer these miscellaneous pieces of writing into shape, make them fit together in some way. But you know as well as I do that I have no gift for that kind of thing. So tell me, what is this really all about? Is there something you are afraid to tell me? I know it is early in the morning, I apologize for that, but please be open with me. Is something wrong?'

There is a long silence. When at last his mother speaks, her voice is perfectly clear, perfectly lucid.

'Very well, I will tell you. I am not myself, John. Something is happening to me, to my mind. I forget things. I cannot concentrate. I have seen my doctor. He wants me to go in to the city for tests. I have made an appointment with a neurologist. But in the meantime I am trying to put my life in order, just in case.

'I can't begin to describe the mess on my desk. What I

sent you is only a fraction of it. If something happens to me the cleaning-woman will throw it all in the trash. Which is perhaps what it deserves. But in my vain human way I persist in thinking that something of value can be made of it. Does that answer your question?'

'What do you think is wrong with you?'

'I don't know for sure. As I said, I forget things. I forget myself. I find myself in the street and I don't know why I am there or how I got there. Sometimes I even forget who I am. An eerie experience. I feel I am losing my mind. Which is only to be expected. The brain, being matter, deteriorates, and since the mind is not unconnected with the brain, the mind deteriorates too. That is how things are with me, in summary. I can't work, can't think in a larger way. If you decide you can't do anything with the papers, never mind, just put them somewhere safe.

'But while I have you, let me tell you what happened last night.

'There was a programme on television about factory farming. Normally I don't watch such things, but this time for some reason I didn't switch off.

'The programme featured an industrial hatchery for chickens – a place where they fertilize eggs en masse, hatch them artificially, and sex the chicks.

'The routine goes as follows. On the second day of their life, when they are capable of standing on their own two feet, the chicks are fed onto a conveyor belt, which moves them slowly past workers whose job it is to examine their sex organs. If you turn out to be female, you are transferred to a box for dispatch to the egg-laying plant, where you will spend your productive life as a layer. If you are male you stay on the conveyor belt. At the end of the conveyor belt you are tipped down a chute. At the bottom of the chute are a pair of toothed wheels that grind you into a paste, which is then chemically sterilized and turned into cattle-feed or fertilizer.

'The camera, last night, followed one particular little chick in his progress along the conveyor belt. *So this is life!* you could see him saying to himself. *Confusing, but not too challenging thus far*. A pair of hands lifted him, parted the fluff between his thighs, replaced him on the belt. *Lots of tests!* he said to himself. *I seem to have passed that one*. The belt rolled on. Bravely he rode it, confronting the future and all that the future contained.

'I can't put the image out of my mind, John. All those billions of chicks who are born into this beautiful world and are by our grace allowed to live for one day before being ground to a paste because they are the wrong sex, because they don't fit the business plan.

'For the most part, I don't know what I believe any longer. What beliefs I used to have seem to have been overtaken by the fog and confusion in my head. Nevertheless, I cling to one last belief: that the little chick who appeared to me on the screen last night appeared for a reason, he and the other negligible beings whose paths have crossed mine on the way to their respective deaths.

'It is for them that I write. Their lives were so brief, so easily forgotten. I am the sole being in the universe who still remembers them, if we leave God aside. After I am gone there will be only blankness. It will be as if they had never existed. That is why I wrote about them, and why I wanted you to read about them. To pass on the memory of them, to you. That is all.'

JEAN PLIYA

THE WATCH-NIGHT

[*To the memory of Prosper Pliya, my father, who was also a guide and friend.*]

WHEN I WAS ten years old, the man I most admired was Zannu. On moonless nights, in a town without any kind of public lighting system, he watched over our sleep, facing a thousand dangers. It was said that armed only with a simple club, he could challenge thieves, defy wild animals and even meet evil spirits without fear or trembling. His self-confidence impressed me so greatly that I decided to get to the bottom of it.

The opportunity offered itself one evening at bedtime. I had just stretched out on a mat beside my little brother David and was whistling the catchy tune of a song learnt at school when my aunt Gussi abruptly entered the room.

'So you are the careless fellow who whistles at night! You'll attract poisonous snakes. Don't you know that they embody dangerous spirits or jinn?'

I stopped whistling at once and sat up, my heart throbbing. My aunt put up the wick of the night-lamp and looked at me sternly.

'But it's not true, auntie. You only want to scare me.'

'Too bad for you,' she said. 'Anyway, if you start again, I'll leave you right this minute.'

'No, please, I won't whistle any more. Say, auntie, why do spirits only come out at night?'

'Would you like to see them?'

'Oh no!'

This set me musing and I looked at my aunt, a short plumpish woman with teeth turned yellow by tobacco. She snorted, took up an end of the wrapper she was wearing and blew her big nose in it. She sat down on the mat and stretched out her legs, obviously delighted to be able to contribute her share to my education. She was convinced that at school I was left in ignorance about the most venerable traditions.

'Auntie,' I started again, 'why don't the spirits do any harm to Zannu? I have heard him whistle at night.'

She smiled with amusement and her fingers rumpled my hair. 'Zannu is a strong man,' she replied, lowering her voice. 'He owns charms and wears juju rings on his fingers.'

'Even with these rings I would still be scared to see the spirits.'

'Not all spirits are evil,' my aunt explained. 'The ones called *aziza* can even become friendly. They may, for example, tell us the secret of plants which make you invisible or change a man into a snake or a lion.'

I listened to my aunt open-mouthed, thinking of Zannu's mysterious powers. Like the ghosts this man slept in the daytime and roamed the dark lanes at night. I was so impressed I even forgot to ask whether his body had ever been found after having been transformed into an animal. I did not doubt for a single moment that such an operation was possible. From then on I made it a point to seek Zannu's company.

On Wednesday and Saturday nights, the eves of days of rest, I would sit by his side on the trunk of the silk-cotton tree which ran horizontally along the enclosing wall. Initially I trembled at the idea that Zannu, calm as he was, might turn into a roaring lion. I would sit down a bit away from him. I would greet Zannu. He would answer with a grunt. I was happy with this token of interest. Once I dared ask him to tell me a story. He kept silent for a moment. By the light of his lamp I watched his neat profile, his greying hair, his loincloth of indigo blue. He was not looking at me. Besides, I wouldn't have been able to stand the flash of his strange eyes.

'Won't you be afraid?' he asked with a faint smile. I drew closer to him and answered 'No' but my voice was shaking slightly. Since then, what marvellous tales I have heard! The stories he told me with a voice soft as a cradle-song frightened me so much that I no longer dared to go alone from the gate to our bedroom.

Seeing me hesitate, Zannu would take me by the hand and lead me. In spite of his presence and the hurricane lamp at the back of the shed where the bags of palm-kernels were stored, I would walk on tiptoe, afraid to see the characters from his tales rise before me: the old leprosy-stricken sorceress sitting half-naked on the river bank, who compels people to wash her back eaten up with scaly sores; the phantom draped in a white shroud; the emaciated masses in times of famine; Yogbo the glutton, the trickster of the prying look. And yet I would never tire of these terrifying stories. They bound me to Zannu and formed the basis of our friendship.

One night, after having accompanied me back, Zannu returned to sit down on the trunk of the silk-cotton tree. Some time later he got up. Holding his left hand on the small of his back, the right arm pointing towards the sky, he stretched himself at length with his back arched and his chest thrust out. He took three puffs from his clay pipe and with his index finger pressed down the half-consumed tobacco; then he grabbed his oversized club and started walking up and down under the mango tree whose highest branches brushed against the roof of our house.

We lived opposite the market of Athieme on the main street which led to the Mono river. My father's shop occupied the ground floor.

Zannu did his sentry-go, coming and going with a springy gait. His club hit the ground at regular intervals. The furnace of his pipe made a hole in the night like glowing embers flying slowly through the air. The watch-night sat down again, squeezing his weapon between his knees and leaning the back of his neck against the rough wall. The thick foliage of the mango tree stirred in the night breeze. In the small, sleeping town only the indefatigable dogs roamed under the market-sheds, their claws clicking on the concrete floor. An attentive ear would also have caught the chirping of crickets.

Suddenly a hooting rent the night. Zannu raised his eyes and for a fraction of a second he saw up there, between the mango tree and the eaves of corrugated iron sheets, two spread wings which disappeared at once. He heard a rustle like the folding of a silk fan. He murmured these strange words, 'Accursed be thy father, accursed thy mother. My flesh is too salty for you to taste. Return to where you come from, bird of ill omen!'

It was the fifth time in a row that this owl had emerged about midnight, flying on noiseless wings, had hooted, performed the same manoeuvre and then faded into the night. The watch-night suspected that it might be perched on the tree. To drive it away, he picked up a handful of pebbles which he threw at it. Nothing stirred. The long leaves of the mango tree rustled gently.

The following morning, Zannu informed my father of the incident. My father thought it ridiculous to worry about a simple bird flying over our house. But the watch-night stated calmly that the owl was nesting under the roof and that it would bring bad luck. My father rubbed his bald head and frowned. As a matter of fact strange noises had been disturbing us in our sleep for some time. It sounded as if a sharp talon was scratching the ceiling. I would stare into the dark, cock my ears and tremble with fright. Daddy had simply declared that it was the dancing of mice. In the end, to calm my fears, he ordered the watch-night to clean out the loft.

For my small brother and myself this was like a feast. We hoped to make extraordinary discoveries up there. Zannu put a bamboo ladder against the wall in a corner of our room and up he went. He drew the nails from some battens and loosened a length of plywood. Mouse droppings, dead cockroaches and grey dust fell down on our hair. Proud to help Zannu we hung on to the ladder, making sure not to look up. As soon as the watch-night had disappeared, I told David not to leave go of the ladder and I climbed up in turn. The spacious loft smelt musty. This smell of old things went to my head. I shied away from the darkness but gradually I could make out Zannu squatting near a box.

'What is it?' I asked. 'What have you got?'

My heart pounded in my chest. Zannu kept silent. A little further away, two rays of sunlight filtered through the roof. Zannu pushed the box into the bright patch of light. Amid broken shells, bird droppings and dried herbs three grotesque-looking little birds were wobbling about. They opened their big yellow beaks set between enormous round eyes. Carcasses of lizards and rats crackled under their feet. Zannu held out to me one of those unshapely packets of straw-yellow down. I shrank back.

'Don't be afraid,' he said. 'It's a little owl.'

Abruptly I made an about-turn and went tumbling down

the ladder. I hurried down into the yard where I made a muddled report to my brother. Without understanding the reason for my terror he was alarmed. Soon Zannu brought along the whole brood, chirping desperately. A terrified David opened his eyes wide and turned away crying. My father ordered the birds to be destroyed. Zannu threw them into the pit-latrine which had been dug in a corner of the compound.

In the evening of that same day panic struck our home. David complained of a violent headache and had to be put to bed. I did not know what to think of to bring him relief. He refused the toys and goodies I brought for him. His body was racked with fever. My mother gave him aspirin tablets and plenty of herb tea. Aunt Gussi, silent and surly, shrugged her shoulders but then started pestering Mummy with questions.

'Do you really think the white man's medicine will cure the little one? We ought to try something else.'

'But what, for heaven's sake?' our mother once asked, out of all patience.

My aunt cast a stealthy glance at the door and replied, 'The whites don't know how to cure all the diseases of the blacks. We ought to consult . . .'

Suddenly she fell silent. My father was coming. Aunt Gussi went out at once.

Despite our watchful care, David's state of health grew worse from day to day. The doctor came to examine him and diagnosed acute anaemia, but he was unable to tell the cause. One evening my aunt could not stand it any longer and invited me to accompany her to a native doctor in a part of town called Gbeji.

'The important thing is to hurry,' she added in a confidential tone of voice. 'Your father is not supposed to see us.'

How proud I was of the trust she put in me! I was ready for the escapade in no time. My aunt draped a wrapper over her shoulders and we left. We walked straight ahead into the darkness, brushing human shapes which emerged and vanished like phantoms. Ten minutes later we entered a vast compound consisting of thatched huts. We made for an impressive dwelling; a woman asked us to wait and went in to announce us. As soon as she came back, we were ushered in. Our guide asked us to take a seat and she put her oil-lamp near us. I thought I heard somebody stir at the back of the room which was in complete darkness. I looked around me, seized with great curiosity.

The hut with its walls blackened by smoke was cluttered up with a medley of objects. On the floor, a mat woven of reeds and jars for decoctions; on the wall, above our heads, a buffalo horn and a black bottle with cowrie shells round its neck and a red parrot feather stuck inside. Bundles of firewood, empty palm-nut shells, bunches of dry leaves and others of roots were piled up in a corner. A little farther away a matchet, a broom and corn-cobs were lying around.

Our wait dragged on.

'Where is the herbalist?' I challenged my aunt. She seemed to be in a pensive mood and simply squeezed my arm.

Just at that moment the wrapper which served as a curtain was pushed aside and I saw a stocky little man with a lamp in his hand. The yellow flame danced deep down in his eyes. I could not take my eyes off this apparition. His big head capped with white hair was bent towards his chest and gave his body a stooping carriage. In his pock-marked face the veins stood out under the skin of the temples and crawled as far as his eyelids. An enormous wrapper girded his loins, formed a voluminous knot below the abdomen and fell in disorderly folds.

After the usual salutations my aunt was just about to explain the purpose of her visit when the old man interrupted her with a gesture and took a double sack of tanned leather from the wall. He sat down cross-legged on the mat, arranged his diviner's gear and set his hand to consulting the oracle. He rubbed a small board of white wood with china clay and washed his hands in a decoction of basil leaves. With his left hand he took a handful of polished palm-nuts. With the other he held out a *bonduc* fruit to my aunt. She put it close to her mouth, murmured some indistinct questions and returned it to him. The diviner fingered the sacred nuts for a brief spell and then traced on the board small vertical lines, either simple or double, running from the upper to the lower part, with his index and second fingers. When he had interpreted the pattern thus obtained, he declared that a spell had been cast on a child of our family. The guilty party, one of our relatives, he specified, was taking revenge for a wrong suffered at our hands.

'My God, how can we save my nephew?' my aunt asked.

'Does he suffer from colic?' the native doctor inquired.

'No, but from a terrible headache. He has lost a lot of weight.'

'That means that the illness is benign. In serious cases the sorcerers have a way of causing violent colics before changing their victim into a domestic animal. Once that stage is reached, absolutely nothing can be done.'

I uttered a cry of terror.

'Well, that's the way it is, little one. The wickedness of man is boundless. At any rate, Gussi, follow my prescriptions faithfully.'

The native doctor handed to my aunt a small bottle of green powder, as well as a mixture of dried leaves and roots. The powder was to be put into incisions on David's chest, back, and both calves. The dried leaves and the roots would be boiled down and the liquid put into his bath water. My aunt paid the native doctor and we hurriedly returned home.

Despite our various precautions my father found out about the new remedies. But he did not protest, seeming resigned to trying anything that might save David. Soon, in fact, my little brother regained his former cheerfulness.

Three weeks after this event, I was coming from the river in glaring sunlight when I noticed from afar an unusual crowd around the big mango tree. What kind of attraction could it be that had thus drained the whole market? I broke into a swift gallop and mixed with the crowd of idlers and market traders. All were looking up to the top branches. Using my elbows I soon found myself next to my aunt Gussi.

'What's going on?' I asked.

'It's an owl. Look there, in a fork!' No matter how hard I stared, I saw nothing. Finally, when I followed the direction of my aunt's index finger pointing towards the tree-top, I caught sight of an oblong, light brown form, a cat's head with outsized pupils, bearing two crests of feathers, the ear-tufts, which moved gently as if wafted by the wind. The shadow of the foliage half hid the motionless bird. How did it happen to get there and why didn't it escape? The jostling of the crowd had reached its climax; I heard a small boy starting to yell. I recognized David's voice. Somebody had stepped on his foot. I cleared a way for myself till I got to him and dragged him to the side. My father called me. I managed to join him with some difficulty.

'Do you know where Zannu lives?' he asked.

'Yes, Daddy.'

'Fetch him for me. He will have to catch that owl!'

I ran at breakneck speed, crossed a bridge and arrived out of breath in front of a house which overlooked the bank of a tributary of the Mono river. I lifted the latch and pushed one of the sides of the front gate. A stone attached to a bicycle chain was hanging on the other side. I had to lean my whole weight against the door to open it. The rectangular hut built of blackish-grey mud stood at the back. I gave some hurried knocks. Zannu appeared, rubbing his sleep-reddened eyes with the back of his hand.

'What's going on?' he queried.

'Come! . . . Come quickly. Daddy is asking for you. There's a big owl in our mango tree.'

'Well, I thought it was an outbreak of fire.'

I was disappointed by the coolness of his reception. I begged him to hurry up, fearing that the bird might fly away before our arrival. He turned back into the hut and took a tiny gourd from the head of his pallet of rushes. By shaking it gently he poured a pinch of powder on his palm and lapped it up. A little girl came in. Zannu told her to watch the house. He lit his pipe when we left. I had to run to keep up with him. Our feet kicked up the crunching gravel. Zannu drew puffs of smoke from his pipe at rapid intervals; they immediately dissolved into thin air.

The crowd in front of our house had grown more dense. When Zannu arrived, people stood aside for him. He emptied his pipe by knocking it against his raised left heel, stuck the stem in his belt and approached the mango tree. Using his arms and feet he climbed up as nimbly as a monkey. When he arrived near the bird of prey, Zannu hugged the tree-trunk with both legs and slowly stretched out his hand. For a moment he stopped in mid-air. The bird stirred . . . No, it was not going to fly away. The hand, which kept coming closer, ever closer, swept it off its feet. There was a disordered flapping of wings, a din of raucous shrieks drowned out by the acclamations of the crowd. White down feathers got scattered, whirling around like falling leaves. Suddenly, the crooked beak slashed the man's hand. Blood flowed at once and Zannu stifled a cry of pain. He finally managed to get hold of the wings, now powerless. The russet and fawn-coloured feathers of its cloak were all ruffled, the talons, like hinged hooks, kept clawing at empty space. The descent from the tree was child's play for Zannu.

People pressed all around him. I was out in front and could thus observe in bright daylight that terror of African nights, the legendary messenger of the sorcerers. It half-opened its golden eyes which at times were veiled by the blinking eyelids. It struggled; its short beak with its large nostrils clicked. Nobody dared touch it. Hands were stretched out jauntily but remained at a safe distance. Zannu entered our house, carrying the bird at arm's length. Aunt Gussi recommended picking up the fallen feathers. My father thought this precaution unnecessary.

'Why should we waste time on such a thing?' he objected.

'Because it's dangerous to let them lie around,' my aunt retorted.

'Stuff and nonsense! How can you believe such humbug?'

'You're joking but this is a serious matter.'

'One would think you'd turned into a sorceress yourself,' my father said jokingly.

My aunt kept silent. However, the mass of the crowd was now scattering, and people were still loudly swapping impressions. Zannu allowed some of our acquaintances to admire his catch. The women uttered shrill cries and drew back. Some people in the audience said that the bird ought to be burned. Others felt pity.

'It's time to get it done and over with,' Zannu cut them short.

He made for the frangipani with twisted branches which flowered in the courtyard. Still keeping the owl's wings apart he seized its neck and with a swift twisting motion snapped its vertebrae.

I was just coming back with some boys with the wood we had collected to make a funeral pyre when a woman trader called Ayele accosted Zannu and asked him for a feather of the bird. She kept a restaurant right in the market, selling akassa balls (corn paste made from meal mixed with water, fermented and boiled) and appetizing soup. Tattooed designs in pairs marked her forehead, temples and cheeks. Her house was next to Zannu's. Since the death of his wife the watch-night would send his only daughter, Cicavi, to buy his meals from Ayele. Zannu asked in a bantering tone, 'What are you going to do with it, my sister?'

'It seems that this feather protects one from juju,' the trader replied.

'In that case, I'd like one, too,' said a farmer who had come to sell his produce.

Aunt Gussi declared that it was imprudent to divert even the tiniest down. My father returned to the charge, 'Don't let's exaggerate, a bird's feather can't harm anyone.'

So the trader and the farmer were both given a feather. We then made a big wood fire kindled with cakes of fibre drenched in palm-oil. The brushwood crackled. The fire, fanned by the wind, started roaring and the flames leapt to heaven with a whistling sound. Zannu threw the dead bird into the blazing fire, and it immediately went up in flames. Soon it was changed into an insignificant-looking heap of ashes. Zannu scattered part of it in the compound. Each of the persons present put a pinch of it on the tip of his tongue. Aunt Gussi powdered her face with it.

But these precautions did not fully reassure me. For

Zannu, the event was nothing but a trite everyday occurrence. If one were to believe him, the last act had just been played.

At nightfall I accosted him smiling to congratulate him. He appeared preoccupied whereas I had expected to see him happy about a job well done. Keeping his eyes fixed to the ground and deeply lost in thought, he hardly answered. I left him, my heart brimful with sorrow.

When returning from school the next day I found Zannu and my father in the shop engaged in serious conversation. The moment my friend was alone, I asked him what was the matter.

'Cicavi, my daughter, is suffering from a violent attack of colic,' he replied.

'Isn't it the killed owl taking revenge?'

Zannu gave a brief, forced smile. 'One can't know straight off; it is necessary to consult the oracle,' he said as he walked away.

At noontime my father took medicines from the family medicine-chest and we set out together for Zannu's.

'I've been to see a diviner,' he told us. 'I wanted to know whether the sickness has natural causes or whether it has been provoked by an enemy. In the latter case I have to discover the culprit. But the diviner was not in and is only expected back late at night.'

In the hut Cicavi was writhing with pain. My father asked her how she felt. She was unable to reply. We had fallen silent for a while when the door opened. Ayele appeared smiling, with a hurried air.

'Good afternoon!' she called. She put down an enamelled iron pan containing dishes on a small wooden table blackened with grease.

'Zannu, I'm bringing you your meal. Why didn't your

daughter come to collect it? Just go ahead and taste my chicken soup!'

Eating was about the last thing in Zannu's thoughts at this moment. He looked at the trader with a vacant stare. My father motioned to the intruder to lower her voice. Ayele checked her high spirits and approached the girl who lay whimpering. She touched her forehead with the back of her hand and pursed her lips.

'What's the matter with her? What medicine has she taken? Has she eaten? Poor child!'

'Things look very bad,' my father said.

Ayele did not press the case further. She wished Cicavi a speedy recovery and left. Zannu made fire in a charcoal-pan and put a greenish powder in the fire. An acrid smoke filled the room. Feeling ill at ease in such an atmosphere I went out discreetly. After dinner, my father and I returned to Cicavi's bedside; her illness had grown worse. A kerosene lamp feebly lit the cracked walls.

Zannu remained seated, his elbows resting on his knees and his chin propped up on his fists. As I was incapable of keeping awake all night, I dozed off incessantly and kept yawning. My eyelids closed of their own accord. I vainly tried to stem the weight of sleep.

The native doctor arrived at two o'clock in the morning. I recognized him at once. His arrival put new life into Zannu. The doctor proceeded to consult the oracle, questioned the sacred nuts, spent a long time deciphering their mysterious augury, then shook his head from left to right. Was he going to pronounce an irrevocable sentence? To my surprise he complained about an obstinate stench of rottenness. Zannu rose and approached the table on which his meal of the previous day had been placed. He took the chicken stew which was already in a state of putrefaction and went out in a hurry. He made for an enclosure which was formed by the hedge adjoining his hut and which served as his bathroom. He dug a hole, poured the stew into it and closed it again. He stamped down the fresh earth with his heel and hurried back to the native doctor, who had just packed up his gear.

'My poor friend,' he said, addressing himself to Zannu, 'you've consulted me a little late. A witch wants to kill your daughter. She's marked you down too. Beware!'

'What woman are you speaking of?' Zannu interrupted him.

'She's a very crafty witch. Her house is nearby.'

Zannu thought for a moment. 'Really, I don't get your meaning,' he said.

'And yet the signs of the oracle are quite clear,' the native doctor insisted. His lips twitched in a bitter smile. All of a sudden Zannu clenched his fist.

'I know the witch,' he snarled. His features had hardened and his eyes were reduced to two thin slits.

'Who is it?' queried the native doctor.

'Ayele, the food seller.' Zannu was positive. 'If I hadn't given her that owl's feather, Cicavi would be safe. She even dared come here to flout me and make sure her heinous crime is working. But no silly woman is going to make game of me.'

Ayele a witch! This seemed an extravagant idea to me. But still the determination of the watch-night impressed me. Zannu, who was on such a familiar footing with the spirits, couldn't make up his mind lightly. The native doctor looked at him questioningly. My father could not hide his interest.

'Ayele isn't just anybody,' he said. 'Think twice before accusing her, Zannu. Besides, do you really think that a bird's feather holds so much importance?'

'No doubt about that,' the native doctor explained. 'If

one kills an owl serving as the messenger of a witch, she can reconstitute the bird with a single feather and pursue her deadly trade.'

'That seems highly improbable,' my father retorted. 'Listen, Zannu, try and find additional proof.'

'I'll soon furnish proof of the most convincing kind.'

'What are you going to do?'

'Defend myself,' Zannu replied with a victorious air, like a wrestler determined to win.

While an eminent native doctor, a diviner with white hair, was ready to give up, Zannu was prepared to take up the challenge. His voice vibrated like that of a captain in battle.

'It's getting late. I have to finish before daybreak. Can you bring me twin gongs, a fresh egg, and a black horse tail?'

'Certainly,' answered the native doctor who readjusted his wrapper and immediately took his leave.

Zannu, totally engrossed in his idea, went right away to the darkest corner of the hut and took down two dusty flasks hanging on pegs which had been rammed into a crack. He also took a matchet. He noticed that I was watching him with wonder.

'Bring the lamp and lend me a hand,' he said.

I jumped up and followed him. Arriving in the middle of the courtyard Zannu began digging a round hole half a metre in diameter.

'You carry on and make it deeper,' he told me, turning towards the gate. Proud to have a hand in Zannu's revenge, I went to work furiously. The dew had moistened the ground. I exerted myself so much that five minutes later I was pouring with sweat.

Zannu brought back an armful of fine lianas, the tender type, the leaves of which recoil at the slightest contact. He wove them into a crown which he arranged around the hole, then lined the hole itself with firewood and dry straw. Soon a powerful, crackling flame lit up the house.

Just at that moment the native doctor reappeared. Never had I seen Zannu so eager. However, not a muscle moved in his face. He squatted in front of the fire and poured a bit of the contents of the two flasks on it. He chewed kola and some grains of meninguette pepper, spat them against the egg, which he then slipped under the blazing fire. He planted the horse tail on the mound of fresh earth, seized the twin gongs together with a gong stick and started walking around the fire, from left to right, while reciting magic formulas.

I shuddered when the gong resounded in the silent night. With half of his body illuminated by the red glare, with the intent gaze of his eyes, his enormous shadow running after him and his hardly audible incantations, Zannu was altered beyond recognition.

The native doctor counted in a subdued voice the strokes of the gong which rang out obsessively, growing stronger and stronger, with a regular cadence, 'King go! King go!' The solemn tolling filled the night like a knell. The smoke was rising in a black column punctuated with yellow sparks. Zannu was still continuing his rounds and the gong kept sounding, thirty-one . . . thirty-two . . . thirty-three . . . Suddenly I heard an ululation just above our heads. In a split-second I was on my feet. Two grey wings were soaring in the sky. The bird described a big circle, swept round and came back at us. I recognized a huge owl with its pupils glittering like stars. Only Zannu did not raise his eyes. 'King go!' the indefatigable gong went on droning. The orbits of the bird of prey grew smaller. At the thirty-ninth stroke, he seemed to stand still at the apex of the column of smoke. The egg burst. A piece of egg-shell burnt my foot. When the gong was just about to strike for the forty-first time, Zannu uttered a cry of defiance, a cry of triumph. At the same moment the bird plummeted straight down and crashed into the flames in a shower of sparks. Zannu brandished a log and clubbed it to death with hectic, furious, irreparable blows. His face dripping with sweat looked radiant.

'Stir up the fire!' he shouted.

I could not stay put in the circumstances. I ran to collect wood but came back empty-handed. The native doctor and my father were smiling. The bird was entirely burnt up by the flames.

'And now it's the witch's turn,' Zannu decided. With two leaps he was in his room. He put the flasks back in their place and slipped on his left arm a red leather ring, a talisman of Hausa make.

'Can I go with you?' I asked Zannu.

'No,' my father cut in. 'This isn't children's business. You stay right here with the native doctor.'

In his hand he carried an electric torch with a chromium-plated casing. He switched it on, then off again. For a moment the hut was cheered up by a lively brightness. Zannu and he left. The night was already taking on a grey hue.

At Ayele's house, Zannu banged on the door with his fist several times and listened attentively. He heard moans.

'Who's there?' a voice asked as from a distance. 'Open the door quickly!'

Zannu broke open the door with a single shove. The white beam of the torch lit up an interior encumbered with dry leaves, roots and pots. A large earthenware jar covered with a wicker sieve occupied one corner. The light focused on a cadaverous face with wild-looking eyes. Lying amid dishevelled wrappers, Ayele was furiously tearing away her dressing-jacket.

'Claws are tearing at my chest. I am suffocating. Save me,' she implored them.

'What have you done to Cicavi?' Zannu asked in the voice of a dispenser of justice.

'Have pity, pity!' the woman trader begged. 'I will set her free. Listen to me, Zannu. Get a bowl and take some herb tea from that jar. I'll send my messenger to Cicavi. Hurry up, I'm dying.'

Zannu took one step but turned back all of a sudden, full of wrath. 'Who's your messenger?' he roared. 'If it's that bird, I tell you it's dead. Dead, you hear me, and reduced to ashes. And now it's your turn to croak, old slut!'

At these words the witch sat up, her features distorted by an infernal hatred. Her bent fingers clawed at his eyes with lightning speed. Zannu dodged her by jerking his head away. Ayele attacked again. The night-watchman caught her by the wrists and sent her sprawling. She winced, clutched her breast with both hands and collapsed, muttering, 'You too will die . . . You've eaten the soup . . . By the power of voodoo, by all that flies by night or crawls with its mouth full of poison, you'll die . . .' The end of her sentence was lost in a gurgling of agony. Zannu gave a sneer. 'Let's go, master! Cicavi's life is hanging on a slender thread.'

The two men walked so fast that one would have said they were running. Far away a dog howled at the passing of death. The front door closed with a bang. I hurried to meet them. From their withdrawn expressions I understood the seriousness of the moment.

'Ayele is dead,' my father said curtly.

Zannu rushed into his hut and took from a box filled with odds and ends a long flask with a shaking black liquid in it. He uncorked it. A smell of grease infected the atmosphere. He knelt on the floor near Cicavi, rubbed her body and covered her with his loin-cloth. Then he pulled her to his chest and started rocking her. For the first time I thought I could discern anxiety on his face. In a low voice I kept repeating, 'Cicavi must recover, Cicavi must recover.'

'I'm waiting for this drug to take effect,' Zannu explained. 'It comes from Nigeria. They tell me it can raise a person from the dead. If it fails, it means that my dead wife wishes to take back her daughter and that it had to happen.'

A strong rattling sound forced him into silence.

'What a terrible woman!' my father remarked. 'Just imagine her feeding the whole town! A first-rate poisoner if ever there was one.'

'This is not a question of poisoning,' the native doctor retorted, 'it's a spell. Did you see the bird perish? Its end signed the witch's death-sentence.'

'It's extraordinary,' my father admitted.

'What a stroke of good luck that I threw away yesterday's meal,' Zannu said.

'Are you saying that Ayele gave you food?' the native doctor queried.

'Of course. I buried the dish behind my hut.'

'Where exactly? You've had a narrow escape.'

'In the bathroom, right next to the hedge.'

'Stay here with your daughter,' the native doctor said. Then, turning to my father, 'Come with me.'

Zannu put Cicavi back into bed. Her body was shivering. I followed the two men. After twenty metres they stopped and began a consultation. I withdrew out of respect for them. I could not make out a word of their whispering.

Coming out of the suffocating heat, I felt the morning freshness like a soothing tonic. The day was about to break. The dawn gave way to a freshly laundered sun. The two men were still talking at the foot of a coconut palm laden with green fruit. In the palm trees stripped of their leaves and gently swaying, weaver-birds were busying themselves around their globular nests. I slowly approached the hedge, watching the talking men out of the corner of my eye. The dew was dripping from the waxy, serrated leaves. Beyond, the east was turning rosy. A cock sang out his cock-a-doodle-doo. The daybreak set half the town aglow.

I retraced my steps. Why was the native doctor concerned about the stew brought by Ayele? Did he want to check whether it was poisoned after all? But hadn't he excluded this possibility?

Meanwhile my father and he had finished their conversation. They finally made for the bathroom, with me at their heels. The slimy, blackish earth was sodden. Water whitened by the lather of soap stagnated in the gutter. One could immediately detect in a corner the place where the earth had been freshly turned. The native doctor tore a stick from the fence and used it to reopen the hole. My father and I bent forward, our hands resting on our knees, gasping for breath. The lumps of earth piled up with a thud. A nauseous smell of rotten stew passed into the air. Green, hairy flies began buzzing. I was just going to stand upright when something utterly strange appeared in the hole. My curiosity got the better of the stench which was seizing me by the throat. Where I knew to be only pieces of chicken, I saw an unheard-of thing. I thought I was the sport of a fantastic illusion. In this hole . . . there at our feet, lay a shoulder with an arm severed at the elbow and two children's legs. On the rotten flesh crawled voracious larvae. I uttered a scream of horror and my teeth began chattering. Hardly listening to the native doctor's curses, I fled head over heels, the flight providing a curious feeling of relief.

When I arrived at Zannu's doorstep, I heard heart-rending sobs which kept me rooted to the spot. For the first time in my life, I was going to see a man weep. And what a man! In the smoke-filled hut where the nearly burnt-out wick was still flickering, Cicavi had just passed away.

GUILLAUME OYÔNÔ-MBIA

THE LITTLE RAILWAY STATION

To Samuel and Marie Ebo

TO THE EYES of the dozing passenger jolted out of his nap by the stopping of the train, this little railway station is in no way different from any of the other stops of comparable importance dotted along the central line. A small brick structure serving both as office and living quarters, with the cooking-shed a few yards away, and surrounded by a vegetable patch. In brief, that semi-rural, semi-urban look so dear to Civil Servants working in the bush. The village in its absolute calm wakes up only at the fixed, or supposedly fixed hours when the train stirs it into short-lived animation. And our passenger usually departs without realizing to what extent, despite appearances, this little station surpasses all others big or small.

For this is the domain of Silas Aloga, better known by the name of Sangô Station-Master.

Twenty years of service have elevated Silas Aloga to the high office we have respectfully referred to. He has thus become the man whom all villagers address with deference in the Station Bar run by Daddy Mayega. For him these village yokels represent an audience always keen to hear the news of the world transmitted by the small transistor radio from which Silas Aloga is never separated. He bought it three years ago to listen to the pop songs which were then in vogue. But since his important promotion he has made it a point to listen also to the 'news in brief' and then to spin it out *ad libitum*, depending on the capacity of the bottle of *majunga* which serves to pep up the conversation, and on the curiosity of his listeners.

Nobody can properly gauge the various responsibilities incumbent on the man in charge of a little station lost in the bush. No passable road. The only outlet for local produce is to sell it to the dozing passengers carried by the trains twice a day.

Silas Aloga is fully aware of the importance of his mission. And it can hardly be overrated. Just imagine all those families in Douala and Yaoundé waiting in vain for the arrival of their dear ones should he, Sangô Station-Master, simply refuse to sell them tickets! Those husbands, still young or already resigned to their fate, would just go on insolently enjoying their newly found tranquillity because their better halves, on holiday with their parents near the little station, would be unable to return in time to re-establish their domestic disharmony. Without any shadow of doubt, Silas Aloga is a public benefactor.

Nothing gives him greater pleasure than those high-class ladies from Yaoundé, hardly recognizable 'under the crushing load of wigs and make-up', coming round regularly on the eve of their departure to tell him, 'Sangô Station-Master, I have to return tomorrow.'

That's all there is to it, but how many people are there who really remember to do so, I'm asking you? Too many of them just plain forget the respect due to the great man who alone has the right to halt the train and to make it start again. Hence Silas Aloga replies to these ladies, after due reflection, 'Hala, Nyango! (All right, madam!) The train will be there!'

And he walks off with a martial gait daring next day's train to disobey him by not arriving. Generally the train will beware of not coming, for certain people insist on calling it 'regular'. Those from the surrounding villages, however, know the exact score since they see Sangô Station-Master speaking on the phone to mysterious people every day and hear him announce afterwards like a conjurer, 'The train is coming!'

One day, one of these high-class ladies already mentioned asked him, 'Sangô Station-Master, do you know that my friend is here, staying with my parents?'

'Your friend?'

'Precisely. You know, the Acting Senior Assistant Secretary General.'

At the unfolding of this title, Silas Aloga, who had already tipped his cap in deference to the lady, took it off completely and exclaimed in a fluster, 'The Acting Senior Assistant Secretary General in person, here in Nyango! And me not knowing anything about it? When does he expect to return?'

'We shan't stay long because of his important functions. We'll be going back by tomorrow afternoon's train.'

'The train will come! . . . It most certainly will,' Silas Aloga asserted.

The great lady gave a smile, thanked him and walked away swaying her hips like those girls who have more than one Acting Senior Assistant Secretary General up their sleeve.

That night in the Station Bar the only topic of conversation was the visitor whose presence was doing the entire village proud. Silas Aloga related the event with an air of self-importance, taking his transistor radio and his bottle of *majunga* to witness whenever it seemed to him that shadows of incredulity were crawling over the faces of his audience. According to him, it was known from an authoritative source that the Acting Senior Assistant Secretary General was on an official tour. All station-masters had received a special news-flash to this effect. Silas Aloga was getting overheated and would end up each sentence by saying, as if he wanted to convince himself of the extraordinary piece of news he was announcing, 'The Acting Senior Assistant Secretary! . . . The Acting . . .'

'The Acting Senior Assistant Secretary General?' one of the customers queried. 'Which one?'

Silas Aloga had not yet asked himself this question but did not want to admit it. He said, as if surprised at the ignorance displayed by the previous speaker, 'What do you mean, which one? Haven't I been telling you it's he himself?'

'Himself?'

'Yes sir, in person!' Silas Aloga affirmed. And he triumphantly drained his glass of wine. Then, while old man Mayega put the third bottle of wine before him, he let the audience into the secret of the conclusions he had reached and also told them about his apprehensions.

Big people like the Acting Senior Assistant Secretary General would never go on tour without drafting on their return to Douala or Yaoundé a circumstantial account dealing with the smallest details they had noticed during their journey. It was to this fact that some of his colleagues owed their being put in charge of big railway stations with air-conditioners, refrigerators, heavily scented lady typists, in short, all modern amenities. Had he been given ample advance warning, our man continued, he would have set his little station in order a bit so that the official visitor would have been struck by his expertise and qualities of leadership. For he was a real disciplinarian if it came to the crunch, he concluded, stroking his luxuriant moustache.

When the station-master had finished speaking, a sympathetic silence settled in the little bar. Daddy Mayega set his mind to thinking. He was far from stupid. When some time ago Silas Aloga had been appointed station-master, he was the first to salute the new cap of the great man destined to become famous under the title 'Sangô Station-Master'. With the astuteness that is the mark of the true businessman he even went further, reserving a special small table near the window for our hero. His wife made it a point to go through the motions of wiping it the moment Silas Aloga's heavy outline loomed up at the door. This little table all for himself had quite naturally enhanced the regular attendance of Sangô Station-Master in the little bar. On the day in question, Daddy Mayega said to him after he had voiced his fears, 'Sangô Station-Master, have you forgotten that the passengers are under your administrative tutelage as long as they remain on your premises? Put them on their best behaviour. How do you expect them to behave themselves if you don't compel them to obey you? Make sure you tell them, particularly tomorrow, to queue in front of the booking-office as they do in the big cities where they have policemen.'

Silas Aloga was struck by the logic of this argument: 'administrative tutelage', that was it! After all, wasn't it absolutely normal? Had anybody ever seen leaders without subjects, without people under their jurisdiction, to put it in a nutshell? He therefore pledged to himself that as from the next day he would make his little station into a model of order and discipline. The only thing that worried him was the well-known attitude of certain youngsters who tended not to be amenable to his authority. Those were of course the students, whose heads were full of ideas totally lacking in respect: they were convinced that once they had bought a ticket they were entitled to take the train just like that. Silas Aloga had a knack of identifying these rebels in a crowd, where they would walk with their hands in their pockets, making such blatantly absurd remarks as 'the railway is at the service of its users', 'equality before the booking-office', and so on. But on the day he would be expecting the visit of the Acting Senior Assistant Secretary General, Silas Aloga promised himself he would show them what stuff he was made of.

Those young rebels will be more obedient, he thought when tossing about in his bed, as soon as all travellers have to submit a stamped application to the station-master two weeks before taking the train. Why not? After all, it's done for taking the boat or the plane.

Silas Aloga was conversant with these latter details because one of his distant nephews, who had wanted to travel to Kinshasa, had been obliged to spend two or three months in Yaoundé filling in forms which subsequently had to be stamped. Carried away by the irresistible current of his ambitious imagination, our hero already saw himself in an ultra-modern railway station, sitting in front of a pile of mail awaiting attention which he would not even have the time to go through, as he would be completely engrossed in revelling in his own importance. A uniformed messenger would enter from time to time to relight his pipe, at the same time bringing a request for an interview from a young woman very keen on attending a surprise party at N'Komgsamba. And he, Silas Aloga, would answer in a voice loud enough to be heard in the waiting-room, 'No time to see anybody! Tell her to come back next Monday!'

First he would have made sure by a quick look at the wall calendar that it clearly showed Tuesday, in other words, that the charming applicant would have a whole week to think of a different method of pleading with him, after nightfall of course, which might actually turn out to be more effective.

With his heart full of such high hopes Sangô Station-Master started off a new day, the day which was to culminate in the advent of the Acting Senior Assistant Secretary General before his modest ticket-window.

* * *

Quite some time before the arrival of the train, the passengers arrived at the station. They made themselves comfortable on old disused boxes, sleepers and other commodities of the same type which the railway authorities, God bless them, unable to get rid of them, had left for their convenience. Some, in an effort to prove to others that they were personally acquainted with the Station-Master, bade him a timorous 'Mayega, Sangô (Good morning, sir)' which was meant to have a ring of familiarity about it. Maybe it had, for the person thus saluted would first raise his eyes from his enormous ledger, then from his spectacles, before deigning to grunt Hmm! while at the same time giving a slight nod. Despite its obvious slightness, this nod sufficed to embolden the travellers. Questions were asked: Will this train arrive today? Is the luggage going to be checked in as usual? Will any tickets be sold?

Silas Aloga, moved to pity, heaved a sigh. Poor ignorant passengers who had been unable to guess that this day was going to be decisive in his career as a station-master! Did they really think that the Acting Senior Assistant Secretary General would conceive a favourable opinion of a station-master who replied to the greetings of those under his jurisdiction? If they had known what was in the offing, he thought to himself, the travellers would have arrived much later.

He therefore continued filling in his ledger with an absolutely useless scribble, hoping that the high visitor would find him engrossed in doing his work and would take good note of it. He was even a bit surprised at not having seen him appear yet.

The passengers, who were gradually getting worried, crowded in a disorderly fashion before the booking-office, which remained obstinately closed. A young man – one of the rebels – looked at his wrist-watch and ventured to remark, 'Oh, the train will be here in twenty minutes!'

The passengers looked at each other dumbfounded. They obviously wondered whether they would have sufficient time to check in their luggage. But Silas Aloga, who had sharp ears, had overheard the young rebel's remark. He came out to put him in his place as he had sworn to himself the night before: 'Maybe it's you who has received the latest instructions. I bet you're the station-master here and I don't matter any more. But what if I told you that the train will be behind schedule?'

The passengers were utterly dumbfounded. They were too modest to think of the marvellous prospect of arriving at Yaoundé in the middle of the night, where at the railway station they would be given a warm reception and provided with free lifts in a Black Maria by the police, who by that time would have sent the taxi-drivers packing. The young rebel was given a good dressing-down. One of those who don't know how to show respect to the mighty of the earth! Why want to antagonize Sangô Station-Master at the risk of causing the train to be late? Some old peasants pleaded with Silas Aloga not to pay attention to this mark of disrespect. 'Today's youth – Sangô! . . .'

Then Silas Aloga surveyed his administrative charges. He all but ordered them to snap to attention. 'Now look at that! What chaos in front of my booking-office window! They wouldn't dare do that sort of thing in Yaoundé, of course, because of the police! But here nobody cares about making a proper queue. You want the Acting Senior Assistant Secretary General to write about me in his report: unable to get people to line up in front of his booking-office window!'

The passengers started queuing at once. They were

holding old one hundred franc notes in sweaty fists. Silas Aloga, already on his way to the ticket-office, stopped in front of the luggage piled up on the scales, 'Whose box is this?'

'It's mine, Sangô Station-Master.'

The owner of the box rushed forward, pushing aside his companions with the authority conferred on him by the honour of being served before anybody else. But on that glorious day the Lord of the little railway station was grimly determined not to recognize any authority beside his own and that of the VIP he was expecting. He challenged the owner of the trunk, a humble farmer who had covered twenty kilometres on foot in the hot sun to catch this train, 'Did you check the padlocks?'

'I . . .'

'Come on, check those padlocks. I don't want anybody to go round saying that the railway employees have robbed you. We value our reputation, we do! . . .'

The farmer checked the padlocks and found to his dismay that he had actually forgotten to lock them. Silas Aloga with a sweeping glance took the crowd to witness this atrocity and walked off thinking that there was no need for any further comment. A woman accosted him. She wanted to weigh in an enormous basket of food.

'Where are you going?'

'To Yaoundé.'

'Have you got a ticket?'

'But . . .'

'You see!' Silas Aloga exclaimed, drawing approval from the crowd. 'Regardless of my instructions, people still want to weigh in their luggage here even before they've bought a ticket.'

'But the ticket-window is not yet open!' one of the

passengers in the queue shouted with such ill-advised haste that he forgot to add 'Sangô Station-Master'. He soon had cause to be sorry, for Silas Aloga laid great store on people addressing him properly. He fulminated, 'The window is not yet open, you say? So this is it! You want the Acting Senior Assistant Secretary General to say that I'm failing in my duty! . . . You just try and spend the whole day here running this station! Yes, running this station and taking all those phone calls!'

The passenger fell silent. Sangô Station-Master, despairing of seeing the great man he was expecting arrive, reluctantly decided to start selling tickets. He entered his office and the passengers finally heard him open the window. The previously impeccable order of the queue was thereby promptly upset. While the crowd pressed in front of his tiny window, Silas Aloga methodically searched through an enormous bunch of keys for the little key that would open the ticket cupboard. He interrupted his activity for a moment to glance at the passengers with the eyes of an ogre and growled, 'How do you people expect me to find my key if you keep obstructing my window?'

To give added emphasis to the majesty of these possessive adjectives he put on a show of closing the little shutter once more, and the queue formed again immediately. Sangô Station-Master recommenced his search. Not that after so many years of good and loyal service he was unable to identify the little key, incidentally quite distinct from the others, which opened the lock in question. On this momentous day he merely wanted to avoid giving the uninitiated the impression that his job was easy. He also hoped that by postponing the beginning of his ticket sales as much as possible, he would have an opportunity of showing the Acting Senior Assistant Secretary General his exceptional qualities, which would earn him the promotion he was now almost certain to obtain.

When after a laborious search Silas Aloga had finally made up his mind to pick the right key, the telephone rang. He dropped the bunch of keys, overjoyed at the prospect of having to start all over again later, and made for the ancient telephone, taking off the receiver.

'Hallo – o –!'

An anguished silence while Sangô Station-Master talked to a distant speaker. Impossible to read the news from his face which remained impassive, except for a long-drawn-out Hmm! issuing from it from time to time. Hanging up, he instantly rushed to the ticket-cupboard which he opened without any further ado and exclaimed, 'If you miss that train, you'll only have yourselves to blame! We've got only ten minutes left!'

Great confusion among the passengers. They knew of course that missing the train on a particular day meant at least a twenty-four-hour wait for the party concerned. Hands were stretched out over the counter waving banknotes that now were even clammier than before.

'Douala . . . Sambadjeck . . . Yaoundé . . .!'

Amid the hubbub of voices only Sangô Station-Master kept an edifying composure of studied calm, worthy of the man about to obtain a big promotion. With measured gestures he would collect the money, check it, listen to the passenger shouting his destination, and finally hand him both his change and the ticket with the reminder that nobody talks to a Station-Master without his cap off.

The tickets were sold. Over to the checking-in of the luggage. Once again Silas Aloga managed to remain unruffled, although he strained his ingenuity to sow panic among his charges just for the fun of calling them to order again with his thunderous voice. Nevertheless he had the impression that a disastrous silence was spreading, and he therefore suddenly left his scale, entered his office and came out again after having talked on the telephone.

'Come on! . . . Hurry up!' This 'Hurry up!' was punctuated by a stroke of his little hammer on a steel bar which was hanging on the veranda and which served as a bell. The alarm was now given. The passengers called out to each other and jostled each other in the station. They moved their luggage close to the rails. Indignantly Silas Aloga realized that his administrative charges no longer paid any attention to him after each one of them had got hold of his ticket. What would the Acting Senior Assistant Secretary General think when faced with such chaos? Our hero rushed forward in search of a victim to be sacrificed to a promotion put in jeopardy. And quite naturally his eyes fell on the young man with the wrist-watch who having finished his preparations was waiting for the train reading a magazine.

'So now we start reading near the line! Don't my notices clearly say that it is dangerous to . . .'

The rebel moved away from the rails. Other passengers followed suit. Silas Aloga, somewhat put out by this obedience which deprived him of the chance of blowing his top a bit more, ran this way and that, hoping to find other pretexts for indignation.

'These small children on their own, with nobody to look after them! So you never listen to the radio! Just wait till I've got an unguarded level crossing installed here so we can also have accidents just as in Douala and Yaoundé! And when the authorities come for the inquiry you'll see who's the boss here!'

He didn't add, for this was understood, that the people under his jurisdiction would still have to wait for a long time for the privilege of a level crossing since this type of innovation rarely preceded the building of a motor road. But his prophecies had the desired effect, for the woman now kept the frolicking children in check.

'It's the same problem everywhere, Mr Station-Master,' a cultured voice said in French behind Silas Aloga. Turning around he finally saw the important couple he had waited for so long to arrive. The Acting Senior Assistant Secretary General and his lady friend were in walking-out dress, that is to say they wore those European winter clothes which have proved so convenient during the dry season in tropical countries. Two or three villagers accompanied them carrying their luggage. The gentleman continued while the station-master saluted him in military fashion (was it his fault if the authorities had failed to send him any policemen to honour this VIP passenger?), 'It's the same thing everywhere. You'll never see people arrive in time at the offices of the public administration or act like everybody else. I, for example, the Acting Senior Assistant Secretary General of . . .'

'But I know you, my lord!' Silas Aloga exclaimed in the manner of somebody who had already been invited for dinner by all the Acting Senior Assistant Secretary Generals in the world. 'You need not introduce yourself.'

'Could I please purchase my tickets?'

'Why, certainly, Mr Acting . . . Senior . . . Sir! Would Nyango mind sitting down on this chair? . . .'

Madam declined and declared that she preferred to stand. Out of politeness she refrained from making it clear that the chair offered by the station-master was too old to match the brand-new natural complexion she had acquired by the clever use of so-called beauty cream.

Meanwhile, Silas Aloga was looking for the change due to the gentleman, who had paid with a five thousand franc note. This did not, however, prevent him from upbraiding two latecomers who were trying to take advantage of the lordly presence to obtain tickets of their own, 'So it's tickets you want! Just when the train's about to arrive! These people can neither read my instructions nor my notices! You're lucky that the general here is also late . . . I mean just in time. Keep quiet while I get the first-class tickets for the lady and the gentleman.'

This reference to the august visitors imposed a respectful silence. And one could hear, distant yet but waxing stronger, the droning of the train. The latecomers at the booking-office were growing restless, and their restlessness was amply justified by the fact that Sangô Station-Master had once more left his window. When handing the first-class tickets to the gentleman, he almost fainted at the spectacle in front of him: like a reincarnated fertility goddess Madam was surrounded by an array of bowls filled with fruit, bunches of bananas, mangoes and so forth which the local farmers wanted her to buy. The icy stare with which she received their advances should have been enough to make them realize that she had even forgotten the names of these uncivilized sorts of food. Silas Aloga rushed out, raving:

'Nyodi! (Off with you!) . . . Nyodi! . . . How long have I been telling you on the notice-board to judge people by appearances! Do Madam's fingernails look like those of a housewife? How do you expect her to peel mangoes with that nail-polish? . . . Nyodi! . . . Master and Madam have been to Mbengué (Europe)! They get their food supplies from Mbengué, you hear? Besides, native food is banned in the first class. First-class passengers eat à la carte! . . . Seven hundred francs excluding wine and service charges.'

These kindly words dispersed the passengers who took up their old positions near the railway line, for the train was now entering the station. Silas Aloga went into his office and came out shortly after waving a little red flag. The two stragglers ran after him crying, 'Sangô . . . oh Sangô . . .!'

Sangô stopped. 'What will you people do without me? For soon I won't be here any more to sell you tickets. To the office now, and stand in a queue!'

Overflowing with gratitude, the passengers stood one behind the other in front of the booking-office. Silas Aloga entered, sold them their tickets in a few seconds and came out just in time to order the train to a halt with the all-powerful blast of his whistle.

'All aboard!' he roared. 'But don't board this train before the first-class passengers! It's forbidden to . . . Decree number . . .'

Nobody paid any more attention to him. In such moments Silas Aloga realized the weakness of the whole administrative set-up. Why hadn't the men who made so many unnecessary speeches themselves arranged for official addresses, followed by compulsory applause, to be delivered by the station-master concerned before the departure of each train? How he would have taken advantage of such an opportunity to thank the Acting Senior Assistant Secretary General and Madam for their visit to his modest railway station! He would also have sneaked in a little discreet remark to the effect that he hoped to be appointed head of a big station in the near future. But in the absence of any speech to be made Silas Aloga decided to look for a passenger in difficulty on the platform and to lend him a helping hand. As was to be expected, his eyes fell on the young rebel with the wrist-watch who was going from one luggage van to another in a vain attempt to berth his moped. The railway authorities are so concerned about the health of the passengers who have checked in their luggage that they kindly request them to load it themselves into the appropriate van. This practice is necessary to keep the railway users in top condition so that they can fully enjoy the comfort of the wooden benches installed in second-class carriages. Hence, when Silas Aloga saw the young rebel in trouble, he rushed forward, wanting the public to notice to what extent his character was free from vindictiveness.

'Well, you're no longer interested in telling the time now, are you? You do realize now that we of the Railway Corporation are not lying idle . . . Hi there, stow away this moped for me!'

The employees in the luggage van, who had previously told the young fellow that this was the wrong carriage, hastened to obey Silas Aloga. Sangô Station-Master went off to look for other opportunities to distinguish himself. Unfortunately for the man of action within him who was bursting with energy, all was as quiet as it usually is in those little railway stations devoid of imagination or ambition where nothing ever happens. By way of consolation he thought proudly of all the activity he had displayed since the arrival of the august visitor. It would be a well-deserved promotion to be sure. Hadn't he proved to be a great disciplinarian, carved out of the stuff of which the bosses of big stations are made? In his imagination he already saw the admiring glances of the customers in Daddy Mayega's little bar when that very night he would tell them about his exploits of the day. He would add, of course, that the Acting Senior Assistant Secretary General had promised not to forget to mention him to his superior officers once he had returned to Yaoundé. And the villagers would loudly approve him since experience had long taught them that this was an infallible way of getting the great man to stand drinks all round.

All these prospects gave him a feeling of elation. As he could not find any more passengers in distress on the platform, he roughly pushed aside the people who still wanted to draw out their farewells and were clinging to the doors.

'Stand back . . . Stand back . . . The train is going to leave!'

He was very anxious for everyone to pay attention to his whistle, or else the effect would be spoiled. But since the regulations required that the train had to be announced at the next station before it could leave, he entered his office. Just as he approached the telephone, it rang.

'Hallo – o – o – o?'

'The station-master please?'

'It's the station-master himself!' Silas Aloga replied, irritated by this pointless question – as if his voice wasn't universally known . . . 'I'm sending off the train.'

'Definitely not! Don't send us the train!'

Silas Aloga gasped: just fancy not sending the train with the famous visitor aboard! He stammered, 'What? . . . What are you saying?'

'There's been a derailment between our station and yours, and we're phoning for a relief-engine.'

'A relief-engine! And me having promised the Acting Senior Assistant Secretary General that the train . . .'

'The Acting Senior Assistant Secretary General of what?'

'Hmm . . . I don't really know. The Acting Senior Assistant Secretary General and Madam. They're travelling first-class. They . . .'

'They'll wait like everybody else! At least twelve hours' delay!'

B. L. HONWANA

PAPA, SNAKE & I

AS SOON AS Papa left the table to read the newspaper in his sitting-room, I got up as well. I knew that Mama and the others would take a little longer, but I didn't feel like staying with them at all.

When I stood up, Mama looked at me and said, 'Come here, let me look at your eyes.'

I went towards her slowly, because when Mama calls us we never know whether she's cross or not. After she had lifted my lids with the index finger of her left hand to make a thorough examination, she looked down at her plate and I stood waiting for her to send me away or to say something. She finished chewing, swallowed, and picked up the bone in her fingers to peep through the cavity, shutting one eye. Then she turned to me suddenly with a bewildered look on her face.

'Your eyes are bloodshot, you're weak and you've lost your appetite.'

The way she spoke made me feel obliged to say that none of this was my fault or else that I didn't do it on purpose. All the others looked on very curiously to see what was going to happen.

Mama peered down the middle of the bone again. Then she began to suck it, shutting her eyes, and only stopped for a moment to say, 'Tomorrow you're going to take a laxative.'

As soon as the others heard this, they began eating again

very quickly and noisily. Mama didn't seem to have anything else to say, so I went out into the yard.

It was hot everywhere, and I could see no-one on the road. Over the back wall three oxen gazed at me. They must have come back from the water trough at the Administration and stayed to rest in the shade. Far away, over the oxen's horns the grey tufts of the dusty thorn trees trembled like flames. Everything vibrated in the distance, and heat waves could even be seen rising from the stones in the road. Sartina was sitting on a straw mat in the shade of the house, eating her lunch. Chewing slowly, she looked around, and from time to time, with a careless gesture, she shooed away the fowls who came close to her hoping for crumbs. Even so, every now and then one of the bolder ones would jump on to the edge of the plate and run off with a lump of mealie meal in its beak, only to be pursued by the others. In their wild dispute, the lump would become so broken up that in the end even the smallest chicken would get its bit to peck.

When she saw me coming near, Sartina pulled her capulana down over her legs, and even then kept her hand spread out in front of her knees, firmly convinced that I wanted to peep at something. When I looked away she still didn't move her hand.

Toto came walking along slowly with his tongue hanging out, and went to the place where Sartina was sitting. He sniffed the plate from afar and turned away, taking himself off to the shade of the wall where he looked for a soft place to lie down. When he found one, he curled round with his nose almost on his tail, and only lay still when his stomach touched the ground. He gave a long yawn, and dropped his head between his paws. He wriggled a little, making sure that he was in the most comfortable position, then covered his ears with his paws.

When she had finished eating, Sartina looked at me insistently before removing her hand which covered the space between her knees, and only when she was sure I was not looking did she spring to her feet with a jump. The plate was so clean that it shone, but after darting a last suspicious glance at me, she took it to the trough. She moved languidly, swaying from the waist as her hips rose and fell under her capulana. She bent over the trough, but the back of her legs was exposed in this position, so she went to the other side for me not to see.

Mama appeared at the kitchen door, still holding the bone in her hand, and before calling Sartina to clear the table, she looked around to see if everything was in order. 'Don't forget to give Toto his food,' she said in Ronga.

Sartina went inside, drying her hands on her capulana, and afterwards came out with a huge pile of plates. When she came out the second time she brought the table-cloth and shook it on the stairs. While the fowls were skirmishing for the crumbs, pecking and squawking at each other, she folded it in two, four, and eight, and then went back inside. When she came out again she brought the aluminium plate with Toto's food, and put it on the cement cover of the water meter. Toto didn't have to be called to eat and even before the plate was put down, he threw himself on his food. He burrowed into the pile of rice with his nose, searching for the bits of meat which he gulped up greedily as he found them. When no meat was left, he pushed the bones aside and ate some rice. The fowls were all around him, but they didn't dare to come nearer because they knew very well what Toto was like when he was eating.

When he had swallowed the rice, Toto pretended he didn't want any more and went to sit in the shade of the sugar cane, waiting to see what the fowls would do. They came nervously towards his food, and risked a peck or two, very apprehensively. Toto watched this without making a single movement. Encouraged by the passivity of the dog, the fowls converged on the rice with great enthusiasm, creating an awful uproar. It was then that Toto threw himself on the heap, pawing wildly in all directions and growling like an angry lion. When the fowls disappeared, fleeing to all corners of the yard, Toto went back to the shade of the sugar cane, waiting for them to gather together again.

Before going to work Papa went to look at the chicken run with Mama. They both appeared at the kitchen door, Mama already wearing her apron and Papa with a toothpick in his mouth and his newspaper under his arm. When they passed me Papa was saying, 'It's impossible, it's impossible, things can't go on like this.'

I went after them, and when we entered the chicken run Mama turned to me as if she wanted to say something, but then she changed her mind and went towards the wire netting. There were all sorts of things piled up behind the chicken run: pipes left over from the building of the windmill on the farm, blocks which were bought when Papa was still thinking of making out-houses of cement, boxes, pieces of wood, and who knows what else. The fowls sometimes crept in amongst these things and laid their eggs where Mama couldn't reach them. On one side of the run lay a dead fowl, and Mama pointed to it and said, 'Now there's this one, and I don't know how many others have just died from one day to the next. The chickens simply disappear, and the eggs too. I had this one left here for you to see. I'm tired of talking to you about this, and you still don't take any notice.'

'All right, all right, but what do you want me to do about it?'

'Listen, the fowls die suddenly, and the chickens disappear. No one goes into the chicken run at night, and we've never heard any strange noise. You must find out what's killing the fowls and chickens.'

'What do you think it is?'

'The fowls are bitten and the chickens are eaten. It can only be the one thing you think it is – if there are any thoughts in your head.'

'All right, tomorrow I'll get the snake killed. It's Sunday, and it will be easy to get people to do it. Tomorrow.'

Papa was already going out of the chicken run when Mama said, now in Portuguese, 'But tomorrow without fail, because I don't want any of my children bitten by a snake.'

Papa had already disappeared behind the corner of the house on his way to work when Mama turned to me and said, 'Haven't you ever been taught that when your father and mother are talking you shouldn't stay and listen! My children aren't usually so bad mannered. Who do you take after?'

She turned on Sartina, who was leaning against the wire netting and listening. 'What do you want? Did anyone call you? I'm talking to my son and it's none of your business.'

Sartina couldn't have grasped all that because she didn't understand Portuguese very well, but she drew away from the netting, looking very embarrassed, and went to the trough again. Mama went on talking to me, 'If you think you'll fool me and take the gun to go hunting you're making a big mistake. Heaven help you if you try to do a thing like that! I'll tan your backside for you! And if you think you'll stay here in the chicken run you're also mistaken. I don't feel like putting up with any of your nonsense, d'you hear?'

Mama must have been very cross, because for the whole day I hadn't heard her laugh as she usually did. After talking to me she went out of the chicken run and I followed her. When she passed Sartina, she asked her in Ronga, 'Is it very hot under your capulana? Who told you to come here and show your legs to everybody?'

Sartina said nothing, walked round the trough and went on washing the plates, bending over the other side.

Mama went away and I went to sit where I had been before. When Sartina saw me she turned on me resentfully, threw me a furious glance, and went round the trough again. She began to sing a monotonous song, one of those songs of hers that she sometimes spent the whole afternoon singing over and over again when she was angry.

Toto was bored with playing with the fowls, and had already finished eating his rice. He was sleeping again with his paws over his ears. Now and then he rolled himself in the dust and lay on his back with his legs folded in the air.

It was stiflingly hot, and I didn't know whether I'd go hunting as I usually did every Saturday, or if I'd go to the chicken run to see the snake.

Madunana came into the yard with a pile of firewood on his back, and went to put it away in the corner where Sartina was washing the plates. When she saw him, she stopped singing and tried to manage an awkward smile.

After looking all around, Madunana pinched Sartina's bottom, and she gave an embarrassed giggle and responded with a sonorous slap on his arm. The two of them laughed happily together without looking at each other.

Just then, Nandito, Joãozinho, Nelita and Gita ran out after a ball, and started kicking it around the yard with great enjoyment.

Mama came to the kitchen door, dressed up to go out. As soon as she appeared, Madunana bent down quickly to the ground, pretending to look for something, and Sartina bent over the trough.

'Sartina, see if you manage not to break any plates before you finish. Hurry up. You Madunana, leave Sartina alone and mind your own business. I don't want any of that nonsense here. If you carry on like this I'll tell the boss.'

'You, Ginho' (now she spoke in Portuguese), 'look after the house and remember you're not a child any more. Don't hit anybody and don't let the children go out of the yard. Tina and Lolota are inside clearing up – don't let them get up to mischief.'

'Sartina' (in Ronga), 'when you've finished with that put the kettle on for the children's tea and tell Madunana to go and buy bread. Don't let the children finish the whole packet of butter.'

'Ginho' (now in Portuguese), 'look after everything – I'm coming back just now. I'm going along to Aunty Lucia's for a little chat.'

Mama straightened her dress and looked around to see if everything was in order, then went away.

Senhor Castro's dog, Wolf, was watching Toto from the street. As soon as he saw Wolf, Toto ran towards him and they started to bark at each other.

All the dogs of the village were frightened of Toto, and even the biggest of them ran away when he showed his temper. Toto was small, but he had long white hair which bristled up like a cat's when he was angry, and this is what must have terrified the other dogs.

Usually he kept away from them, preferring to entertain himself with the fowls – even bitches he only tolerated at certain times. For me he was a dog with a 'pedigree', or at least 'pedigree' could only mean the qualities he possessed. He had an air of authority, and the only person he feared was

Mama, although she had never hit him. Just to take him off a chair we had to call her because he snarled and showed his teeth even at Papa.

The two dogs were face to face, and Wolf had already started to retreat, full of fear. At this moment Dr Reis's dog, Kiss, passed by, and Toto started to bark at him too: Kiss fled at once, and Wolf pursued him, snapping at his hind-quarters, only leaving him when he was whining with pain. When Wolf came back to Toto they immediately made friends and began playing together.

Nandito came and sat down next to me, and told me, without my asking, that he was tired of playing ball.

'So why have you come here?'

'Don't you want me to?'

'I didn't say that.'

'Then I'll stay.'

'Stay if you like.'

I got up and he followed me. 'Where are you going? Are you going hunting?'

'No.'

'Well, then?'

'Stop pestering me. I don't like talking to kids.'

'You're also a kid. Mama still hits you.'

'Say that again and I'll bash your face in.'

'All right, I won't say it again.'

I went into the chicken run, and he came after me. The pipes were hot, and I had to move them with a cloth. The dust that rose was dense and suffocating.

'What are you looking for? Shall I help you?'

I began to move the blocks one by one and Nandito did the same. 'Get away!'

He went to the other end of the run and began to cry.

When I had removed the last block of the pile I saw the snake. It was a mamba, very dark in colour. When it realized it had been discovered it wound itself up more tightly and lifted its triangular head. Its eyes shone vigilantly and its black forked tongue quivered menacingly.

I drew back against the fence, then sat down on the ground. 'Don't cry, Nandito.'

'You're nasty. You don't want to play with me.'

'Don't cry any more. I'll play with you just now. Don't cry.'

We both sat quietly. The little head of the snake came slowly to rest on the topmost coil, and the rest of its body stopped trembling. But it continued to watch me attentively.

'Nandito, say something, talk to me.'

'What do you want me to say?'

'Anything you like.'

'I don't feel like saying anything.'

Nandito was still rubbing his eyes and feeling resentful towards me.

'Have you ever seen a snake? Do you like snakes? Are you scared of them? Answer me!'

'Where are the snakes?' Nandito jumped up in terror, and looked around.

'In the bush. Sit down and talk.'

'Aren't there any snakes here?'

'No. Talk. Talk to me about snakes.'

Nandito sat down very close to me.

'I'm very frightened of snakes. Mama says it's dangerous to go out in the bush because of them. When we're walking in the grass we can step on one by mistake and get bitten. When a snake bites us we die. Sartina says that if a snake bites us and we don't want to die we must kill it, burn it till it's dry, then eat it. She says she's already eaten a snake, so she won't die even if she gets bitten.'

'Have you ever seen a snake?'

'Yes, in Chico's house. The servant killed it in the chicken run.'

'What was it like?'

'It was big and red, and it had a mouth like a frog.'

'Would you like to see a snake now?'

Nandito got up and leaned against me fearfully. 'Is there a snake in the chicken run? I'm scared – let's get out.'

'If you want to get out, go away. I didn't call you to come in here.'

'I'm frightened to go alone.'

'Then sit here until I feel like going out.'

The two of us stayed very quietly for a while.

Toto and Wolf were playing outside the fence. They were running from one post to another, going all the way round and starting again. At every post they raised a leg and urinated.

Then they came inside the chicken run and lay on their stomachs to rest. Wolf saw the snake immediately and began to bark. Toto barked as well, although he had his back turned towards it.

'Brother, are there always snakes in every chicken run?'

'No.'

'Is there one in here?'

'Yes.'

'Well then, why don't we go out. I'm scared!'

'Go out if you want to – go on!'

Wolf advanced towards the snake, barking more and more frenziedly. Toto turned his head but still did not realize what was wrong.

Wolf's legs were trembling and he pawed the ground

in anguish. Now and again he looked at me uncomprehendingly, unable to understand why I did not react to his hysterical alarm. His almost human eyes were filled with panic.

'Why is he barking like that?'

'Because he's seen the snake.'

The mamba was curled up in the hollow between some blocks, and it unwound its body to give itself the most solid support possible. Its head and the raised neck remained poised in the air, unaffected by the movement of the rest of its body. Its eyes shone like fires.

Wolf's appeals were now horribly piercing, and his hair was standing up around his neck.

Leaning against the fence, Tina and Lolota and Madunana looked on curiously.

'Why don't you kill the snake?' Nandito's voice was very tearful and he was clutching me around the neck.

'Because I don't feel like it.'

The distance between the snake and the dog was about five feet. However, the snake had inserted its tail in the angle formed between a block and the ground, and had raised its coils one by one, preparing for the strike. The triangular head drew back imperceptibly, and the base of the lifted neck came forward. Seeming to be aware of the promixity of his end, the dog began to bark even more frantically, without, however, trying to get away from the snake. From a little way behind, Toto, now on his feet as well, joined in the barking.

For a fraction of a second the neck of the snake curved while the head leaned back. Then, as if the tension of its pliant body had snapped a cord that fastened its head to the ground, it shot forward in a lightning movement impossible to follow. Although the dog had raised himself on his hind legs like a goat, the snake struck him full on the chest. Free of support, the tail of the snake whipped through the air, reverberating with the movement of the last coil.

Wolf fell on his back with a suppressed whine, pawing convulsively. The mamba abandoned him immediately, and with a spring disappeared between the pipes.

'A nhoka!'* screamed Sartina.

Nandito threw me aside and ran out of the chicken run with a yell, collapsing into the arms of Madunana. As soon as he felt free of the snake, Wolf vanished in half a dozen leaps in the direction of Senhor Castro's house.

The children all started to cry without having understood what had happened. Sartina took Nandito to the house, carrying him in her arms. Only when the children disappeared behind Sartina did I call Madunana to help me kill the snake.

Madunana waited with a cloth held up high while I moved the pipes with the aid of a broomstick. As soon as the snake appeared Mandunana threw the cloth over it, and I set to beating the heap with my stick.

When Papa came back from work Nandito had come round from the shock, and was weeping copiously. Mama, who had not yet been to see the snake, went with Papa to the chicken run. When I went there as well, I saw Papa turn the snake over on to its back with a stick.

'I don't like to think of what a snake like this could have done to one of my children.' Papa smiled. 'Or to anyone else. It was better this way. What hurts me is to think that these six feet of snake were attained at the expense of my chickens . . .'

At this point Senhor Castro's car drew up in front of our

* nhoka – a snake.

house. Papa walked up to him, and Mama went to talk to Sartina. I followed after Papa.

'Good afternoon, Senhor Castro . . .'

'Listen, Tchembene, I've just found out that my pointer is dead, and his chest's all swollen. My natives tell me that he came howling from your house before he died. I don't want any back-chat, and I'm just telling you – either you pay compensation or I'll make a complaint at the Administration. He was the best pointer I ever had.'

'I've just come back from work – I don't know anything . . .'

'I don't care a damn about that. Don't argue. Are you going to pay or aren't you?'

'But Senhor Castro . . .'

'Senhor Castro nothing. It's 700 paus.* And it's better if the matter rests here.'

'As you like, Senhor Castro, but I don't have the money now . . .'

'We'll see about that later. I'll wait until the end of the month, and if you don't pay then there'll be a row.'

'Senhor Castro, we've known each other such a long time, and there's never . . .'

'Don't try that with me. I know what you all need – a bloody good hiding is the only thing . . .'

Senhor Castro climbed into his car and pulled away. Papa stayed watching while the car drove off. 'Son of a bitch . . .'

I went up to him and tugged at the sleeve of his coat.

'Papa, why didn't you say that to his face?'

He didn't answer.

* * *

* 700 'paus' – slang for 700$ (about £8).

We had hardly finished supper when Papa said, 'Mother, tell Sartina to clear the table quickly. My children, let us pray. To-day we are not going to read the Bible. We will simply pray.'

Papa talked in Ronga, and for this reason I regretted having asked him that question a while ago.

When Sartina finished clearing away the plates and folded the cloth, Papa began, '*Tatana, ha ku dumba hosi ya tilo misaba . . .*'*

When he finished, his eyes were red.

'Amen!'

'Amen!'

Mama got up, and asked, as if it meant nothing, 'But what did Senhor Castro want, after all?'

'It's nothing important.'

'All right, tell me about it in our room. I'll go and set out the children's things. You, Ginho, wake up early tomorrow and take a laxative . . .'

When they had all gone away, I asked Papa, 'Papa, why do you always pray when you are very angry?'

'Because He is the best counsellor.'

'And what counsel does He give you?'

'He gives me no counsel. He gives me strength to continue.'

'Papa, do you believe a lot in Him?'

Papa looked at me as if he were seeing me for the first time, and then exploded. 'My son, one must have a hope. When one comes to the end of a day, and one knows that tomorrow will be another day just like it, and that things will always be the same, we have got to find the strength to keep

* *Tatana, ha ku dumba hosi ya tilo misaba* – Father, we put our trust in Thee, Lord of Heaven and earth.

on smiling, and keep on saying, "This is not important!" We ourselves have to allot our own reward for the heroism of every day. We have to establish a date for this reward, even if it's the day of our death! Even today you saw Senhor Castro humiliate me: this formed only part of today's portion, because there were many things that happened that you didn't see. No, my son, there must be a hope! It must exist! Even if all this only denies Him, He must exist!'

Papa stopped suddenly, and forced himself to smile. Then he added, 'Even a poor man has to have something. Even if it is only a hope! Even if it's a false hope!'

'Papa, I could have prevented the snake from biting Senhor Castro's dog . . .'

Papa looked at me with his eyes full of tenderness, and said under his breath, 'It doesn't matter. It's a good thing that he got bitten.'

Mama appeared at the door. 'Are you going to let the child go to sleep or not?'

I looked at Papa, and we remembered Senhor Castro and both of us burst out laughing. Mama didn't understand.

'Are you two going crazy?!'

'Yes, and it's about time we went crazy,' said Papa with a smile.

Papa was already on the way to his room, but I must have talked too loudly. Anyway, it was better that he heard, 'Papa, I sometimes . . . I don't really know . . . but for some time . . . I have been thinking that I didn't love you all. I'm sorry . . .'

Mama didn't understand what we had been saying, so she became angry. 'Stop all this, or else . . .'

'Do you know, my son,' Papa spoke ponderously, and gesticulated a lot before every word. 'The most difficult thing to bear is that feeling of complete emptiness . . . and one suffers very much . . . very, very, very much. One grows with so much bottled up inside, but afterwards it is difficult to scream, you know.'

'Papa, and when Senhor Castro comes? . . .'

Mama was going to object, but Papa clutched her shoulder firmly. 'It's nothing, Mother, but, you know, our son believes that people don't mount wild horses, and that they only make use of the hungry, docile ones. Yet when a horse goes wild it gets shot down, and it's all finished. But tame horses die every day. Every day, d'you hear? Day after day, after day – as long as they can stand on their feet.'

Mama looked at him with her eyes popping out.

'Do you know, Mother, I'm afraid to believe that this is true, but I also can't bring myself to tell him that it's a lie . . . He sees, even to-day he saw . . . I only wish for the strength to make sure that my children know how to recognize other things . . .'

Papa and Mama were already in their room, so I couldn't hear any more, but even from there Mama yelled, 'Tomorrow you'll take a laxative, that'll show you. I'm not like your father who lets himself get taken in . . .'

My bed was flooded in yellow moonlight, and it was pleasant to feel my naked skin quiver with its cold caress. For some unknown reason the warm sensation of Sartina's body flowed through my senses. I managed to cling to her almost physical presence for a few minutes, and I wanted to fall asleep with her so as not to dream of dogs and snakes.

Translated by Dorothy Guedes

SAIDA HAGI-DIRIE HERZI

GOVERNMENT BY MAGIC SPELL

At the village

WHEN SHE WAS ten, Halima learned that she was possessed by a jinni. The diagnosis came from the religious healer of the village, the Wadaad. Halima had been ill for several months. The Wadaad had tried all his healing arts on her till he had understood that there could be no cure: Halima was not ill in the ordinary sense of the word; she was possessed – possessed by the spirit of an infant, which she had stepped on by accident, one night in front of the bathroom. Fortunately for Halima, the sage expounded, the jinni was of the benevolent sort, one that was more likely to help than to harm her. But it would never leave her – not leave her voluntarily, not even yield to exorcism. And it would forever be an infant jinni.

With that Halima became famous. The story of her jinni was known from one end of the village to the other within hours after the Wadaad had told her mother. Everyone talked about Halima and her jinni – what it might do and what it might be made to do, for her and for the village. In no time at all, the villagers had convinced themselves and each other that Halima had the power to foretell the future and to heal the sick. And it was not long before Halima herself was convinced.

Before long, Halima began to act the part. At times she would sit staring off into space. People assumed that she was listening to her jinni. Or she would actually go into a trance – she would talk, though no one was there to talk to;

she would shout at the top of her voice and sometimes she would even cry. Those who witnessed these scenes were filled with holy dread. All were careful not to disturb Halima, during those moments or at any other time, for fear that they might offend the jinni. If people talked about Halima they did so in whispers, behind her back.

Halima made believe that the spirits of the infant's parents visited her during those moments of trance. They came to enquire of the infant, she told people, came to teach her how she could make the jinni happy. At the same time, Halima affirmed, they told her all manner of things about life in general, about the people of the village, things past, things present and things yet to come.

A question that was on the minds of many people in the village was who was to marry Halima when she reached the marriageable age. No one doubted that she would marry. It was what women were for – marriage and childbearing. But there was the problem of the jinni. Wouldn't it be dangerous to be married to a woman possessed? Would there be men brave enough to want to marry Halima?

When Halima did reach the marriageable age, a problem presented itself which no one had anticipated. Halima did not *want* to get married. There were indeed men brave enough to want to marry her, but Halima turned them all down. The Wadaad himself proposed to her. He, people thought, would have been the ideal husband for Halima: he, if anyone, should have been able to cope with a woman possessed. But Halima turned him down too.

Not that possession by a jinni spirit was something unusual in Halima's village. Stories of jinnis abounded – of people who were actually possessed by jinnis, of people who had jinni spirits that were like invisible twin brothers, or people who had jinni spirits as servants. It was common knowledge that one of Halima's own forefathers had had a jinni twin brother called Gess Ade, and one of her mother's grandfathers had had, in addition to a jinni twin brother, three devoted jinni servants called Toore, Gaadale, and Toor-Ourmone respectively. When Halima's mother had problems, she called on those three for help and protection. The ancestors of several clans were believed to have been born twins, a jinni being the twin partner of each of them. The tribe of Halima's brother-in-law had a twin jinni by the name of Sarhaan.

When animals were sacrificed, the jinni twins had to get their share. In return, the jinnis were expected to give support and protection to the clan. First the animals would be butchered. Then, the ritual songs having been sung, the carcasses would be cut open and the inner organs removed. These were to be given to the jinnis. Admonitions would be mumbled such as 'Let's not forget Gess Ade's share; or Toore's, Gaadale's, Ourmone's . . .'

The parts set aside for the jinnis would be taken to a remote place up in the hills, and, because they invariably and mysteriously disappeared, the villagers were sure that the jinnis devoured them. No one, therefore, would dream of cheating the jinnis of their share. This had been so for generations and would continue to be so. Children were made to memorize the ritual songs so as to keep the ancestral rites intact from generation to generation.

When Halima was under the spell of her spirits, all her emotions seemed intensified. She experienced a feeling of power, as though she could do things beyond the reach of ordinary human beings. She felt good then. Moreover, whatever she undertook, her spirits seemed to lend a helping hand. Because the fortunes of her family, indeed those of the whole clan, prospered at the time, Halima as well as other people assumed that it was the spirits' doing. In time, Halima came to be regarded as a blessing to her family, an asset to the whole clan. And she gloried in the special status her spirits gave her.

To the capital

It was because of her special power that Halima was summoned to the capital. A big part of her clan was there. The most important and the most powerful positions in the government were held by people of her clan. It had all started with one of their men, who had become very powerful in the government. He had called his relatives and found big government jobs for them. They in turn had called relatives of theirs till the government had virtually been taken over by Halima's people. And that had meant quick riches for everyone concerned. Nor had they been very scrupulous about getting what they wanted: anything that had stood in their way had been pushed aside or eliminated. At the time when Halima was summoned, her clan controlled the government and with that the wealth of the country so completely that no one dared to challenge them any more and they could get away with murder. Still they wanted to secure for themselves the extra protection of Halima's supernatural powers.

They had tried to get Halima's father to come to the capital as well. He was a man of stature, whose presence would have done honour to the clan. But he did not want to go. Old and resentful of change, he did not want to leave the peace and security of his village for the madness of the big city. But he was also afraid for his reputation. It was solid in his village but joining this gang might tarnish it, something he did not want to risk so near the end of his life. However, though he did not want to go himself, he had no reservations about sending his son and his daughter there. On one hand he hoped that they might get a slice of the big pie for themselves and so for the family. On the other hand he thought it would do no harm to have Halima there to protect the clan and to ensure its continued domination. Perhaps she could come to a deal with her spirits – she to continue looking after their infant and they to look after the welfare of the clan.

Halima did let herself be persuaded to go, but, before she went, she consulted her spirits. They asked her to perform two rituals. One was to prepare 'Tahleel', a special type of water, over which certain rituals were performed. People drank it or bathed in it to benefit from its powers. The second was to perform daily annual sacrifices to Gess Ade, the clan's twin spirit. Select parts of the innards of thousands of animals – hearts, kidneys, intestines and others – were to be offered to him every day on the eastern shore.

When Halima and her brother were ready to go, a cousin of theirs came from the big city to fetch them. From this cousin, who was an important government official, the two learned many things. They learned about the great privileges their people enjoyed in the city. They got an idea what wealth they had amassed since the clan had come 'to power'. They found out how completely the clan was in control of the government. They were awed, the more so when their informant told them that the clan had 'achieved' all this greatness in ten short years and that most of the people who now held important government positions were illiterate.

In the city, the two were given a beautiful villa complete with lots of servants and security guards. Within days, Halima's brother obtained an important government position of his own. He was made the head of the department that handled the sale of all incense, both inside and outside the country. Its official name was Government Incense Agency.

And Halima wasted no time carrying out the two requests of her spirits. She asked two things from the leaders of the clan. She asked them to bring all the water resources of the city together in one central pool to facilitate the performing of the 'Tahleel' and she requested the building of a huge slaughterhouse at the eastern shore. The leaders readily granted her requests since they were convinced that Halima's ministrations were of crucial importance for the continued success of the clan.

To centralize the city's water system, two huge water reservoirs were created, one in the eastern half and one in the western half of the city. Eventually all the wells of the city were destroyed, even the ones in private houses, and all water systems were connected to the two reservoirs. This way all the water consumed in the city came from the same source, and when Halima put the spell of her 'Tahleel' on the two reservoirs, it reached everyone.

One of the effects of the 'Tahleel' was to cure people of curiosity. Those who drank it stopped asking questions. Above all they stopped wondering about the actions of the clan's leading men. They became model subjects doing without question, without objection, what they were told to do. And Halima kept putting ever new spells on the water, faster than the old ones wore off. Though no one but she herself knew what kind of magic she put on the water, rumours abounded. One rumour had it that she performed certain incantations over the bath water of the leader and then released it into the reservoirs. There was no doubt in her mind and in the minds of the leaders that as long as everyone drank the water that carried her 'Tahleel' everything would go according to their plans.

When the new slaughterhouse went into operation, all other slaughterhouses were closed down. Unfortunately the new slaughterhouse was close to the Lido, the most popular of the city's beaches. In no time at all, the waters off the Lido swarmed with man-eating sharks, drawn there by the waste of blood and offals discharged by the slaughterhouse. After a number of people had been killed by the predators people stopped going to the Lido. There was no comment from the government. Quite obviously the slaughterhouse, where the sacrifices to Gess Ade were performed, was more important to the rulers of the country than the beach.

Every so often Halima would come to the slaughterhouse to check on the performance of the animal sacrifices. Here too she modified the rituals periodically to strengthen their effect.

As things kept going well for the tribe and her, Halima became more and more sure that she was the cause of it all. The clan's leaders too were convinced that they owed their continued success to Halima and her spirits. They heaped honours on her. They consulted her on all important issues and her counsel often proved invaluable. It was Halima, for instance, who thought up the idea of the shortages to keep the common people subdued. Shortages of all basic commodities were deliberately created and they kept people busy struggling for bare survival. They did not have time or energy to spare worrying about the goings-on in the government. The leaders of the clan felt more secure than ever.

Nearly twenty years have passed since Halima first went to the city. She is still performing her rituals, and the affairs of the clan are still prospering. Its men still hold all the important posts in the government and they still control the wealth of the country. As for the rest of the nation – they are mostly struggling to make ends meet, something that's becoming more and more difficult. And if there should be a few that might have time and energy left to start asking questions, Halima's Tahleel and her various other forms of magic take care of them. The men of the clan continue to govern with the help of Halima's magic spell.

DAMBUDZO MARECHERA

PROTISTA

THERE WAS A great drought in our region. All the rivers dried up. All the wells dried up. There was not a drop of water anywhere. I lived alone in a hut next to the barren fig-tree which had never been known to have any fruit on it. Now and then it would show signs of being alive but these always withered and were carried away by the relentless winds from the south-east which were dry and dusty and would sting into the very coolness of our minds. Those winds, they were fierce and scathing and not a drop of moisture was left.

My hut was on a slight rise on the shoulder of the Lesapi Valley. The valley was red and clayey and scarred with drought fissures from the burning sun and the long cold nights when I lay awake thinking of Maria the huntress who had one morning taken down her bows and arrows and had gone out into the rising sun and had never been seen again. But before she left she had drawn a circle in red chalk on the wall by my bed and said: 'If the circle begins to bleed and run down the wall that means I am in danger. But if it turns blue and breaks up into a cross then that means I am coming home.'

The drought began the very day she left me. There was not a green blade of grass left. There was not a green leaf of hope left; the drought had raised its great red hand and gathered them all and with one hot breath had swept all the leaves into a red dot to the pencil-line of the horizon where Maria had last been seen taking aim with her bow and arrow at a running gazelle.

And twelve long lean years had passed by somehow.

I still had three more years to serve. I had been exiled to this raw region by a tribunal which had found me guilty of various political crimes. Maria had been my secretary and my wife and had for long endured the barren fire of exile with me. And the sun burnt each year to cinders that darkened the aspect of the region. I began to forget things. My dreams still clung defiantly to the steel wire of old memories which I no longer had the power to arrange clearly in my mind. My imagination was constantly seared by the thought of water, of thirst, of dying barren and waterless and in the grave to be nothing but dehydrated 'remains'. It was not so much forgetting as being constantly preoccupied with the one image of water. And water in my mind was inextricably involved with my thoughts about Maria, about my own impotence, about the fig-tree, and about the red soil of the Lesapi Valley. The years of my life that had gone were so much time wasted, so little done, so many defeats, so little accomplished; they were years I would have preferred to forget if they did not in themselves contain my youth and the only time Maria and I had been happy together. And now, disjointed, disconnected, they came back to me unexpectedly and with such a new grain in them that I hardly recognized them for what they were. There was the story my father had told me, when I was barely six years of age, about the resilience of human roots: a youth rebelling against the things of his father had one morning fled from home and had travelled to the utmost of the earth where he was so happy that he wrote on their wall the words 'I have been here' and signed his new name after the words; the years rolled by with delight until he tired of them and thought to return home and tell his father about them. But when he neared home his father, who was looking out for him, met him and said 'All this time you thought you were actually away from me, you have been right here in my palm.' And the father opened his clenched hand and showed the son what was written in this hand. The words – and the very same signature – of the son were clearly written in the father's open palm: 'I have been here.' The son was so stunned and angry that he there and then slew his father and hung himself on a barren fig-tree which stood in the garden. I dreamed of this story many times, and each time some detail of it would change into something else. At times the father would become Maria the huntress; the son would be myself; and the fig-tree would become the tree just outside my own hut. But sometimes the son would become Maria and I would be the father whose clenched hand contained everything that Maria was.

The scarred hand of exile was dry and deathlike and the lines of its palm were the waterless riverbeds, the craters and fissures of dry channels scoured out of the earth by the relentless drought. My own hands, with their scars and callouses and broken fingernails, sometimes seemed to belong not to me but to this exacting punishment of exile. And yet they had once tenderly held Maria to me; and she had been soft and warm and wild and demanding in these very same hands. These hands that now were part of the drought, they had once cupped the quickening liquids of life, the hearty laughter of youth, the illusory security of sweet-smelling illusions. These hands that now were so broken, they had once tried to build and build and build a future out of the bricks of the past and of the present. These hands that had never touched the cheek of a child of my own, they were now utterly useless in the slow-burning furnace of the drought whose coming had coincided with Maria's going away from me.

Her arms were long and thin and the fingers were long and finely moulded though her nails, like mine, had long since lost their natural lustre and had become broken and jagged. And she was gentle, fiercely so, for she knew her great strength. She was a head taller than I and her long full legs sometimes outstrode me when we went out for a walk in the Lesapi Valley. I had named the valley Lesapi after my birth-place where once I had learned to fish, to swim and to lie back into the soft green grass and relax, with my eyes closed and my head ringing with the cawing of the crows and the leisurely moo of cows grazing on Mr Robert's side of the river, where it was fenced and there was a notice about trespassers. And in the summer the white people held rubber-boat races on the river and sometimes I was allowed to watch them swirling along in the breezy hold of the river. But somebody drowned one day and my father told me not to go down to the river any more because the drowned boy would have turned into a manfish and he would want to have company in the depths of the waters. Water was good, but only when it did not have a manfish in it. My first nightmare was about a white manfish which materialized in my room and licked its great jaws at me and came towards my bed and said: 'Come, come, come with me', and it raised its hand and drew a circle on the wall behind my head and said, 'That circle will always bleed until you come to me.' I looked at his hand and the fingers were webbed, with livid skin attaching each finger to another finger. And then he stretched out his index finger and touched my cheek with it. It was like being touched by a red-hot spike; and I cried out, but I could not hear my own voice: and they were trying to break down the door, and I cried out louder and the wooden door splintered apart and father rushed in with a world war in his eyes. But the manfish had gone; and there was a black frog squatting where he had been. The next day the medicine-man came and examined me and shook his head and said that an enemy had done it. He named Barbara's father, and my father bought strong medicine which would make what had been done to me boomerang on Barbara's father. They then made little incisions on my face and on my chest and rubbed a black powder into them, and said that should I ever come near water I must say to myself: 'Help me, grandfather.' My grandfather was dead, but they said that his spirit was always looking and watching over me. They made a fire and cast the black frog into it, and the medicine-man said he would seed its ashes in Barbara's father's garden. But he could do nothing about the circle on the wall, because although I could clearly see it no one else could. Shortly after this, my eyes dimmed a little and I have had to wear spectacles since then; at the time, however, it only made the little circle jump sharply at me each time I entered my room. The spot where the manfish had touched me swelled with pus, and mother had to boil water with lots of salt and then squeeze the pus out and bathe it with the salted water; after that it healed a little, and ever since I have always had a little black mark there on my face. Soon afterwards Barbara's father went mad and one day his body was fished out of the river by police divers who wore black fishsuits. There were various abrasions on his face and the body was utterly naked, and something in the river seemed to have tried to eat him – there were curious toothmarks on his buttocks and his shoulders had been partially eaten; the hands looked as though something had chewed them and tried to gnaw them from the arms.

Every morning, when the sun rose, there was a fine mist

in the valley, and the interplay of the sun's rays on it created fantastic images within the mist. And they invariably looked like people I had once known. The shapes within the mist were somewhat formless, and yet with such a realistic solidity to them that I could never quite decide what to think. I had named the valley to give it the myths and faces of moments in my own life. But as the years went by, the waterless valley – paralysed by the cramping effects of an overwhelming oppression – emitted its own symbolic mists which overpowered my own imagination, and at last so erupted with its own smoke and fire and faces and shapes that I could not tell which valley was the real Lesapi. I had been physically weakened by the great shortage of water and the shortage of food. Besides, I had never been very strong. And this eerie region which was so stricken by the sun seemed to have a prodigious population of insects: flies, mosquitoes, cicadas, spiders, and scorpions. The cicadas were good to eat; the rest tormented me with their sudden stinging. The massive difference between the temperature of the days and the temperature of the nights was also a severe torture. And the manner in which I had been brought up was not calculated to cramp and stifle the imagination; rather my imagination has always been quick to the point of frightening me. All this made the valley come out alive at my very doorstep. The circle which Maria had drawn on the wall seemed alive; it was in constant motion, changing colour, breaking and rearranging itself into a cross, moving again into a circle and bleeding and running down the wall till I cried in my sleep. It seemed I was in many places at one and the same time; my sleeping and waking had no difference between them. There was a sharp but remote flame of pain inside my head; it seemed I was not so much talking to myself as talking to the things of that valley.

I woke up one morning and at once felt in myself that something was wrong. I could not move; I could move neither my body nor my hands nor my feet. At first I thought something had in the night strapped me down to the ground, but I could feel no bonds binding me. When I realized what had happened I almost cried out – but held my breath because there was no one to hear me. Not only had my hair grown into the floor like roots, but also my fingers and my toes and the veins and arteries of my body had all in my sleep grown into the earth floor. I had been turned into some sort of plant, I thought. And as soon as that thought seared through my head I immediately could feel that my skin had turned into bark. It has happened at last, I said to myself. As I did so I noticed that the circle on the wall had begun to bleed and was running down the wall: something had happened to Maria. I could not feel my eyes, nor my ears, but, strangely, I could see and I could hear. I do not know how long I lay there; nor what days or weeks passed as I lay there fighting back the feverish delirium that soon swamped me. And I was staring fixedly at Maria's life bleeding on the wall; and stared at it so much that I could see nothing else but that red circle bleeding slowly down the wall.

It was like sleeping with one's eyes open.

The footsteps outside had stopped at my door and I could hear heavy breathing. The roof rattled a little as the south-east wind swept by. And then the breathing stopped. The wind stopped too, and the roof did not rattle any more. It suddenly dawned on me that the footsteps were actually inside me; they were my old heart beating, my old things come home. The door had not opened, but I could see her clearly. She was mere bones, a fleshless skeleton, and she was sitting on a tree-trunk. I was the tree-trunk. I do not know how long she sat there. She was weeping; clear tears, silvery and yet like glass, coming out of the stone of her eyeless sockets; and her small gleaming head rested in the open bones of her palms, whose arms rested lightly on her knees. And she held between her front teeth a silver button which I recognized: I had years before bought her a coat which had buttons like that. It was the sight of her forlornly chewing that button which filled me with such a great sadness that I did not realize that my roots had been painlessly severed and that what was left to do was to bind my wounds and once more – but with a fresh eye – walk the way of the valley. The roof was rattling once more; the south-east winds were singing a muffled song through the door. And those horrid footfalls retreated until their distant echo beat silently in my breast.

After that, the sun never came up. I do not know where it had decided to go. Perhaps it fell into the sea where the great manfish lives. Anyway, the night did not come either; it had retreated to the bedrock of the deepest sea where the great manfish came from. There was in the sky so much of its face that even the stars had grown vicious and turned into menfish. And they all wanted company; they were all hungry for me, thirsty for me. But I kept a careful watch and always chewed the silver button, because that alone can keep them away. Yesterday I met Barbara's father in the valley:

'I'll get you in the end, you rascal!' he screamed.

But I bit the silver button and turned myself into a crocodile and laughed my great sharp teeth at him.

He instantly turned himself into mist, and I could only bite chunks of air. While I was cursing him, a voice I did not recognize said:

'You thought it was all politics, didn't you?'

But there was no one there.

I sneered:

'Isn't it?'

And I sullenly turned myself back into human shape. I had decided to write all this down because I do not know when the stinking menfish will get me. Maria, if ever you find this – my head is roaring with fever and I scarcely know what I have written – I think the menfish are out to undermine my reason – if ever you find this – I think Barbara's father is coming to get me and the sky and the earth and the air are all full of monsters like him and me – like him – I wish I had been able to give you a child – my head! – all grown-ups are menfish, but remember perhaps there is still a chance that the children – my head!

I have been a manfish all my life. Maria, you did well to leave me. I must go.

JACK COPE

POWER

FROM THE GUM tree at the corner he looked out over, well – nothing. There was nothing more after his father's place, only the veld, so flat and unchanging that the single shadowy koppie away off towards the skyline made it look more empty still. It was a lonely koppie like himself.

The one thing that made a difference was the powerline. High above the earth on its giant steel lattice towers, the powerline strode across the veld until it disappeared beyond the koppie. It passed close to his father's place and one of the great pylons was on their ground in a square patch fenced off with barbed wire, a forbidden place. André used to look through the wire at the pylon. Around the steelwork itself were more screens of barbed wire, and on all four sides of it enamel warning-plates with a red skull and crossbones said in three languages, DANGER! And there was a huge figure of volts, millions of volts.

André was ten and he knew volts were electricity and the line took power by a short cut far across country. It worked gold mines, it lit towns, and hauled trains and drove machinery somewhere out beyond. The power station was in the town ten miles on the other side of his father's place and the great line simply jumped right over them without stopping.

André filled the empty spaces in his life by imagining things. Often he was a jet plane and roared around the house and along the paths with his arms outspread. He saw an Everest film once and for a long time he was Hillary or Tensing, or both, conquering a mountain. There were no mountains so he conquered the roof of the house which wasn't very high and was made of red-painted tin. But he reached the summit and planted a flag on the lightning conductor. When he got down his mother hit his legs with a quince switch for being naughty.

Another time he conquered the koppie. It took him the whole afternoon to get there and back and it was not as exciting as he expected, being less steep than it looked from a distance, so he did not need his rope and pick. Also, he found a cow had beaten him to the summit.

He thought of conquering one of the powerline towers. It had everything, the danger especially, and studying it from all sides he guessed he could make the summit without touching a live wire. But he was not as disobedient as all that, and he knew if he so much as went inside the barbed-wire fence his mother would skin him with the quince, not to mention his father. There were peaks which had to remain unconquered.

He used to lie and listen to the marvellous hum of the powerline, the millions of volts flowing invisible and beyond all one's ideas along the copper wires that hung so smooth and light from ties of crinkled white china looking like chinese lanterns up against the sky. Faint cracklings and murmurs and rushes of sound would sometimes come from the powerline, and at night he was sure he saw soft blue flames lapping and trembling on the wires as if they were only half peeping out of that fierce river of volts. The flames danced and their voices chattered to him of a mystery.

In the early morning when the mist was rising and the first sun's rays were shooting underneath it, the powerline sparkled like a tremendous spiderweb. It took his thoughts away into a magical distance, far – far off among gigantic machines and busy factories. That was where the world opened up. So he loved the powerline dearly. It made a door through the distance for his thoughts. It was like him except that it never slept, and while he was dreaming it went on without stopping, crackling faintly and murmuring. Its electricity hauled up the mine skips from the heart of the earth, hurtled huge green rail units along their shining lines, and thundered day and night in the factories.

Now that the veld's green was darkening and gathering black-and-gold tints from the ripe seeds and withering grass blades, now that clear warm autumn days were coming after the summer thunderstorms, the birds began gathering on the powerline. At evening he would see the wire like necklaces of blue-and-black glass beads when the swallows gathered. It took them days and days, it seemed, to make up their minds. He did not know whether the same swallows collected each evening in growing numbers or whether a batch went off each day to be replaced by others. He did not know enough about them. He loved to hear them making excited twittering sounds, he loved to see how they simply fell off the copper wire into space and their perfect curved wings lifted them on the air.

They were going not merely beyond the skyline like the power, they were flying thousands of miles over land and sea and mountains and forests to countries he had never dreamt of. They would fly over Everest, perhaps, they would see ships below them on blue seas among islands, they would build nests under bridges and on chimneys where other boys in funny clothes would watch them. The birds opened another door for him and he liked them too, very much.

He watched the swallows one morning as they took off from their perch. Suddenly, as if they had a secret signal, a whole stretch of them along a wire would start together. They dropped forward into the air and their blue-and-white wings flicked out. Flying seemed to be the easiest thing in the world. They swooped and flew up, crisscrossing in flight and chirping crazily, so pleased to be awake in the morning. Then another flight of them winged off, and another. There was standing-room only on those wires. Close to the lofty pylon and the gleaming china ties another flight took off. But one of the swallows stayed behind, quite close to the tie. André watched them fall forward, but it alone did not leave the line. It flapped its wings and he saw it was caught by its leg.

He should have been going to school but he stood watching the swallow, his cap pulled over his white hair and eyes wrinkled against the light. After a minute the swallow stopped flapping and hung there. He wondered how it could have got caught, maybe in the wire binding or at a join. Swallows had short legs and small black claws; he had caught one once in its nest and held it in his hands before it struggled free and was gone in a flash. He thought the bird on the powerline would get free soon, but looking at it there he had a tingling kind of pain in his chest and in one leg as if he too were caught by the foot. André wanted to rush back and tell his mother, only she would scold him for being late to school. So he climbed on his bike, and with one more look up at the helpless bird there against the sky and the steel framework of the tower, he rode off to the bus.

At school he thought once or twice about the swallow, but mostly he forgot about it and that made him feel bad. Anyway, he thought, it would be free by the time he got home. Twisting and flapping a few times, it was sure to work its foot out; and there was no need for him to worry about it hanging there.

Coming back from the crossroads he felt anxious, but he did not like to look up until he was quite near. Then he shot one glance at the top of the pylon – the swallow was still there, its wings spread but not moving. It was dead, he guessed, as he stopped and put down one foot. Then he saw it flutter and fold up its wings. He felt awful to think it had hung there all day, trapped. The boy went in and called his mother and they stood off some distance below the powerline and looked at the bird. The mother shaded her eyes with her hand. It was a pity, she said, but really she was sure it would free itself somehow. Nothing could be done about it.

'Couldn't—?' he began.

'Couldn't nothing, dear,' she said quite firmly so that he knew she meant business. 'Now stop thinking about it, and tomorrow you'll see.'

His father came home at six and had tea, and afterwards there was a little time to work in his patch of vegetables out at the back. André followed him and he soon got round to the swallow on the powerline.

'I know,' his father said. 'Mama told me.'

'It's still there.'

'Well—' his father tilted up his old working-hat and looked at him hard with his sharp blue eyes '—well, we can't do anything about it, can we, now?'

'No, Papa, but—'

'But what?'

He kicked at a stone and said nothing more. He could see his father was kind of stiff about it; that meant he did not want to hear anything more. They had been talking about it, and maybe – yes, that was it. They were afraid he would try to climb up the pylon.

At supper none of them talked about the swallow, but André felt it all right. He felt as if it was hanging above their heads and his mother and father felt it and they all had a load on them. Going to bed his mother said to him he must not worry himself about the poor bird. 'Not a sparrow falls without our Good Lord knowing.'

'It's not a sparrow, it's a swallow,' he said. 'It's going to hang there all night, by its foot.' His mother sighed and put out the light. She was worried.

The next day was a Saturday and he did not have to go to school. First thing he looked out and the bird was still there. The other swallows were with it, and when they took off it fluttered and made little thin calls but could not get free.

He would rather have been at school instead of knowing all day that it was hanging up there on the cruel wire. It was strange how the electricity did nothing to it. He knew, of course, that the wires were quite safe as long as you did not touch anything else. The morning was very long, though he did forget about the swallow quite often. He was building a mud fort under the gum tree, and he had to carry water and dig up the red earth and mix it into a stiff clay. When he was coming in at midday with his khaki hat flapping round his face he had one more look, and what he saw kept him standing there a long time with his mouth open. Other swallows were fluttering and hovering around the trapped bird, trying to help it. He rushed inside and dragged his mother out by her hand and she stood too, shading her eyes again and looking up.

'Yes, they're feeding it. Isn't that strange,' she said.

'Sssh! Don't frighten them,' he whispered.

In the afternoon he lay in the grass and twice again he saw the other swallows fluttering round the fastened bird with short quivering strokes of their wings and opening their beaks wide. Swallows had pouches in their throats where they made small mud bricks to build their nests, and that was how they brought food to it. They knew how to feed their fledglings and when the trapped bird squeaked and cried out they brought it food. André felt choked thinking how they helped it and nobody else would do anything. His parents would not even talk about it.

With his keen eyes he traced the way a climber could get up the tower. Most difficult would be to get round the barbed-wire screens about a quarter of the way up. After that there were footholds in the steel lattice supports. He had studied it before. But if you did get up, what then? How could you touch the swallow? Just putting your hand near the wire, wouldn't those millions of volts flame out and jump at you? The only thing was to get somebody to turn off the power for a minute, then he could whip up the tower like a monkey. At supper that night he suggested it, and his father was as grim and angry as he'd ever been.

'Crumbs,' André said to himself. 'Crumbs! They are both het up about it.'

'Listen, son,' his father had said. He never said 'son' unless he was really mad over something. 'Listen, I don't want you to get all worked up about that bird. I'll see what can be done. But you leave it alone. Don't get any ideas into your head, and don't go near that damned pylon.'

'What ideas, Papa?' he asked, trembling inside himself.

'Any ideas at all.'

'The other birds are feeding it, but it may die.'

'Well, I'm sorry; try not to think about it.'

When his mother came to say goodnight to him he turned his face over into his pillow and would not kiss her. It was something he had never done before and it was because he was angry with them both. They let the swallow swing there in the night and did nothing.

His mother patted his back and ruffled his white hair and said, 'Goodnight, darling.' But he gritted his teeth and did not answer.

Ages seemed to him to have passed. On Sunday the bird was still hanging on the lofty powerline, fluttering feebly. He could not bear to look up at it. After breakfast he went out and tried to carry on building his fort under the gum tree. The birds were chattering in the tree above him and in the wattles at the back of the house. Through the corner of his eye he saw a handsome black-and-white bird fly out in swinging loops from the tree and it settled on the power-line some distance from the tower. It was a butcher-bird, a Jackey-hangman, a terrible greedy pirate of a bird. His heart fell like a stone – he just guessed what it was up to. It sat there on the wire impudently copying the calls of other birds. It could imitate a toppie or a robin or a finch as it liked. It stole their naked little kickers from their nests and spiked them on the barbed wire to eat at pleasure, as it stole their songs too. The butcher-bird flew off and settled higher up the wire near the pylon.

André rushed up the path and then took a swing from the house to come under the powerline. Stopping, he saw the other birds were making a whirl and flutter round the cannibal. Swallows darted and skimmed and made him duck his head, but he went on sitting there. Then some starlings came screaming out of the gum tree and flew in a menacing bunch at the butcher-bird. They all hated him. He made the mistake of losing his balance and fluttered out into the air and all the birds were round him at once, darting and pecking and screaming.

The butcher-bird pulled off one of his typical tricks: he fell plumb down and when near the ground spread his wings, sailed low over the shrubs, and came up at the house where he settled on the lightning conductor. André stood panting and felt his heart beating fast. He wanted to throw a stone at the butcher-bird but he reckoned the stone would land on the roof and get him in trouble. So he ran towards the house waving his arms and shouting. The bird cocked its head and watched him.

His mother came out. 'Darling, what's the matter?'

'That Jackey, he's on the roof. He wanted to kill the swallow.'

'Oh, darling!' the mother said softly.

It was Sunday night and he said to his mother, 'It's only the other birds keeping him alive. They were feeding him again today.'

'I saw them.'

'He can't live much longer, Mama. And now the Jackey knows he's there. Why can't Papa get them to switch off the electricity?'

'They wouldn't do it for a bird, darling. Now try to go to sleep.'

Leaving for school on Monday, he tried not to look up. But he couldn't help it and there was the swallow spreading and closing its wings. He quickly got on his bike and rode as fast as he could. He could not think of anything but the trapped bird on the powerline.

After school, André did not catch the bus home. Instead he took a bus the other way, into town. He got out in a busy street and threading down through the factory area he kept his bearings on the four huge smokestacks of the power station. Out of two of the smokestacks white plumes were rising calmly into the clear sky. When he got to the power station he was faced with an enormous high fence of iron staves with spiked tops and a tall steel gate, locked fast. He peered through the gate and saw some black men off duty, sitting in the sun on upturned boxes playing some kind of draughts game. He called them, and a big slow-moving man in brown overalls and a wide leather belt came over to talk.

André explained very carefully what he wanted. If they would switch off the current then he or somebody good at climbing could go up and save the swallow. The man smiled broadly and clicked his tongue. He shouted something at the others and they laughed. His name, he said, was Gas – Gas Makabeni. He was just a maintenance boy and he couldn't switch off the current. But he unlocked a steel frame-door in the gate and let André in.

'Ask them in there,' he said, grinning. André liked Gas very much. He had ESCOM in big cloth letters on his back and he was friendly, opening the door like that. André went with Gas through a high arched entrance and at once he seemed to be surrounded with the vast awesome hum of the power station. It made him feel jumpy. Gas took him to a door and pushed him in. A white engineer in overalls questioned him and he smiled too.

'Well,' he said. 'Let's see what can be done.'

He led him down a long corridor and up a short cut of steel zigzag steps. Another corridor came to an enormous panelled hall with banks of dials and glowing lights and men in long white coats sitting in raised chairs or moving about silently. André's heart was pounding good and fast. He could hear the humming sound strongly and it seemed to come from everywhere, not so much a sound as a feeling under his feet.

The engineer in overalls handed him over to one of the men at the control panels and he was so nervous by this time he took a long while trying to explain about the swallow. The man had to ask him a lot of questions and he got tongue-tied and could not give clear answers. The man did not smile at all. He went off and a minute later came and fetched André to a big office. A black-haired man with glasses was sitting at a desk. On both sides of the desk were telephones and panels of push-buttons. There was a carpet on the floor and huge leather easy chairs. The whole of one wall was a large and exciting circuit map with flickering coloured lights showing where the power was going all over the country.

André did not say five words before his lip began trembling and two tears rolled out of his eyes. The man told him, 'Sit down, son, and don't be scared.'

Then the man tried to explain. How could they cut off the power when thousands and thousands of machines were running on electricity? He pointed with the back of his pencil at the circuit map. If there were a shutdown the power would have to be rerouted, and that meant calling in other power stations and putting a heavy load on the lines. Without current for one minute the trains would stop, hospitals would go dark in the middle of an operation, the mine skips would suddenly halt twelve thousand feet down. He knew André was worried about the swallow, only things like that just happened and that was life.

'Life?' André said, thinking it was more like death.

The big man smiled. He took down the boy's name and address, and he said, 'You've done your best, André. I'm sorry I can't promise you anything.'

Downstairs again, Gas Makabeni let him out at the gate. 'Are they switching off the power?' Gas asked.

'No.'

'*Mayi babo!*' Gas shook his head and clicked. But he did not smile this time. He could see the boy was very unhappy.

André got home hours late and his mother was frantic. He lied to her too, saying he had been detained after school. He kept his eyes away from the powerline and did not have the stomach to look for the swallow. He felt so bad about it because they were all letting it die. Except for the other swallows that brought it food it would be dead already.

And that was life, the man said. . . .

It must have been the middle of the night when he woke up. His mother was in the room and the light was on.

'There's a man come to see you,' she said. 'Did you ask anyone to come here?'

'No, Mama,' he said, dazed.

'Get up and come.' She sounded cross and he was scared stiff. He went out on to the stoep and there he saw his father in his pyjamas and the back of a big man in brown overalls with ESCOM on them: a black man. It was Gas Makabeni!

'Gas!' he shouted. 'Are they going to do it?'

'They're doing it,' Gas said.

A linesman and a truck driver came up the steps on the stoep. The linesman explained to André's father a maintenance switch-down had been ordered at minimum-load hour. He wanted to be shown where the bird was. André glanced, frightened, at his father who nodded and said, 'Show him.'

He went in the maintenance truck with the man and the driver and Gas. It took them only five minutes to get the truck in position under the tower. The maintenance man checked the time and they began running up the extension ladder. Gas hooked a chain in his broad belt and pulled on his flashlight helmet. He swung out on the ladder and began running up it as if he had no weight at all. Up level with the pylon insulators, his flashlight picked out the swallow hanging on the dead wire. He leaned over and carefully worked the bird's tiny claw loose from the wire binding and then he put the swallow in the breast pocket of his overalls.

In a minute he was down again and he took the bird out and handed it to the boy. André could see even in the light of the flashlamp that the swallow had faint grey fringes round the edges of its shining blue-black feathers and that meant it was a young bird. This was its first year. He was almost speechless, holding the swallow in his hands and feeling its slight quiver.

'Thanks,' he said. 'Thanks, Gas. Thanks, sir.'

His father took the swallow from him at the house and went off to find a box to keep it out of reach of the cats.

'Off you go to bed now,' the mother said. 'You've had quite enough excitement for one day.'

The swallow drank thirstily but would not eat anything, so the parents thought it best to let it go as soon as it would fly. André took the box to his fort near the gum tree and looked towards the koppie and the powerline. It was early morning and dew sparkled on the overhead wires and made the whole level veld gleam like a magic inland sea. He held the swallow in his cupped hands and it lay there quiet with the tips of its wings crossed. Suddenly it took two little jumps with its tiny claws and spread its slender wings. Frantically they beat the air. The bird seemed to be dropping to the ground. Then it skimmed forward only a foot above the grass.

He remembered long afterwards how, when it really took wing and began to gain height, it gave a little shiver of happiness, as if it knew it was free.

JAMAL MAHJOUB

ROAD BLOCK

THE STORYTELLER DROVE a Toyota Hilux, red with a horn that played seven different tunes. Everything that wasn't chrome was painted a gaudy silver. In the back of the pickup he had red lights that spun like catherine wheels, and in the front he had a string of coloured fairy lights that were draped across the acrylic fur of the dashboard. The tailboards were covered in scrawled poems in Arabic lines; passages from the Koran where the word Allah appeared frequently. Though if Allah were in fact to cast his eye this way he might not have been too impressed with this storyteller.

His father of course was the original Storyteller. They still remember him in the small innumerable villages that cling to the sides of the Red Sea Hills and drop away into the Nubian Desert. Famous among the Beja tribes through which he used to travel on foot telling his tales in exchange for a square meal. One of the last greats, they refer to him, though most of those who might remember are either dead or have gone insane with age.

His son was a man who lived by his wits, a smuggler. He ran a ring of sizeable proportion importing whisky and almost anything else that you were willing to pay for. They operated out of the old port at Suakin, a ghost town.

It was after the curfew hour, the early hours of the morning in fact, when he came hurtling out of the darkness on a quiet stretch of road that would take him away from the coast.

He was late because he had spent rather longer than he had expected with one of the girls at Mama Samina's. The narrow road stretched out in front of him and, despite the fact he was a little late, he was singing to himself in the cool dusty air of a December night.

The road block was a square shed of bare brick and a large mimosa tree. There were only two men there at one time. Bona sat with his rifle across his knees and tried to lean his chair back against the wall of the building. His partner had gone to bed complaining that his tapeworms were acting up and giving him pain. Bona hated his partner who was fat and smelled. They were from different ends of the country. Bona was an Azande from the far south, his partner was a northerner. As for any kind of tribal dislike between them, Bona was more bothered by the fact that his partner ate like a pig and smelt like one too. The sooner their spell here was up the better as far as he was concerned.

The lights from the Toyota were getting nearer. The Storyteller had forgotten about the road block as it was quite a recent addition. By the time he realized what it was he knew that he would already have been seen. It was easy enough to pull off the road and make a wide detour of the sentry post and rejoin the road later on. However, he didn't know the ground round here all that well and he didn't want to risk hitting a pothole or even getting hit by a stray bullet. His cargo of Scotch whisky was far too valuable to risk in some mad race in the dark. He slowed down and switched off his lights. With luck they would all be asleep.

Bona saw the lights go off and he stood up slowly. Cocking the old Lee Enfield over his shoulder so that it hung forwards across him, he rested his hand on the gun the way he had seen it in one of those Italian cowboy films. He stepped into the middle of the road and stood, legs akimbo, facing down the dark alleyway of the night.

The Storyteller saw the figure outlined in the darkness as he crawled slowly towards the checkpoint. Cursing under his breath, he switched on the sidelights and saw the tall thin man who was waving him to stop with a laconic flick of the wrist. He stopped when the plastic horns mounted on the radiator were almost touching the statue-like policeman.

Bona stepped aside and crooked the barrel of his gun at the figure in the driving seat. 'Out,' he indicated with his rifle.

As he climbed out, the Storyteller was cursing himself for his stupidity, thinking about where this man's partner was. He was wondering about what to offer as a bribe.

Bona was thinking about how the sharp leather of his boots cut into his bare feet. He was thinking about the way he looked, trying to remember if the rifle had been cleaned recently.

'Where are you going this time of night?'

'Home. I fell asleep in town but I have been working all day at the port.'

Bona glanced at the tarpaulin-covered shape in the back of the pickup.

'You've been working at the port today?'

The other man nodded. 'I work for the hospital.'

'Which hospital is that?' asked Bona carefully. He moved towards the back of the Toyota. The Storyteller reached for a cigarette, the bolt snapped back as Bona cocked the rifle.

'Just a cigarette,' said the other man, holding up the packet. Bona shook his head at the offer and waited while the Storyteller lit his. Placing the packet back in the pocket of his gjallabia, he rested a hand on his hip, inches away from the pistol that he kept under cover strapped to his waist. He smiled at the policeman.

'Which hospital?'

'The American Hospital, at Quaz Rajab. That's where I live.'

'I didn't know there was an American Hospital here.'

'Really? It's quite new, I suppose.'

Bona licked his gums, at the front where his two front teeth had been removed as a young man. He watched the driver very carefully as he sucked on his cigarette and exhaled, foreign cigarettes.

'And what is there here, things for the hospital?'

'Medicine.' He tapped his chest. 'For the sick, for coughs and chest infections.' Bona nodded understandingly. He stepped over and tugged at the cover, indicating it should be opened up. 'Let me see,' he said.

The Storyteller dropped his cigarette into the dust and moved across to untie the canvas cover, flipping it back so that the sentry could see the boxes. He held a hand out for Bona to inspect the contents. 'There you are.'

Bona stepped back and squinted in the bad light.

'Don't be vague,' he read slowly in English, 'ask for Haig.'

The Storyteller rested his hand back on the Browning automatic. He hadn't expected the man to be able to read English – whoever heard of a stupid policeman being able to read English? He scratched his head.

Bona looked up at the driver. The Storyteller looked back at him.

'What does it mean?' He pointed with his hand. 'Don't be vague,' he read again.

The sentry stood back and waited. The Storyteller scratched his head with his one free hand. He looked at the boxes, then back at the skinny black southerner with the trousers that stopped halfway down his legs on their way to his boots, so that there were about six inches of exposed legs: two skinny bone legs the size of twigs.

The sentry shrugged and shifted the weight of his rifle. He was waiting. The Storyteller rubbed his neck. 'Don't be vague, ask for Haig?' he repeated. He spoke very little English and could hardly read what it said – he repeated the words the sentry had used.

'It means,' he said, 'that you should never let yourself become ill, and you must always drink your medicine.' He nodded enthusiastically, quite pleased at how convincing he sounded. Bona shifted his rifle again and sucked his gums for a moment.

'Let me see this wonderful medicine.'

'You want to see it? It's just cough medicine, brown liquid.'

Bona raised the barrel of his rifle until it was pointing squarely at the other man's chest. There was no way he could pull the pistol out faster than the sentry could shoot him dead; all he had to do was squeeze the trigger.

The Storyteller raised up his hands and showed his palms.

'No problem, officer,' he smiled. 'If you want to see, then you shall see. I shall open these boxes for you myself,' he continued, 'one by one,' he added dramatically, shaking a finger to emphasize his conviction.

Bona smiled and cocked his head to indicate that he could start opening boxes straight away. The Storyteller had no choice. He stepped forward now and pulled the canvas away with a jerk of his hand, his irritation showing for a brief moment. The sentry looked away and smiled inwardly to himself. The cardboard was slit and the box opened. Dozens of tiny minatures gleamed in the starlight. With one hand on the trigger, Bona leaned over and plucked a bottle from the array. He held it up so the whisky glowed in the light. He twisted the cap off with his teeth and held the neck up to his nose.

'Cough medicine?' he asked again.

The Storyteller nodded resignedly. Bona tilted his neck back and poured the contents down his throat, draining the bottle in one go. He swallowed and licked his lips. Then he threw the empty bottle over his shoulder into the darkness. He cleared his throat.

'Cough medicine,' he nodded, and stepped back raising the rifle again.

This was the moment that the Storyteller had been trying to prepare himself for. He would have to shoot the man dead. He closed his finger round the butt of the pistol. Bona was talking again.

'All the same, are they? All the same kind of medicine?'

The Storyteller nodded, his finger finding the trigger.

'I'll have that one,' said Bona quickly.

'What?'

'That box there, I'll take that one.' He glanced back at the sentry post just to check if his partner had woken up, though he knew the pig would be asleep until midday tomorrow. 'Just lift it over the side and leave it in the dust.'

The Storyteller hesitated and then moved rapidly, pulling the case forward and over the tailboard. Bona nodded, then he waved a hand down the road and stepped away, lowering the rifle. The two men stood facing each other for a moment, then without saying a word the Storyteller pulled the canvas back in place and tied it down. He climbed into the cab and started the engine, punching it into gear and roaring away down the road into the welcome darkness. Above the racing engine and the howl of the wind past the open window of the car, he thought he could hear the sound of laughter. In the mirror he could just make out the figure of the sentry returning to his post with his prize under one arm.

The man they now called the Storyteller didn't really share the same gift as his father, but then that was what the pistol was for.

CHIMAMANDA NGOZI ADICHIE

GHOSTS

TODAY I SAW Ikenna Okoro, a man I had long thought was dead. Perhaps I should have bent down, grabbed a handful of sand, and thrown it at him, in the way my people do to make sure a person is not a ghost. But I am a Western-educated man, a retired mathematics professor of seventy-one, and I am supposed to have armed myself with enough science to laugh indulgently at the ways of my people. I did not throw sand at him. I could not have done so even if I had wished to, anyway, since we met on the concrete grounds of the university Bursary.

I was there to ask about my pension, yet again. 'Good day, Prof,' the dried-up-looking clerk, Ugwuoke, said. 'Sorry, the money has not come in.'

The other clerk, whose name I have now forgotten, nodded and apologized as well, while chewing on a pink lobe of kola nut. They were used to this. I was used to this. So were the tattered men who were clustered under the flame tree, talking loudly among themselves, gesturing. The education minister has stolen the pension money, one fellow said. Another said that it was the vice chancellor who had deposited the money in high-interest personal accounts. They cursed the vice chancellor: His penis will quench. His children will not have children. He will die of diarrhoea. When I walked up to them, they greeted me and shook their heads apologetically about the situation, as if my professor-level pension were somehow more important than their messenger-level or driver-level pensions. They called me Prof, as most people do, as the hawkers sitting next to their trays under the tree did. 'Prof! Prof! Come and buy good banana!'

I chatted with Vincent, who had been our driver when I was faculty dean in the eighties. 'No pension for three years, Prof,' he said. 'This is why people retire and die.'

'*O joka*,' I said, although he, of course, did not need me to tell him how terrible it was.

'How is Nkiru, Prof? I trust she is well in America?' He always asks about our daughter. He often drove my wife, Ebere, and me to visit her at the College of Medicine in Enugu. I remember that when Ebere died, he came with his relatives for *mgbalu* and gave a touching, if rather long, speech about how well Ebere had treated him when he was our driver, how she gave him our daughter's old clothes for his children.

'Nkiru is well,' I said.

'Please greet her for me when she calls, Prof.'

'I will.'

He talked for a while longer, about ours being a country that has not learned to say thank you, about the students in the hostels not paying him on time for mending their shoes. But it was his Adam's apple that held my attention; it bobbed alarmingly, as if just about to pierce the wrinkled skin of his neck and pop out. Vincent is younger than I am, perhaps in his late sixties, but he looks older. He has little hair left. I quite remember his incessant chatter while he drove me to work in those days; I remember, too, that he was fond of reading my newspapers, a practice I did not encourage.

'Prof, won't you buy us banana? Hunger is killing us,' one of the men gathered under the flame tree said. He had a familiar face. I think he was my next-door neighbour

Professor Ijere's gardener. His tone had a half-teasing, half-serious quality, but I bought groundnuts and a bunch of bananas for them, although what all those men really needed was some moisturizer. Their faces and arms looked like ash. It is almost March, but the harmattan season is still very much here: the dry winds, the crackling static on my clothes, the fine dust on my eyelashes. I applied more lotion than usual today, and Vaseline on my lips, but still the dryness made my palms and face feel tight.

Ebere used to tease me about not moisturizing properly, especially in the harmattan, and sometimes after I had my morning bath, she would slowly rub her Nivea on my arms, my legs, my back. We have to take care of this lovely skin, she would say with that playful laughter of hers. She always said my complexion had been the trait that persuaded her, since I did not have any money like all those other suitors who had trooped to her flat on Elias Avenue in 1961. 'Seamless,' she called my complexion. I saw nothing especially distinctive in my dark umber tone, but I did come to preen a little with the passing years, with Ebere's massaging hands.

'Thank you, Prof!' the men said, and then began to mock one another about who would do the dividing.

I stood around and listened to their talk. I was aware that they spoke more respectably because I was there: carpentry was not going well, children were ill, more moneylender troubles. They laughed often. Of course they nurse resentment, as they well should, but it has somehow managed to leave their spirits whole. I often wonder whether I would be like them if I did not have money saved from my appointments in the Federal Office of Statistics and if Nkiru did not insist on sending me dollars that I do not need. I doubt it; I would probably have hunched up like a tortoise in its shell and let my dignity be whittled away.

Finally I said goodbye to them and walked towards my car, parked near the whistling pine trees that shield the Faculty of Education from the Bursary. That was when I saw Ikenna Okoro.

He called out to me first. 'James? James Nwoye, is it you?' He stood with his mouth open and I could see that his teeth are still complete. I lost one last year. I have refused to have what Nkiru calls 'work' done, but I still felt rather sour at Ikenna's full set.

'Ikenna? Ikenna Okoro?' I asked in the tentative way one suggests something that cannot be: the coming to life of a man who died thirty-seven years ago.

'Yes, yes.' Ikenna came closer, uncertainly. We shook hands, and then hugged briefly.

We had not been good friends, Ikenna and I; I knew him fairly well in those days only because everyone knew him fairly well. It was he who, when the new vice chancellor, a Nigerian man raised in England, announced that all lecturers must wear ties to class, had defiantly continued to wear his brightly coloured tunics. It was he who mounted the podium at the Staff Club and spoke until he was hoarse, about petitioning the government, about supporting better conditions for the non-academic staff. He was in sociology, and although many of us in the proper sciences thought that the social sciences people were empty vessels who had too much time on their hands and wrote reams of unreadable books, we saw Ikenna differently. We forgave his peremptory style and did not discard his pamphlets and rather admired the erudite asperity with which he blazed through issues; his fearlessness convinced us. He is still a shrunken man with froglike eyes and light skin, which has now become discoloured, dotted with brown age spots. One heard of him in those days and then struggled to hide great disappointment upon seeing him, because the depth of his rhetoric somehow demanded good looks. But then, my people say that a famous animal does not always fill the hunter's basket.

'You're alive?' I asked. I was quite shaken. My family and I saw him on the day he died, 6 July 1967, the day we evacuated Nsukka in a hurry, with the sun a strange fiery red in the sky and nearby the *boom-boom-boom* of shelling as the federal soldiers advanced. We were in my Impala. The militia waved us through the campus gates and shouted that we should not worry, that the vandals – as we called the federal soldiers – would be defeated in a matter of days and we could come back. The local villagers, the same ones who would pick through lecturers' dustbins for food after the war, were walking along, hundreds of them, women with boxes on their heads and babies tied to their backs, barefoot children carrying bundles, men dragging bicycles, holding yams. I remember that Ebere was consoling our daughter, Zik, about the doll left behind in our haste, when we saw Ikenna's green Kadett. He was driving the opposite way, back onto campus. I sounded the horn and stopped. 'You can't go back!' I called. But he waved and said, 'I have to get some manuscripts.' Or maybe he said, 'I have to get some materials.' I thought it rather foolhardy of him to go back in, since the shelling sounded close and our troops would drive the vandals back in a week or two anyway. But I was also full of a sense of our collective invincibility, of the justness of the Biafran cause, and so I did not think much more of it until we heard that Nsukka fell on the very day we evacuated and the campus was occupied. The bearer of the news, a relative of Professor Ezike's, also told us that two lecturers had been killed. One of them had argued with the federal soldiers before he was shot. We did not need to be told this was Ikenna.

Ikenna laughed at my question. 'I am, I am alive!' He seemed to find his own response even funnier, because he laughed again. Even his laughter, now that I think of it, seemed discoloured, hollow, nothing like the aggressive sound that reverberated all over the Staff Club in those days, as he mocked people who did not agree with him.

'But we saw you,' I said. 'You remember? That day we evacuated?'

'Yes,' he said.

'They said you did not come out.'

'I did.' He nodded. 'I did. I left Biafra the following month.'

'You left?' It is incredible that I felt, today, a brief flash of that deep disgust that came when we heard of saboteurs – we called them 'sabos' – who betrayed our soldiers, our just cause, our nascent nation, in exchange for a safe passage across to Nigeria, to the salt and meat and cold water that the blockade kept from us.

'No, no, it was not like that, not what you think.' Ikenna paused and I noticed that his grey shirt sagged at the shoulders. 'I went abroad on a Red Cross plane. I went to Sweden.' There was an uncertainty about him, a diffidence that seemed alien, very unlike the man who so easily got people to *act*. I remember how he organized the first rally after Biafra was declared an independent state, all of us crowded at Freedom Square while Ikenna talked and we cheered and shouted, 'Happy Independence!'

'You went to Sweden?'

'Yes.'

He said nothing else, and I realized that he would not tell me more, that he would not tell me just how he had left the campus alive or how he came to be on that plane; I know of the children airlifted to Gabon later in the war but certainly not of people flown out on Red Cross planes, and so early, too. The silence between us was tense.

'Have you been in Sweden since?' I asked.

'Yes. My whole family was in Orlu when they bombed it. Nobody left, so there was no reason for me to come back.' He stopped to let out a harsh sound that was supposed to be laughter but sounded more like a series of coughs. 'I was in touch with Dr Anya for a while. He told me about rebuilding our campus, and I think he said you left for America after the war.'

In fact, Ebere and I came back to Nsukka right after the war ended in 1970, but only for a few days. It was too much for us. Our books were in a charred pile in the front garden, under the umbrella tree. The lumps of calcified faeces in the bathtub were strewn with pages of my *Mathematical Annals*, used as toilet paper, crusted smears blurring the formulas I had studied and taught. Our piano – Ebere's piano – was gone. My graduation gown, which I had worn to receive my first degree at Ibadan, had been used to wipe something and now lay with ants crawling in and out, busy and oblivious to me watching them. Our photographs were ripped, their frames broken. So we left for America and did not come back until 1976. We were assigned a different house, on Ezenweze Street, and for a long time we avoided driving along Imoke Street, because we did not want to see the old house; we later heard that the new people had cut down the umbrella tree. I told Ikenna all of this, although I said nothing about our time at Berkeley, where my black American friend Chuck Bell had arranged for my teaching appointment. Ikenna was silent for a while, and then he said, 'How is your little girl, Zik? She must be a grown woman now.'

He had always insisted on paying for Zik's Fanta when we

took her to the Staff Club on Family Day, because, he said, she was the prettiest of the children. I suspect it was really because we had named her after our president, and Ikenna was an early Zikist before claiming the movement was too tame and leaving.

'The war took Zik,' I said in Igbo. Speaking of death in English has always had, for me, a disquieting finality.

Ikenna breathed deeply, but all he said was '*Ndo*,' nothing more than 'Sorry.' I was relieved he did not ask how – there are not many hows anyway – and that he did not look inordinately shocked, as if war deaths are ever really accidents.

'We had another child after the war, another daughter,' I said.

But Ikenna was talking in a rush. 'I did what I could,' he said. 'I did. I left the International Red Cross. It was full of cowards who could not stand up for human beings. They backed down after that plane was shot down at Eket, as if they did not know it was exactly what Gowon wanted. But the World Council of Churches kept flying in relief through Uli. At night! I was there in Uppsala when they met. It was the biggest operation they had done since the Second World War. I organized the fund-raising. I organized the Biafran rallies all over the European capitals. You heard about the big one at Trafalgar Square? I was at the top of that. I did what I could.'

I was not sure that Ikenna was speaking to me. It seemed that he was saying what he had said over and over to many people. I looked towards the flame tree. The men were still clustered there, but I could not tell whether they had finished the bananas and groundnuts. Perhaps it was then that I began to feel submerged in hazy nostalgia, a feeling that still has not left me.

'Chris Okigbo died, not so?' Ikenna asked, and made me focus once again. For a moment, I wondered if he wanted me to deny that, to make Okigbo a ghost-come-back, too. But Okigbo died, our genius, our star, the man whose poetry moved us all, even those of us in the sciences who did not always understand it.

'Yes, the war took Okigbo.'

'We lost a colossus in the making.'

'True, but at least he was brave enough to fight.' As soon as I said that, I was regretful. I had meant it only as a tribute to Chris Okigbo, who could have worked at one of the directorates like the rest of us university people but instead took up a gun to defend Nsukka. I did not want Ikenna to misunderstand my intention, and I wondered whether to apologize. A small dust whirl was building up across the road. The whistling pines above us swayed and the wind whipped dry leaves off the trees farther away. Perhaps because of my discomfort, I began to tell Ikenna about the day Ebere and I drove back to Nsukka after the war ended, about the landscape of ruins, the blown-out roofs, the houses riddled with holes that Ebere said were rather like Swiss cheese. When we got to the road that runs through Aguleri, Biafran soldiers stopped us and shoved a wounded soldier into our car; his blood dripped onto the back seat and, because the upholstery had a tear, soaked deep into the stuffing mingled with the very insides of our car. A stranger's blood. I was not sure why I chose this particular story to tell Ikenna, but to make it seem worth his while I added that the metallic smell of the soldier's blood reminded me of him, Ikenna, because I had always imagined that the federal soldiers had shot him and left him to die, left his blood to stain the soil. This is not true; I neither imagined such a thing, nor did that wounded soldier remind me of Ikenna. If he thought my story strange, he did not say so. He nodded and said, 'I've heard so many stories, so many.'

'How is life in Sweden?' I asked.

He shrugged. 'I retired last year. I decided to come back and see.' He said 'see' as if it meant something more than what one did with one's eyes.

'What about your family?' I asked.

'I never remarried.'

'Oh,' I said.

'And how is your wife doing? Nnenna, isn't it?' Ikenna asked.

'Ebere.'

'Oh, yes, of course, Ebere. Lovely woman.'

'Ebere is no longer with us; it has been three years,' I said in Igbo. I was surprised to see the tears that glassed Ikenna's eyes. He had forgotten her name and yet, somehow, he was capable of mourning her, or perhaps he was mourning a time immersed in possibilities. Ikenna, I have come to realize, is a man who carries with him the weight of what could have been.

'I'm so sorry,' he said. 'So sorry.'

'It's all right,' I said. 'She visits.'

'What?' he asked with a perplexed look, although he, of course, had heard me.

'She visits. She visits me.'

'I see,' Ikenna said with that pacifying tone one reserves for the mad.

'I mean, she visited America quite often; our daughter is a doctor there.'

'Oh, is that right?' Ikenna asked too brightly. He looked relieved. I don't blame him. We are the educated ones, taught to keep tightly rigid our boundaries of what is considered real. I was like him until Ebere first visited, three weeks after her funeral. Nkiru and her son had just returned to America. I was alone. When I heard the door downstairs close and open and close again, I thought nothing of it. The evening winds always did that. But there was no rustle of leaves outside my bedroom window, no *swish-swish* of the neem and cashew trees. There was *no* wind outside. Yet the door downstairs was opening and closing. In retrospect, I doubt that I was as scared as I should have been. I heard the feet on the stairs, in much the same pattern as Ebere walked, heavier on each third step. I lay still in the darkness of our room. Then I felt my bedcover pulled back, the gently massaging hands on my arms and legs and chest, the soothing creaminess of the lotion, and a pleasant drowsiness overcame me – a drowsiness that I am still unable to fight off whenever she visits. I woke up, as I still do after her visits, with my skin supple and thick with the scent of Nivea.

I often want to tell Nkiru that her mother visits weekly in the harmattan and less often during the rainy season, but if I do, she will finally have reason to come here and bundle me back with her to America and I will be forced to live a life cushioned by so much convenience that it is sterile. A life littered with what we call 'opportunities'. A life that is not for me. I wonder what would have happened if we had won the war back in 1967. Perhaps we would not be looking overseas for those opportunities, and I would not need to worry about our grandson who does not speak Igbo, who, the last time he visited, did not understand why he was expected to say 'Good afternoon' to strangers, because in his world one has to justify simple courtesies. But who can tell? Perhaps nothing would have been different even if we had won.

'How does your daughter like America?' Ikenna asked.

'She is doing very well.'

'And you said she is a doctor?'

'Yes.' I felt that Ikenna deserved to be told more, or maybe that the tension of my earlier comment had not quite abated, so I said, 'She lives in a small town in Connecticut, near Rhode Island. The hospital board had advertised for a doctor, and when she came they took one look at her medical degree from Nigeria and said they did not want a foreigner. But she is American-born – you see, we had her while at Berkeley, I taught there when we went to America after the war – and so they had to let her stay.' I chuckled, and hoped Ikenna would laugh along with me. But he did not. He looked towards the men under the flame tree, his expression solemn.

'Ah, yes. At least it's not as bad now as it was for us. Remember what it was like schooling in *oyibo*-land in the late fifties?' he asked.

I nodded to show I remembered, although Ikenna and I could not have had the same experience as students overseas; he is an Oxford man, while I was one of those who got the United Negro College Fund scholarship to study in America.

'The Staff Club is a shell of what it used to be,' Ikenna said. 'I went there this morning.'

'I haven't been there in so long. Even before I retired, it got to the point where I felt too old and out of place there. These greenhorns are inept. Nobody is teaching. Nobody has fresh ideas. It is university politics, politics, politics, while students buy grades with money or their bodies.'

'Is that right?'

'Oh, yes. Things have fallen. Senate meetings have become personality-cult battles. It's terrible. Remember Josephat Udeana?'

'The great dancer.'

I was taken aback for a moment because it had been so

long since I had thought of Josephat as he was, in those days just before the war, by far the best ballroom dancer we had on campus. 'Yes, yes, he was,' I said, and I felt grateful that Ikenna's memories were frozen at a time when I still thought Josephat to be a man of integrity. 'Josephat was vice chancellor for six years and ran this university like his father's chicken coop. Money disappeared and then we would see new cars stamped with the names of foreign foundations that did not exist. Some people went to court, but nothing came of that. He dictated who would be promoted and who would be stagnated. In short, the man acted like a solo university council. This present vice chancellor is following him faithfully. I have not been paid my pension since I retired, you know. I'm just coming from the Bursary now.'

'And why isn't anybody doing something about all this? Why?' Ikenna asked, and for the briefest moment the old Ikenna was there, in the voice, the outrage, and I was reminded again that this was an intrepid man. Perhaps he would walk over and pound his fist on a nearby tree.

'Well' – I shrugged – 'many of the lecturers are changing their official dates of birth. They go to Personnel Services and bribe somebody and add five years. Nobody wants to retire.'

'It is not right. Not right at all.'

'It's all over the country, really, not just here.' I shook my head in that slow, side-to-side way that my people have perfected when referring to things of this sort, as if to say that the situation is, sadly, ineluctable.

'Yes, standards are falling everwhere. I was just reading about fake drugs in the papers,' Ikenna said, and I immediately thought it a rather convenient coincidence, his bringing up fake drugs. Selling expired medicine is the latest plague of our country, and if Ebere had not died the way she did, I might have found this to be a normal segue in the conversation. But I was suspicious. Perhaps Ikenna had heard how Ebere had lain in hospital getting weaker and weaker, how her doctor had been puzzled that she was not recovering after her medication, how I had been distraught, how none of us knew until it was too late that the drugs were useless. Perhaps Ikenna wanted to get me to talk about all this, to exhibit a little more of the lunacy that he had already glimpsed in me.

'Fake drugs are horrible,' I said gravely, determined to say nothing else. But I may have been wrong about Ikenna's plot, because he did not pursue the subject. He glanced again at the men under the flame tree and asked me, 'So, what do you do these days?' He seemed curious, as if he was wondering just what kind of life I am leading here, alone, on a university campus that is now a withered skin of what it used to be, waiting for a pension that never comes. I smiled and said that I am resting. Is that not what one does on retiring? Do we not call retirement in Igbo 'the resting of old age'?

Sometimes I drop by to visit my old friend Professor Maduewe. I take walks across the faded field of Freedom Square, with its border of mango trees. Or along Ikejiani Avenue, where the motorcycles speed past, students perched astride, often coming too close to one another as they avoid the potholes. In the rainy season, when I discover a new gulley where the rains have eaten at the land, I feel a flush of accomplishment. I read newspapers, I eat well; my house-help, Harrison, comes five days a week and his *onugbu* soup is unparalleled. I talk to our daughter often, and when my phone goes dead every other week, I hurry to NITEL to bribe somebody to get it repaired. I unearth old, old journals in my dusty, cluttered study. I breathe in deeply the scent of the neem trees that screen my house from Professor Ijere's – a scent that is supposed to be medicinal, although I am no longer sure what it is said to cure. I do not go to church; I stopped going after Ebere first visited, because I was no longer uncertain. It is our diffidence about the afterlife that leads us to religion. So on Sundays I sit on the veranda and watch the vultures stamp on my roof, and I imagine that they glance down in bemusement.

'Is it a good life, Daddy?' Nkiru has taken to asking lately on the phone, with that faint, vaguely troubling American accent. It is not good or bad, I tell her, it is simply mine. And that is what matters.

Another dust whirl, both of us blinking to protect our eyes, made me ask Ikenna to come back to my house with me so that we could sit down and talk properly, but he said he was on his way to Enugu, and when I asked if he would come by later, he made a vague motion with his hands that suggested assent. I know he will not come, though. I will not see him again. I watched him walk away, this dried nut of a man, and I drove home thinking of the lives we might have had and the lives we did have, all of us who went to the Staff Club in those good days before the war. I drove slowly, because of the motorcyclists who respect no rules of the road, and because my eyesight is not as good as it used to be.

I made a minor scratch as I backed my Mercedes out last week, and so I was careful parking it in the garage. It is twenty-three years old but runs quite well. I remember how excited Nkiru was when it was shipped back from Germany, where I bought it when I went to receive the Academy of Science prize. It was the newest model. I did not know this, but her fellow teenagers did, and they all came to peer at the speedometer, to ask permission to touch the panelling on the dashboard. Now, of course, everyone drives a Mercedes; they buy them secondhand, rearview mirrors or headlights missing, from Cotonou. Ebere used to mock them, saying our car is old but much better than all those *tuke-tuke* things people are driving with no seat belts. She still has that sense of humour. Sometimes when she visits, she tickles my testicles, her fingers running over them. She knows very well that my prostate medication has deadened things down there, and she does this only to tease me, to laugh her gently jeering laugh. At her burial, when our grandson read his poem, 'Keep Laughing, Grandma', I thought the title perfect, and the childish words almost brought me to tears, despite my suspicion that Nkiru wrote most of them.

I looked around the yard as I walked indoors. Harrison does a little gardening, mostly watering in this season. The rose bushes are just stalks, but at least the hardy cherry bushes are a dusty green. I turned the TV on. It was still raining on the screen, although Dr Otagbu's son, the bright young man who is reading electronics engineering, came last week to fix it. My satellite channels went off after the last thunderstorm, but I have not yet gone to the satellite office to find somebody to look at it. One can stay some weeks without BBC and CNN anyway, and the programmes on NTA are quite good. It was NTA, some days ago, that broadcast an interview with yet another man accused of importing fake drugs – typhoid fever medicine in this case. 'My drugs don't kill people,' he said, helpfully, facing the camera wide-eyed, as if in an appeal to the masses. 'It is only that they will not cure your illness.' I turned the TV off because I could no longer bear to see the man's blubbery lips. But I was not offended, not as egregiously as I would have been if Ebere did not visit. I only hoped that he would not be let free to go off once again to China or India or wherever they go to import expired medicine that will not actually kill people, but will only make sure the illness kills them.

I wonder why it never came up, throughout the years after the war, that Ikenna Okoro did not die. True, we did sometimes hear stories of men who had been thought dead and who walked into their compounds months, even years, after January 1970; I can only imagine the quantity of sand thrown on broken men by family members suspended between disbelief and hope. But we hardly talked about the war. When we did, it was with an implacable vagueness, as if what mattered were not that we had crouched in muddy bunkers during air raids after which we buried corpses with bits of pink on their charred skin, not that we had eaten cassava peels and watched our children's bellies swell from malnutrition, but that we had survived. It was a tacit agreement among all of us, the survivors of Biafra. Even Ebere and I, who had debated our first child's name, Zik, for months, agreed very quickly on Nkiruka: what is ahead is better.

I am sitting now in my study, where I marked my students' papers and helped Nkiru with her secondary school mathematics assignments. The armchair leather is worn. The pastel paint above the bookshelves is peeling. The telephone is on my desk, on a fat phone book. Perhaps it will ring and Nkiru will tell me something about our grandson, how well he did in school today, which will make me smile even though I believe American teachers are not circumspect enough and too easily award an A. If it does not ring soon, then I will take a bath and go to bed and, in the still darkness of my room, listen for the sound of doors opening and closing.

FRANCIS BEBEY

EDDA'S MARRIAGE

WHAT YOUNG EDDA really wanted was a wife; a wife who would be all his own, who belonged to him alone as a woman should belong to a man. He wanted a woman who would render him all the services a good spouse is supposed to render her husband, a woman who would always keep his hut clean and tidy and prepare his meals as custom dictates.

What Nkollo wanted was a woman also. Of course not for himself, since Nkollo was Edda's father and, after all, the young man's mother was still alive. A man will not marry a second time as long as his first wife is still by his side, particularly if she does not make life hard for him and on top of this has had the wise idea of giving him an heir. Men always love to have an heir although their conscience reminds them from dawn to dusk that they really do not possess anything worth inheriting once they are gone. Man's mind is always imbued with this instinct of self-preservation which prompts even the shabbiest individual to leave a trace of his sojourn in this world and not to quit this life until this has been guaranteed. Then with a stout heart he can wait for the last breeze to sweep away his hopes forever.

What old Nkollo really wanted then was not a wife for himself but a wife for his son, and of course for the rest of the community as well. It had always been like that: with us nobody had ever managed to be the sole master of his own wife. Nobody had ever dared to make a decision concerning his wife without consulting the community or at least the wise opinion of old Bilongo, the patriarch.

But Edda had grown up in the city where he was staying with his uncle Mendona. And it was in the city that he had learned that one could order one's wife about, make her come and go according to one's own pleasure, abuse her or treat her well according to one's whims without bothering about other people's suggestions. He had appreciated the manner in which his uncle Mendona managed to beat up his wife when his food was not ready in time. In the city the man from the bush ends up knowing the significance of time. We have a saying here that the city opens the eyes of the blind man who came from the most remote corner of our country. Edda was lucky to have known the city . . . he was incredibly lucky.

The entire village admired this young man who had come back to his home town just a few days ago to stay only for a short time. They admired him because he dressed differently from the other young men of the same age group, because he did not look at things and people the way they did, and because he was well-versed in all matters concerning the white man's world.

And since everybody admired and loved this young man so much, Edda thought that he might be permitted to do in the village what was hardly even permitted in the big city. He asked his father to give him a wife who he intended to take back with him. As you well know it was common in the village for the young men always to wait for their fathers to take the initiative in suggesting marriage. This had to happen one day or another. It never occurred to them to pop the question themselves. Edda thought it silly to permit the old to steer the boat of youth. One morning he simply decided that he was going to get married.

Old man Nkollo respected his son who had been brought up in the city and who knew all the things only the white men knew. He did not see anything unusual in his son wanting to marry at seventeen. One year later this would have been the common thing, anyhow! And besides, young people nowadays were so different from those in the old days!

But father and son did not view the future wife in the same way. One wanted her for the good of the entire community, the other could never conceive of his wife preparing meals for all his cousins as if she were a communal spouse.

Whatever the differences, the essential principle remained the same: Edda was going to have a wife. A wife all to himself as he saw it, and a wife for himself and the community according to old man Nkollo's wish. The next thing to be decided was who would go and choose this wife.

Nkollo went to see old Bilongo, the patriarch, and told him of his son's intention to get married. All the men of the village were immediately summoned to a big meeting to decide upon the conditions for Edda's marriage, after the village where they wished to ask for Edda's wife had been chosen. For the last two years we had taken all our wives from among the people of Afana or Effidi. The last marriage celebrated in our village had been Atabi's. His wife came from Afana. What a bad deal . . . We had never paid such a high dowry. Having learnt that we had had a good harvest and knowing that two or three of our men worked in the city, the Afana assumed that our little village of Meloundi owned all the artesian wells overflowing with money on this earth. We shall always remember that marriage, particularly since Atabi's wife, whom we had had such a hard time convincing to join us, created quite some problems, and was hardly the best example of female submissiveness. 'Never again one of these geese from Afana,' it had been said without reticence during the big meeting with Bilongo.

There remained the people of Effidi and Zaabat. We already had some wives among us from Effidi. We agreed that they were quite all right.

Our experience with the people of Zaabat, on the other hand, was not far from being a disappointment. However, we were not going to implore once more these Effidi to give us one of their daughters. The earth has its own laws, one of which says that one should neither give nor take always from the same person. Therefore, we obviously were forced to turn to the Zaabat. These people I did not like at all. But I am sure that the entire assembly would have attacked me bodily had I made so bold as to oppose their almost unanimous decision to send a delegation to Zaabat. I therefore contented myself with crossing the forefinger and middle finger of my right hand, swallowing saliva, and imploring heaven not to make us regret the grave decision we had just taken.

One morning old Nkollo, accompanied by two of our men, left Meloundi to go to Zaabat where he was going to find a wife for his son. When he came back from his trip he informed us that we were all invited to Zaabat nine days from then.

It's a long way from Meloundi to Zaabat: some hundred landmarks. But what were a hundred kilometres for walkers like us, particularly as we were walking in a group and with such a noble objective as finding a wife? The one, however, who did not join this group was Edda himself. All along this trip I had asked myself to what degree he was actually poking fun at us with this story that he wanted a wife. You never know with these city slickers what may suddenly come up in their heads. What if he only had the simple idea of getting us on the road for nothing? What if he had suddenly decided not to want a wife any more? What a shame for our village to arrive in Zaabat without being able to show our merchandise, without being able to say: 'That's him, our young gentleman from the city! Now let's see a wife to match . . .' This is normally said in a proud voice when the young husband-to-be is present, dressed in beautiful khaki shorts standing out among men wearing only loincloths. But what was to become of us now without Edda?

The next day we arrived about five o'clock in the afternoon. It was Saturday. We planned to start negotiations the following day. We had walked a long time in the blazing sun. If we had the same luck tomorrow we were sure to bring back Edda's future wife without any problem. But Lord, where was this Edda? I still was not able to trace him anywhere. It was most agonizing that nobody knew his whereabouts. Not even his father knew it, nor his 'little father' – his father's brother – not even his own mother.

About six o'clock – by now we were seriously worried – a lorry dropped Edda in the village square just like a live bag of cocoa to the great surprise – but a pleasant surprise at that – of everyone. We were all relieved, indeed. What champions those city people are!

The cock-crow was too long in coming, it seemed to me, because I had been awake most of the night. Actually I had been awake since the moment I lay down on a mat on the ground. These Zaabat people could not find anything better for potential in-laws than cold mats on the ground! I just burned to let them know how I felt about this during the friendly encounter which was to see us face to face the next morning. They were going to learn some manners about how to receive their guests! I was ready to get up immediately but peeping through the cracks in the wall I gained the impression that it was still too early.

. . . Finally the great meeting under a giant mango tree got under way.

'I have brought along my son so that you can provide him with a wife.' Obviously you must have recognized old Nkollo's voice. 'And I am accompanied by all my people, as you can see!'

'Listen, Nkollo!' I said aloud, 'Don't forget to tell your hosts that they ought to take better care of the people they invite. Last night I slept on a clammy mat right on the ground. Had I known this I would have got my son to bring along my bamboo bed.'

'Oh, but what does this man think? Does he believe that we don't have beds? Listen to that . . . Where does he come from?'

I had already set fire to the powder keg from the first minute of our assembly. Nkollo knew as well as I did that I surely hadn't helped things. The dowry for Edda's wife most likely was going to cost us twice as much now as it would have if I hadn't said a word. But still, why did they have to give me only a mat on the cold ground? It is true that the mat was not clammy as I had claimed, but it is equally true that I had a bamboo bed at home which could have been brought by my son.

So many people started now to buzz in the Zaabat camp that I was grateful to Patriarch Effoudou when he commanded his men to be silent. The meeting had barely begun. Why were people in such a hurry to make trouble? And on top of this, trouble about totally irrelevant things? If the Zaabat owed us reparation, one could see to it later. Perhaps we could deduct the rebate from the amount of the dowry which we were going to fix during this same meeting.

'Well said, Effoudou!'

Nkollo must have thought the same thing when he turned to me and spoke softly: 'Stop putting your foot in it; you know that my cocoa harvest was not the best this year.'

I kept silent.

The others talked while I gazed at the girls sitting round and tried to figure out which one old Nkollo had chosen for his son during his last visit with the Zaabat.

There were some beautiful girls among them! But I could not forget that in our community we had not much use for beautiful women. We have had enough problems with them: many of our youngsters frequently quarrelled and beat each other up over a girl. So we did not allow women to sow discord among us any longer . . . What's more – and each one of us knew this well enough – beautiful women could not keep house any better than the others.

The youngsters of Zaabat were sitting in the background of the opposite camp as if to show us that they were well brought up. The only ones missing at this meeting, which was strictly reserved for grown-ups, were the children.

'Here is my son! He is a young man from the city . . . what I want to say is that he has lived in town since early childhood. His uncle, a hospital attendant, took good care of him. Would you be so kind as to give us one of your daughters and allow our son to take her back with him?' This is what old Nkollo asked.

He had spoken well. If his son could expose problems in as clear a way, he would most certainly be a most intelligent man.

For a moment the men of Zaabat looked at each other as if to find out who was to speak first. They were sitting down, each of them as dark as we were. Some of them wore multi-coloured loincloths but were naked from the waist up. Others had wrapped a whitish calico piece around them with the two extremities solidly tied at the nape of the neck. Their chief was holding a huge fly whisk in his hand. It had been decorated by the best craftsman in the village. The men's naked torsos shone in the strong sunlight due to the palm-oil with which they had rubbed their bodies.

The shy girls were adorned as well as they could be. They had kept their smiles for other occasions, for more solemn moments. Attentively they listened to whatever was said about them without, however, saying a single word. For a moment their apparent modesty made me believe that we were not doing so badly after all in coming to this village for Edda's wife. But I should have kept in mind how deceptive looks can be. I was going to have occasion to verify this right here a few moments later.

A man of the Zaabat rose, turned towards his clansmen while adjusting his loincloth, and looked at them questioningly as if to make sure that they allowed him to speak.

'If you have come to look for a wife from among us,' he said, 'it means that you take us to be fine people. We, too, under the circumstances, take you for fine people. You seem to us intelligent and well behaved . . . We should be really glad to give you one of our daughters if we could make sure that, once among you, she would be the worthy wife you seem to be looking for. But we have to tell you with great regret that none of our daughters has ever been to the city. They know absolutely nothing about the white man's ways. How come then that you look for a wife among us savages?'

'You are right,' murmured the Zaabat. 'These people have a way of treating us which is definitely unpleasant. How could they – in the first place – dare to tell us that their son comes from the city? . . . As if we had never seen people from the city among us? . . .'

Now our reply had to rectify immediately this misunderstanding which had arisen right from the onset. The enemy proved hard to beat but we had faced other enemies ever since we had been negotiating on behalf of our boys and girls wanting to get married.

Old Nkollo now spoke again, trying to redress the situation! 'If you have misunderstood me, do say so! I never intended to say that you are savages, I don't even think so. I simply told you the truth about our son whom we propose to be the husband of one of your daughters. If you believe that I have done badly, all you have to do is pardon me. We are all brothers and should be able to pardon one another.'

'In that case,' one of the Zaabat exclaimed, 'we too are going to extol the merits of our girls. They know very well how to keep house, do the washing, harvest potatoes and cassava. They know everything a good housewife ought to know. Can your girls match them?'

'That is not the point, brother,' one of our men said. 'That is not the point at all. We did not ask you to take one of our girls. We came to tell you that we would consider ourselves lucky to be allowed to lead away one of yours. And it is precisely because we do know that your girls make such excellent housewives that we came to see you rather than go to any other village.'

How stupid they seemed to be, these Zaabat . . . How arrogant on top of it . . . They did not even seem to realize what the discussion was about . . . I wonder which way the discussion would have gone if we had spoken to each other as reasonable human beings. But that's how the Zaabat were. It was difficult to rank them among the human race despite the effort we had put into visiting them. This was actually not the first time we had done business with them; we already had had tremendous difficulties with them in previous negotiations and this is why I had asked myself from the beginning why old Nkollo and the village council wanted Edda's wife to be chosen from among these people . . . Now they did not even bother to treat us as we deserved. Their attitude towards us was simply an insult . . . And on top of this, that cold mat right on the floor! An entire night without sleep to find nothing but total incomprehension the following morning . . . I definitely must have been right in thinking that the Zaabat were not worthy of our interest.

'That is not the point,' Abel said once again.

'He is right,' Effoudou, the patriarch of our enemies, said. He was apparently the only Zaabat man able to understand anything. He was doing his level best to cover up the stupidity of these people. I just wondered what would happen to the Zaabat without their patriarch Effoudou.

Once more he succeeded in calming down this wild sea of conversation between his people and ours. But unfortunately this did not last very long. At last, when the discussion was making some sort of progress, the women suddenly joined in. They added just a little too much salt and thus changed the taste of the whole sauce.

Actually they had nothing to do with these negotiations, which were strictly men's business. They had no right to speak nor to show their opinions in any other way. The old Africa of our ancestors had decided – and reasonably so – that it was not necessary to permit women to speak just to see them start a war.

The proof?

That Sunday morning when we, the men, were just trying to make up to the Zaabat so as not to have to pay too big a dowry, the women of our community started fighting the women of the opposite camp. It was at first a silent fight but it soon burst from silence into loud noise.

While one of our men addressed the Zaabat, I was surprised to see one of their women get up and threaten one of our women:

'Listen, you, if you give me such looks again, you'll see what will happen! I told you, didn't I? If you . . .'

'And you? What about you? How did you look at me? What did you stare at me with, if not with those witch's eyes which you rolled as if I had harmed you?'

The men in the two camps, after first being nonplussed, did not remain silent spectators for very long. While these two women threatened each other, it became clear that we had come in vain, that Edda's wife was never going to come from Zaabat. No, I could never imagine our son being married to one of these Zaabat women who dared to open their mouths in public at a meeting strictly reserved for men – it doubtless would have made his life unbearable. These women did not inspire me with any confidence at all. Incidentally, that is not at all surprising. The two or three specimens of Zaabat women had never satisfied us in the past either.

But this most certainly was not the moment for speculation. Unless, of course, I wanted to miss some of the charming things that were being said on both sides, as if the two quarrelling women had contaminated all the rest.

'Who do you think you are? Do you actually think that you are superior to us? . . .'

'And who has told you that you are worth more than we are? Who told you this lie that you are worth anything at all?'

'Come on, you bitch! I am telling you that you're not going to leave this village alive if you go on like this.'

'Permit me to laugh, dear mother . . . let's have a look at this woman who claims to have a husband: you are as ugly as I don't know what. And you seriously dare to claim you have a husband?'

'That's what you are going to see right now! Wait, I am coming!'

And she rushed forward to grab her. I think she wanted to skin her alive. It is true that these Zaabat women, who abused our wives in our presence, deserved an exemplary punishment from them.

So she rushed forward to grab her and skin her alive. But her husband was not keen on seeing an accident happen among the women.

'Stop it, wife!' he said. 'She is crazy. Leave her alone! If her husband were worth a penny, he'd show up. But where is he? . . .'

A character from Zaabat got up from those sitting in readiness for war.

'I am her husband! What do you want from me? Speak up! What do you want? Speak up so that everyone can hear you!'

'I don't have anything special to announce,' our man said carelessly. 'I simply remarked to my wife that I do not speak to people who are below me. That's all!'

'You excel me? You? Just listen to that! He is above me! My brothers, do tell him that he does not know who he is talking to! You are above me? I own a huge cocoa-plantation. What do you own?'

'I own a cocoa-plantation, too. But it's much bigger than yours. Tell me again that I don't excel you . . . Look, men, have a glimpse at this beast who tries to address me as if he were—'

'You dare to call me a beast? You? Look at this owl bringing us bad luck!'

'This does not alter the fact that the owl surpasses you by

far. I have a house built with cement and my wife has the most beautiful umbrella in Meloundi.'

Deep down I said to myself that the last remark was sort of awkward and that our brother could have avoided this. What an idea to make us recall in front of our enemies all the fights and jealousies connected with old Adele's umbrella. This was when her husband some time ago had announced that he had bought for his wife the most beautiful umbrella ever seen . . . Really, it was hardly worth our while to come all the way from Meloundi to Zaabat to listen once more to this story which was to demonstrate that none of our men except old Adele's husband had good taste. Fortunately our horrible ememies did not pick on this less flattering trait in us. They were content enough to continue with the oral exhibition of their possessions.

'Get away with your umbrella!' he said. 'What's an umbrella? I own a record-player and records . . . Can you beat me with this one? And if so, how? What do you really own?'

'At night I have light from a Tilley lamp. Do you own such a precious lamp?'

'You're talking drivel . . . Look at him! He wants to make himself important. A Tilley lamp! Just a Tilley lamp . . . Don't you know that I have much better things? I own an accordion. Do you have an accordion? Do you actually have enough money even to afford an accordion? Would you know how to play one?'

'Whatever you may say, you just remain a braggart! You'll never reach my level. I have a bicycle and I always put on shoes which have been well polished whenever I use this bike. Do you have anything comparable, you beast?'

The man hesitated shortly as if he had exhausted his repertory. But fortunately his wife knew what he owned.

She whispered in his ear to tell him what he seemed to have forgotten. And immediately he was his old self again.

'I have a tropical helmet,' he said. 'It is completely white and you can come and admire me on the fourteenth of July. Can you still beat me? Tell me, can you surpass me now, not even having an ordinary hat to protect your old brains with?'

The man from our village who had valiantly kept up the bout till now, suddenly fell silent. This obviously indicated that he had nothing left to show off with. He was clearly beaten. The other man with his tropical helmet had won the contest.

We were then going through that heroic period of our lives which brought us into contact with 'civilization'. In our country there were not yet enough courageous people to offer the world the simple and revolutionary truth that we, too, were civilized . . . in our own way, of course. Since this memorable day, I have encountered men and women who eulogized the remarkable wisdom of the Bantu, the inexhaustible source which the music of the black people of Africa represents, the perfect social organization of the Pygmies in Gabon, the originality of Benin art, and the legendary hospitality of Africans. Meanwhile the world knows all this. But at that time our children wasted their time in school. When they came home after school they taught us how dear July 14th was to us and that we should pay attention to this national day. We shook hands with the civilized world, willy-nilly, and religiously respected its great day of revolution . . . which over the years was going to prepare us for other revolutions. If I take a map of Africa today, I read names totally unknown to the rest of the world at the time when young Edda wanted to take his wife from among the Zaabat.

We were just traversing at that point the heroic period

of our lives which made us enter the civilization of another world. The white helmet was to protect us from sun-stroke, and made us forget that long before this helmet had been invented, our ancestors had been proud to be able to walk in the hot sun with their heads shaven and bare. Our respect and love for that white contraption was endless and we never failed to acquire it the day when the cocoa and palm-nut harvest had made us a few pennies richer. But this sign of expensively purchased prestige was far from being within reach of everybody's purse. And this is why this man, a stout defender of Zaabatian superiority, was right in throwing the colonial trump card on the table.

Just try to find a fitting reply to a Zaabat who owns a white helmet which he still wears each July 14th . . . The defeat of our brother was our own defeat. But of course we never would bow to these inferior beings – or victorious enemies. We merely set out for home immediately.

Edda's wife was not with us. This was all right since each of us asked himself what old Nkollo really had in mind when he decided to find his son's future wife among savages. The one who really surprised us, to the point of virtually being expelled from our community, was young Edda. Hardly three weeks after this checkmate with the Zaabat, this young man from the city came to pay us a visit. He was accompanied by a very beautiful woman – one had to admit this – but she had a belly which was slightly bigger than the belly of a normal young girl.

Old Nkollo kept swearing that he was unaware of what was going on, nor did he admit that he was going to be a grandfather, nor that his son had narrowly avoided being a bigamist.

Translated by Georg M. Gugelberger

ADEWALE MAJA-PEARCE

THE HOTEL

IT WAS A TOWN like all the other Northern towns he had passed, but it was uncomfortable in the train so when they pulled into the station he got off and found a hotel.

Behind a desk in the entrance of the hotel sat a woman. She looked up at him and smiled.

'Are you looking for a room?' she asked.

'Yes.'

'This way.'

She led him up some stairs and then along the dark corridor.

'You're lucky. There's a big conference tomorrow and all the rooms except this one are taken,' she said and unlocked the door. He entered and put down his bag. There was a table, a chair, a bed and nothing else.

'The toilet and bathroom are at the end of the corridor,' she said, and opened the window that overlooked the courtyard. A boy, about ten years old, was bouncing a ball against a wall.

'My son,' she said, and went over to the bed. She pulled the cover back and checked the sheets.

'I hope you will be comfortable here,' she said.

'I expect so,' he said.

'If you are hungry you will find an inexpensive eating-house halfway down the street on the left,' she said.

'Thank you,' he said, and she left.

He took off his shoes and lay down on the bed. Night fell.

He switched on the light and took a book from his bag. He tried to read but the sentences made no sense. He decided to go out.

In the foyer he met the woman again. She looked up at him and smiled.

'I'm just going out for a stroll,' he said.

'Would you like to leave your key here?' she asked. He gave it to her and she hung it on a nail.

The moon had risen and the sky was littered with stars. The daytime heat had lifted, and a cool breeze blew from the desert. Here and there tall men in white robes hurried along. He walked aimlessly until he came to the edge of a cultivated field. He lit a cigarette but as he drew in his breath the smoke caught in his throat and he realized he had been weeping. He turned back to the hotel.

The woman was not in the foyer. He took his key from the nail and climbed the stairs. He lay on his bed a long while and heard male voices and then he fell asleep.

He woke with the dawn. His dreams had been vivid but all that remained with him were images that confused him. He listened to the others bustling about, shouting and laughing. So he waited for a long time until they finally left. Then he went for a shower and afterwards sat on the bed and thought about catching the train; but since he had broken the journey he lacked the energy to start all over again.

About ten o'clock the woman knocked on the door.

'I'm sorry to disturb you but I've come to clean the room,' she said.

'Okay,' he said.

'Will you be staying another night?' she asked.

'If that's all right,' he said.

'I hope you weren't disturbed last night. They made a lot of noise,' she said.

'No, I wasn't disturbed,' he said.

'They checked out this morning so you will be here on your own in peace,' she said.

He went for lunch. Then he went back to his room and remained there all day. In the evening he heard the sound of the ball bouncing off the wall. Later, he heard the woman call the boy in.

This went on for a week. Each day was exactly like the last.

One morning the woman said, as she walked into his room: 'If I can do anything to help you please don't hesitate to ask me,' and then, as though embarrassed, she looked away.

'There's nothing, but thank you,' he said.

'I would be happy if you would come and eat with us this evening,' she said.

He hesitated.

'It won't be much, just chicken and rice,' she said, still not looking at him.

'Thank you,' he said.

He waited until he heard her call the boy in, and then he went down. She had two rooms and an outside kitchen. The room they ate in was also the room she slept in, while the boy had the other room to himself.

After they had eaten she sent the boy to bed. They sat in silence until she asked:

'What brought you to our town?'

He shrugged and said: 'Chance.'

'How do you like it?' she asked.

'Not much,' he said.

'I don't like it either,' she said. 'It was my husband's town, that's how I came here, but since he died I've been reluctant to leave. This hotel gives me my livelihood although the responsibility is sometimes too much.'

‘How long ago did he die?’

‘Five years this December,’ she said.

‘I’m sorry,’ he said. Once again they fell silent. Then she said:

‘It’s hard on the boy, without a father.’

‘Yes,’ he said, and then on an impulse he kissed her on her cheek. She put her arms around him and burst into tears.

Later, as they lay in bed, she said: ‘It’s not a bad way to live, running a hotel.’

‘No,’ he said.

‘You can keep your own hours and between two people the work is nothing.’

In the morning he went up to his room and checked the timetable, and then he put his wallet in his pocket and went downstairs. The boy had left for school and the woman had cooked his breakfast. As he ate she spoke of the plans she had for redecorating the hotel. She quoted prices but he paid little attention.

At noon he told her that he was going out. She wanted to accompany him but he told her he wanted to be on his own.

Walking rapidly in the suffocating heat the dust got into his mouth and in his eyes. He got to the platform in time to hear the train approaching.

OKEY CHIGBO

THE HOUSEGIRL

LOOK, I DON'T want what I am going to tell you repeated anywhere. The last time I told anyone anything, that terrible gossip Nkechi Obiago got to hear it through God knows who, and now the whole world knows my life history. First of all, did I tell you that Madam has returned from Lagos? You should see the things she brought back. *Chineke!* Lagos na so so enjoyment! All kinds of beautiful trinkets that shone as if the sun and moon had come down to adorn Madam's portmanteau; all kinds of dazzling things from that wonderful heaven on earth where everyone wears the latest fashions and discards them in a week. She gave Obiageli a beautiful gown with enough wonderful colours to shame all the pretty flowers in our village of Aniugwu. Obiageli was ordered to give one of her old gowns to that witch Selina.

As usual, there was nothing for me. You know how it goes. Selina gets everything just because she is from Madam's hometown. My seniority as number one housegirl does not mean anything to Madam. The world knows how competent I am in cooking: Master is often asking for my delicious *egusi* soup, but does Madam care? The world knows how well I do the household chores, but does Madam care? Have you ever seen Selina sweep a room? It is as if her mother never taught her anything. I sometimes ask her who she is leaving the dust in the corners for. But that is another story.

* * *

Anyhow, you remember when Madam's son Callistus returned? It was about three months ago, I think. He was doing poorly in school at Enugu, so Master either pulled him out, or he got expelled for failing his exams. It is not that he does not have a head for books; it is just that he is such a wild boy, he never reads. Did you know he was running about with a harlot woman instead of reading his books? This harlot woman was also Chief M. A. Nwachukwu's girlfriend, the very same chief who fired a double-barrelled shotgun at a man he caught leaving his fifth wife's bedroom. You know the very chief I am talking about. Cally is lucky he did not get caught by Chief Nwachukwu. Obiageli says Cally must have been giving the harlot woman money because he was always broke. What a silly boy, eh? Can you imagine us 16-year-old housegirls giving our little wages to boys? Ha! We will make them give us money first.

Oby-girl says that he used to write Madam every week begging for money, telling all kinds of lies about new school uniforms and new books. She would send it because he is her favourite son. She is also making a lot of money as an Army contractor, but when I ask about my pay, she either ignores me or tries to bite my head off. Oh hard cruel world! Just because I ask for what is mine, she snaps at me. Do you know that since my father died, she has not paid me a penny? Oh hard cruel world! I have no one to defend my interests. Don't mind me, please. I will continue with the story as soon as I have wiped my tears.

Cally stayed home while his father decided what to do with him. I used to listen to him boast about the harlot woman when his friends came visiting. I would pretend to sweep the room next to his, and you know me, I would open my ears wide. You can trust me in these matters. If there is anything worth hearing in that house, I will hear it. The things those boys used to talk about. *Chineke!* Those boys are more rotten than overripe fruit with maggots in it.

One morning I found him sitting at the dining table resting his elbows on the table, and carrying his face in his palms. He looked like he alone had been given the task of shouldering all the world's troubles. When I asked what was wrong he did not reply. He just rose and walked away. I did not think too much about it, but went on to complete my morning duties by sweeping his room. Well, who did I find there but the headmistress of witches herself, Selina Okorie, doing the job. Or rather, she had stopped work by his table and was looking at something on it. I have to tell you that ever since Cally returned from Enugu, she had been trying to get into his good graces, running all kinds of errands for him, arranging his room for him whenever he messed it up, and always hanging around him to ask in her sweetest voice, 'Cally, is there anything you want? Can I wash your clothes? Can I prepare some *ugba* for you?' That kind of behaviour might have bothered some people, but it did not bother me because I am too big to be bothered by such things. But I am not surprised that Cally took no notice of her because her protruding teeth – which make her look like Agaba the dread spirit mask – are enough to frighten the stoutest heart.

I stood for some time at Cally's door, watching her, and she seemed to be reading something on the table. After a while I could not stand it any longer, and went in.

'SELINA OKORIE!' I shouted, and she leaped up in consternation, grabbed her broom and started to sweep rapidly. She slowed down when she saw me, then stopped. 'What are you looking at on that table?' I continued. 'I will tell Callistus. Thief! Idiot of no consequences!' As you can see, I am very good at insulting people in English. I did not complete elementary five for nothing.

'Your mother, idiot of no consequences,' she replied coolly. I tell you that girl can do things to drive someone mad. The blood immediately rushed to my head.

'What!' I cried. 'What did my mother do to you that you should bring her into this?'

'You insulted me first.'

'Yes, but I did not insult your mother.'

'Well, a light tap often buys a big slap.'

'You will get an even bigger slap from me then,' I shouted and flew at her.

Her *chi* must have been very alert that day, because she slipped through my grasp before I could box her ears shut, and escaped into the yard. I made sure that she was gone, then returned to complete the sweeping. As God is my witness, I did not intend to read what was lying on Cally's table. God knows I am not a sinful person, but if a letter is left carelessly open on a table, what is to prevent the devil from pushing an innocent girl like me in its direction? Of course, I first wrestled strenuously with the devil who clearly wanted me to read the letter, but you know how it goes.

I started to read the letter.

It was from his harlot woman in Enugu. She called him her 'dearest darling'. Ha! I am sure she has twenty other dearest darlings. The letter said that she was getting married to Chief M. A. Nwachukwu. *Chineke!* Money! Some people love it O! How can any woman leave a beautiful young boy like Cally for an old man like Chief M. A. Nwachukwu whose thing does not stand up any more? It's true! That's what Oby-girl said. And Oby should know, she has seen many . . . no, I did not say anything, I do not want to get into trouble. I am not like that terrible gossip Nkechi Obiago, who is full of more news than a radio.

Anyway, the harlot woman's letter said that she did not want Cally to see or contact her again 'in everyone's best interest'. Oho-o! I thought when I read it. So that is why he was so unhappy today. But it is good, I thought. It is not right for them to be together. Some women of nowadays, they have no shame. How can a 25-year-old *agaracha* be going with a 17-year-old boy, and be taking all his money? It is not right.

Later I passed him as he headed for his room and said, 'I know your entire history, your intimate and deepest secrets.'

'What do you mean?' he asked, looking at me suspiciously.

'Just be aware that I know everything about you,' I said. He frowned and looked into his room.

'Dearest darling,' I sang, and began to walk away quickly.

'Wha-what? What have you . . .' he shouted. 'Come here!' I scampered off, laughing like a hyena, and he charged after me, bellowing at the top of his voice, 'Comfort! Comfort, I will kill you for reading my letter!'

He caught me at the steps leading outside, pulled me to the ground and started to tickle my ribs. By now, I was laughing till tears ran down my cheeks while we rolled around on the ground. What are you looking at me like that for? Please wipe that sinful look off your face, it was all innocent fun. Your mind always goes to bad things. We rolled to a stop against a pair of legs in well-pressed trousers, and looked up. It was Master! Papa Callistus!

'Ah, I see you are getting along very well with the ladies, Cally,' he said, nodding his head very gravely. 'Just bear in mind if you get any of them pregnant, you will have to marry her.' I felt like asking him why he has not married Miss Onyejiekwe the teacher. Don't tell anyone, but do you know that the baby she had recently is said to be Master's? It is true! Nkechi told me.

A few days after this, Madam left for Lagos. The day before she left, I went into the parlour where she was with her friend Mama Moses the market woman. You know Mama Moses: she is big enough to fill a room and a parlour, so she occupied one couch all by herself. Madam on the other hand daily resembles the dry fish we use to make soup (I feel free to insult her because she is bad to me), and was seated in a small corner of the opposite chair. Madam is getting thinner every day despite her successful business, because her wooden heart is sucking up all the kindness in her body. Look at Mama Moses her friend – getting rounder every day even though she is not as successful, because she is so kind and good. Just the other day, she bought Nkechi a pair of 'higher heel' to wear to church. Can you imagine Madam doing that for any of *her* housegirls? All I can say is that if you are good, *Chineke* will reward you with the well-fed look of the wealthy, and if you are bad, *Chineke* will make you look hungry like the starving poor no matter how rich you are.

Anyway, that evening the two 'Business Madams' were discussing their business when I came in to pour the fourth bottle of stout for Mama Moses (that woman can take her drink better than any man in Aniugwu). Madam told her to drink as much as she wanted because business was going very well. Madam told Mama Moses that she was making the trip to Lagos to meet one Army major-general who would help her get a new contract that would give her bags and bags of money. When I heard this, my heart beat faster, and I solved some arithmetic in my head: if her business is working well, and she is expecting bags of money soon, then this is the time to ask her for some of my money. This is also the time to ask her of the promise she made to my father before he died. I don't know if I have told you this, but she promised to take me into her business and teach me how to become a big business madam like her. This is why I am still with her; I would have gone to work for someone else, but I do not want to remain a housegirl all my life. So that night, after Mama Moses left, I decided to ask about the money.

After seeing Ma Moses off, Madam went straight to her room to pack and make final preparations for the trip. I must confess that when the time came to go and ask her, my heart started beating poom-poom, poom-poom like that big drum young boys play during the New Yam feast. I walked past her room seven times, but could not make my heart strong enough to go in. I was about to abandon the idea when she suddenly called from inside the room: 'Who is there?'

My legs started to carry me away, but I forced them to stop. Why was I running? I asked myself. All I wanted was my money.

'It is me, Comfort.'

'What do you want?'

'I want to ask you for something.'

'Yes, go on.'

'It is about . . . well, you know how . . . do you remember . . .'

'WELL, WHAT IS IT? Hurry up, I have not finished packing yet.'

'It-it . . . Madam, it is about my money.'

'Is that why you are bothering me? GET OUT OF HERE!! Can't you find a better time to talk about it? Can't you see I am busy?'

I bolted out of the room, out of the house into the cool night air of the backyard, where I threw myself on the ground and began to weep. Cally found me there a short while later trying to compete with the heavy rains of last week.

'Comfort, what is the matter?' he cried, dropping to his knees and peering into my face.

'Nothing,' I replied, not wanting to tell him bad things about his mother.

'Stop crying and let us go back into the house,' he said, taking me by the hand. 'Won't you tell me what is wrong? Did Mama beat you?'

I felt like telling him because he is such a good-hearted person, and I knew he would sympathize with me, but I did not wish to talk at that time because I knew I would say bad things about his mother.

'I will tell you tomorrow,' I said as we trudged slowly back to the house.

All the servants got up at 4.30 the next morning to prepare for Madam's departure. Everything was hurry-hurry and quick-quick. You know how Madam is when she has something to do: she wants everybody to quick-march like soldiers. Romanus the driver drove her car out to wash it; Selina heated water for Madam's bath and then ironed her clothes; I fried *akara* and prepared hot *akamu* for breakfast. It was still very dark with the night insects still chirping, and the roosters just starting to crow, just around the time when spirits, both good and evil, abandon their wanderings abroad and return to their homes in the earth. Madam did not seem worried about meeting any spirits as she sat in the 'owner's corner' and Romanus drove the car out of the compound.

We watched the lights of the car disappear into the darkness on its way to that marvellous city where no one sleeps, then turned back into the house. I pretended to go to the kitchen to prepare the ingredients for the day's meals but as soon as I was sure no one was looking, I crept back to the parlour where I sleep, spread out my sleeping mat behind the long couch, wrapped myself snugly in my cover cloth and slipped into a comfortable and sweet sleep. This is why I am always happy when Madam travels – I can sleep a little longer and not have to wake up at 5.30. *Chineke* knows I am not a soldier man or a rooster that I should be waking up so early every day.

It seemed I had just fallen asleep when Madam returned to the house! She must have forgotten something, I thought, I must get up before she catches me sleeping. I tried to get up, but seemed glued to the mat, and she marched into the room and switched on the light.

'COMFORT!'

I leaped six feet into the air, shouting, 'Madam *biko-o*!' with my arm upraised to ward off the expected slap.

But when my eyes got used to the bright sunlight streaming in from the open window, there was only Selina cackling hysterically in the corner.

'Madam *biko-o*!' she mimicked between bursts of laughter. I tell you, it was too much to bear. I had to tell her a few good words.

'Selina Okorie,' I began.

'Yes, Madam Sleep,' she replied.

'Selina, do not insult me because I am your senior in everything, including age: 365 days is no joke, so please respect your elders. Remember it is me who shares out the meals now that Madam is out. If you do not look out, the meals that mice eat will be enormous compared to what I will give you.' She behaved herself after that for the rest of the day.

Later on that day, Cally called me into his room to ask why I was crying the night before. 'It is past now, don't worry about it,' I told him.

'Come on, tell me. It is Mama, isn't it? I know it is. You can tell me, I won't say anything to her.' I was silent.

'Tell me,' he insisted.

'Show me a picture of your har . . . your girlfriend, the one who is marrying Chief Nwachukwu.'

'Will you tell me what is wrong if I show you?'

'Yes.'

'Liar. You are more cunning than the tortoise of children's fables.'

'I promise, I will tell you after I see the pictures.'

He showed me a colour photograph of her. She is very beautiful with an oval-shaped face and a very fair complexion.

I said to him: 'She is very lovely, but I don't like the way she dresses. Why does she wear a skirt that is slit up to the waist, and a blouse that exposes all her breasts? She might as well just parade naked in front of everyone.' He laughed and made a playful grab at me which I easily evaded. I then told him that I had not been paid since my father died suddenly about a year ago. My father used to come at the end of every month to collect the money from Madam, ten naira a month, and he would give me three naira to spend. I used to be rich in those days. I could afford to buy earrings, bracelets, and chewing gum.

'How much does mother owe you now?' he asked.

'One hundred and fifty naira,' I replied, and he whistled.

'OK. I will see what I can do.'

'Just don't tell anyone I told you anything,' I said to him and turned to leave. 'By the way, I hope you have stopped crying over that girl. Do not worry about her, she is too *agaracha* for you, and all she wants is money. I am sure you will find many girls in Enugu who are nicer and more beautiful than she is. Look, I will cook your favourite dishes for you while Madam is away, and when I have time, I will come and sit with you and we shall tell stories. Very soon you will forget your *agaracha* friend.' He smiled and I left the room.

A few hours later, as I was passing the room, he pulled me inside and, to my great surprise, pressed a folded wad of notes into my hand. I uttered a short cry, and let it drop to the ground as if it were a red-hot piece of charcoal straight from the fire. He picked it up and gave it back to me. I counted thirty naira, and demanded to know where he got it, but he would not tell. I then told him I would not accept the money since I did not know where it came from, and he quickly said it was what remained of his pocket money.

I did not believe that story, but my heart was beating very fast as I stared at that money in my hand and my heart seemed to be saying, poom-poom, earrings, bracelets, poom-poom, earrings, bracelets . . . I solved the arithmetic in my head in this way: who knows where Cally got the money? He may have stolen it from his father's wallet, he may have broken into Madam's strong box, and he is so wild that boy, that he may even have friends who counterfeit money! But on the other hand, it may really be what is left of his pocket money. I will keep it for a while; if anyone reports missing thirty naira, I will give the money back to Cally, if not, I will spend it.

Unfortunately, I did not take the devil and his evil ways into account. He knows how to lead young girls astray just when they think they have the situation under control. The next day, Obiageli asked me to go to the market alone to buy ingredients for soup; usually I go with her or with Madam. I pleaded with her to come with me, but she wanted to go and visit a friend who she had not seen for a long time. So I had to go alone. The devil immediately entered my heart, and I tied up the thirty naira in the hem of my wrapper intending to take it to the market with me. 'If I leave it here, Selina might find it,' I reasoned.

After buying the okra and palm oil for the soup, I made a detour through the trinket stalls 'just to see what is available in case I find out I can keep the money'. It is not good for young housegirls like us to be without money for a long time, especially when there are so many nice things to buy, and other housegirls like Nkechi Obiago walk around in 'higher heel', and wear nice earrings. Lack of money makes us envious, and the bad ones among us may steal, while the others will spend foolishly whenever they get a little money. I left the stalls with only five naira left in the hem of my wrapper, and two pairs of imitation gold earrings.

* * *

If you know the devil and his cunning ways, you will realize that after you have done a bad thing as a result of his tempting, he runs away laughing, and the blindness with which he has covered your eyes is lifted so you can see the foolishness you have committed. It soon dawned on me that I could not show off my new treasures to the other housegirls and bask in their envious glances, because Selina would surely report it to Madam. I was gripped by a terrible fear: what if the money did not belong to Cally, and he had stolen it from Master or Madam? What if one of them found their money missing and called the police? Would Cally admit to the deed? I told myself that he was a good boy and he would, but what if they found out when he was not in town, gone off to school or somewhere? What would I do? Master or Madam would surely call the police. And they would send those policemen who don't wear uniforms and go around pretending to be ordinary people, those policemen who can just look at your face and know immediately that you stole money. I began to tremble with fear. I was ready to cry because I did not want to go to prison.

I walked into the house expecting someone to confront me and say 'Comfort! Where is the thirty naira?' But nobody did; the house was quiet, and seemed empty until I saw Selina come out of Cally's room. 'You!' I shouted. 'Did I not tell you not to go to Cally's room, you sorceress?'

'I can go wherever I like,' she snapped defiantly. 'And where I go is none of your business.'

'Watch your tongue, or I will slap that devil out of your head.'

'Just try,' she replied, staring at me fiercely and cocking her fist.

* * *

I wanted to give her a few good slaps, but felt it was not a wise idea since I had not put away the earrings and they might be discovered in a struggle. Also at that moment, Cally poked his head out of his room, and said, 'What are you two fighting about? Comfort, leave her alone, I asked her to clean my room.'

I went to his room that night to tell him about the earrings. He laughed when I told him how I was unable to help myself when I saw them. He asked me to put them on, which I did, and stood admiring myself in front of the mirror on his table. You must promise never, never to tell anyone what I am going to tell you now. As I was watching myself in the mirror, he came up behind me and started to rub my stomach with his hands, and then worked his way up to my breasts. Yes, he actually touched them. He really is a wild animal, that Cally. I pleaded with him, 'Please, Cally, don't do that, it is wrong.' But he did not seem to hear. 'Cally, stop. It is a sin.' Eventually he stopped, and we stood around avoiding each other's eyes. It was the first time he had ever tried such a thing with me. I know that I am plump and have a full figure which makes all the houseboys try to steal looks when I bend to pick something from the ground, but I did not know that Cally looked at me that way.

After a long embarrassing silence, he put his hand in his pocket and took out ten naira.

'Take this,' he said.

'Why? What do you think I am?' I cried.

'Just take it. It is simply more of the money Mama owes you, so take it and don't be silly.'

'Don't be silly yourself! I won't take it!' I said angrily and left the room. But I took the money later. He followed me everywhere and eventually I had to take it. He made me take it. And if you really want to know (because your mind always wants to know bad things) we played the touching game again. Many times. I cannot tell you any more, but just remember that I am a good girl and I have my limits.

A short while before Madam's return, Cally was sent off to Owerri in Imo State where his uncle teaches at a secondary school. The man is Papa Cally's brother, and a very strict disciplinarian who does not spare the cane even on grown boys like Cally. That is why Papa Cally sent Cally there. If that uncle does not make Cally study his books, nothing in this world will.

After Madam's return and the big distribution of gifts (with none for me as I told you) everything seemed to return to normal until a few days ago. I was in the kitchen cooking, and Selina and Madam were in her room. It seems that Selina was rearranging her wrapper when some money fell out of it. The foolish girl had put it there and forgotten about it.

'Selina, where did you get this ten naira from?' Madam said sharply.

'My ten naira,' I thought when I heard her. 'That witch must have taken it from my box!' I crept closer to listen to what was going on.

'Selina, I asked you where you got this ten naira? Has the devil taken your tongue? You better answer before I slap it out of your mouth!'

'I found it lying on the road.'

'Liar!' (SLAP!) 'Liar!' (SLAP! SLAP!) 'I noticed that some money has been taken from my strong box. That's where you found it, isn't it? Speak!' (SLAP!) 'Speak, you ungrateful wretch that I rescued from poverty. Don't I send your mother money regularly? Why then do you steal from me?'

'Madam *biko-o*! Cally gave me the money, Cally gave it to me!'

'Yes, go ahead, blame it on Cally because he is not here. Why would Cally give you ten naira? You are a terrible liar and a thief! I am going to lock you up. Get into that room and stay there. There will be no food for you today, and I will send you back home tomorrow.'

My body trembled like someone suffering from malaria when I heard this. At first, I had thought, that witch Selina has stolen my money and now God is punishing her for taking what is not hers. But then, I started to solve some arithmetic in my head, and reasoned thus: if she took the money from my box, why did she not say so and get me into trouble? Maybe she was telling the truth. Maybe Cally did give her the money. I decided to go and see if the money was still in my box, but just as I left the kitchen, I heard Madam call, 'Comfort!' My heart skipped a beat and I replied, 'Madam *bi* . . . I am coming!' and ran to her rooom, my heart pounding.

'Stop cooking,' she said. 'Go over to Mama Moses' and bring back the yams she brought me back from Abakaliki. Go immediately so you can be back before the soup is ready. I will watch the soup while you are gone.' I dashed out of the house as fast as I could, heaving a sigh of relief. But on the way, my anxiety returned. Was it my money or not? Even if it wasn't, I could still get into trouble because it was now clear that the money Cally gave me was taken from Madam's strong box. Should I go and own up and save Selina? She is not really a bad girl; it is only envy that makes us enemies. But even if I tell Madam that Cally gave me money too, will she believe it? She does not like to believe anything bad about him, and would be more likely to believe that Selina and I stole the money and now want to blame it on Cally because he is not home. I could ask her to write to Cally to confirm that he gave us money. But then Madam will never do that, not for her housegirls. She can get new housegirls too easily. And besides, I was sure she was searching for a chance to get rid of me.

With these thoughts buzzing around my head like a swarm of big, dirty houseflies, I returned from Mama Moses with the yams. When I got to the kitchen, Selina was sitting before the pot of soup, stirring it nonchalantly. 'You got out!' I gasped.

'Yes I did,' she replied. 'You thought I was done for, didn't you? Well, for your information, God does not allow good people like me to be punished for nothing.'

It turned out that Obiageli had returned from school to find Selina in 'detention', and had asked why. When Madam told her, she laughed, and said that Selina must be speaking the truth because Obiageli had caught Cally taking money from Madam's strong box when Madam was in Lagos. Selina was let out of the room with a strong warning never to take money from anyone in the household without knowing its source. No one was more relieved than me when I heard that. I found the ten naira untouched in my box, and promised myself to be very careful with it, and keep it secret from everyone in the house.

Everything now seems all right except for Selina. She seems to be crying a lot these days; her complexion is also getting fairer and her breasts seem to be getting bigger.

M. G. VASSANJI

LEAVING

KICHWELE STREET WAS now Uhuru Street. My two sisters had completed school and got married and Mother missed them sometimes. Mehroon, after a succession of wooers, had settled for a former opening batsman of our school team and was in town. Razia was a wealthy housewife in Tanga, the coastal town north of Dar. Firoz dropped out in his last year at school, and everyone said that it was a wonder he had reached that far. He was assistant bookkeeper at Oriental Emporium, and brought home stationery sometimes.

Mother had placed her hopes on the youngest two of us, Aloo and me, and she didn't want us distracted by the chores that always needed doing around the store. One evening she secured for the last time the half a dozen assorted padlocks on the sturdy panelled doors and sold the store. This was exactly one week after the wedding party had driven off with a tearful Razia, leaving behind a distraught mother in the stirred-up dust of Uhuru Street.

We moved to the residential area of Upanga. After the bustle of Uhuru Street, our new neighbourhood seemed quiet. Instead of the racket of buses, bicycles and cars on the road, we now heard the croaking of frogs and the chirping of insects. Nights were haunting, lonely and desolate and took some getting used to. Upanga Road emptied after seven in the evening and the sidestreets became pitch dark, with no illumination. Much of the area was as yet uninhabited and behind the housing developments there were overgrown bushes, large, scary baobab trees, and mango and coconut groves.

Sometimes in the evenings, when Mother felt sad, Aloo and I would play two-three-five with her, a variation of whist for three people. I had entered the University by then and came back at weekends. Aloo was in his last year at school. He had turned out to be exceptionally bright in his studies – more so than we realized.

That year Mr Datoo, a former teacher from our school who was also a former student, returned from America for a visit. Mr Datoo had been a favourite with the boys. When he came he received a tumultuous welcome. For the next few days he toured the town like the Pied Piper followed by a horde of adulating students, one of whom was Aloo.

The exciting event inspired in Aloo the hope that not only might he be admitted to an American university, but he could also win a scholarship to go there. Throughout the rest of the year, therefore, he wrote to numerous universities, culling their names from books at the USIS, often simply at random or even only by the sounds of their names.

Mother's response to all these efforts was to humour him. She would smile. 'Your uncles in America will pay thousands of shillings just to send you to college,' she would say. Evidently she felt he was wasting his time, but he would never be able to say that he did not have all the support she could give him.

Responses to his enquiries started coming within weeks and a handful of them were guardedly encouraging. Gradually Aloo found out which were the better places, and which among them the truly famous. Soon a few catalogues arrived, all looking impressive. It seemed that the more involved he became with the application process, the more tantalizing was the prospect of going to an American university. Even the famous places did not discourage him. He learnt of subjects he had never heard of before: genetics, cosmology, artificial intelligence: a whole universe was out there waiting for him if only he could reach it. He was not sure if he could, if he was good enough. He suffered periods of intense hope and hopeless despair.

Of course, Aloo was entitled to a place at the local university. At the end of the year, when the selections were announced in the papers, his name was on the list. But some bureaucratic hand, probably also corrupt, dealt out a future prospect for him that came as a shock. He had applied to study medicine, he was given a place in agriculture. An agricultural officer in a rural district somewhere was not what he wanted to become however patriotic he felt. He had never left the city except to go to the national parks once on a school trip.

When Aloo received a letter from the California Institute of Technology offering him a place with a scholarship, he was stupefied at first. He read and reread the letter, not believing what it seemed to be saying, afraid that he might be reading something into it. He asked me to read it for him. When he was convinced there was no possibility of a mistake he became elated.

'The hell I'll do agriculture!' he grinned.

But first he had to contend with Mother.

Mother was incredulous. 'Go, go,' she said, 'don't you eat my head, don't tease me!'

'But it's true!' he protested. 'They're giving me a scholarship!'

We were at the table – the three of us – and had just poured tea from the thermos. Mother sitting across from me stared at her saucer for a while then she looked up.

'Is it true?' she asked me.

'Yes, it's true,' I said. 'All he needs is to take 400 dollars pocket money with him.'

'How many shillings would that make?' she asked.

'About three thousand.'

'And how are we going to raise this three thousand shillings? Have you bought a lottery? And what about the ticket? Are they going to send you a ticket too?'

As she said this Aloo's prospects seemed to get dimmer. She was right, it was not a little money that he needed.

'Can't we raise a loan?' he asked. 'I'll work there. Yes, I'll work as a waiter. A waiter! – I know you can do it, I'll send the money back!'

'You may have uncles in America who would help you,' Mother told him, 'but no one here will.'

Aloo's shoulders sagged and he sat there toying with his cup, close to tears. Mother sat drinking from her saucer and frowning. The evening light came in from the window behind me and gave a glint to her spectacles. Finally she set her saucer down. She was angry.

'And why do you want to go away, so far from us? Is this what I raised you for – so you could leave me to go away to a foreign place? Won't you miss us, where you want to go? Do we mean so little to you? If something happens . . .'

Aloo was crying. A tear fell into his cup, his nose was running. 'So many kids go and return, and nothing happens to them . . . Why did you mislead me, then? Why did you let me apply if you didn't want me to go . . . why did you raise my hopes if only to dash them?' He raised his voice to her, the first time I saw him do it, and he was shaking.

He did not bring up the question again and he prepared himself for the agricultural college, waiting for the term to begin. At home he would slump on the sofa putting away a novel a day.

If the unknown bureaucrat at the Ministry of Education had been less arbitrary, Aloo would not have been so broken and Mother would not have felt compelled to try and do something for him.

A few days later, on a Sunday morning, she looked up from her sewing machine and said to the two of us: 'Let's go and show this letter to Mr Velji. He is experienced in these matters. Let's take his advice.'

Mr Velji was a former administrator of our school. He had a large egg-shaped head and a small compact body. With his large forehead and big black spectacles he looked the caricature of the archetypal wise man. He also had the bearing of one. The three of us were settled in his sitting-room chairs staring about us and waiting expectantly when he walked in stiffly, like a toy soldier, to welcome us.

'How are you, sister?' he said. 'What can I do for you?'

Aloo and I stood up respectfully as he sat down.

'We have come to you for advice . . .' Mother began.

'Speak, then,' he said jovially and sat back, joining his hands behind his head.

She began by giving him her history. She told him which family she was born in, which she had married into, how she had raised her kids when our father died. Common relations were discovered between our families. 'Now this one here,' she pointed at me, 'goes to university here, and *that* one wants to go to America. Show him the documents,' she commanded Aloo.

As if with an effort, Aloo pushed himself out of the sofa and slowly made his way to place the documents in Mr Velji's hands. Before he looked at them Mr Velji asked Aloo his result in the final exam.

At Aloo's answer, his eyes widened. 'Henh?' he said, 'All A's?'

'Yes,' replied Aloo, a little too meekly.

Mr Velji flipped the papers one by one, cursorily at first. Then he went over them more carefully. He looked at the long visa form with the carbon copies neatly bound behind the original; he read over the friendly letter from the Foreign Student Adviser; he was charmed by the letters of invitation from the fraternities. Finally he looked up, a little humbled.

'The boy is right,' he said. 'The university is good, and they are giving him a bursary. I congratulate you.'

'But what should I do?' asked Mother anxiously. 'What is your advice? Tell us what we should do.'

'Well,' said Mr Velji, 'it would be good for his education.' He raised his hand to clear his throat. Then he said, a little slowly: 'But if you send him, you will lose your son.

'It's a far place, America,' he concluded, wiping his hands briskly at the finished business. 'Now what will you have – tea? orange squash?'

His wife appeared magically to take orders.

'All the rich kids go every year and they are not lost,' muttered Aloo bitterly as we walked back home. Mother was silent.

That night she was at the sewing machine and Aloo was on the couch, reading. The radio was turned low and through the open front door a gentle breeze blew in to cool the sitting room. I was standing at the door. The banana tree and its offspring rustled outside, a car zoomed on the road, throwing shadows on neighbouring houses. A couple out for a stroll, murmuring, came into sight over the uneven hedge; groups of boys or girls chattered before dispersing for the night. The intermittent buzz of an electric motor escaped from mother's sewing machine. It was a little darker where she sat at the other end of the room from us.

Presently she looked up and said a little nonchalantly, 'At

least show me what this university looks like – bring that book, will you?'

Mother had never seen the catalogue. She had always dismissed it, had never shown the least bit of curiosity about the place Aloo wanted so badly to visit. Now the three of us crowded around the glossy pages, pausing at pictures of the neoclassic facades and domes, columns towering over humans, students rushing about in a dither of activity, classes held on lush lawns in ample shade. It all looked so awesome, and yet inviting.

'It's something, isn't it?' whispered Aloo, hardly able to hold back his excitement. 'They teach hundreds of courses there,' he said. 'They send rockets into space . . . to other worlds . . . to the moon—'

'If you go away to the moon, my son, what will become of me?' she said humorously, her eyes gleaming as she looked up at us.

Aloo went back to his book and Mother to her sewing.

A little later I looked up and saw Mother deep in thought, brooding, and as she often did at such times she was picking her chin absentmindedly. It was, I think, the first time I saw her as a person and not only as our mother. I thought of what she must be going through in her mind, what she had gone through in bringing us up. She had been thirty-three when Father died, and she had refused several offers of marriage because they would all have entailed one thing: sending us all to the 'boarding' – the orphanage. Pictures of her before his death showed her smiling and in full bloom: plump but not excessively fat, hair puffed fashionably, wearing high heels and make-up. There was one picture, posed at a studio, which Father had had touched up and enhanced, which now hung beside his. In it she stood against a black background, holding a book stylishly, the nylon pachedi painted a light green, the folds falling gracefully down, the borders decorated with sequins. I had never seen her like that. All I had seen of her was the stern face getting sterner with time as the lines set permanently and the hair thinned, the body turned squat, the voice thickened.

I recalled how Aloo and I would take turns sleeping with her at night on her big bed; how she would squeeze me in her chubby arms, drawing me up closer to her breast until I could hardly breathe – and I would control myself and hope she would soon release me and let me breathe.

She looked at me looking at her and said, not to me, 'Promise me . . . promise me that if I let you go, you will not marry a white woman.'

'Oh Mother, you know I won't!' said Aloo.

'And promise me that you will not smoke or drink.'

'You know I promise!' He was close to tears.

Aloo's first letter came a week after he left, from London where he'd stopped over to see a former classmate. It flowed over with excitement. 'How can I describe it,' he wrote, 'the sight from the plane . . . mile upon mile of carefully tilled fields, the earth divided into neat green squares . . . even the mountains are clean and civilized. And London . . . Oh London! It seemed that it would never end . . . blocks and blocks of houses, squares, parks, mountains . . . could any city be larger? How many of our Dar es Salaams would fit here, in this one gorgeous city . . .?'

A bird flapping its wings: Mr Velji nodding wisely in his chair, Mother staring into the distance.

EMMANUEL BOUNDZÉKI DONGALA

JAZZ AND PALM WINE

IT ALL STARTED with two luminous spheres in the sky, turning on their own axes like spherical fireflies. First they slowly passed over the woman who was working in her field, then they landed softly beside her. Panic-stricken at the approach of the creatures who stepped out, she fled, leaving behind her her most treasured possessions, including her she-donkey.

The creatures, two of them to be precise, advanced towards the she-donkey and with their hands on their navels (presumably a gesture of respect among them) bowed their heads while one of them pushed the button of its built-in mini-cassette; a sentence came out in Kiswahili: 'Would you mind taking us to your president?'

The startled donkey kicked off in the direction of the village, and the two creatures followed her, thinking that she had understood and was leading them to the president of men.

Meanwhile the woman had arrived in the village panting for breath, her breasts flapping and her face lacerated by the thorny shrubs of the bush. Her shouting alerted the whole village.

'Hurry, hurry,' she cried, 'weird creatures coming! They are similar to us but they are blue, blue like tempered steel. Their physical features are like ours but they have green hair. They walk jerkily and are terrifying.'

The entire village was roused; the children hid under the

beds; the women hung up amulets and charms everywhere and fled into their houses; some of the men armed themselves with bows and arrows, others with lances, while the war veterans, drawing on the military expertise they had acquired in the service of the fatherland in two world wars, brought out their rusty old rifles and posted themselves around the town.

And the donkey arrived braying; she stopped abruptly, her body riddled with bullets and arrows. The two creatures also stopped. They did not have time to speak or to make a gesture. They were likewise riddled with bullets, arrows and lances, and fell to the ground, one face downwards, and the other on its back, while turquoise-green blood flowed in thick clots from multiple wounds.

At the same moment, as if those who had stayed aboard were conscious of the fate that had befallen their comrades, the two spaceships rose and disappeared in the gathering twilight.

2

THEY CAME FROM everywhere; from the four corners of the sky they came, criss-crossing it, blinking their lights and sweeping around in crazy patterns before landing softly. They came down in tens, hundreds and thousands, and covered the whole savanna of the Zaïre basin, overflowing onto the far bank of the river beyond Kinshasa. Those who fell into the river went under or were carried off, slowly at first, and then swept away by the turbulence of the whirlpool that thrust them into the waterfalls further down the river, where they smashed against gigantic blocks of granite; others exploded the moment they touched down on the water and broke into a display of brilliant lights which made the slumbering hippopotamuses and crocodiles grunt with anger while the aquatic birds sleeping on the water-lilies chirped in shrill fright.

And they still kept coming, in tens, hundreds and thousands; the horizon was blacked out. They fell on Brazzaville, on Kinshasa. In Brazzaville they fell on top of tall buildings, broke to pieces and caught fire. They fell on the palace of the Head of State, went through the roof and crashed into his bedroom before blowing up; he had a narrow escape. They fell on the embassy of the Soviet Union and on De Gaulle Square; finally they fell on the radio station which was no longer broadcasting because the air was too heavily charged with static . . .

Chaos was just around the corner.

3

THE UNITED STATES proposed what they called 'saturation bombing', a refined type of carpet-bombing such as they had first practised in Germany and brought to perfection in Vietnam; too bad if some natives lost their hides in the proccss; after all, didn't the world go round as usual, despite the massacre of millions of Red Indians, and hadn't America become the leading world power?

The Russians, on the other hand, were all for the good old method of a wholesale intervention of tanks and armoured vehicles which had stood them in such good stead in Hungary and Czechoslovakia.

China, which had been specially invited for the occasion in view of the seriousness of the situation, proposed to flush out the Zaïre basin with millions of men. Although some tens of millions would be killed, a sufficient number would still remain to defeat the invaders.

Cuba, seconded by Vietnam and North Korea, suggested the use of the guerrilla method: when the invader pushes forward, we withdraw, in this way we shall be able to assess his strong points and his weaknesses.

South Africa in turn simply proposed the setting-up of barbed wire fences, a kind of Verwoerd line surrounding the contaminated area, to be manned by white soldiers all round; and since the operation had got started anyway, one might as well enclose in this zone all black people, all Arabs, all Chinese, all American and Asian Indians, all Papuans, all Malays . . . (The delegate had to stop here to get his breath back, so long was his list.)

The delegate from Ovamboland pointed out to him that this exercise involved more than three quarters of humanity, but the South African delegate replied that the gentleman from Ovamboland had used the term 'humanity' in a rather loose sense and that even if he accepted the construction put on it, it still would not be too much of a sacrifice to save the white race. The Afro-Asian delegates walked out of the assembly in protest . . .

They kept coming, in tens, hundreds and thousands. They spilled over from the Zaïre basin, reaching Douala, Abidjan, Timbuktu, and Ouagadougou. They now covered the whole of the northern part of the continent. But they were also moving south and posing an immediate threat to the Katanga mines . . .

Meanwhile, the deadlock continued. The Soviet delegate accused the United States of not having done anything to forestall the invasion and added that he would not be surprised if the Yankees were behind all this; the fact that the Soviet embassy at Dongola in Sudan had been hit by ninety-nine of these strange spaceships was merely additional proof to bolster these suspicions.

The American delegate parried by saying that the U.S. embassy had also been hit; at any rate it was public knowledge that the Russians' only objective was to sabotage the security council. Who knew whether the whole operation wasn't a smokescreen for the grand design to sovietize the world? But the Soviet delegate should remember one thing: 'Better dead than Red!'

The delegate from Swaziland, who because of his thirty-three children (including quintuplets) and his fourteen wives was used to the endless bickerings of a harem, interrupted the Soviet and U.S. delegates to prevent such an important debate from degenerating into a slanging match. At any rate, it was useless to palaver much longer about the root-cause of this calamity for he, having consulted the spirits of his ancestors who knew all about human sufferings, had received the answer that the whole invasion was nothing but witchcraft used by the white racists to exterminate the coloured nations, just as they had massacred yellow people at My Lai, Zulus at Sharpeville and Black Panthers in the United States.

This speech, which was transmitted by the United Nations Broadcasting Corporation via the artificial satellite Terra 1, caused a deep stir in Harlem, where Black Power militants started demonstrating with portraits of Malcolm X, Lumumba and Bobby Hutton floating overhead.

The French delegate, representing France Everlasting, champion of the Third World and the Third Way, warned the Assembly against accepting an exclusively Soviet-American solution, which would be even more catastrophic than the menace weighing on the world right now.

The deadlock continued.

Up north they were encroaching on Europe. In the little village of Colombey-les-deux-Églises they fell all around a private estate called La Boissérie belonging to a certain general, at Aulnay-sous-Bois they fell onto the LCHP (Low Cost Housing Project to the initiated) of Monsieur and Madame Millet, and at Montpellier on the School of Chemistry. Over in Germany, at Augsburg, Brecht's birthplace, they landed on the house of Fraulein Barbara Weckbach who ran head over heels to her boyfriend Maggi. At Litchfield, a small American country-town, they crashed on the house of Dr Lovejoy who fled panic-stricken to safety with his whole family to his English neighbour's house. In Africa the airdrops went on unabated. In the Republic of Benin they arrived right in the middle of a military coup; the Katanga mines were crawling with them and a first batch was reported to have plunged into the Limpopo River . . .

The Belgian delegate insisted that a decision be taken immediately even if it meant a unilateral initiative limited to NATO (the North Atlantic Treaty Organization). At the news that Johannesburg had been invaded, the South African delegate, whose raw beefsteak complexion had turned a ghastly pallor, rose and declared that he was prepared to accept any constructive proposal, even if it came from a non-white.

The Kenyan delegate finally got up and moved that in keeping with African tradition one should attempt to find the chieftains of the invaders and the elders among them; they should then be invited to sit around the big tree in the centre of a village square, and it would be possible to palaver with them over some calabashes of palm-wine. Meanwhile, there would be ample opportunity to study them at leisure.

The motion was unanimously carried.

4

YOU CAN SAY that again! Jazz and palm wine. The palm wine put them into a very receptive frame of mind (in line with the research done at the laboratories of St Emilion by the French wine-growers), and they just loved drinking it. John Coltrane's music immersed them in a kind of nirvana (Kathmandu laboratory, Nepal) and subsequently put them into a trance; then they were given the finishing touches by the cosmic music of Sun Ra (Goddard Laboratories in the United States). Apart from that, nothing worked; they were no longer sensitive to wounding, piercing or burning . . . they liked neither whisky, nor water, nor women . . . nothing but jazz and palm wine.

Millions of Coltrane discs were waxed in secret. Tropical agriculture had never seen such a boom and the world had never been so short of soil specialists and agriculturists. Sun Ra especially was treated like a king, and his solar bank had never been so much in demand.

5

THE DAY OF the festival arrived. To celebrate the tenth anniversary of the conquest of the Earth, the Great Conquest as it was called in official documents, all presidents and heads of state of the whole world were assembled in Brazzaville, the point of departure of colonization. The South African president was allowed to attend on condition that he would not shake hands with Sun Ra who was then everybody's idol. Despite his tears and genuflections, the organizers remained adamant. Speeches were made praising the scientific know-how, the courage and intelligence and so on of the conquerors, without whom the world would not be what it was today.

'We earth-dwellers have become cultural mulattoes on a cosmic scale, trying to assimilate the best of two worlds, on the one hand the tremendous intellectual and scientific contribution of our illustrious friends, the conquerors of the universe, drawing their light from the suns of Vega and Sirius, and on the other hand from the earth culture where everything is based on the binary rhythm of day and night, a culture of moonshine (the time for love, sex and other non-scientific activities) and of sunlight (the time of loneliness, alienation and scientific achievement).'

And the speeches continued in this vein, speeches made by captain-presidents, major-presidents, colonel-presidents, general-presidents, and even civilian-presidents, poet-presidents and poet-ministers.

At the end of the ceremony came the hour of libations. The paramount chief of the conquering tribe jocularly recalled that in the earth legends there existed a god called Bacchus who was the patron of wine. To show their respect for the traditions of the natives all over the earth, they were going to pay homage to him by tasting the only enjoyable and truly original product they had found on earth: palm wine. An earth delegate told him that there existed on earth another tradition of no lesser significance, that of planting a moist kiss on the neck of one's host, which he promptly did. The paramount chief of the invaders then raised his glass and started to drink. Thereupon everybody rushed at the billions of gallons of palm wine which had been distributed free of charge throughout the world. And they drank, drank, and drank . . .

Suddenly from everywhere, from the houses, the bowels of the earth, from space and beyond, exploded the spell-binding sounds of Coltrane. And the creatures' heads started swaying, a fixed stare in their eyes, and soon over an area of tens, of hundreds, of millions of square kilometres one saw nothing but bodies in a trance, in the grip of a dance of possession. Not even the President of the United States could resist; he clapped his hands and tap-danced with his cowboy boots yelling in his best nasal whine, 'I've got rhythm, man! And soul!'

Then Sun Ra swung into action with his rocket-like orchestra. The moment he had attained the speed of light, all that was not human and of this earth began to evaporate and disappeared in space.

[An accident that happened at that very moment has remained unexplained to this day: the South African delegate suddenly turned an immaculate white and then evaporated. Several hypotheses have been advanced but research has mostly been focused on the following two questions:

a) Was it the effect of the palm wine?

b) Was he a stranger in the world of men?

Pending a scientifically irrefutable answer, a preventive *cordon sanitaire* called the Verwoerd line has been drawn around the country.

It still exists.]

People began to dance with one another, to embrace and to sing of their newly-won freedom. In this way, Sun Ra became the first black man, and a jazz-musician to boot, to occupy the post of President of the United States, in the same way, the best palm wine drinker of the year is regularly appointed Secretary-General of the United Nations, and jazz has conquered the world.

Epilogue

One year after this adventure John Coltrane was canonized by the Pope under the name of St Trane and the first movement of his work 'A Love Supreme' came to replace the 'Gloria' in the Catholic mass.

Biographical Notes

CHINUA ACHEBE

Novelist, poet, short-story writer, he was born in Ogidi, Eastern Nigeria, in 1930. He studied English, history and African traditional religions at the University of Ibadan. *Things Fall Apart* was published in 1958, *No Longer at Ease* in 1960, *Arrow of God* in 1964 and *A Man of the People* in 1966. *Anthills of the Savannah* came out in 1987. He was awarded the Man Booker International Prize in 2007. In 2012 he published *There Was a Country: A Personal History of Biafra.* He died in 2013.

CHIMAMANDA NGOZI ADICHIE

She was born in Eastern Nigeria in 1977. She studied at the University of Nigeria and received her MA at Yale. Her works include *Purple Hibiscus* (2003), *Half of a Yellow Sun* (2006), *The Thing Around Your Neck* (2009), *Americanah* (2013) and *Mama's Sleeping Scarf* (2023). She won a MacArthur Fellowship in 2008.

AMA ATA AIDOO

Poet, playwright, novelist, short-story writer and academic, she was born in 1942 in Abeadzi Kyiakor, in central Ghana. She studied English at the University of Ghana, Legon. Her first play, *The Dilemma of a Ghost*, was published in 1965. *Our Sister Killjoy* came out in 1977, and *No Sweetness Here* in 1970. *Changes* appeared in 1991. It won the Commonwealth Writers' Prize for Best Book (Africa). She died in 2023.

FRANCIS BEBEY

Poet, novelist, short-story writer and guitarist, he was born in Douala, Cameroon, in 1929. He studied broadcasting at the University of Paris and New York University. While working for UNESCO he documented traditional African music. His first novel, *Le fils d'Agatha Moudio* (Agatha Moudio's Son), won the Grand prix littéraire d'Afrique noire in 1968; *L'Enfant pluie* (The Child of Rain) won the Prix Saint Exupéry in 1994.

OLYMPE BHÊLY-QUÉNUM

Diplomat, journalist and esteemed short-story writer, he was born in Ouidah, Benin, in 1928. He worked for UNESCO in Paris. His first novel, *Un Piège sans fin* (*Snares Without End*), was published in 1960. *Le Chant du lac* (The Song of the Lake) appeared in 1966 and won the Grand prix littéraire d'Afrique noire. *C'était à Tigony* (*As She Was Discovering Tigony*) came out in 2000.

OKEY CHIGBO

He is a writer of short stories born in Enugu, Nigeria, in 1955. He studied economics at Simon Fraser University in Vancouver. His stories have been published in Canada and the United States. He is a freelance journalist and former editor of *Metropolitan Toronto Business Journal* and of *CPA Magazine*.

J. M. COETZEE

He was born in Cape Town, South Africa, in 1940. He studied English and mathematics at the University of Cape Town. *Dusklands* was published in 1974. *Life & Times of Michael K* came out in 1983, and *Disgrace* in 1999 – both won the Booker Prize. He was awarded the Nobel Prize in Literature in 2003. The 'Jesus' trilogy was published between 2013 and 2019. *The Pole* appeared in 2023.

JACK COPE

Novelist, short-story writer and journalist, he was born in Natal, South Africa, in 1913. *The Fair House* appeared in 1955. In 1982 he published *The Adversary Within: Dissident Writers in Afrikaans*. Short-story collections include *The Tame Ox* (1960) and *The Man Who Doubted and Other Stories* (1967). *The Rain-Maker* appeared in 1971.

MIA CUOTO

Poet, short-story writer and novelist, he was born in Beira, Mozambique, in 1955. He studied medicine at the University of Lourenço

Marques. *Raiz do Orvalho*, poems, was published in 1983, and *Vozes Anoitecidas* (*Voices Made Night*), stories, in 1986. *Terra Sonâmbula* (*Sleepwalking Land*) came out in 1992, and *Jerusalém* in 2009. He won the Neustadt International Prize for Literature in 2014.

MOUHAMADOUL NOUKTAR DIOP
He is a Mauritanian writer of short stories.

EMMANUEL BOUNDZÉKI DONGALA
Novelist, short-story writer and chemist, he was born in Brazzaville, Congo, in 1941. He received his BA in chemistry from Oberlin College. *Un fusil dans la main, un poème dans la poche* (A Gun in the Hand, a Poem in the Pocket) was published in 1973. *Jazz et vin de palme* (*Jazz and Palm Wine*) came out in 1982, and *Johnny chien méchant* (*Johnny Mad Dog*) in 2002. It won the Cezam prix littéraire inter CE in 2004.

AHMED ESSOP
He was born in India in 1931. He studied at the University of South Africa. *The Hajji and Other Stories* was published in 1978, winning the Olive Schreiner Award in 1979. *The Visitation* appeared in 1980. *History and Satire in Salman Rushdie's The Satanic Verses* was published in 2009. He died in 2019.

NADINE GORDIMER
Novelist and short-story writer, she was born in 1923 in Springs, Transvaal, South Africa. She studied for a year at the University of the Witwatersrand. *Face to Face* came out in 1949, and *The Lying Days* in 1953. *The Conservationist* won the Booker Prize in 1974. *Burger's Daughter* was published in 1979. *The Essential Gesture: Writing, Politics and Places* appeared in 1988. In 1991 she won the Nobel Prize in Literature. She died in 2014.

ABDULRAZAK GURNAH
Novelist and short-story writer, he was born in Zanzibar in 1948. He studied at Christ Church College, Canterbury. *Memory of Departure* came out in 1987. Other notable novels include *Paradise* (1994), *By the Sea* (2001), *Desertion* (2005) and *Afterlives* (2020).

He edited *The Cambridge Companion to Salman Rushdie* (2007). He won the Nobel Prize in Literature in 2021.

BESSIE HEAD

Novelist, short-story writer and journalist, she was born in Pietermaritzburg, in South Africa, in 1937. She trained as a teacher and from 1964 lived and worked in Botswana. *When Rainclouds Gather* was published in 1968, *Maru* in 1971, and *A Question of Power* in 1973. *The Collector of Treasures*, stories, came out in 1977. In 2003 the South African Order of Ikhamanga Gold was posthumously bestowed on her for her exceptional literary contributions. She died in 1986.

SAIDA HAGI-DIRIE HERZI

Short-story writer and feminist, she was born in 1950 in Mogadishu, Somalia. She studied English literature at the King Abdulaziz University in Jeddah. Her first story, 'Against the Pleasure Principle', was published in *Index on Censorship* in 1990. Her stories have been widely anthologized.

LUÍS BERNARDO HONWANA

He was born in Maputo, Mozambique, in 1942. He studied law at the University of Lisbon. He became Minister for Culture in 1986. *Nós Matámos o Cão-Tinhoso* came out in 1964 (translated as *We Killed Mangy Dog and Other Stories* in 1969.) *A Veha Casa de Madeira e Zinco* (The Old House of Wood and Zinc) was published in 2017.

JOMO KENYATTA

He was born in 1897 in Kiambu, Kenya. He studied at Moscow's University of the Toilers of the East and the London School of Economics. In 1938 he published *Facing Mount Kenya*, which is both autobiography and an anthropological study of the Kikuyu. He was the first president of Kenya from 1964 to 1978. He died in 1978.

CAMARA LAYE

He was born in Kouroussa, Guinea, in 1928. He studied motor

mechanics and engineering. *L'Enfant noir* (*The African Child*), 1953, won the Prix Charles Veillon in 1954. *Le Regard du roi* (*The Radiance of the King*) came out in 1955, and *Dramouss* (*A Dream of Africa*) in 1966. He died in 1980.

DORIS LESSING

She was born in Kermanshah, Iran, in 1919 and moved to what was then Rhodesia in 1925. In 1937 she worked as a telephone operator in Salisbury. She settled in London in 1949. *The Grass Is Singing* was published in 1950, and *This Was the Old Chief's Country* in 1951. She published more than 70 works in a wide range of genres. *The Golden Notebook* (1962), *Briefing for a Descent into Hell* (1971) and *Memoirs of a Survivor* (1974) are among the most notable. She won the Nobel Prize in Literature in 2007. She died in 2013.

HENRI LOPÈS

A future prime minister of the People's Republic of Congo, he was born in Kinshasa, in 1937. His short-story collection *Tribaliques* (*Tribaliks: Contemporary Congolese Stories*) was published in 1971, the satirical novel *Le Pleurer-rire* (*The Laughing Cry*) in 1982 and *Le Méridional* in 2015. He died in 2023.

CLÉMENTINE NZUJI MADIYA

Poet and short-story writer, she was born in Tshofa, in the Belgian Congo, in 1944. She studied at the Lovanium University. Her first books of poems, *Murmures* (Whispers), was published in 1968, and *Lenga et autres contes d'inspiration traditionnelle* (Lenga and Other Traditional Stories) in 1976.

JAMAL MAHJOUB

He was born in London in 1960 to British and Sudanese parents. He studied geology at the University of Sheffield. His first novel, *Navigation of a Rainmaker*, came out in 1989. *The Carrier* (1998) won the Prix de l'Astrolabe in France. *Nubian Indigo* was published in 2006.

ADEWALE MAJA-PEARCE

Writer, critic and journalist, he was born in London in 1953 and grew up in Lagos in Nigeria. He recived an MA in African Studies from SOAS. *Loyalties and Other Stories* was published in 1986. In 1990 he edited *The Heinemann Book of African Poetry* and in 1991 he published *Who's Afraid of Wole Soyinka? Essays on Censorship. My Father's Country* (1987) and *The House My Father Built* (2014) are memoirs.

DANIEL MANDISHONA

He was born in Harare in 1959. He studied graphic design and architecture at University College London. *White Gods, Black Demons*, a story collection, was published in 2009. He died in 2021.

DAMBUDZO MARECHERA

Short-story writer and poet, he was born in Rusape, Zimbabwe, in 1952. *The House of Hunger* (1978) won the Guardian Fiction Prize. *Black Sunlight* came out in 1980, *Mindblast* in 1984, and *The Black Insider* posthumously in 1992. He died in 1987.

EZEKIEL (ES'KIA) MPHAHLELE

Writer, educationalist and activist, he was born in Pretoria in 1919. He studied English, psychology and African administration at the University of South Africa. In 1959 he published *Down Second Avenue*, and in 1967 *In Corner B and Other Stories. The Wanderers* came out in 1971. *Father Come Home* appeared in 1984. In 1998 Nelson Mandela awarded him the Order of the Southern Cross. He died in 2008.

GRACE OGOT

Short-story writer, novelist, diplomat and broadcaster, she was born in 1930, in Asembo, Kenya. *The Promised Land* came out in 1966, and *Land Without Thunder* in 1968. *An Island of Tears* appeared in 1980. She died in 2015. Three new novels were published posthumously in 2018.

BEN OKRI

Novelist, poet, short-story writer, he was born in Minna, Nigeria, in 1959. He studied comparative literature at the University of Essex. *Flowers and Shadows* came out in 1980, and *Stars of the New*

Curfew in 1988. *The Famished Road* (1991) won the Booker Prize. *African Elegy*, poems, came out in 1992, *The Freedom Artist* in 2019, and *The Last Gift of the Master Artists* in 2022. He was knighted for services to literature in 2023.

SEMBÈNE OUSMANE

Novelist, short-story writer and film maker, he was born in Ziguinchor, Casamance, in Senegal, in 1923. *Le Docker noir* (*The Black Docker*) was published in 1956, and *Xala* in 1973. *Les Bouts de bois de Dieu* (*God's Bits of Wood*) came out in 1960. His films *Xala* and *Black Girl* are classics of world cinema. He died in 2007.

DAVID OWOYELE

He was born in Northern Nigeria and worked in the information services. His first collection of stories, *Seven Short Stories*, was published in 1969.

GUILLAUME OYÔNÔ-MBIA

Short-story writer and playwright, he was born in Cameroon in 1939. He studied English literature in Britain and taught at the University of Yaoundé. His plays include *Trois prétendants . . . un mari* (1962; *Three Suitors . . . One Husband*) and *His Excellency's Train* (1969). *Chroniques de Mvoutessi* (Chronicles of Mvoutessi) came out in 1971–2. He died in 2021.

JEAN PLIYA

Novelist, playwright and short-story writer, he was born in the Republic of Benin in 1931. He studied history and geography at the Universities of Dakar and Toulouse. His play *Kondo, le requin* (1964) won the Grand prix littéraire d'Afrique noire in 1967. *L'Arbre fétiche* (*The Fetish Tree*), stories, came out in 1971. He died in 2015.

TAYEB SALIH

Novelist and short-story writer, he was born in Karmakol, Sudan, in 1929. He studied at the Universities of Khartoum and London. *Mawsim al-Hijrah ilâ al-Shimâl* (*Season of Migration to the North*) was published in 1966, as was *Urs' al-Zayn* (*The Wedding of Zein*).

A memoir, *Mansi: A Rare Man in his Own Way*, appeared in 2004. He died in 2009.

NGŨGĨ WA THIONG'O

Novelist, short-story writer, playwright, he was born in Kamirithu, in Kenya, in 1938. He studied English at Makerere University, Kampala, Uganda. *Weep Not, Child* was published in 1964, *A Grain of Wheat* in 1967, and *Petals of Blood* in 1977. Around 1970 he began to write in Gĩkũyũ. *Detained*, his prison memoir, came out in 1981 and *Decolonising the Mind: The Politics of Language in African Literature* in 1986. *Mũrogi wa Kagogo* (*Wizard of the Crow*) was published in 2006.

M. G. VASSANJI

Novelist and short-story writer, he was born in Kenya in 1950 and raised in Tanzania. He studied at MIT, specializing in nuclear physics. He co-founded a literary magazine, has written ten novels, three volumes of short stories, and is a member of the Order of Canada. *The Gunny Sack* came out in 1989 and *Uhuru Street,* stories, in 1992. *And Home Was Kariakoo: A Memoir of East Africa* appeared in 2014 and *Nostalgia* in 2016.

ACKNOWLEDGMENTS

CHINUA ACHEBE: 'The Voter' (first published in *Black Orpheus*, number 17, 1965) from *Girls at War and Other Stories*, Heinemann, 1972. Copyright © 1972, 1973 by Chinua Achebe. The Wylie Agency.

CHIMAMANDA NGOZI ADICHIE: 'Ghosts' from *The Thing Around Your Neck*, Fourth Estate, 2009. Reprinted by permission of HarperCollins Publishers Ltd. Copyright © 2009, Chimamanda Ngozi Adichie. 'Ghosts' from *The Thing Around Your Neck* by Chimamanda Ngozi Adichie. Copyright © 2009, Chimamanda Ngozi Adichie, used by permission of The Wylie Agency (UK) Limited. Reprinted with permission from Narrative Landscape Press. Reprinted with permission of Penguin Random House Canada.

AMA ATA AIDOO: Ama Ata Aidoo, 'Two Sisters' from *No Sweetness Here and Other Stories.* Copyright © 1970 by Ama Ata Aidoo. Reprinted with the permission of The Permissions Company, LLC on behalf of The Feminist Press at the City University of New York, www.feministpress.org. All rights reserved.

FRANCIS BEBEY: 'Edda's Marriage' originally published as 'Le mariage d'Edda' in *Embarras & Cie: nouvelles et poèmes*, Éditions CLE, Yaoundé, Cameroun, 1968. English translation by Georg M. Gugelberger published in *Jazz and Palm Wine*, ed. Willfried F. Feuser, Longman, 1981.

OLYMPE BHÊLY-QUÉNUM: 'A Child in the Bush of Ghosts' originally published as 'Promenade dans la forêt' in

Liaison d'un été, Éditions Sagerep, Paris, 1968. © by Sagerep – *Afrique Actuelle*. English translation published in *Jazz and Palm Wine*, ed. Willfried F. Feuser, Longman, 1981.

OKEY CHIGBO: 'The Housegirl' first published in *The Heinemann Book of Contemporary African Stories*, ed. Chinua Achebe and C. L. Innes, Heinemann, 1992. Copyright © Okey Chigbo.

J. M. COETZEE: 'The Glass Abattoir' from *The Pole and Other Stories*, published by Harvill Secker. Reprinted with permission from David Higham Associates. Copyright © J. M. Coetzee, 2016, 2017, 'Moral Tales' © J. M. Coetzee, 2017. All rights reserved. Arranged by Peter Lampack Agency, Inc.

JACK COPE: 'Power' from *The Man Who Doubted and Other Stories*, Heinemann, 1967. With consent of Penguin Random House UK and by permission of the Estate of Jack Cope.

MIA COUTO: 'The Birds of God' from *Vozes Anoitecidas*, first published in Portuguese by Associação dos Escritores Moçambicanos, Maputo, and by Editorial Caminho, Lisbon, 1986. *Voices Made Night*, English translation by David Brookshaw, published by Heinemann (African Writers Series), 1990. Copyright © Mia Couto. English translation copyright © David Brookshaw.

MOUHAMADOUL NOUKTAR DIOP: 'The Pot of Gold', published in *Présence Africaine*, 45, 1st Quarterly, 1963; English translation published in *Jazz and Palm Wine*, ed. Willfried F. Feuser, Longman, 1981.

EMMANUEL BOUNDZÉKI DONGALA: 'Jazz and Palm Wine' first published as 'Jazz et vin de palme' in *Presence Africaine*, 73, 1st Quarterly, 1970; English translation published in *Jazz and Palm Wine*, ed. Willfried F. Feuser, Longman, 1981.

AHMED ESSOP: 'Hajji Musa and the Hindu Fire-Walker' from *The Hajji and Other Stories*. Ravan Press, Johannesburg, 1978, Picador Africa, 2004. © Copyright Ahmed Essop, 1978.

NADINE GORDIMER: 'Amnesty' first published in *The New Yorker*, August 19, 1990. © 1990 by Felix Licensing BV. Subsequently collected in *Jump and Other Stories,* 1991 (Bloomsbury, London; Farrar, Straus & Giroux, New York). A. P. Watt / United Agents.

ABDULRAZAK GURNAH: 'Cages' first published in *The Heinemann Book of Contemporary African Short Stories*, ed. Chinua Achebe and C. L. Innes, Heinemann, 1992. Copyright © Abdulrazak Gurnah, 1992. The author c/o Rogers, Coleridge & White Ltd, 20 Powys Mews, London W11 1JN.

SAIDA HAGI-DIRIE HERZI: 'Government by Magic Spell'. Copyright © Saida Hagi-Dirie Herzi. *The Heinemann Book of Contemporary African Short Stories*, ed. Chinua Achebe and C. L. Innes, Heinemann, 1992.

BESSIE HEAD: 'Jacob: The Story of a Faith-Healing Priest' from *The Collector of Treasures and Other Botswana Village Tales*. Waveland Press, 1977. Reprinted with permission from Waveland Press. 'Jacob: The Story of a Faith-Healing Priest' from *The Collector of Treasures and Other Botswana Village Tales*, Heinemann (African Writers Series), 1977. Reproduced with permission of Johnson & Alcock Ltd.

L. B. HONWANA: 'Papa, Snake & I', copyright © Luís Bernado Honwana, 1969. Originally published in Portuguese as 'Papa, Cobra, Eu' in *Nós Matámos o Cão-Tinhoso* (1964), published in English as *We Killed Mangy-Dog and Other Mozambique Stories* (Heinemann African Writers Series), Heinemann, 1969, in a translation by Dorothy Guedes. Reprinted with permission of A. P. Watt.

JOMO KENYATTA: Excerpt(s) from *Facing Mount Kenya*

by Jomo Kenyatta, copyright © 1938 by Jomo Kenyatta. Used by permission of Alfred A. Knopf, an imprint of the Knopf Doubleday Publishing Group, a division of Penguin Random House LLC. All rights reserved. 'The Gentlemen of the Jungle' from *Facing Mount Kenya* by Jomo Kenyatta, published by Martin Secker & Warburg, London, 1938. © Jomo Kenyatta, 1938. Reprinted by permission of The Random House Group Limited.
CAMARA LAYE: 'The Eyes of the Statue' first published as 'Les Yeux de la statue' in *Présence Africaine*, No. 13, April–May 1957. English translation by Una MacLean first published in 1959 in the magazine *Black Orpheus* and reprinted in *Black Orpheus: An Anthology of African and Afro-American Prose*, Longmans of Nigeria, 1964.
DORIS LESSING: 'A Sunrise on the Veld' from *This Was the Old Chief's Country*, Copyright © 1951, Doris Lessing. HarperCollins UK. From *African Stories* by Doris Lessing. Copyright © 1951, 1953, 1954, 1957, 1958, 1962, 1963, 1964, 1965, 1972, 1981 by Doris Lessing. Reprinted with the permission of Simon & Schuster LLC. All rights reserved. Reprinted with permission from Jonathan Clowes Limited.
HENRI LOPÈS: 'The Plot' first published as 'Le Complot' in *Tribaliques* (pp. 93–102), Éditions CLE, Yaoundé, 1971. English translation published in *Jazz and Palm Wine*, ed. Willfried F. Feuser, Longman, 1981.
CLÉMENTINE NZUJI MADIYA: 'Ditetembwa' from *Lenga*, Éditions St Paul-Afrique, Lubumbashi, 1976. English translation published in *Jazz and Palm Wine*, ed. Willfried F. Feuser, Longman, 1981.
JAMAL MAHJOUB: 'Road Block'. Copyright © Jamal Mahjoub. A. M. Heath. First published in *The Heinemann Book of Contemporary African Short Stories*, ed. Chinua Achebe and C. L. Innes, Heinemann, 1992.

ADEWALE MAJA-PEARCE: 'The Hotel' from *Loyalties and Other Stories* (1986). Copyright © Adewale Maja-Pearce. Reprinted with permission from the author.

DANIEL MANDISHONA: 'A Wasted Land' first published in *The Heinemann Book of Contemporary African Stories*, Heinemann, 1992. Copyright © Daniel Mandishona.

DAMBUDZO MARECHERA: 'Protista' from *The House of Hunger* by Dambudzo Marechera, copyright © 1978 by Dambudzo Marechera. Used by permission of Pantheon Books, an imprint of the Knopf Doubleday Publishing Group, a division of Penguin Random House LLC. All rights reserved. *The House of Hunger* by Dambudzo Marechera first published by Heinemann (African Writers Series), 1978. Text copyright © Dambudzo Marechera, 1978.

EZEKIEL (ES'KIA) MPHAHLELE: 'The Coffee-Cart Girl' from *In Corner B* (East African Publishing House, Nairobi, 1967). Phoenix Publishers.

GRACE OGOT: 'The Green Leaves' from *Land Without Thunder*, East African Publishing House, Nairobi, 1968.

BEN OKRI: 'Incidents at the Shrine' from *Incidents at the Shrine*, Secker & Warburg, 1968. Georgina Capel Associates Limited.

SEMBÈNE OUSMANE: 'Tribal Marks' originally published in French as 'Le Voltaïque' in *Voltaïque* by Sembène Ousmane, Présence Africaine, 1962. English translation published in *Jazz and Palm Wine*, ed. Willfried F. Feuser, Longman, 1981.

DAVID OWOYELE: 'The Will of Allah' from *Seven Short Stories*, Northern Nigerian Publishing Company, Zaria, 1969.

GUILLAUME OYÔNÔ-MBIA: 'The Little Railway Station' originally published in French as 'La Petite Gare' in *Chroniques de Mvoutessi*, Vol. 1 (pp. 25–43), Éditions CLE, Yaoundé, 1971. English translation published in *Jazz and*

Palm Wine, ed. Willfried F. Feuser, Longman, 1981.
JEAN PLIYA: 'The Watch-Night' originally published in French as 'Le Gardien de nuit' in *L'Arbre fétiche* (pp. 67–9) by Jean Pliya, Éditions CLE, Yaoundé, 1971. Reprinted with permission.
TAJEB SALIH: 'A Handful of Dates' from *The Wedding of Zein and Other Stories*, translated by Denys Johnson-Davies, Heinemann (Arab Authors Series), 1978. Originally published in Arabic in Beirut, 1966. With permission from the Estate of Tajeb Salih and United Agents.
NGŨGĨ WA THIONG'O: 'The Martyr' from *Secret Lives and Other Stories,* Heinemann (African Writers Series), 1975. The Ngũgĩ wa Thiong'o Foundation. Reprinted with the permission of Watkins/Loomis Agency Inc. The New Press. East African Educational Press.
M. G. VASSANJI: 'Leaving' from *Uhuru Street*, Heinemann (African Writers Series), 1991. With permission of McClelland and Stewart (PRH Canada), Toronto and Transatlantic Agency, Toronto.

Titles in Everyman's Library Pocket Classics

Bedtime Stories
Selected by Diana Secker Tesdell

Berlin Stories
Selected by Philip Hensher

The Best Medicine: Stories of Healing
Selected by Theodore Dalrymple

Cat Stories
Selected by Diana Secker Tesdell

Christmas Stories
Selected by Diana Secker Tesdell

Detective Stories
Selected by Peter Washington

Dog Stories
Selected by Diana Secker Tesdell

Erotic Stories
Selected by Rowan Pelling

Fishing Stories
Selected by Henry Hughes

Florence Stories
Selected by Ella Carr

Garden Stories
Selected by Diana Secker Tesdell

Ghost Stories
Selected by Peter Washington

Golf Stories
Selected by Charles McGrath

Horse Stories
Selected by Diana Secker Tesdell

London Stories
Selected by Jerry White

Love Stories
Selected by Diana Secker Tesdell

Music Stories
Selected by Wesley Stace

New York Stories
Selected by Diana Secker Tesdell

Paris Stories
Selected by Shaun Whiteside

Prague Stories
Selected by Richard Bassett

Rome Stories
Selected by Jonathan Keates

Scottish Stories
Selected by Gerard Carruthers

Shaken and Stirred: Intoxicating Stories
Selected by Diana Secker Tesdell

Stories of Art and Artists
Selected by Diana Secker Tesdell

Stories of Books and Libraries
Selected by Jane Holloway

Stories of Fatherhood
Selected by Diana Secker Tesdell

Stories from the Kitchen
Selected by Diana Secker Tesdell

Stories of Motherhood
Selected by Diana Secker Tesdell

Stories of the Sea
Selected by Diana Secker Tesdell

Stories of Southern Italy
Selected by Ella Carr

Stories of Trees, Woods, and the Forest
Selected by Fiona Stafford

Venice Stories
Selected by Jonathan Keates

Wedding Stories
Selected by Diana Secker Tesdell

Saki: Stories
Selected by Diana Secker Tesdell

John Updike:
The Maples Stories
Olinger Stories